#1 PLAYER

USA *Today* Bestselling Author

T. GEPHART

#1 Player
Published by T Gephart
Copyright 2017 T Gephart

ISBN-10: 0–6480231–2-5
ISBN-13: 978–0-6480231–2-8

#1 PLAYER

DEDICATION

To my Mum,

Who doesn't run a whorehouse, but who waved me goodbye—with love and understanding—when I was 18 (and 20, 21, and 23) because my heart was desperate to wander. I needed to find my place in the world, turns out it was here all along.

CHAPTER #1

EVERY YEAR, RICHARD Benton invites the beautiful and noteworthy to fill the hallowed ballroom of The Plaza for his coveted New York Impresses event. A literal who's who, where the worlds of Hollywood, politics, sports and music collide in one big hot mess of who has the biggest ego. Here's a hint . . . none of us give a shit.

Ugh.

        \<delete\> \<delete\> \<delete\>

My finger hammered on the key until I was once again looking at a blank page.

Lance Priestly had concertgoers on their feet as he shook his Levi-clad ass at Madison Square Garden on Friday. The not-so-bright Tennessee native, who is short on talent but big on sex appeal, flashed his dumb-but-still-charming smile at the crowd, gaslighting hundreds of otherwise smart people.

God damn it!

        \<delete\> \<delete\> \<delete\> \<delete\>

The flashing black line ate the words, banishing them to the never-to-be-read abyss.

Manhattan, NYC—Lila Callan, journalist for The New York Times, was found dead at her desk earlier this afternoon by her editor, Dick Voss.

While Lila had dreamt of a promising career contributing to the world in a meaningful way, she soon found that sharp editorial pieces and in-depth reporting were left to the senior members of the writing staff, leaving her shit out of luck. Of course, her personal brand of flare and insight was welcome in the arts section where she was relegated until Karen Harrow came back from procreating for a second time in eighteen months. RIP Karen's vagina, we were all pulling for you, boo.

Lila's cause of death is still pending a coroner's inquiry, but early speculation leads investigators to believe she literally died of boredom. Expired in a lethargic sea of malaise, and a bunch of other two-dollar words she'll never be able to use while describing Bella—last-name-un-pronounceable—'s tiny ass or RuRu LaRu's bountiful bosom.

She leaves behind two loving parents, a small posse of cherished friends, and a vibrator called Ryan—Ryan York, he was not named after you, so deflate your ego.

Her final thoughts were of an earth-shattering orgasm while clutching a Pulitzer Prize—sadly she perished with neither.

May her soul rest in eternal peace.

My hand hovered over the send button, itching to submit the editorial, which would most likely be accepted as my resignation . . . but I didn't.

It would be stupid. More than stupid, it would be career suicide. Because, as much as I was bored out of my ever-loving mind, I was one of the lucky ones. Landing a job at *The New York Times* was the Holy Grail. Usually you had to wait until some crusty senior journalist retired or moved on to pen some novel about a past president or the changing political climate. So, that I was even here in the first place was a miracle in itself. Most editors had taken one look at me, seen my blonde hair, blue eyes, and slender frame and assumed I'd sucked cock to get my 4.0 GPA. Because clearly you couldn't be smart *and* attractive, someone call CNN to confirm.

So yes, I knew things could be worse, even if my current mood didn't reflect my feelings of good fortune. And working at *The Times* had always been my dream, so there was no way I would toss away the opportunity. Even if it was going to take a while before I graduated from the kiddie table.

But help me, Lord Jesus, I was bored.

My long-time best friend and usual partner-in-crime, Tia, had hooked up with a movie star. You heard that correctly. A movie star. The sexy, rich, successful kind, who was better looking than should be humanly allowed. So it's hardly surprising that our adventures of general mayhem had been curtailed. While she split her time between L.A. and New York, sharing her bed with Eric Larsson—the hot, sexy movie star in question—I spent quality time with a vibrator, eating cold Chinese takeaway, drinking alone while I met deadlines. Not even *good* deadlines, I doubted my editor would even notice if I didn't submit my shitty think piece on who was seen at the latest opening of whatever.

Ugh.

Maybe I needed a new vibrator.

"Lila, can I see you in my office?" Dick Voss, my boss and editor, poked his head over the divider of my cubical.

"Sure, be right there." I smiled sweetly, grabbing a notepad and pen in case the mind-numbing shit he was about to share was important. *Ha, doubtful.*

"Hey, Dick, what's up?" I lowered my butt into the seat opposite him.

"Lila, I've told you at least a hundred times, it's Richard, not *Dick.*" His eyes narrowed as he watched me sit. "I'm beginning to think you call me that just to get a reaction."

"Moi?" My hand daintily rested on my chest while an adequate amount of shock flashed across my face. "I would never dream of such insubordination. It was just a slip of the tongue. I assure you it won't happen again."

We both knew I was lying.

I called him Dick because he was one. While he wasn't a misogynistic A-hole like some of the other *good ole boys* in the industry, he was an equal-opportunity prick. Mean, with a tunnel-visioned view that unless you were over the age of forty-five you had nothing worthwhile to contribute—he had a strong distaste for millennials. My twenty-eight years made me just right for his personal brand of loathing. Add in my smart mouth, a better-than-average intelligence and I was probably his least-favorite person. Which of course meant I had a civil duty to antagonize him, flying the flag for young people everywhere. And it also helped pass the time.

"Regardless, I didn't call you here for that." He rocked slowly in his office chair as a sly grin crept on his face. "I have an assignment for you."

"What?" The look of shock no longer manufactured as I sat up straighter in my chair. "An assignment?"

In all the years I'd been working at *The Times*, I'd never been *given* an assignment. Tossed suggestions about what I should be writing—aplenty, but something just for me—nada.

"I thought that would get your attention." His lips spread, his teeth yellowed from excessive coffee and tobacco making an appearance. "I need you to cover the MCM charity event." He steeled his fingers in true villainous fashion. "In Hollywood."

MCM, one of the largest studios in Hollywood, threw a charity gala every year to raise money for whichever pet cause their CEOs felt would give them the biggest publicity. Biggest dog and pony show where an award *wasn't* given out, and for the starting price of three thousand dollars a ticket, you too could rub shoulders with the famous elite. Except it was invitation only. What? They weren't going to let just any old nobody in there with all the beautiful people. And if that wasn't limiting enough, it was also strictly a no-press zone, with cameras and reporters banished to the other side of the red carpet.

"Yeah, last time I checked they didn't let the press inside." I smiled, conveniently playing the dumb-blonde routine despite knowing exactly what he was suggesting.

Don't get me wrong, I absolutely abhorred women who pretended to be inadequate or stupid, it was demeaning. But in some instances, I allowed the loophole. *This* was one of those times.

"They don't, but I figured with your connection—" He waved his hand in the air. "—you could get the inside scoop. Imagine the headlines now." The look of satisfaction barely contained on his smug-ass face.

"Dick." He was acting like one so that's what I was calling him. "Assuming I could get access with my *connection*." No prizes for guessing he meant I Barbie doll'd up and put the hard word on my BFF and her super-hot leading man. "I'm not in the habit of using my friends for a story. And even if I did lose my mind, became a money-hungry bottom dweller and turned on the people I cared about to further my career, my name would be toast."

"*Richard*," he corrected me, the vein in his neck twitching. "And wasn't it you who was complaining just the other day how you wanted something meatier, more relevant to report on?"

Oh, please tell me he was not equating *that* to *this*. "I was talking about the new health care bill before the senate, or maybe the pharmaceutical company jacking up the price on life-saving drugs. Or even investigating the movement of aluminum helmet wearers who believe the Hadron Collider has shifted us to a parallel universe." I was a sucker for a conspiracy theory.

"Those stories are all taken." The leather of his chair creaked as he leaned back, no warmth to his smile. "So, you can head to L.A. and write the story I've given you or find me something as equally juicy. But I want it entertainment-based, and interesting. We have enough people in this city popping antidepressants, the art section isn't supposed to have them reaching for another hit of Valium."

"Fine." The eye roll unavoidable as I rose to my feet. "I'll be on the first flight tomorrow." I didn't wait to be excused, giving him a half-hearted wave as I saw myself out.

The nerve of that man. I childishly flipped off the closed door as soon as I'd shut it. There was a snowball's chance in hell I was going to sell out the closest thing I had to a sister for some bullshit fluff piece. I was still seething as I walked back to my desk.

"Hey, Lila." Chris from sports leaned up against the wall of my cubicle, his big biceps bulging against the sleeves of his polo. "How are you doin'?"

"Hey, Chris." I did my best to force the smile. "Doing great."

He was cute in a quarterback sort of way. Tall, athletic, with hair so shiny I could use the reflection to reapply my lipstick. But I was almost positive he was more in love with himself than he could ever be with any woman. And jocks really weren't my thing, which is why I'd been dodging his advances for the past three months.

"So, I was thinking." His eyes dropped to my boobs, his lips spreading into a grin. "The Giants, Jacksonville game is this Sunday at MetLife. Thought you might like to join me."

Wow, he'd finally worked up the nerve to ask me out and that was the best he could do? I was thinking maybe dinner, or a movie where he tried to slide into second base by the time the credits rolled, but a game? Did he even know me?

"Aren't you working that game?" I eyed him suspiciously, the question more rhetorical since he'd told me on more than one occasion that he covered almost every game both at home and on the road.

"Well, yeah." The cocky grin made two dimples pop on his cheeks. "I can get an extra pass for the box. You have press credentials, so it will be no sweat."

"Well, gee." I gave the offer some thought for a minute longer than it deserved. "As much as I would love to." Watching football rated just above a root canal. "I'm heading out of town tomorrow. Maybe some other time."

"That blows." Chris looked genuinely disappointed, girls turning him down probably a new occurrence. "Where are you going? You coming back any time soon?"

"L.A.," I answered, the thought of seeing Tia and chasing some warmer weather making the idea more appealing. "Not sure how long I'll be gone, but maybe we could do something when I get back?"

Why I had to go and add the last part was beyond me. I was almost positive I wasn't interested in Chris in any way that was romantic. But, while there was little chance of a relationship blossoming between me and Captain Polo Shirt, it had been a while since I'd dated. And it might be nice to have sex with a real penis for a change. All those muscles. Hopefully the one that counted flexed in all the right places too.

"Yeah, that would be great." His chest puffed out, his confidence restored. "You know, for a second there I thought you might have been blowing me off." He shook his head, discounting the thought anyone could be immune to his charm. "But then I realized how ridiculous that would be."

"Yeah." I tried to stifle my grimace. "Totally ridiculous." I punched him lightly in his big, bulgy arm, wondering how much worse the day was going to get. "I'll call you."

"Why don't you give me your number, just in case you lose mine." He gave me a wink, not so subtly reminding me I'd yet to use the number in the three months since he'd given it to me.

"Suuuuure." I hoped the cringe was only inward and not plastered all over my face. "I'll write it down for you." I flipped over my notepad and scribbled my number against my better judgment.

Maybe it wouldn't be so bad? While he didn't seem overly

bright, he'd always been polite. And sure, he did spend an obscene amount of time checking out my boobs—hard to avoid those suckers, I'd been blessed/cursed with ample boobage—but he'd been nothing but nice to me. Plus, he was attractive; most of the men around the office looked like a walking advertisement for either cholesterol medication or erectile dysfunction. *See your doctor to check if inflate-a-dick is right for you.*

I should give him a chance. It wasn't like every man I dated had to turn into some long, serious relationship. Besides, it had been so long since I'd had real sex it was possible I regained my virginity. I made a mental note to investigate hymen regeneration later.

"Here it is." I tore the page and handed it to him, the piece of paper folded neatly before sliding into his pocket.

"Thanks. Enjoy L.A." He tapped the side of my cubicle and then sauntered off, a satisfied grin on his face.

Ugh.

I had issues.

While yes, I was less than twenty-four hours from getting on a plane for a story I hadn't yet conceived, but it was the interaction between Chris and I that was weighing heavily on my mind.

I had a somewhat skewed view on relationships. It wasn't that I was a prude, oh no, I loved sex as much as anyone. Probably more so—which I totally blamed on genetics—but I just couldn't do the casual sex thing.

Not. At. All.

I tried a few years ago, went home with a guy I barely knew who I'd met at a party. By the time we got to the sex part I was so far from aroused, not even lube helped. It felt too contrived, too forced. And without the emotional connection, I just couldn't come. It was one of the worst sexual experiences of my life, and losing my virginity had been no picnic, so that was saying something.

Funny how it becomes a hang up when your mother runs a

gentleman's club in Vegas and most of the boys you grew up with assumed you were a whore.

Of course, my mother had never been a prostitute either—that had been my grandma—my mom had been the enterprising young woman who decided if grandma was going to sell her ass, she might as well be making a profit. So while other teenagers were working part-time jobs at the mall, my mom was coordinating grandma's johns. Which I guess made her a pimp.

But not content with thinking small, she took some classes in community college and before you knew it, she'd parlayed her little business into a major Nevada attraction. And while it was completely legal—almost everything was in Vegas—she got the law's attention in a different way, the local sheriff falling desperately in love with her. Yeah, you heard that right, my father was a sheriff while my mother was a madam.

What sounded like a tagline for a dodgy B-grade movie—and don't even start with a Freudian analysis—was actually my life, and had I not been raised in an obscene amount of love, I would probably be in therapy.

And other than a strong aversion to one-night stands, I'd escaped relatively unscathed. Although it was also probably one of the reasons why I hadn't had a serious boyfriend until I'd moved away from home and gone to college in New York.

Moving away had been intentional. While not all women in Vegas wore sequins on their boobs, I just didn't fit in in the desert. So the big city it was, and there was none better than NYC. Ironically, it felt more like home than *home* ever did, which is why I didn't move back after I graduated. That, and obviously I wanted to be a big-time journalist.

Shaking off thoughts that were way too deep for a Thursday, I ignored the noise of the office and picked up my cell and dialed.

"Hey, sunshine, you sick of being blissfully happy yet?" I sighed into the phone, missing her and her crazy more than I could ever put into words.

"Lila!" Tia squealed back. "I swear you must have ESP or something because I was just about to call you."

"Really, everything okay in LaLa Land?" It had only been a few days since we last spoke, but with Tia you could never tell. If there was ever a person who could find herself in trouble in such a short amount of time, it would be the one on the other end of the phone.

"Everything is perfect." I could hear the smile in her voice. "But I need to go to this stupid charity thing for the studio and deciding what to wear is making me crazy." She breathed, exasperated. "The stylist they sent wants to make me look like a porn star. And when I told her the designer dress she'd chosen was slutty, she gave me judgey eyes. I need you and your honest opinion, I don't trust these people."

"Well, you can count on me to let you know if you're dressing like a hooker. I mean, if anyone should know it's me, right?" I laughed, neglecting to mention Dick and his idea about the charity event I was positive was the same one she was talking about. "Besides, I miss your face, which is why I was calling. I'm coming to L.A. to visit."

"Shut. Up. You're coming here? Oh, thank you, Lord and all the saints! When are you getting here? Don't even think of booking a hotel, you know I'm still annoyed from the last time you did that." She fired out words faster than I could answer.

"I thought you would appreciate the space. I know you don't get a lot of time with Eric when he's filming. I didn't want to throw a damper on your plans of crazy monkey sex with the boyfriend." I couldn't help but laugh.

"Girlfriend, how long have you known me?" Tia chuckled. "Not even the Viking gods have that kind of power. Now, tell me when you're getting here, we have serious plans to make."

"I need to book my ticket, but expect me sometime tomorrow." I sank into my office chair and started looking at flights. "I'll send you my flight details."

"Shit, I promised Eric's mom I'd go with her to Santa Barbara tomorrow. She wanted to do some wine tour thing. I'm not sure how long I'll be gone. I can cancel?"

"Don't be silly, there's no need to cancel, especially a wine tour. Just bring back a decent bottle and I'll get a cab from the airport."

"I will only get the good stuff, and no, you won't get a cab." Her tone letting me know it wasn't up for further discussion. "I'll send Ryan. I'm sure he'll be happy to come get you."

"Okay," I answered a little quicker than I should. "I mean, whatever."

Ryan York was Eric Larsson's right-hand man. Part driver, part entourage and all hotness, it was literally a sin the man wasn't burning up his own silver screen.

Standing six-two, with light brown hair, dark brown eyes and a body that had obviously spent a lot of time in the gym, he was a walking, talking, sexual fantasy. And hand on heart, he was legitimately the most attractive man I'd ever seen. Even hotter than Eric, if that was humanly possible.

With a wicked sense of humor and smile to match, it was noooooo hardship to spend time with him whenever our paths crossed. In fact, I looked forward to it, loving the eye candy and masturbation material he provided. I'd lied about my vibrator earlier; it totally *was* named after him.

And while working for their highly successful friend might be a problem for some men, Ryan wore it like a badge of honor. The whole loyalty and duty thing an additional turn on, because clearly he needed more reasons to soak my panties.

"Yeah, I figured you'd be fine with that." She laughed, not

even pretending to not notice my enthusiasm at the mention of his name. "Something you want to share?"

"Sadly, nothing." I sighed, the lack of *something* partly my own doing.

I hadn't exactly told him how I felt, and Ryan was flirty with everyone. His attention and sexy smile were not exclusively for me, the other recipients more than happy to take him up on his offer of being *friendly*.

Ryan wasn't *only* a flirt, but also an active participant in the carousel of casual sex. I'd seen the signs, the frequent late-night text messages he seemed to get—the cheeky grin spreading across his face before silencing his phone. And if that was what I'd noticed, imagine what I hadn't.

"You know he's interested." Tia's voice lowered and I wasn't sure if the man in question was around or she was just being discreet.

"I have boobs and a pulse, Tia. Of course he's interested." I rolled my eyes, having a fairly good idea of the scope of Ryan's *type*.

Not that I blamed him. He was young, good looking and had access to hordes of beautiful women, enjoying the buffet of vaginas made sense. And I couldn't even hate him, because he wasn't a dick about it—being respectful and freaking charming was also in his bag of tricks.

Besides, I had no one to blame but myself for my lack of Ryan-branded satisfaction. I'm sure if I gave him even the slightest chance we'd be having hot sex with reckless abandon like he probably did with other women. Except there was no way I wanted to be one of *them*. No, I would rather suffer in monogamous silence with a vibrator and stare at him creepily like an idiot. God that sounded tragic. I really did need to date. And hopefully find a boyfriend who could make me come *and* stick around, I needed the package deal.

"Anyway, it doesn't matter." I pushed ideas of Ryan and his hotness out of my mind, more important things requiring the mental space. "I better go book this flight, I still need to get home and pack."

"And pack something nice, I want you to come to this charity thing with me."

"Tia, the tickets start at three grand."

Sure, I could raid my savings account for the ticket and a dress, but it wouldn't help the feelings of deceit bubbling inside of me. Because even though I wasn't going to write the story, the whole thing felt underhanded.

"I can't go. And don't even think of buying me a ticket," I warned her knowing how quickly she could go off on a tangent when her mind was set.

"What makes people think they can tell me how I should be spending my money? First, Eric having a conniption because I paid for groceries, and now you with the *don't buy me a ticket*." She laughed, obviously not as annoyed as she sounded. "He has a table, trust me, it's his money not mine. So stop arguing, go pack, book your flight and get here so you can save me from this god-awful stylist."

"Fine, fine." I waved her off, knowing the argument was best saved for later. "We'll discuss when I land. Restock your liquor cabinet." Drinks were going to be needed.

"Babe, Eric has a cellar. Not even *you* could drink this place dry."

"Sounds like a challenge to me. I'll see you soon."

We quickly exchanged goodbyes and ended the call. Meanwhile my fingers got busy on my laptop as I booked a six a.m. flight to LAX out of JFK. I already was going to be hating life with the early morning, throw in a time change and tomorrow was going to be a barrel of laughs. Still, there was one silver lining, the drive and accompanying driver from the airport worth the lack of sleep even if the *ride* wasn't the one I really wanted.

Ugh.

It was definitely a night for Ryan tonight. Sadly, it was going to have to be the motorized version that sat in the bottom drawer of my nightstand.

CHAPTER #2

I HATED EARLY mornings.

The darkness outside, the puff of visible breath that expelled from my lungs every time I opened my mouth—it was like starring in my own horror movie. My lack of sleep, contributing to the carnage.

And let's not even talk about what obscene hour I had to wake up so I could shower and make myself look human. There was no way was I stepping off the plane in a pair of yoga pants and a messy hair bun when Ryan freaking York would be on the other side of the journey. But even though my pulse spiked and my nether regions clenched just at the mention of his name, turning into a Disney caricature, whistling happy tunes about catching the early worm or some shit wasn't happening. There was only so much joy I was capable of before ten a.m. and I was currently maxed out.

The minute I'd arrived, I immediately regretted my outfit choice. The leather jacket, knee-high boots and dress I'd worn when I'd left my apartment had been perfect for a fall New York morning. But in California, I was roasting alive as I wrestled my way through the airport to the meeting point.

"Hey, princess." Ryan slipped his shades down the bridge of

his nose, peeking over the lenses as the rumble made its way up his throat. "I heard you're looking for a ride."

Oh. Help. Me. Jesus.

Every single muscle in my body seized at the sound of his voice, my legs freezing in place as my eyes ran up and down the length of his body. He was gorgeous, smoldering in a pair of faded jeans and a T-shirt that hugged every curve of his abs like my tongue was aching to do.

His eyes were on me, doing a survey of their own, as a sexy smirk played on his lips. And while my brain knew flirting was his baseline, my hormones ignored that detail, my girlie bits salivating more than one of Pavlov's dogs.

"Ryan." My hand gripped my suitcase, more for stability than anything else. "I need to take off my clothes."

Oh, I knew what I was saying. While I could have blamed the heat, fatigue, the time zone, or maybe that fucking T-shirt—I had full control over my mouth. The words had been intentionally suggestive and slightly inappropriate, because if he was going to slay me with the sexy talk right off the bat, then I had to combat it with something of my own.

"Well, Lila." His jaw tightened, my name sounding dirtier than it should. "You've come to the right place. I have a PhD in undressing."

Oh. I bet he did.

Our game wasn't new. We'd tossed innuendo at each other like Hallmark threw out greetings, and while he was arguably a better player than I was, I didn't care. The stupid thrill it gave me more fulfilling than the orgasms I'd been receiving from his battery-operated counterpart, even if I knew I was probably only the flavor of the month. Hell, the fact it lasted this long was probably because I *hadn't* slept with him. That, or we didn't see each other enough for him to be sick of me yet. Or—I wasn't sure how many alternate possibilities I was up to now—he just really enjoyed toying with me. I didn't exactly hate *playing* with him either even though I knew it probably wasn't going anywhere.

"I think I can manage." I said words I didn't mean as I looked for a nearby bathroom. "But I really do need to change."

He grinned, saving me from another verbal onslaught as he nodded to a bathroom sign I had obviously missed. Then taking the suitcase out of my hand he wheeled it to the door for me, standing to the side as he waited.

"I'll just wait here, take your time."

"Thanks, I'll be quick."

Ignoring the sexual tension that crackled between us, I wheeled my suitcase into the bathroom and found an empty stall.

I needed to get out of my clothes and into something cooler before I gave my vagina heatstroke. And if I was truthful, only part of it was garment related.

With limited space, I quickly stripped, immediately feeling better as the cool air hit my hot skin, and redressed into something more weather appropriate.

And then with a quick repack and check of the mirror, I was back outside the bathroom to find Ryan leaning sexily up against the wall with his phone in his hand.

"Wow." The appreciation in his eyes now visible with the sunglasses he'd been wearing missing in action. "I think I'm in love with your dress."

"Thank you." My hands smoothed down the fabric, secretly thrilled he liked it. "She's dry clean only, way too high-maintenance for you."

"Directions are for suckers." He took the suitcase out of my hands and tipped his head toward the door. "Besides, I'm a firm subscriber that rules are lame and they should always be broken. I bet half the shit printed on labels is a lie."

Of course, he was right. About the dress, *not* the rules. I'd washed the dress by hand and nothing bad had happened, but I worried about what my mouth would do if I started talking about hands and what he might do with them. It was a minefield of bad decisions, and one I wouldn't be making today.

We walked out of the terminal and into the morning sun. His black Hummer was parked relatively close as he loaded my suitcase into the back while I climbed into the passenger seat.

"So, tell me something." My head twisted to face him as he slid into the driver's seat and fastened his seat belt.

"Okay." He shrugged, not missing a beat as the smile spread across his lips. "I have a really big cock."

"What the hell?" The air from my lungs expelled in a rush while my brain warned my eyes not to glance down to confirm. Okay, so maybe I'd looked before and from early investigations he was telling the truth, but now he had said it out loud it was harder not to go there. Damn it, now I really wanted to look. "Why would you even tell me that?"

Don't look at his crotch.

Do *not* look at his crotch.

Do not—too late. My eyes floated to the fly of his jeans.

"You told me to tell you something." He smirked, catching my not-so-discreet glances. "So I did."

"It was a rhetorical question."

"You shouldn't have paused then." He started the ignition, the smoldering continued as he side-eyed me, easing out of the parking spot. "You said tell you something, and then you paused. If you wanted to ask something else, or you were particular about what it was you wanted to know, you should have probably just asked."

Speechless.

I'd been with him maybe thirty minutes? Forty-five at a stretch, and he'd already told me he had a large cock and offered to undress me. Granted, I had been a willing participant, wading into the murky water along with him. But while I should have been horrified and possibly offended, I was neither. My eyes still staring at his lap, trying to x-ray vision through those fantastic jeans.

"Lila, you *do* realize you're checking out my dick." He chuckled, forcing my attention back to his eyes. "I'm totally fine with it, but I just want to be sure you weren't stroking out or anything."

"Nice choice of words," I squeaked out, my eyes shooting upward, not allowing my gaze to dip lower than his chin. Clearly, my eyes couldn't be trusted to behave, so I needed to set up an exclusion zone.

"Thanks, it was intentional." The edges of his lips twisted as we pulled into traffic.

He was so much better at this than me. His effortlessly sexy and playful banter forced me to up my game. Because that's what this was, a game. And as tempting as it was to lose myself in the performance of it all, nothing serious would ever eventuate.

Because Ryan didn't do serious.

While he hadn't had a girlfriend in a while, he'd never seemed lacking for female company. They didn't seem to mind being his playthings, and I didn't want to be part of his harem.

That's not what I wanted, right?

Unless, did I?

"So, back to my original question." I held up my hands, stopping him before he volunteered something else I shouldn't want to know, but very much did. "And before you give me any other unsolicited information, let me be clear. I was going to ask you about the MCM charity thing."

"Boring." He groaned. "Why the hell would you want to know about that? I thought you were my people, Lila." He shook his head, a small smile hinting he wasn't as disgusted as he pretended. "You know, we sit on the sidelines and scoff at the famous people."

"Your best friend is famous," I pointed out, the same guy who was also paying his salary.

"Exactly, but I've been calling him an asshole from before the money rolled in, just doing my part in keeping it real."

I loved how unaffected he was by it all. That he'd somehow assimilated to his lifestyle with no bitterness, no pretense—and he still called his super-famous best friend an asshole without hesitation.

"Eric is not an asshole." I eased into my seat, the slow rush of air brushing past my lips as I breathed out. "He's smart and sexy and sooooo talented. I can't wait to see him again." My hands clutched dreamily under my chin.

Eric was indeed all of those things, but I had no feelings for him other than a casual appreciation for his good looks—he was hot and I wasn't blind—and gratitude, because he made Tia happy.

But I couldn't help but needle Ryan, knowing the line to his bedroom had sometimes included a woman or two who had used him in order to get to Eric. And the one thing he wouldn't be was someone's consolation prize.

"Again you disappoint me." Ryan shook his head, rolling his eyes. "I had such high hopes for us too and yet, you wound me."

"Oh, stop." I gently pushed against his arm, loving that I had a legitimate excuse to touch him. "*I* know your ego isn't that fragile, and *you* know I was joking."

"You want to kiss and make up?" He turned his head, a smile that could obliterate panties playing across his lips. "I can pull over."

YES!

Who cared if it was only one time? I bet it would be worth it, my lips not even caring about the average kisses that would probably follow. Because Ryan York looked like the kisses he'd deliver would be unforgettable. No one could have a mouth like that and *not* know how to use it. I bet he knew *exactly* what to do with it, and kissing would only be the start.

"Maybe later." Words I hadn't wanted to say were volunteered by my mouth. Because clearly I was too smart for my own good. "I'll take a rain check."

"Suit yourself." Ryan shrugged, completely unaffected as his eyes returned to the road.

I marveled at his ability to be so cool, so collected, when being around him made me feel like a hot mess. Thank God I still had the ability to camouflage my attraction so he didn't see me as the mumbling moron he reduced me to whenever I got too close.

"So, the charity event." I tried again, forcing my mind out of neutral. "What's it like?"

There was zero chance of me writing the story Dick had wanted me to write. An exposé on one of Hollywood's biggest night of nights was not happening. But it did get me thinking maybe I could work a different angle. An unbiased insider's view into the lives of the rich and the beautiful, not as a gossip piece but an illustration on their normality—a peek behind the curtain. It was still just rough thoughts in my head but if the information was given willingly and not under false pretenses, then surely that was okay, right? And no one would be more impartial than I was, and it would finally present the group of seemingly pedestaled humans in an accurate light.

His head turned and he looked at me strangely, like something in my voice tipped him off or he could read my mind.

"First rule of Fight Club, Lila." His eyebrow rose, his voice sending a shiver down my spine. "You do not talk about Fight Club."

"Fine." I sighed, trying to play it off like it was no big deal. "It would have been off the record."

"You're a reporter. *Nothing* is off the record." His lips twitched into a grin. "But enough talking about you, we should be talking about me. Tell me, how much did you miss me?"

And with that, we slipped into an easy conversation about

nothing important. I lied and told him I hadn't given him a second thought and then conveniently diverted it back onto him. Asking him how he'd been and how life had been treating him in general. He was relaxed, speaking freely as he got me up to speed since we'd last seen each other a couple of weeks or so ago in New York. Women or dating weren't mentioned, the subject conveniently sidestepped as he spoke about other things. And either he was a choirboy who went home early for church—not a chance—or he was being discreet.

I should have been thankful, but I couldn't help being curious. Wondering if the information omission had been intentional because it was me. If not for Tia—who was better at collecting intelligence than the FBI—I'd never even known about the revolving door of women.

While his BFF had happily settled down with a significant other, Ryan showed no signs of following suit. Still, if everyone was a consenting adult, then he really wasn't doing anything wrong.

"So, I heard you've got a new girlfriend," I baited, knowing full well it was a lie. "What did Tia say her name was?" I tapped my fingers on my lips pretending I didn't remember the redhead he'd apparently dated a couple of weeks ago. "Celeste?"

"Tia has a big mouth." Ryan raised an eyebrow, his face betraying nothing. "And she isn't, wasn't and will never be my girlfriend."

"Wow, my mistake then." I pretended his strong denial didn't thrill me. "I guess there are plenty more fish in the sea." Sadly, it was probably his desire to sample more of the *pond* that saw him throw poor Celeste back.

"Well, lucky for you I'm not interested in a girlfriend. I'm a free agent."

Yeah, I'll bet. Free to play the field, sow his wild oats, or whatever else he wanted to do. Just like I could do.

Except that I wasn't, and didn't want to.

And that sort of annoyed me.

Which made no sense, because what was he supposed to do? Be a celibate mind reader who kept his dick under lock and key on the chance I got my shit together *and* told him I was actually interested? Yes, that's what he should be doing. Waiting for a fictional relationship which he'd already stated he wasn't interested in—he's a free agent, remember—and for me to have this casual fling I was probably incapable of. Oh, and we'd probably ruin our friendship and make it awkward for our mutual best friends.

And I used to think I was so rational.

Pushing all of that aside, I turned the conversation to safer territory, and asked him about his plans for the coming week. Thankfully, those plans didn't involve other women, or if they did, he didn't mention them.

We returned to playing our game of flirty innuendo until we pulled up to the big black iron gates of the Larsson mansion. And even though I'd seen it all before, it was no less impressive as Ryan parked the car and we made our way to the front door.

Eric's house was huge by anyone's standards. With so many rooms you needed a GPS to find your way around, it was equally beautiful and intimidating. If the house itself wasn't spectacular enough, the stunning manicured lawns, and a lagoon-style pool which overlooked the Hills surely would do it. The seduction by real estate wasn't necessary, but if there was any doubt, any decent New York woman would cream her pants at the large walk-in closets.

Then there was Ryan's place, a small cottage nestled away opposite the house. It too was stunning, but with less fanfare or grandeur, although I'd yet to see inside. It—like his penis—had been a self-appointed no-fly zone, enforced because I knew I couldn't be trusted.

"Lila," Eric said as he welcomed me at the door, wrapping his arms around me in a friendly hug. "Tia has messaged me about forty times asking if you'd arrived yet. She's been drinking." His smile hinted that his girlfriend was probably going to be loaded by the time she got back. "I'm beginning to think her going to Santa Barbara with my mother wasn't such a good idea."

"Seriously, Larsson." Ryan laughed, stepping past us as he carried my suitcase into the house. "You already have one woman, try leaving something for the rest of us."

"He has issues." Eric rolled his eyes, waiting for me to step inside before following me. "Feel free to ignore him."

Ignore him? Why didn't Eric just ask me to stop breathing because those two things had equal chances of happening.

"It's fine." I laughed, trying to not be obviously awkward. "You're not working today?"

Eric and Tia split their time between coastlines, with their address dictated by Eric's filming schedule. Tia—a columnist for *The New York Post*—could work anywhere and therefore wasn't shackled to a desk. Something I sometimes envied.

"Just about to leave, I had a late start and thought I'd wait around and say hi." He gave me a blinding Larsson smile. "Make yourself at home. I'll see you later tonight."

"Thanks," I responded, giving his arm a squeeze. "Don't be offended if I'm unconscious. I'm on east coast time."

"None taken. Ryan will entertain you if you get bored." His head tipped to the man in question who was still standing beside my suitcase. "Play nice."

"I always do." Ryan opened the door, giving Eric a casual wave. "See you later, my lord."

"Bye," Eric said smiling, flipping off Ryan as he walked outside.

And then we were alone.

Me.

Him.

The big empty house.

"You look nervous." Ryan folded his arms across his delicious chest, his biceps straining against the arms of his T-shirt. "You want to talk about it?"

Lord.

The last thing I wanted to do was talk. I wanted him to stop looking at me with those beautiful brown eyes and kiss me like he'd offered to do in the car. To take my mouth and then my body in a way that was even too obscene to say out loud. I wanted dirty, hot, porno sex so that tomorrow I would walk funny and my voice would be hoarse from screaming his name.

So, no.

I didn't want to talk.

But I guess that's all I had, because unfortunately I didn't do casual sex, which was exactly what it would be.

Asshole.

Me, I meant.

"I should . . ." *Lick you, kiss you, take that shirt you're wearing and fashion it into a shrine?* "Go put my suitcase upstairs."

"Hey." He grabbed my arm, stopping me before getting the suitcase I'd mentioned and going to get lost upstairs. "I was just playing around before, you know that right?"

"Of course." A nervous laugh bubbled up my throat. "We're totally cool."

Great. Now I was talking like someone from the valley. All I needed to do was twist my hair and pop a hip and use "like" every other word. Now was not the time to feed into the stereotype of my blonde-hair blue-eyed looks.

"Yeah, I don't believe you." He stalked closer, his eyes studying me like my face might yield answers. Lord, why did he have to pick today to be so perceptive?

I had a choice to make.

Tell him something—a lie—and hope I could be convincing

so shit didn't get weird. Or tell him the truth and let shit get weird.

Both those options sucked.

And neither involved us getting naked, so I guess I was shit out of luck.

"I need a story."

Okay, so we were going to go down that road. Technically not a lie, and it *was* my reason for being here.

"What kind of story?"

"Well, my editor wants me to infiltrate the MCM charity event and give a tell-all account. And before you look at me with judgey eyes, it wasn't going to happen," I added, not wanting him to even think for a second I would use my relationship with either Eric or Tia for a story.

"I wasn't going to give you judgey eyes." He moved closer, his hand gripping my arm tighter.

"No?"

"No, that's too passive aggressive for me." His mouth twitched. "I would have told you to your face I was judging you."

"I wouldn't have done it."

"I wouldn't have let you."

I wasn't sure if it was those words, his proximity or that I was sharing my *feelings*. Not the ones that pertained to him, but feelings none the less. In any case, none of it should have been hot but yet, as I stood there, my core was burning like I had ingested a vat of gunpowder and he'd casually tossed in a match. Worst part of all, I had no desire for it to stop.

"So . . . now what?" he asked, not moving his hand or his body out of the blast zone.

"I have to figure something else out." God, this would be easier if he'd stop looking at me. *Look away, look away.* "He wants an entertainment piece but not gossip, and nothing depressing."

"Which explains the impromptu visit."

"Yes."

Normally, talking things out made me feel better. And had my best friend not been off somewhere drinking adult grape juice, my heart to heart would have been with her. It's what I'd planned to do when she got back, hopefully when she was sober so we could make good choices.

But talking it over with Ryan didn't ease me in the same way. My hot and bothered state complicated the discussion, making it difficult for me to concentrate on words, which were necessary if I wanted a resolution.

"So you need a story."

"Yes."

I was down to single-word answers and there wasn't a thing I could do about it. Years of education was no match for the six-foot-two sex god and the fire he'd set to my core.

"Fine, we'll get you a story." There was no hesitation, like he could run down to the store and pick it up with a quart of milk.

"It's not that easy." I had to look away, needing a reprieve from all that was Ryan York so I could think clearly. "And it's not your problem, it's mine."

"But I know now, so I'm already involved. And more importantly, you could use the help."

At least he was honest, and on both accounts, correct. I *could* use the help whether I begrudgingly wanted to admit it or not. And he wasn't the kind of guy to sit idly on the sidelines either, which just made me more crazily attracted to him than I already was.

"Fine." I wasn't sure if I was thrilled or terrified that I was going to be working so closely with Ryan. But the smile on my face was probably not a good sign. "As long as you're clear that I'm taking the lead on this."

"You've just been looking for an excuse to dominate me, haven't you?" He laughed, his eyes moving restlessly down my body.

"All you had to do was ask, princess."

The man was killing me.

Killing me.

But I wouldn't crack.

"Don't get too excited, this is work." The reminder served a dual purpose for both him and myself; my own levels of delight highly inappropriate. "Now let's go sit down and talk this out."

"Too late." He smirked. "I'm already excited," he called over his shoulder as he turned around and headed to the living room.

"Great."

I was either an idiot or delusional.

CHAPTER #3

WITH PARENTS WHO still lived in Vegas, you would think I'd be more adapted to the flights and time zone changes. But I wasn't. My eyelids started to droop just after dinner and neither Eric nor Tia had come home yet.

Ryan and I spent the day camped out in the living room, my idea for the story discussed in detail. He listened to my pitch—unmasking the famous people—and even had some good suggestions of his own.

He ordered pizza and opened a bottle of wine, our relaxed dinner allowing us to talk about things other than work. I liked talking to him and the way he looked at me when he listened, as if absorbing every word.

He had the most amazing brown eyes. Deep and rich like chocolate, the expensive kind that was so creamy and delicious you didn't care how much wider it made your ass. And the rest of him was just as addictive too. I needed to keep a tally of my glances and ration them out like Weight Watchers points. I was pretty sure I'd already blown my daily allowance as my eyes traveled up his deliciously strong forearms, his big hands resting leisurely on his knees.

I'd even kept a responsible distance away from him, opting for the armchair rather than the couch. But those eyes and body were like a vortex, and I could have been slinging burgers in Reno and still felt the heat from them.

It became more difficult as the hours wore on—the time change, the early morning, the additional concentration it took to keep my mouth to myself—and I was becoming increasingly exhausted. All of those contributing factors increased the chances of a slip, one where I fell into his lap and sucked his cock.

"You want me to take you to bed?"

"Huh?" My head snapped up and I wasn't sure if I'd heard it right, or if my subconscious had started throwing in suggestions of its own. Because maybe him taking me to bed wasn't such a bad idea. No. It was. *Bad, Lila.*

"I said, did you want to go to bed?" he clarified. "Clearly you're tired and I've never had a girl fall asleep on me, so we shouldn't start that now." His eyes shone with wicked intention. "Last thing I need is the bad press."

Yeah, wouldn't want someone to get the wrong idea and have him need to prove me wrong. It's not like I didn't already have a vivid imagination of how amazing he'd be. Women were probably able to stay awake for a week after being with him purely from the adrenaline. I, unfortunately, hadn't had a proper hit.

"I'm sorry." I yawned, scrubbing my face, unable to will myself more alert. "I'm running low on stimulants today."

The minute I'd said it, I knew it was a mistake. A complete rookie error—stimulants and stimulate, not the kind of words that would be overlooked.

"You know that is begging for me to say something, right?" He could barely contain the grin. "And I'm trying to be good, so it's killing me to keep my mouth shut. Which means, I'm going to need some recognition or something—acknowledging you tossed me the perfect pass and I didn't go for a slam dunk."

"It has been acknowledged." I nodded, his good behavior noted and appreciated. "You and your mouth are awesome."

Shit. And double shit.

"Again, you're giving me waaaay too much to work with."

Wasn't that the truth. Who needed enemies, when with enough sleep deprivation and lack of caffeine, I'd hang myself. I knew what my last meal would be—Ryan York's delicious body, consumed one lick at a time.

"And on that note, I should probably go to sleep."

I needed to cut my losses, start fresh tomorrow when I was rested and wasn't liable to say stupid stuff. Besides, I needed to take the edge off this sexual frustration, have some quality time with the showerhead and its multiple *massage* settings. *Yeah, I'd like that.* I slowly rose from the armchair and stretched.

"You need a hand?"

"Mmm, no." The words lazy in my mouth as I closed my eyes. "I've got it covered. I'll take care of it in the shower."

"What?"

"Nothing." My eyes sprung open, hoping he'd developed a hearing disorder or something. Lord, at least let him keep up the pretense of ignorance, that would be the polite thing to do. "I meant I'm good."

"Ok-ay." The smile hinted he wasn't an idiot. "Let me carry your bags up then."

Not a good idea. We'd already established I had left my A-game back on the east coast and the breathy confessions, even in the vaguest possible form, weren't helping my cause. If I got him near a bed, who knew what I'd volunteer. And if I had to guess, his *hand* wouldn't be what I'd be asking for.

"It's fine, you've already done enough." My attempt to move past him foiled as he stood in my way. "I can get my case up the stairs."

"Why don't you just let me do it. It will make me feel manly and I won't have to worry about you sleepily missing a stair or some shit and breaking your neck. I'd rather avoid difficult conversations, and if you died or something, that would make it kind of unavoidable."

"You just keep wearing me down," I conceded, too many times in less than twenty-four hours that he'd convinced me to do exactly what he'd wanted.

He was slick about it too. Making it seem like it was a better idea if I yielded to him, and honestly, I wasn't putting up much of a fight. But as tempting as it was, I could see how it could be dangerous.

"Princess, I'm not even trying."

He looked over his shoulder as he walked back to the doorway where my suitcase and handbag were dumped.

I followed him up the stairs, his tall, strong body, agile as it climbed. I loved the way his shoulders flexed, the steady movements of his arms and legs—everything so controlled and so goddamn hot I couldn't stand it.

The *princess* thing wasn't new. He seemed to have an aversion to using people's real names and had thrown it around a few times. I'd figured it was because he assumed I was high maintenance—the nice clothes, heels, long hair, makeup, etc. and decided to bestow on me a moniker that seemed fitting. Of course he'd never confirmed it, and I got a stupid thrill out of hearing it so I didn't ask, even if it was wildly inaccurate.

FYI, I was *far* from high maintenance.

He strode casually into the room I usually used when I stayed with Tia and lowered my suitcase on the floor. His feet stayed in placed as he watched me walk in. It would be so easy to push him down on the bed and do whatever the hell I wanted with him. And if the look on his face was anything to go by, I doubted he'd fight me.

I wanted to.

I was tempted.

"You need anything else?" He stepped closer, the distance between us almost nonexistent as his heady scent invaded my space.

He smelled so good, fresh and clean and manly—and I wasn't sure how much of it was cologne and how much was just him. I leaned closer, just wanting to inhale a bit more so I could lock up the memory and store it for later.

"God, you smell good."

It wasn't an accident. They hadn't casually slipped out of my mouth. I'd wanted to say those words and damn the consequences, I wanted *consequences*, I wanted them all over me in the worst way.

Maybe just this one time?

Maybe we could do it and nothing bad would happen. I mean, he was used to hook-ups all the time, maybe we could have amazing sex and all the scenarios which made it terrible—I'd be just another notch in his belt, he'd lose interest in me, we'd mess up our friendship etc. etc.—wouldn't have to eventuate. We could be an anomaly. Not break the rules, but *change* the game.

"Lila?" And it was clear the question he was asking wasn't my name.

"I said you smelled good." My face moved inches from his neck and took a deep inhale.

It was exaggerated, like Rachael Ray taking a whiff of her chocolate caramel mud cake.

All I had to do was kiss him.

Plant my lips on his neck and let my mouth take over.

I bet he tasted as good too.

"Lila!"

My name punched through the silence followed by the thundering of footsteps. The moment vanished, taking with it my lowered defenses and stupidity.

I couldn't sleep with Ryan.

What the hell was I thinking?

He blinked, not responding to our soon-to-be company as he moved his mouth closer and whispered in my ear, "Now that's *my* rain check."

There wasn't any time to argue—assuming I wanted to, which I didn't—taking a step away just as Tia stormed through the door and threw herself at me.

"Leeeeeellllaaa." Her arms clung to my neck, her legs not doing a good job of keeping her upright. "Oooooooh, you look so good." Her face was flushed as she took a step back. "Doesn't she look good, Ryan?"

"She sure does." He grinned, leaning up against the wall as his eyes traveled suggestively up my body.

"Fun time in Santa Barbara, huh?" I laughed, ignoring Ryan and his sexy eyes. I'd deal with them later.

"I think I drank too much." She giggled, leaning in closer. "Eric's mom can really put it away. I mean she had five sons, I'd have drank a lot too."

"Sounds like a good time, sweet cheeks. I hope neither of you were driving."

"Please, I can barely operate a can opener right now, a car would have been out of the question." She waved her arms erratically. "No, Ryan's mom, Donna, drove." She smiled at him sweetly.

"Oh, really?" I turned to him, the detail not important but interesting all the same.

"Our moms hang out, I've told them it will only lead to bad things, but no one seems to listen." He shrugged with an easy sigh.

"Incidentally, Ryan, between your mom and Eric's, I got some seriously good dirt." Tia narrowed her eyes, a devious smile on her lips. "And if you decide to ever release that video you have of me singing, *you* will never date in this town again."

"And I rest my case." He smiled, tipping his chin to Tia. "All right, ladies, unless you need me to show you where the closest exits are or help you raise your tray tables, I'm going to jet."

"I think we've got it." I waved him off, my plans for an erotic shower and collapsing into bed temporarily shelved. Well, I guess if nothing else, it would keep me out of trouble.

"Awesome. Tia," he gave her a gentle shoulder shake, "you might want to drink some coffee or something."

"Nah, I had an espresso martini, I've totally got this." She gave him a thumbs up that convinced neither of us she had *anything* other than a future hangover.

"Yep." He stepped toward to the door. "Call if you need anything." The last part directed at me.

"All good." I watched him walk out, all six-foot-two of sexiness, as I mentally listed all the *needs* that might justify a call. All of them sexual, so I probably needed to hide my phone from myself just in case.

"You need help getting to your room?" Dirty thoughts were pushed aside as I faced a very drunk and gravity-challenged Tia.

"Pfft, it's still early." She looked at me like I was the crazy one. "I'm going to wait up for Eric. We're going to have hot sex."

"Oh, I'm sure that's *exactly* what's going to happen." I pitied her boyfriend when he walked through the door. Assuming she didn't fall asleep first, she was going to throw her vagina at him first and ask questions later. "Don't puke in his lap though, it will probably be a mood killer."

"Yeah, he's going to be late. I think I have a few hours to sober up." She wobbled, unsteady on her feet.

"Maybe you should get a nap before he gets home." I stopped short of telling her napping sounded like a solid plan and I could use the rest myself. "That would be the smart thing to do."

"Come on, Lila, we both know I'm terrible at choosing the smart option."

"True." I shook my head, unable to suppress the laugh. "So, what do you want to do? Although I have to be honest with you, I'm exhausted."

"Oh, shit. I'm sorry." She looked panicked, grabbing my hand. "I should let you sleep. We'll catch up tomorrow."

"I'm so glad to be here with you." I pulled her in for a hug, having missed her crazy and warmth in my life. I didn't get to see her nearly enough and hoped she didn't take my need to power down as a sign I didn't care.

"Me too." She hugged me back, tapping me awkwardly on the shoulder. "Tomorrow we're gonna hang out all day."

"Sure, whatever you want."

"Okay, goodnight, Lila."

"Night."

CHAPTER #4

I TOSSED AND turned most of the night.

The expensive mattress and fine Egyptian cotton sheets where I was attempting to sleep were negated by my restless mind and the hormone party currently taking up residence in my body.

Not even the impressive showerhead with all its massage settings in my private adjoining bathroom helped. All it did was give me a couple of mediocre orgasms, a sore wrist and pruned skin. Nothing even close to making me feel better.

So, it was with mixed emotions that I descended the stairs the next morning, no more refreshed than when I climbed them, looking for caffeine and a decent distraction.

"You're up early." Eric was sipping coffee as I walked into the kitchen. "Sleep well?"

He was already dressed, wearing a pair of designer jeans and T-shirt; his famous movie-star smile and tussled hair making him look better than he should, given the time of the morning.

I still wasn't used to the whole thing. I had been accustomed to seeing him on a screen, and now I was staying at his house. And I would never admit it in this lifetime or the next, that even with all that star power, Ryan was still better looking.

"Fine," I lied, looking enviably at the coffee pot. "I always need a day or so to get back into the swing of things. Tia still asleep?"

"Yeah." He didn't even try to hide his grin. "She had an interesting night."

Yeah, I'll bet, and if the smile on his face was anything to go by, I'd say he didn't hate her *interesting* night all that much either.

"So, I wanted to tell you something, before Tia got up."

I'm not sure why I felt it was important, but it was. Maybe because I assumed Ryan might have mentioned it and I wanted him to hear my side. Or maybe because I didn't want him to ever think I was someone he couldn't trust.

"Sounds serious." His coffee cup lowered as he gave me his full attention.

"It's about this gala thing you guys are going to." My voice was unsteady, moving through the words with no confidence. Perhaps I should have waited to have the conversation until after the coffee.

"Last I heard, you were coming too." His eyebrow rose, challenging me to say something different.

"Okay, so here's the thing." I was thinking of bypassing the coffee and heading straight to vodka. "I'm happy to come—to be honest, I'm as curious as hell—but my editor wanted the inside scoop. And even though I've already said I wouldn't write about it—there is literally no chance I will do a dirty exposé—I just wanted to tell you. Because . . . you should know."

Drinking would have definitely been a smart option.

"Do you think by telling me I'm going to let you off the hook, withdraw Tia's invitation?" He leaned back against his kitchen counter, surprisingly wearing a smile.

"I don't know. Maybe."

Was that what I was doing? Unintentionally avoiding the situation so the decision was made for me? Well, shit. That wasn't usually my style.

"You've known her a lot longer than I have, so this should come as no surprise to you. But if she wants you there, neither you nor I are going to stop that." He laughed, rightfully assuming that neither of us was going to have a choice.

"Handling" Tia was like trying to defuse a bomb while wearing oven mitts—well above my level of expertise.

"Gee, big help you are," I scoffed, feeling more at ease by just having the conversation.

"Yep, but if you want my help on anything else, let me know." He lowered his cup into the sink. "Ryan will be here around ten to take you ladies out."

Just the sound of his name sent a shiver down my spine.

I hadn't planned on seeing him today, hoping to give my lady parts a break from the hormone assault he threw at us whenever he was in the room.

"Oh?" I grabbed a cup from the cupboard and poured some coffee, my attempt at acting casual.

"Yeah, Tia needs a dress for the gala." He bit back his grin. "And she informed the stylist she wasn't interested in her services or her selection of dresses."

Ha! I was almost positive those were *not* the words she would have used.

"I'm sure she wasn't that polite."

"No," he laughed, "which is why you two are going to go out and spend an obscene amount of money on whatever stuff you both need. I don't care what you guys buy, as long as she's happy."

Oh, that was dangerous, and suddenly the idea of going shopping for a gala dress wasn't so bad. I didn't usually like to take advantage of a man and his wallet, preferring to *independent women"* my way like Destiny's Child. But I figured there should be exceptions to every rule.

"I'll keep her away from the makeup counters." It was the least

I could do, it's where she'd do the most damage anyway.

"Good plan."

"You know, we're more than capable of taking out one of those fancy cars of yours." I took a sip of my coffee, trying to subtly take care of the Ryan situation. "We don't need a driver."

"Come on, Lila." He lowered his gaze and met my eyes. "You're a smart woman, you know Ryan isn't *just* a driver."

Ooooooo, well this was news. I mean I assumed he ran errands and stuff like that, you know, to keep him busy and justify his paycheck. But now I was curious as to what other activities were listed on his resume.

"What, like security?" The idea making me hotter than it should.

"Let's say he has more training in hand-to-hand combat and personal security than he does in driving. And he's been at the wheel since he took his old man's Ford for a joyride when he was ten."

And now he had my attention. My lady parts and my brain fought for dominance, one wanting to know exactly what his skill set was, while the other fantasized about him topless in camo pants infiltrating hostile territory and rescuing a hostage with his bare hands. I'll let you guess which one belonged to whom.

"Wow. I just assumed he was . . ." I deliberately left the sentence trailing, not wanting to say the word *entourage*.

"Yeah, part of the ruse." Eric folded his arms across his chest, an amused look on his face. "We both went for the same role right out of college, a movie about marines in Iraq. I got a major role and he a minor one, but we were both sent to do some training with the real deal. He took it super serious, which considering his personality should have been a hunch. He ended up getting in tight with those guys, took what we learned for the movie and kicked it up a few notches in his private time. I needed someone to watch my back when I was traveling, so it seemed like the perfect solution."

"Holy shit. This is amazing." The lady parts were currently winning out. No wonder he was so freaking fit. I wondered if he Instagrams his workouts, I was going to be investigating the minute Eric walked out the door. "Does Tia know?"

It was information I would have liked—for reasons—and it wasn't something I would have easily forgotten. So, if she had known, she hadn't mentioned it.

"Yeah, she knows." He looked at me carefully, like he was gauging whether I was pretending to be surprised or his girlfriend had legitimately kept it from her best friend. She had by the way, but I would deal with that later.

"I had to explain why I wanted Ryan to drive her around rather than let her go by herself. There are some crazy fans out there who aren't excited I've got a girlfriend. We both specifically asked her to keep that information to herself, the more people who know, the less affective his role is."

"So, you would rather people think he's some glorified hanger on?" It's what I'd guessed when I'd first met him, then later I assumed Eric liked having someone normal around just to keep him grounded. Oh, and given a chance, I'd like Ryan to *ground* me.

Mmmm, well.

Wow.

The fantasy about Ryan in camo pants was back, and I had to wonder if he owned a pair. Maybe I could pick some up for him while on our little dress excursion, multitasking our outing. Not that I had an explanation as to why I'd be buying him pants. I would need to work on my excuse.

"Yep, that's exactly what we want." Eric pulled me from my dirty thoughts before adding, "So, now *you* know." A pointed look was thrown my way, a hint that he didn't just let *anyone* into his circle.

My mind was awash with thoughts. Granted, most of them

dirty, but now I knew the reason, I wasn't surprised Tia had kept her mouth shut. While she was liberal with what she usually told me, she was hardcore at keeping confidences. It was one of the reasons why I had originally trusted her with my background and past.

Eric was the big time, and there were a lot of people whose intentions might not be friendly. So, having undercover security made sense. The less people that knew . . .

"I'm not going to print any of that, or tell anyone, if that's what you're worried about."

Not that I would ever exploit him, but I felt compelled since he'd been so honest with me that I reassured him all that stuff was off limits.

"If I was worried I wouldn't have told you."

And even though it was only the two of us in the kitchen, my mind was elsewhere. I had ADRHD, Attention Deficit Ryan Hyperactivity Disorder, and the only cure was a shot of the man himself. *I'd like to take my inoculation orally, doctor.*

"Hey." Tia emerged, hair all askew, squinting like the sunlight was personally offensive. "My head hurts."

"I've got you." I nodded, making my way to the fridge and taking out orange juice. "Larsson, grab me some vodka, will you? I need to make Tia some breakfast."

I started pouring, knowing exactly what was going to help her wicked hangover.

"Maybe lay off the vodka," he suggested, wrapping his arms around Tia. "You know, just try drinking the juice straight?"

"Oh, no, no, no." I gasped in horror. I mean, it was one thing to allow him to steal away my best friend to his mansion in the hills, but drinking straight juice with a hangover? Next he'd be suggesting a freaking kale smoothie. "Why don't you go to work, I've got this."

"Fine." He shook his head, planting a kiss on Tia, completely ignoring me. "I'll be late tonight. Don't wait up."

She mumbled something back that was probably not fit for public consumption because the smile on his face could melt the Polar Ice Caps.

Thankfully I didn't have to suffer through too much of the display before Eric disappeared.

"Soooooo." I started opening random cupboards searching for some sort of alcohol to doctor up the juice. "I know about Ryan," I casually threw over my shoulder, my search not being fruitful.

"What about Ryan?" She shrugged, walking over to the freezer and pulling out a bottle of Grey Goose.

"Oh, that like Liam Neeson from *Taken*, he has a *particular set of skills*." And I wondered exactly how far those skills extended.

"Lila." She started to apologize. "I couldn't—"

"It's fine," I waved her off, not at all upset, "I get why you couldn't tell me but now that I know, you need to tell me everything."

"Well, the whole *he wants to be an actor* is bullshit." She moved in closer like she was thrilled she was finally allowed to spill. "He hasn't wanted to act in years. He knows some kind of Israeli military martial arts and could probably kill you with a kitchen spoon or something. If he ever gets tired of this gig with Eric, he could totally be an assassin." Her eyes widened, more than likely with excitement.

"I would think bodyguard or work for the Secret Service would have made more sense, but sure, assassin."

Ryan didn't need to be elevated to any higher hotness level than he already was. His face, body and stellar personality already took care of that. But add in the new secret information, and he was in a completely new realm. Now he needed his own warning label, and a fire extinguisher.

While I made us screwdrivers—I wasn't nursing a hangover,

but since I wasn't driving, a cheeky morning cocktail wasn't a bad thing—while Tia filled me in.

Key points.

Eric was required to have security for insurance purposes, apparently the studio got concerned he might be the target of a crazy stalker. Ironic considering who he was dating, but I digress. He also needed a driver and didn't like the idea of hiring a bunch of people he didn't know and most importantly didn't trust. So, it made sense for him to hire his best friend, who not only knew him better than anyone but also was trained in both areas. They had decided to keep the details under wraps though because Eric hated the need for security—and probably didn't want to look like a pussy—and Ryan liked to trade off on the aforementioned pussy by being the hot friend who hung with Eric rather than worked for him. Smart plan. Hell, they fooled me.

"Hmmm." I sipped my drink—yes there was vodka in it, but it had the juice, so totally acceptable for breakfast. "I wonder if girls knew all the macho shit we know, if it would get him more or less interest." Who was I kidding? Women practically threw themselves at him now. Any *more* interested, and he'd have to sell tickets.

Irrationally, it irked me. Not because I wanted him, no, of course not. I mean, yes I wanted him—sexually—but that was more of a curiosity thing. An appreciation for his fine form, to see how all of *that* would measure up. And I meant that literally. But I didn't *want* him, want him.

"Hey, you with me?" Tia waved her hand in front of my face, my daydream of wanting/not wanting Ryan taking me away from the present conversation. "Do you want breakfast or should we get something while we're out?"

"Let's eat here. I have a feeling we're going to be busy while we're out."

Maybe I might try to test how slick Ryan really was. Sure, I was in L.A. for work, to find a story and all of that, but no one said I couldn't have a little fun while I was at it.

CHAPTER #5

RYAN WALKED THROUGH the door a little after ten wearing a pair of jeans that had been stitched by the hand of God and a T-shirt that had no business being sexy. While images of him wearing a black suit and talking into his cuff entertained me, I gave him a friendly but reserved greeting.

There was no hug, which was a shame because it punished me as much as it did him, but alas, I was playing the long game. Why? I still wasn't sure but it was too late to change tactics now.

Tia, Ryan and I loaded into his blacker-than-black Hummer and headed to Beverly Hills. We sat in the back seat with Ryan obviously up front, but we chatted amicably on the drive. He'd given me more than just a few looks in his rearview mirror. Nothing crazy, and it could have been his need to check traffic, but I liked the idea of him wanting to look at me, so that was what I was going with.

After parking, we started our little expedition at Sak's Fifth Avenue on Wilshire.

Ryan accompanied us to the ladies section, his face beaming as he spied the lingerie department. "You could model something for me if you want," he whispered in my ear. "I'll give you my honest opinion."

"Maybe I will." I grinned like an idiot, irrationally excited at the prospect I knew wasn't going to happen. I mean, Tia was with us, that would be weird. And honestly, that was probably the only thing saving us right now—an audience. "There's a guy at work that has asked me out. It's always good to be prepared."

It was childish, and I stupidly played the oldest trick in the book, trying to make him jealous because I had nothing better in my bag of tricks. It wasn't what I had wanted to resort to and was immediately disappointed with myself.

"Well, he's not here now is he, princess?" His eyes darkened, his smile not slipping. "So, I don't give a shit."

"It's not nice to keep secrets." Tia glared, noticing our quiet whisperings as she strode to the designer section. "Either tell me, or do what regular people do and text each other covertly."

"Lila was telling me about the guy who asked her out," Ryan volunteered. "He sounds like a douche."

"I have barely said anything about him, how do you know he's a douche?" I planted my hands on my hips.

"Is this the sports guy?" Tia stopped sifting through clothes racks, lifting her head to give me her full attention. "Because I thought we already agreed that probably wouldn't work out."

"I'm not going to marry him, Tia." I rolled my eyes. "Dating him was allowed."

"I agree with Ryan, he sounds like a douche, don't waste your time." She shrugged returning to her search for a dress.

"Two against one." Ryan didn't even try to hide his satisfied smirk. "Glad we got that settled."

"Nothing was settled." I turned my attention to the closest rack. "My love life isn't a democracy."

It was stupid bringing up another guy. Besides being cliché—and not in a good way—it had totally missed its purpose. If Ryan was jealous, he wasn't showing it. Instead it dragged up attention

I didn't want.

"Oooooo, Tia." I pulled out a red Dolce & Gabbana full-length gown, using its couture beauty as a distraction. "This would look amazing on you."

"You think?" She scrunched her nose, not convinced. "I don't know if I have any shoes that go with it."

"So, we buy shoes." I held it up in front of her. "Just try it on."

"Ladies, can I help you?" A sales associate wandered over, looking at the dress in my hands with interest.

"My friend here is going to a gala." I motioned to Tia. "She needs a dress."

"She's going too." Tia pointed back at me. "So we need *two* dresses."

"And you, sir?" Her attention turned to Ryan, giving him a broader smile than was needed. I bet she had some suggestions on what he could *try on* in the fitting room.

"I'm set, I've already got my dress," he crooned so smoothly I'm surprised the sales associate didn't dissolve into a puddle.

"Oh." She laughed, tipping her head back in an exaggeration of mirth that was totally unnecessary. "I meant a tux, we have a men's department I'd be happy to direct you to. Or if there was something else you needed . . ."

"That's so helpful of you." I smiled sweetly, my grip on the hanger tightening. "But he has everything he needs, so if you could help us, that would be great."

I didn't even care how it sounded, possessive, rude, entitled—who gave a shit? I was probably never going to see this woman again, and she had all but offered to ditch us and go blow him. Okay, maybe that was a slight exaggeration, but I didn't like the attention he was getting.

"Of course." She turned back to us, her fake smile stretching wider. "A gala, right? Sounds exciting, are you all going together?"

Her attention deviated, her eyes landing on Ryan's rather impressive chest.

"You know, maybe we'll look around a little first." Tia gave her a fake smile of her own. "I'll call you if we need help."

"Are you sure?" The sales associate looked slightly panicked, probably mentally calculating the loss of commission.

"Yep, we're good. Thanks." I turned back to the rack to a Versace catching my eye, sensing her retreat more than seeing it.

Good, leave already, because this was my time to ogle Ryan. I didn't want to share it with anyone else.

"Maybe I needed a tux?"

I didn't need to turn around to know he was grinning.

"I'm sure she would have personally measured you as well, see how many inches you needed in the crotch area." My fingers curled around the fabric, not really interested in the dress anymore.

"Maybe I needed that too." He laughed, his breath hot in my ear as he leaned in.

Yeah, I bet.

"Hmmm, well I'm sure she hasn't wandered too far, maybe you can call her back." I acted bored, not willing to allow him to see I was annoyed or even admit it to myself.

I was being dumb. Of course he was interested, she had been relatively attractive and extremely willing—what's not to like. And he probably dated—I used the term loosely—other women just like her, A LOT of them.

I knew this, but having it in front of me was something else. It spiked irrationality in me I had no hope of containing, and I was acting like a brat.

Ignoring him and my mood, I instead put all my effort into finding a dress. My interest in attending the gala now at an all-time low. The thought of seeing Ryan all dressed up in a tux probably looking delicious and having a bunch of famous beautiful women fawning over him, yeah that sounded like a fun night out.

This whole idea, coming out to L.A. and working on a story, now seemed like the lamest one I'd ever had. I blamed Dick, and I was going to pour ExLax in his coffee next time I saw him. Then we'll see who gave whom the shits.

"Found anything?" Tia called out, a couple of dresses draped over her arm as she got closer.

"Not really." Not that I'd actually been looking, moving hangers back and forth didn't really count.

As my head moved away from the clothes and took in my surroundings, I'd noticed Ryan had gone. He wasn't standing beside Tia or near me, and as I scanned the area, all I saw were waves of couture, not a hot six-foot-two hottie in sight anywhere.

"Where did Ryan go?" I asked, not bothering to moderate how interested I sounded. I *was* interested.

"Oh, he walked off a little earlier. I think he was bored. He won't be far." She craned her neck to look around but didn't seem concerned.

Well, I guess he took my advice and went to find whatever her name was and bang in the dressing room or something.

How nice for him.

I hope she has crabs.

"Hi. I'm Ellen." A pretty, leggy, redhead walked up slowly, her smile bright and genuine unlike the last woman who'd approached us. "Ryan thought you might be able to use some help." She looked to her side, Ryan standing beside her. "You're both going to the MCM Gala, right?"

"Yeah," Tia answered cautiously, like me, she didn't trust easily.

"My cousin goes every year." Ellen leaned in. "I got to sneak in one year as his date." A secretive glance was shared between her and Ryan.

"Oh, well that must have been fun," I added, my sincerity

missing in action. I didn't want to even entertain on how they knew each other. I assumed it was sexual. Lord, was there anyone in this town the man wasn't sleeping with?

"Yeah, it was. Ryan is a lot of fun, but you already know that."

Whoa. What?

"Ryan's your cousin?"

I wasn't sure whose mouth it came out of first. Both Tia and I equally surprised at the new information.

"Guilty as charged. You didn't think it was a coincidence you came here and not one of the boutiques, right? Sorry I didn't get here sooner, I was tied up with another customer." She elbowed him gently before taking the dresses from Tia.

"We were entertained in your absence. Someone had offered to help us already." Ryan bit back his grin.

"I'm sure." She rolled her eyes. "Did she offer you a hand job?"

"I assumed she was angling for a blowjob," I added rather cheerily, Ryan's cousin freaking awesome beyond words.

"Ladies." Ryan gripped his chest. "The things you say. I am shocked."

"I agree with hand job actually," Tia weighed in. "That lipstick she was wearing would totally transfer. It would make a mess of her face."

"Good point, Tia." I nodded in agreement. "I assumed she still had a few more hours left on the cock . . . I mean, clock."

Ellen and Tia both laughed—Ryan didn't.

"Should we call her back and ask?" He slid his hands into his pockets, calmly surveying the area. "For research purposes of course."

"Yeah, let's not." Ellen waved off Ryan and then clapped her hands. "Okay. Dresses. Let's get you both into fitting rooms and get you a few different options."

"As long as I don't look like a hooker, I'm good." Tia willingly followed Ellen.

"I'll second that." I too ambled toward the fitting rooms, Ryan close behind me.

"You can take a seat, cuz." Ellen pointed to the comfy couch. "This might take a while."

"With pleasure." He lowered himself into the seat as the three of us disappeared into the fitting rooms.

Ellen was great, picking out a number of different outfits for each of us, all of which were formal enough for a gala but played to our individual strengths. It was fun trying on clothes I would never in a million years have considered, the extra zero on the price tag making them out of my usual price range.

With each option I tried on, I'd show Ellen and Tia. At least that was the reason I told myself why I needed to stride out of the changing room and turn around, displaying every inch of the dress, which inadvertently gave Ryan a fashion show. It wasn't for his benefit, no, I just needed feedback from the girls as to what looked good on me.

I watched him. Watched as his eyes traveled over the length of my body with each outfit change, loving the weight of his gaze on me. It was superficial and I knew that, and I must have been the shallowest person alive because I didn't care.

I liked it.

Wanted more of it.

And didn't want to share it with anyone.

"That one," Ryan coughed, as I emerged from the fitting room in a full-length Herve Leger Bandage dress, the metallic material tight against my body like a second skin.

"You think?" I turned around slowly, giving him a look from all angles. "I'm not usually a gold person."

"Oh, that's so hot." Tia came out to inspect, her body covered in a stunning red Alexander McQueen. "You have to get that one."

"I think you both found your dresses." Ellen smiled at us, a look of satisfaction on her face. "Beautiful, both of you."

"I concur." Ryan nodded, his eyes not leaving my body.

"Then I guess we're done." My hand floated down to my hip as I gave him a few more seconds of the view.

"Good, let's get you both some shoes and accessories." Ellen shooed Tia back into the fitting room. "It will complete the outfit."

Ryan rose to his feet, moving closer. "You need help unzipping, princess?"

"I think I'll manage."

"You sure?"

To be honest, I wasn't sure. The dress wasn't the easiest to get into, so getting out of it would be a challenge. But if I asked him to help me, I'd be tempted to ask his hands to do other things. And unlike some people—previously unnamed sales associate—I wasn't going to give him a blow or hand job in the fitting rooms. Not because I was classier than that—because I wasn't—but because I was worried I wouldn't be able to stop.

"I've got it under control," I lied, and disappeared back into my fitting room.

What was I doing?

How can I be interested in him, jealous of the attention he gives another woman but happy to maintain the status quo? Actually I wasn't happy. I wasn't sure *what* I wanted. Did I need a reminder?

Casual sex—I didn't.

Girlfriends—he didn't.

Ruin a good friendship and possibly make a mess of things— surely that was something neither of us wanted. Why was it so hard this time around?

It was official—I had completely lost control of my mind and body.

It was going to get complicated.

CHAPTER #6

WE MANAGED TO get through the rest of the shopping trip relatively unscathed. Both Ryan and I were on our best behavior and I even discussed my story idea with Tia. You know, the reason why I was here in the first place.

Ryan listened intently, hearing my pitch for the second time while I told Tia, who nodded excitedly about what I was intending to write.

The problem with good ideas was they were often subjective. What might have appeared to be a solid plan yesterday was not necessarily brilliant with the dawning of a new day. And my proposal—the real life and times of Hollywood—might sound awesome, but I had overlooked a small and very important fact.

Other than Eric, I didn't *know* any famous people. Hell, before Tia started dating him, the closest I'd ever been to fame was when a douchebag YouTuber felt me up in a nightclub. I kneed him in the balls and he coughed out expletives, we didn't bother exchanging numbers.

And with zoom lenses lurking through every hedge, I was positive any famous people I *did* meet would probably not have a strong desire to talk to the press. Especially if it wasn't a proper interview, promoting their latest movie or whatever.

So, I was going to need an *in*.

It was still on my mind—various ways to meet the famous people and gain their trust—as we made our way back home, a shiny silver Mercedes with a very attractive man at the wheel catching my eye.

"Shit, was that Dean Watt?" My head craned, my body shifting in my seat to gain a better look.

"Yeah, he lives on the next street." Ryan pulled up to Eric's large black gates, the metal rolling to the side so we could drive in.

"Oh, really?"

I'm not sure why I was surprised. The area Eric lived was sprawling with mansions.

MANSIONS.

Chances were, those fancy homes didn't include a couple of cardigan-wearing Volvo drivers who liked to do crossword puzzles and dine on potluck dinners.

"Princess, you really need to stop looking so impressed." Ryan stopped the car in front of the house.

"I'm not impressed, I was just . . . you know, thinking about the story."

It wasn't a lie.

Dean Watt had a nice guy reputation, and a good relationship with the press. If anyone were going to give me the time of day, it would be someone like him. With a smile that had probably paid for some dentist's yacht, and lowered a few panties, he would be a good entry-level interview. If he had any skeletons in the closet, they were very well hidden.

"Did you want to drive past his house? We could cruise by," Ryan asked, hesitating before killing the ignition.

"I can't just knock on the door."

That would be crazy. It's not like I was selling him a box of

Girl Scout cookies. There was a process, agents, people you needed to talk. I wasn't reporting for TMZ.

"We don't have to knock, we can just scope out the place." Ryan shrugged like he wasn't suggesting illegal activity.

"You mean stalk him?"

"Oooooooo, we should stalk him." Tia leaned forward, contributing for the first time to the discussion. It wasn't a good contribution.

"Hey, I'm not the one throwing out the labels. I'm just saying we drive past." Ryan smirked, knowing full well he was dancing the line.

Wrongly, it excited me. The idea of a covert operation thrilled me beyond measure. Unless you counted my Tuesday morning margaritas, it had been a while since I'd done anything remotely interesting. I was going to take very little convincing.

"What happened to the first rule of Fight Club?" I cocked my head, wondering why he was willing to put his ass on the line.

"Oh, I'm not telling you shit." His big throaty laugh echoing through the cabin of the Hummer. "If you see things with your own eyes then I'm absolved of any responsibility."

"Seriously, Ryan?"

I had no idea if he was baiting me or tossing out a line and seeing if he could reel me in.

"Where's your sense of adventure? We see his house and you can write about how he still needs to wheel out his trashcan on garbage day." His eyebrow rose.

He almost had me.

Yep, I had sat in the car believing he'd happily be a coconspirator and violate whatever personal *code* by pointing out Dean's house.

But the whole time, he'd been playing me. Having fun at my expense.

"You're not taking this seriously." My hand popped opened

the door and I pushed myself out of the car.

Irritated, and maybe a little embarrassed I'd been so easily duped, I grabbed my garment bag and the other bags we'd acquired on our shopping adventures, and pushed myself out of the door. By the time I stepped out onto the driveway, Tia had already walked around the side of the car.

"If you want me to Google him, I can probably find his address." Tia leaned in, walking beside me as we made our way to the front door. "It's not a skill that is easily forgotten."

"Maybe we should." I ignored Ryan, who had shut off the ignition and was coming up behind us. "We don't need *anyone's* help."

"For the record, I was serious and we could have already been there. But sure, you two go for it." Ryan outstretched his arms, waiting for us to walk inside. "I'm dying to see how this works out."

It was irrational, but now it was about proving a point. And while our—Tia's more so than mine—situations might have changed, and we were in a different geographical location, we could CSI the shit out of Dean, or whoever we needed to find. Without Ryan's or anyone else's assistance.

Tia, excited by our new project, dumped the bags and grabbed her laptop. Meanwhile, I helped myself to the liquor collection and started mixing cocktails. It was like the band had gotten back together and this was our reunion tour.

If I ever said I didn't appreciate our crazy-ass adventures, I'd lied.

I loved them.

Lived for them.

Those pockets of insanity fed my soul in a way *normality* couldn't.

Again, I had to wonder if genetics didn't play a part. *Thanks a lot, Grandma.*

We poured shots as we stood at the kitchen bench, both Tia

and I laughing as we typed into the search engine.

Ryan looked on with amusement, turning down our offer of tequila. "Someone needs to babysit." He smirked, pulling up a chair and watching.

"Hey, look at this picture?" Tia laughed, turning the screen around so I could get a better view. "He wears Armani underwear, you can see the waistband."

"We are supposed to be finding out his address not his underwear preference, that information is not helpful." I laughed, slightly tipsy but nowhere close to being drunk.

I wasn't sure if it was my hometown—the capital city of parties and excess—or my upbringing that gave me an obscene tolerance for alcohol. It was unfortunate that I usually ran out of money at the bar before I got a real buzz going. And while I had been loaded many times, it wasn't a state I gravitated to easily. I was thinking of donating my body to medical science when I died, maybe I had an extra liver I didn't know about.

"He's kind of hot, Lila." Tia squinted at the screen, the quest to find Dean's address taking longer than expected. We probably should have cut her off sooner.

"You are both killing me." Ryan shook his head, moving over to the laptop and closing it.

I'd almost forgotten he was there, too involved in my partaking of shots and trying to triangulate Dean's address using Google Earth to notice the voyeur.

Ok, maybe I hadn't miraculously forgotten him, but more chosen to ignore him when I caught him sexting in my peripheral version. Not that I knew it was sexting for sure, but it was what my overactive imagination had conjured up.

"We had it almost narrowed down," I huffed, annoyed he'd shut us down when we'd been so close.

He was just jealous we were going to find Dean without him,

and wanted to stop us. But he could take his sexy I-know-every-thing and shove it.

"I told you he lives a couple of streets away, you didn't need Google for that." He wrapped his arm around my waist and stilled me.

Wow, we were close.

I wished I'd been drunk.

Even with my five feet, nine inches, he still towered over me, his body dangerously close to mine.

I liked the way it felt, his hands on me.

And I wanted to be able to blame inebriation or clouded judgment so I could bury my face in his neck and suck his skin.

God, he smelled good.

And he looked even better.

"Stop being so bossy." I half-heartedly pushed him away, my fingers gripping his T-shirt, not committed to the cause of stopping the contact. No, they were hell bent on holding on as long as they could, which was why I had avoided physical contact to start with.

"Just go get in the car." He didn't ask, swiveling my body until I was facing the door. Tia, no longer interested in our assignment, poured herself another shot as she giggled and waved us off. *Damn it*, I was on my own.

Thoughts of protesting didn't even enter my mind, too consumed with enjoying his hands on me as I leaned back against his chest. His fingers were wrapped tight around my hips while my traitorous legs moved like I was a puppet on a string, bending and yielding to his every command as we walked toward the door.

"You know if I wanted to be ordered around, I would call my boss." My mouth filed the grievance my body clearly wasn't capable of. More so there would be a record of it, so I could say I attempted to stop it. Not that I wanted to, and not that I wasn't desperate for it to continue.

"And if you were really pissed off about it, we wouldn't be doing this."

Damn it, he had me there.

"Fine, let's go stalk the man." My arms waved with reckless abandon. "I wasn't doing anything important anyway."

"Thank you, I'm honored." He bowed at the waist, popping open the passenger side door and waiting for me to get inside.

"Whatever," I grumbled under my breath as he walked around to the driver's side.

I might have been acting annoyed but secretively I loved it. The faint warmth of tequila coursed through my veins but his scent and smile were far more intoxicating.

He slid into the car and started the ignition, grinning as we again drove out the large iron gates. That smile was probably going to be my undoing.

On the surface I was cool and calm, sitting idly while I looked bored. But inside my chest cavity it was a different story, my heart beating so wildly with excitement that I wasn't sure I wasn't having a heart attack.

Not because of Dean. Sure, it would be cool to check out where he lived and possibly chance a fluke encounter. But it was being in the car with Ryan, our own little covert operation, that had me really excited. *Like a crack commando team who escaped a maximum-security prison to survive as soldiers of fortune in the underground of L.A.*

"You okay?" He side-eyed me as we cruised along the streets, the blackened windows making us almost insulated. Or was it invisible? Either way it was totally badass.

"Perfect." My face pressed against the side window as I scoped out the large houses trying to remember which ones I had seen on Google Earth. Some of it looked familiar, I knew Tia and I had been close.

He laughed, but continued driving, turning a corner as we rounded onto another street.

"Okay, up there on the right is his place."

We slowed, the engine idling as we came to a stop.

"I love it when a plan comes together," I whispered, unlatching my seat belt.

"What did you say?" Ryan leaned over the console, my A-Team reference hopefully going unnoticed.

"Nothing." I shook my head; maybe I wasn't as sober as I thought. Still, not drunk enough to not know what I was doing. "Wow, his lights are on. I think he's home."

"You want to get out and take a closer look?" he baited, the Hummer stalled into submission as he killed the ignition.

"Are you *trying* to get me arrested?" My body twisted to face him, making my pulse speed up even more.

Thank God I didn't have a heart condition, because my fluctuating arrhythmia would have given Dr. House a hard-on.

"If you're chicken, just say you're chicken."

His mouth was right at my ear, his hot breath prickling my skin and if we weren't sitting conspicuously in front of someone's house, it might have been erotic. Or maybe it still was, but I was talking myself into keeping my clothes on and my hands to myself.

"I'm not fucking chicken." I smiled, my internal temperature spiking as my hand went to the door handle. "You want to do this? Fine, get out."

Doing my best not to slam the door, I exited the Hummer. My feet gingerly hit the sidewalk as I kept my eyes glued to the house a few feet up.

It was a cross between fucking ridiculous—like spying on an old boyfriend who dropped you three days before prom—and freaking euphoric—like a DEA drug raid. Both of those scenarios more excitement than I'd experienced in the past few weeks.

"Get lower." Ryan took my hand as he led me to the front of the house, the exterior security lighting kicking in.

"What the hell are you doing?" I whispered, following Ryan as he crouched down, inching his way into Dean's bushes. And no, that wasn't a euphemism for something, he was literally hiding in some movie star's bushes!

"Shhh, you're going to get us caught." He yanked me down beside him, my knees hitting the dirt.

Two thoughts went through my head.

One, I should have changed. My pale blue dress and strappy sandals had been ideal for roaming racks of couture, not so much for commando crawling underneath an Italian Cypress. And the other, this was hot as fucking hell.

I was caught somewhere between reality and fantasy. Intellectually I knew this was a bad idea. It hadn't been the plan. We were going to cruise past, check out the address and see how "normal" it was.

I possibly—maybe for a second—toyed with the idea that if he was out and about, like if he'd been night gardening or something— long shot I know—that maybe we'd say hello. For politeness sake.

But there wasn't a chance I was going to knock on his door or press the call button of his intercom. Pretending I was there to check his cable or survey him regarding his choice of phone companies barely worked in the movies, it didn't stand a chance in real life.

Instead, we were trespassing, with tree branches poking me in the ass and dirt on my knees, while I spied on a man I didn't know with another man I was desperate to sleep with. Absurdity didn't even come close.

Whether it was the security lights illuminating or he felt a disturbance in the force, Dean came closer to the window that faced where we were hunkered down, his eyes scanning the horizon.

"Wow, he's super cute." I peeked out from the bushes,

wondering if he felt us watching him. My earlier internet search still lingered in my head, filling in the gaps of what my pupils couldn't see. He had such rich dark eyes. Not as sexy as Ryan's but at least I was able to voice my appreciation for them freely without worry about repercussions.

"He's fucking average at best, Lila. Don't be so impressed." Ryan scoffed beside me, clearly not on Team Dean.

"Average?" I whisper yelled. "Didn't he win bachelor of the year two years ago?"

"So? They gave it to Larsson last year, clearly they have no taste," he whispered back, grinning.

"You are a strange man, you know that." My eyes narrowed, shaking my head before I returned my gaze to Dean who was still at the glass. Though stacked side by side, Ryan was a million times hotter.

"Don't pretend that you don't like it." He chuckled, his voice husky in my ear.

I felt the vibrations travel through me, his hot breath stroking me erotically as I looked at another man. God, either sitting this close to him in the dark on this stakeout was super hot, or I was drunker than I thought. And spoiler alert, I could still walk a straight line and recite the alphabet backwards.

"Shit, he is looking right at us. Get down." I grabbed Ryan's arm and yanked him further into the shrubbery.

While I had been on my mental vacation pretending to contemplate Dean's cuteness—when I'd really been thinking about Ryan—we'd attracted some attention.

And I wasn't sure if my audible appreciation for his fine form had reached his ears, or if he'd seen the crazy people—i.e. us—skulking in his bushes, but it was obvious he wasn't harmlessly checking out his hedges. And how thrilled was I? It had been a while since I'd been tackled to the ground by LAPD and been tasered on someone's front lawn. Oh wait, that had *never* happened because I knew better.

Damn it, Ryan.

"Well, if you hadn't been perving at the man, maybe he wouldn't have looked over." He had the freaking nerve to blame me, moving his hand around my waist and pulling me closer.

"I was NOT perving," I shot back, indignant he had somehow tried to pin this on me.

No, your Honor. I was an innocent bystander, lured by the sexy man's hypnotic voice and outstanding good looks and goaded into participation. I would never be part of such a clear breach of someone's privacy.

"*Wow, he's super cute,*" he mimicked, a stupid grin on his face as he clutched his hands to his chest. "Yeah, you weren't looking at all."

"Shut up." I pushed his chest, the toned planes of his muscles feeling delicious under my fingertips. Well, at least there was some positive to all of this.

"Oh, I think he's coming out." Ryan lifted his head above the hedge line quickly, his eyes widening as he lowered his mouth to my ear. "He's walking this way."

"Fuck." My grip tightened on his T-shirt. This was *not* how it was supposed to go down.

"What? Now, princess?" One of his brows rose as a smirk played on his lips. "I'd say there's a better time and place but if you want to, I won't say no."

Oh. My. God.

He couldn't be serious. Who thought about having sex while in the middle of committing a crime? What was even worse was, for a second, I'd actually considered it myself.

"Shut up, shut up," I whisper yelled to both him and my subconscious.

I wrote news stories; I didn't want to become a headline in one. I bet Dick would have a fucking field day with this, reprimanding me for not having supporting pictures. Asshole.

"Hey, is there anyone out here?" Dean's voice boomed in our general direction. And by the sound of it, he was close.

Ryan lifted his finger to his grinning lips with a silent shhh that didn't need to be spoken. I wasn't sure how he could be amused when my heart was beating so loudly there was no way Dean couldn't hear.

Or maybe he could, which is why when I peeked through the bushes we were currently using as camouflage, I saw he had moved closer. His tall, sort-of-cute body literally two feet away from us.

Please don't let him see us. Please don't let him see us.

I wasn't sure who I was offering those prayers up to, I was almost positive anyone upstairs had washed their hands of me. Nope, if there was a God, he or she was laughing their ass off, tossing me a "you're on your own, dumbass" as they settled in with some popcorn. Damn it. I really needed to start making better choices.

"What the fuck?" Dean's voice was no longer a couple of feet away, a surprised pair of dark eyes staring directly above us.

This was it.

This was how my fall from grace started.

I had successfully dodged scandal despite my upbringing—my prostitute grandmother and my madam bordello-owning mother. To become undone by stupidity and an aversion to being called chicken.

If there were any mercy, I'd hope they let me tidy up before the mug shot.

"Ryan, you bastard. Can't you ring the doorbell like a normal person?" Dean laughed. "This shit is getting old."

What?

WHAT?

I froze in silence as my mind and mouth hovered in disbelief, not fully understanding what was going on.

"Come on, dude." Ryan—who hadn't suffered the same mute stupor I had—rose from the scratchy twigs and brush. His hand smacked loudly on Dean's shoulder. "How are you supposed to find your security weaknesses if no one puts them to the test? You should be thanking me."

"What?" I finally found my voice only to be let down by a limited vocabulary as I rose slowly to my feet. "What is going on?"

"Oh, hey there." A goofy smile spread across Dean's lips. "Sorry, I should have introduced myself. I'm Dean." His hand swung out in front of him.

"Hi, I'm Lila," I answered, my mind still in free fall as I unintentionally ignored his offer of a handshake. "Ryan." I turned, his sexy smirk growing wider. "Care to fill me in?"

"Nothing much to tell." He brushed off his jeans, stepping out onto Dean's front lawn. "We should probably go inside though, huh? We don't want to look like a pair of stalkers." He bit back his grin as he held out his hand.

"Are you serious?" I batted away his hand, smacking him in the chest as I joined them both on the lawn. "Dean, you might want to turn around. I don't want any witnesses when I kill him."

Caught halfway between relieved and angry, I punched a laughing Ryan in the arm as I brushed off my dress. "You!"

"You'll have to excuse Lila." Ryan grabbed my hands, my feeble assault halted as he pulled me close to his chest, holding me captive. "She has anger management issues."

I was going to kill him.

Twisting in his arms, I turned to face Dean who was looking on with interest. More than likely because of the sideshow of insanity that had stepped from behind his hedges, it wasn't the sort of thing that was easy to ignore. "My issues are actually just Ryan related, I have no problem with *other* men or my temper."

It was a paradox.

I was furious he'd led me to believe we were essentially trespassing, moments away from potential and serious trouble, and ridiculously glad we had a reason to touch each other. I may have rubbed my ass against his crotch in revenge; I just wasn't sure which one of us I was punishing.

"Well, that's good to know." Dean smiled, unaffected by the crazy playing out in front of him. "You guys want to come in for a drink or want to mess up my landscaping some more?"

"Lila?" Ryan asked, his arms remaining locked around my body. "You going to play nice?"

No. Nice was not how I wanted to play.

My body stilled as my lips curled into a smile, reality settling in. I was face to face with an actor.

Someone who ordinarily I wouldn't be speaking to. And possibly needed ten different phone calls and a pledge of my first-born child just to even dream of getting this kind of unfettered access. So, while the methods might have been questionable, the end result had been positive. Besides, I still had a story I needed to write.

"Yes. Of course." My voice so laden with sweet I was surprised I didn't develop diabetes. "I would love to come in for a drink. So lovely of you to offer."

Ryan hesitated like he didn't trust me, granting me parole from my Ryan prison by first loosening his grip before dropping his hand to my waist.

I should have complained, given him shit about being restrained, but I didn't. No guesses for why. My subconscious just shook its head at me, not buying my submissiveness as my effort to not make a scene.

"Great." Ryan's hand slid to my hip. "A drink it is."

Dean was likely rethinking his drink invitation as his eyes darted between the two of us. We were acting weird by anyone's measure.

"All right then. Let's go inside." He turned and headed toward his front door.

"You heard the man." Ryan squeezed my hip, keeping his voice low. "I'll take the adulation later."

"You might be waiting a while." The words were choked out between my teeth behind my grin, keeping the conversation as private as I could.

"Lucky for you, I'm patient," he whispered, guiding me to where Dean was waiting at his open door. "Hope we haven't put you out, buddy. I probably should have called first." He tapped Dean on the shoulder as he led me into the entranceway.

Dean's house was a Spanish mission-style with high gloss floors and airy open space. It was stunning, and probably worth a few million, but more modest than the place I'd been staying. Which made sense considering Forbes hadn't even listed Dean, and Eric was a regular fixture on its Top 100. Who said reading the financials was a waste of time when you wrote in the art's section.

"Let's chill in the living room." Dean tipped his chin down the hall. "You guys want a beer?"

"Always." Ryan's hand stayed low on my back as he guided me to the living room, Dean disappearing into the kitchen as we situated ourselves on his large leather couch.

My eyes scanned the room out of habit, collecting information as it floated through the space. He clearly lived alone; the coffee table filled with *Sports Illustrated* back copies and car magazines while the décor screamed done-by-an-interior-designer. Still, it was neat, which was more than I could say for most men who lived alone.

"What a lovely home." I accepted the cold frosted bottle as Dean reentered the room. "Great earthy colors. The walls just seem to breathe."

Of course, I didn't give a rat's ass about his walls or his house, but I was the master of making small talk. And if I wanted my audience with him to last longer than five minutes then I had to at least not sound like a reporter.

"Thanks." He handed another beer to Ryan. "I had someone do it for me. I'm not great with picking shit that matches."

Cue my complete lack of surprise.

"Well, compliments to the designer then." I lifted my beer as he took the chair opposite. "I'm sorry if we crashed your evening plans."

"Nah, I was going to watch Sports Center and run lines." He settled in, taking a sip of his beer. "I have an early shoot tomorrow so was keeping it low key. So, Lila, are you an actress?"

"No, I'm not an actress, I'm a reporter."

Ordinarily I would have cushioned the blow. My job title was usually met with a healthy dose of caution, and I'd heard "this is off the record" more than my own name.

But, I was acutely aware that if I was going to gain Dean's or anyone else's trust in order to do my think piece, then I was going to have to be completely transparent.

"I work for *The New York Times*," I continued, filling the silence.

"Really?" Dean shuffled back into his seat, looking at me with more interest than he had when I'd walked in. "You don't look like a reporter."

Interesting.

I expected if he were too polite to toss me out, then he'd at least reiterate that everything he said or did was off limits. But he didn't, instead regarding me with a curiosity I couldn't quite work out.

"What's a reporter supposed to look like?" I asked, curious I hadn't needed to do the *this-is-off-the-record* speech yet.

"I don't know." He laughed, shrugging. "Not like you."

"He's trying to be smooth, not tell you you're beautiful." Ryan leaned in, mock whispering, "These actors are all the same. You think they'd be better at the pick-up."

"Dude." Dean threw his hands up and chuckled. "I wasn't trying to hit on your girlfriend. You're sitting right next to her, what kind of jerk do you think I am?"

"Oh, I'm not his girlfriend." I laughed, relaxing for the first time since I'd left the house on this crazy adventure.

"Don't laugh too hard, princess. I'd make an excellent boyfriend." Ryan rolled his eyes, hiding his smile as he lifted his beer to his lips.

Of course, he was overlooking the most important part. That to *be* an actual boyfriend, one must have a relationship. Preferably one that lasted longer than a night or two. So, I would say his idea of how *excellent* he'd be and reality were incredibly skewed. Unless he was talking about being a sex partner or lover in which case, I'm positive he would be out of this world amazing.

The hand that wasn't holding my bottle waved between us. "You actually thought we were a couple?"

"Well, yeah." Dean's brows knitted in confusion. "He doesn't usually bring girls around when he's busting my balls. I assumed you had to be someone *special*."

I sucked in a breath, almost choking on the statement. Oh, I was waaaay too elated by that revelation for it to be healthy. The thought Ryan didn't usually introduce his women to his friends, and yet he introduced me? Did that mean he didn't see me as a possibility? Or he saw me just as a friend and this whole flirting thing really was just a game. Or maybe, I *was* different—hopefully in a good way. Shit. I should forget it. It probably meant nothing and I was over analyzing.

"Aww, that's so sweet." I clutched my bottle to my chest, the warm and fuzzy feeling genuine, even though I may have been embellishing a little. "I'm special." I glanced between them adoringly.

"I thought you said you *weren't* hitting on her?" Ryan raised an eyebrow, taunting him.

"I'm not."

"Only because you are terrible at it."

"So, Dean." I rested my hand on Ryan's knee, putting a stop to the mildly entertaining testosterone show. "What are you working on? Anything interesting."

I was dipping a toe in, seeing if the mention of work made him tightlipped so I could gauge if even bringing up the story was worth the effort. After all, he hadn't freaked out when he found out I was reporter, but he was probably being polite because I was a friend of Ryan's.

"A limited series. Pays the bills and I get to stay local. Plus, it's a great director, he likes to shoot in long continuous takes. It's actually really cool." He offered information without censor.

I guess he wasn't telling me anything secretive, all of it could be found on his IMDb page. But it could be partly because he didn't feel threatened by me, right? I wanted to take some of the credit.

"It sounds great." I pressed a little further. "And what do you like to do in your spare time, when you're not working?"

He chuckled, taking another sip of beer before lowering the bottle from his lips. "Is this an interview?"

Yep, too much.

And not my best angle. I had better moves than that, and had I not been playing hide-n-seek in his fucking hedges I might have been more prepared.

"No, sorry. It's a habit," I swallowed, "but I'm going to be honest with you. I'm here in L.A. on a story."

There was no point stringing it out any longer.

"Don't lie to the man, Lila," Ryan added, nudging me with his elbow before leaning forward. "She's here in L.A. because she's bored out of her mind, so of course she came to see me."

"Actually if that were true, I'd be here to see Tia," I pointed out, even though he was a very welcome addition.

"Me, Tia, same, same. Semantics." Ryan shrugged dismissively.

"Anyway . . . the story." I tried my best to get back on track, difficult with Ryan's thigh rubbing up close to mine. "It's a piece on what life is like for actors—people of a certain amount of fame— and what your reality is like."

Dean's brows knitted as he rubbed the back of his neck. "Like do I take out my own trash or something like that?"

Curious he'd pick *that* scenario out of a million others when it had been the exact same one Ryan suggested. Maybe famous people had fixations on trash? Or it was a strange coincidence. Definitely something worth investigating.

"Sort of. A little more involved." I scooted forward in my seat, lowering my beer bottle onto the coffee table. The lack of coasters also confirmed he lived alone. "I was hoping to give you a voice, say things you previously couldn't."

Dean barked out a nervous laugh. "Wow, Lila. That's . . . My agent would probably kill me. Everything I say or do out there affects my ability to be employed. I stop being a person the minute I step out my door, then all of a sudden, I'm a brand."

That was exactly the stuff I was looking for. Raw, juicy, honest. I wanted more than surface stuff, the type of information they'd post on social media if they didn't have to worry about hurting their chances for future employment. A rant if you will.

Or even just a warts-and-all account of what life was really like. I bet most people wouldn't expect a hot successful actor was sitting in his house on a Sunday night watching television. This was the kind of story a writer begged to write, the previously untold account. And readers were hungry for it, even if they didn't know it yet.

"We could keep all names anonymous, no one would ever know who said what. I could get other people too, it won't just be you."

It wasn't how I originally intended it. Names, photos—it would give it a more human feel. But I understood the need to keep their identities suppressed and I could roll with the improv no problem.

"You knew about this?" Dean looked at Ryan, his interest in his beer seeming to be lost as he abandoned it on the coffee table.

He didn't seem pissed off, more caught off guard and I had to wonder if Ryan hadn't stuck his neck out too far for me.

"Yeah, we talked about it." Ryan's eyes shot to me as he lost the sarcasm and I felt a moment of panic. Crap. I shouldn't have said anything yet. He had gone out on a limb and I had inadvertently thrown him under the bus.

His gaze softened, those beautiful brown eyes filling with warmth as his hand lightly tapped my knee in reassurance. If he was mad, he wasn't showing it, turning his focus to Dean. "All jokes aside, I think it's a great idea. Think about it. How many times have you wanted to respond to a rumor or tell everyone to go fuck themselves when they asked you what deodorant you use? You can have your say."

Dean shook his head, not seeming to buy it. "You don't think this is going to end badly, a whole bunch of speculating?"

"Dude, it's Hollywood." Ryan spread out his arms indicating the space. "Rumor and speculation is as much a part of this town as the palm trees and those letters on the hill. I'll vouch for her, she's not one of them."

Of all the things he'd ever said to me, those words were probably the most amazing. I'd never asked him to do it. Hell, I'd never asked *anyone* to do it, but that he trusted me and was willing to put his reputation on the line made my heart squeeze.

Dean's eyes narrowed, tipping his chin at Ryan. "That's a big call coming from you. Is Eric going to be involved?"

Shit. I hadn't even gone there. Not because I didn't trust him, but I didn't want to put him in the difficult position of either agreeing out of obligation or it being awkward if he turned me down.

"I'm not going to reveal any of my sources, whether they contribute or not."

It wasn't outright lying, but if I was going to work on the assumption of anonymity then surely that protection extended to everyone. That it helped me in the pickle I was in, also a bonus.

"So, how does this work?" Dean's foot tapped nervously, his knee jiggling as he spoke. "You follow me around or something?"

I tried to keep the excitement out of my voice, hopefully that him asking questions was a sign he was considering it.

"No, I was thinking more a series of interviews. We can just talk, I'll take notes so we don't have to worry about recordings falling into the wrong hands."

"Do I get to read it?"

"If you want, but I get full creative control. I won't write anything inaccurate and I promise to be impartial but you're going to have to trust that I won't screw you over. I know it's a big ask, but my name is the only one going to be on the chopping block, I can guarantee it."

Dean's eyes fell to the beer bottle on the table. His stare intense, like he was contemplating its weight or the color of the label. Or he was trying to get it to levitate off the wood. Theoretically, it was possible, so you never could tell.

"Okay." The one word left his lips in a rush.

"Okay?"

I wasn't sure how much he was agreeing to, but it was a start.

"But I'm going to need you to sign an NDA." His eyes locked on mine. "I know you said my name won't be attached and I believe you, but I'm not stupid either."

"Sure, whatever you need." I waved my hand. I didn't care if he made me sign ten NDAs, as long as it got us there in the end, it would be worth it.

"Get your questions together and let me know when you want to do this. Ryan has my number. We can do it here, less eyes."

"Of course, that works."

Again, I would do it standing on my head if it made him feel better.

"Don't make me regret this."

I sensed the edge in his voice, the tension in his posture, and while he agreed, he wasn't completely comfortable with the idea. It was natural and I had expected that, but if I was going to get to the good parts underneath the surface then I was going to have to find a way to gain his trust.

"I won't, I promise." And every single word of that promise was sincere. It wouldn't just be Dean I was screwing over. Ryan, Eric, Tia—if this blew up, it would leave the kind of damage I doubted I'd ever be able to repair.

"Fine, let's change the subject." Dean waved his hand dismissively through the air as a smile settled onto his lips. It was the first time I got a glimpse into the charm I had read about. "So, Lila, are you single?"

"Really, you're going to go there?" Ryan laughed beside me.

"Just yanking your chain, dumbass."

CHAPTER #7

FORGET CLOUD NINE, I was on cloud thirty-five.

I could barely remember the drive home, my mind and mouth moving at supersonic speed as thoughts tumbled in my head. Ryan let me vocally spew my ideas as he listened intently. If he was bored or annoyed, he didn't show it, nodding in all the right places as I dominated the conversation.

That boredom I'd experienced last week was gone, in its place a renewed excitement I hadn't felt in months.

I rationalized it was about the story. A chance to not only show off my literary prowess but also do something positive. And that Dick would have to finally give me adulation I felt I deserved was an added bonus. Asshat.

But it was also about the company. Since Tia left New York, I hadn't had a friend I'd been really able to confide in. Sure, we spoke on the phone and I visited and so did she, but it wasn't the same. And while Ryan was exceptionally good to look at, I couldn't deny he was fast becoming a very good friend too.

"I can't believe he agreed." I threw myself at Ryan without thinking, wrapping my arms around him in a hug. "Thank you so much for your part in this."

For reasons I didn't dare to ask, he'd walked me up to my bedroom. The rest of the house dark when we'd arrived home.

His arms instinctively closed around me, accepting my weight as he looked down at me. "No big deal, I just put the wheels in motion, you did the rest."

"Yeah, about that." My hands pushed against his chest, freeing myself reluctantly from the hug. "Hiding in his freaking bushes when we could have just walked up to the door? That was not cool."

If I'd been mad, the emotion had dissolved hours ago but I wasn't letting him know that. He grinned, like he knew I was bluffing and walked us backward into my bedroom and closed the door behind us. My hand instinctually turned on the light; it would have been too much to be that close to him in the dark.

"Walking up to his door would have been so predictable. I wanted to give you a little adventure. Tell me you weren't excited?"

Oh, I'd been excited all right. Just not for the reason he was probably thinking. Or maybe he was. I didn't know and being this close to him didn't do wonders for my mental clarity.

Say something.

"My dress got dirty."

Really? That's the best I had?

His eyes rolled over the front of my pale blue dress, inspecting smudges of dirt on the front. Or not. I don't think I got any dirt on my tits and that's where his eyes seemed to be spending most of their time.

"Well, for that, I am sorry." He moved closer. Any closer and we'd be touching and touching was *not* a good thing. "If you take it off, I'll get it dry cleaned for you."

Help me, Jesus. Help. Me.

I was already suffering weakened resolve, throwing temptation at me like that was just not cool.

"I'll take care of it myself." Like a rock star, I didn't stutter, making the words sound normal, like I wasn't affected.

Meanwhile, down below I had Hoover Dam level flooding and I was almost positive my underwear was toast.

His head lowered, his lips spreading into a wicked grin. "Do you do that a lot? Take care of *it* yourself."

I swallowed. Hard. Trying to un-think every dirty thought I'd ever had about the man so I'd be able to speak. And with willpower of three hundred Spartans, I pulled open the door.

"Goodnight, Ryan."

He looked at the open doorway and then back to me, his are-you-sure not needing to be spoken. Just as well too, because I was most definitely *not* sure.

"Fine, fine. Goodnight." He shrugged and turned, leaving me and my out of control libido as he left the room.

Fuck the three hundred Spartans, *he* had the fortitude of Zeus or Brad Pitt's character in that movie *Troy*—never has a man in a leather skirt looked so good.

I wonder what Ryan would look like in a leather skirt?

Shit.

It was getting harder to fight.

Maybe I was overthinking this.

We were two consenting adults, so what if it was just a fling? If there was ever a man worthy of having a fling with, it was Ryan. And we could totally have sex and it not be awkward. It didn't even have to be sex, maybe I could get away with kissing him.

No actually, I wanted the sex.

But only if he wanted it, I mean I wasn't going to beg. Who was I kidding? What man didn't want sex?

"Shit."

This had bad idea written all over it and I didn't care, I'd deal with the repercussions tomorrow as I shelved whatever objections I'd considered in the past.

The hall was dark as I silently crept out of my bedroom. Tia and Eric's room was at the other end of the hall and their door was closed. It wasn't late, but they liked to spend whatever time they had together holed up in private. Can't say I blamed them and in this instance I was thankful. Because no one would even hear me as I embarked on my second covert mission of the evening.

Quietly, I tiptoed down the stairs, crossing the floor barefoot as I unlocked the double glass doors that lead into the backyard. The moonlight caught the pool water, the surface sparkling as I passed the tiled edge, making my way to the cottage on the other side.

Light poured out of the windows where the drapes hadn't been pulled as I snuck around to the front wooden door undetected. I hesitated for a second, raising my fist to the door and hovering before knocking.

It was too late now to change my mind, my fist rapping against the wood, making my peace with crossing whatever invisible line had stood there before.

"Princess?" Ryan answered the door, his shirt as MIA as my inhibitions.

"Can I come in?"

The question was a formality, as I didn't wait for his response. Instead I squeezed past him, our bodies brushing against each other for a second as I stepped inside.

It was a second too long.

I felt him.

Hard.

And I wasn't talking about his washboard abs either, no matter how impressive they were.

"You want a tour?" He pushed the door closed as he turned to look at me, his sexy smile ever present.

"I'm not here to look at your house."

"I wasn't talking about my house."

God I wanted to kiss him.

To rub myself up against him like some crazy ass scratching post and get rid of this itch. Because we both knew why I was there. And I no longer cared about being one of the many or another notch on his belt. In that moment, those thoughts were pushed aside in favor of the immediate satisfaction I knew he would give me. And to hell what he'd given anyone else.

"Yes."

The strangled word had barely left my mouth as he pulled me against him.

It was like an explosion.

My body slammed into a wall of muscle as my breath quickened, my skin prickling as his hand touched me. My brain short-circuited, equally impressed and aroused by all that firmness.

"Well, Lila."

God, when did my name start sounding so freaking erotic? I was going to orgasm and he hadn't touched me yet. This was so much better than my vibrator.

"Let me start with my mouth."

I didn't get a chance to protest—not that I would have—with his mouth taking mine with no hint of apology. It was hot, hungry and just on the cusp of rebellion. It took everything I had not to become unhinged.

"Ry—" The rest of his name was swallowed in a moan as my fingers threaded through his hair. It was silky and smooth, and amazing just like the rest of him.

"Don't speak," he mumbled against my lips, tossing around proper syllables I wasn't capable of as his hand wrapped around my neck and brought me closer.

I. Was. On. Fire.

Whatever I had been thinking—did I *even* have a game plan when I walked in here?—was tossed aside as I was consumed whole by the inferno that was Ryan York.

And man, did he know how to kiss.

While other men had fumbled around my mouth like they were giving me a dental exam, Ryan's lips and tongue worked in symphonic perfection, stroking me sexually to madness.

Who even knew how to do that? Certainly none of the men I'd ever dated.

And if this is what he could do with his mouth, Lord have mercy on what he could do with the rest of his body.

For research purposes, and for the good of all womankind, I was going to have to find out.

"Bedroom." A primal moan broke free from my mouth.

With one hand still locked around my neck and the other at my waist, Ryan back-walked us through what I assumed was some sort of living area to where I hoped we might find a bed.

Hell, it didn't even have to be a bed. He could have lead me to a dining room table, a couch, or a medieval torture device and I wouldn't have cared at this point.

We continued our walk of entanglement until the back of my knees hit a mattress. Or at least I assumed it was a mattress. Confirmation would have required looking, and looking meant tearing my eyes away from the exquisite perfection that was his face. It was decided it wasn't important enough that I know.

"Mmmm," he hummed, pulling his mouth away as his eyes hungrily rolled up and down my body. I might have been fully dressed, but the way he looked at me made me feel naked.

"Yes." I answered a question that hadn't been asked. I liked the way it sounded out loud and figured I'd be saying it a lot so I might as well get started.

My equilibrium tilted as I felt myself drop, my body falling backward until the pillowy mattress absorbed my weight.

From my new vantage point, he looked huge as he stood at

the edge of the bed. So much exposed toned skin and I wanted to trace every line with my tongue.

What the hell had I been thinking denying myself this? I had literally been handed a gift, and instead of grabbing onto it with both hands—something I was very much going to do—I had tossed it aside like a spoiled brat. That ungratefulness was ending right the hell now.

"Lila." His knees planted themselves either side of my legs as he lowered his body down on me.

God, he could just say my name for the rest of the night and it would be totally fine. Who needed conversation?

It seemed he agreed, with his mouth finding mine, his current kisses no less spectacular than the earlier ones.

I loved him on me, the weight of him against me while I writhed underneath. My fingers pressed deep into the muscles of his back as my imagination ran riot, the safety valve completely disengaged as every single dirty thought I ever conjured came rushing to the surface.

Oh.

Oh.

Oh.

That *wasn't* my imagination. His hand had snaked down to the front of my dress and pressed against the juncture between my thighs, the thin fabric hindering the friction of his beautiful agile fingers.

"I need to take it off," I moaned in desperation, my need to get naked and keep touching him at odds with each other. I should have walked in naked or something, it would have saved time. I needed to work on my seduction techniques.

"Princess." He chuckled, his lips moving to my neck while his hand finger-walked underneath the hem of my dress. "You want me to help you?"

"Please." I arched my back, allowing him access, his other hand lowering the zipper and pulling my dress down from my shoulders.

My arms were pinned by my dress, my bra-covered breasts exposed as his mouth moved back toward me. His lips were my new favorite thing. Screw raindrops on roses and whiskers on kittens, if I was Maria Von Trapp, I would have been singing about those lips and possibly those hands. Oh, and the abs got an honorary mention too.

"These are exactly how I imagined them." He kissed the swell of my breasts gently before biting the lace of my bra. "You have perfect fucking tits."

I wasn't sure if I should thank him or beg him to keep kissing me. In the end I didn't need to make the decision with his mouth again taking over.

My arms struggled against the material of my dress, the straps pulled tight against my elbows so I couldn't lift them. It was sensory deprivation at its worst and as much as I desperately wanted to touch him, I couldn't.

"I need to get all the way out of this dress," I part spoke and part moaned as he continued to lavish my breasts with expert attention. And I shit you not, it took every ounce of concentration I had just to make sure those words were in the correct order.

He didn't bother looking up, pulling the cup of my bra down and exposing my puckered nipple. I felt his smile against my skin. "No, I think we should leave it exactly like this."

"Ryan, please. Do you want me to beg?"

Because I would. I didn't care if every single Suffragette was rolling around in her grave tut-tuting my need to feel my naked body against his but I would do whatever I had to.

"I've got you, princess, don't worry." He winked as his mouth went back to work.

My eyes closed as he took my nipple into his mouth, sucking it hard while his hand played with the other. I had no choice but to lie there and take it, stuck between delicious arousal and excruciating frustration. I needed more.

Insanity.

I was literally teetering on the brink of insanity as he continued to play, the feeling of euphoria building between my legs despite it not getting his attention yet.

Until.

"Oh fuck!"

My back arched as every muscle in my body tightened.

While I'd been distracted, the hand that had been on my breast had moved. Stealthy, like their owner, his fingers had magically reappeared underneath my dress and pushed aside my panties, thumbing gently across my clit.

I wasn't sure how we'd gotten from me walking in, to kissing, to his hand up my dress but it was the best freaking segue of my life. Either he was a master seducer, or I was, but I wasn't about to ask him to stop so we could work it out. In fact, I didn't care how or who got us here, so lost in delirium he could have asked for a kidney at this point and I would have cut it out myself.

"Ryan, Ryan, Ry—"

I wasn't sure if I was asking for something or chanting, his name my mantra as every single cell in my body came online simultaneously. I was wound so tight I wasn't sure I'd survive the actual orgasm. No one had actually died from sex, right? God, I'd hate to be the first.

A finger slid in and then a second, the invasion making me shudder. *It's not even his dick for Christ's sake*, my mind yelled, *how is this even possible?*

"Fuck, Lila." He grunted, his hand unrelenting. "You're so wet."

"Ryan, please."

I wasn't even sure what I was begging for.

For sex?

An orgasm?

To never forget how this felt for the rest of my life?

In a rush my panties were gone, tossed aside as he bunched up my dress.

Between the pool of material at my waist and my arms still trapped by the straps, I was going to torch this Marc Jacobs shift if I ever got out of it.

"I need to taste you, Lila. I've been dying to."

Words. I heard words that didn't make sense as his lips went to where his hands had abandoned, and he let his mouth take over. Sucking and licking, he didn't stop, overloading me with sensations until I finally exploded on his mouth.

There'd been no opportunity to even tell him I was close. My ability to speak reduced to moans or primal growls, connecting with our evolutionary predecessors as I communicated with grunts.

My body shook as he continued to lap, a skilled combination of lips and tongue that would have made a world-class clarinet player jealous. And he was playing me for all it was worth, my body echoing of the greatest oral sex of my life.

No, scratch that.

The best *sex* period.

"Oh God." My breathing was still out of control. "Oh. My. God."

"Too much?" He raised his head with a satisfied grin on his face.

Too much? Was he kidding? "No, I don't think you knocked every cognitive thought out of my head, so we're good." I did my best to muster a laugh, difficult when you were out of breath, your body was tingling and you still didn't have the use of your arms.

I didn't even want to imagine what I looked like, wriggling on that bed like a wild seal. It couldn't have been sexy.

"Please help me out of this dress." No amount of glaring at the constrictive fabric would loosen its hold.

"Sure." Ryan's agile fingers gripped the hem and pulled it over my head, freeing me from the makeshift restraint. "The offer of getting it dry cleaned still stands."

"I'm going to burn it." I laughed stretching out my arms before wrapping them around his neck, bringing him closer. "That wasn't very nice."

"Really? That orgasm I gave you would argue otherwise." His head dipped, kissing me gently. "And I'll give you another, just to prove I'm right."

"You don't get to tie me up this time." My fingers slid down the length of his back, his muscles rippling under my fingertips. "And not that I'm complaining, but the next one you give me can't be with your mouth."

I hated to sound ungrateful, but if I had crossed the line from friend to fling, I wanted the full-service experience. Crap. That sounded shallow. Thank God I didn't say it out loud.

His hands gripped me around the waist and lifted me higher on the bed, my head hitting a pillow as I watched him. I was acutely aware that other than a poorly worn bra—the cups pushed underneath my breasts—I was completely naked.

"Is that so?" He repositioned himself on the bed, rolling his body to the side. "Leaves a lot of room for interpretation, you sure you want to give me that kind of leeway?"

"Yes."

No hesitation.

For someone who didn't do casual sex, it sure as hell didn't seem like it when I threw my body at him like a stunt double.

"I trust you."

"Good." His fingers moved across my body, my skin tingling under his touch. "Let's get this bra off you."

His hand disappeared around my back and with a flick it was gone.

"You need to be naked," I moaned, my fingers roaming down his abs to rest on the waistband of his jeans.

He smirked, kicking off his shoes. "Can you say that again so I can record it as my ringtone?"

"Get naked and we'll talk about it."

He didn't need to be asked again. Lifting off the bed as he tore off his jeans and boxer briefs, tossing aside his clothes and pulling off his socks.

The end result, absolutely breathtaking.

"Wow."

Ryan wasn't a man; he was a fucking action figure. His body was a parade of defined, cut muscles and rope-like limbs. Except instead of GI Joe's disappointing plastic mound there was very hard, very impressive cock.

The kind that got you pregnant just by looking at it.

And hell, now I couldn't stop.

"Please tell me you have condoms. Like a lot of them."

He laughed, his beautiful body shaking. "You asking me or my cock?" He snapped his fingers in front of my face. "Eyes up, princess. I'm feeling objectified."

"I'm sorry." I mumbled a half-hearted apology, my eyes yo-yoing between his chest and his—Shit, I'd lasted maybe three seconds.

I was trying, honestly. And it's not like I hadn't seen a few real penises in my lifetime—probably in the thousands, if you counted Tumblr—but even with my vast visual research, I doubted there was one as spectacular as Ryan's. Hell, most of them weren't even attractive, yet his needed its own Instagram account. Its perfection, unparalleled.

"Lila, you want to have sex or stare at my dick some more? I mean, you're doing wonders for my ego, but I'd much rather put him to good use."

My eyes shot to his face, the grin across his lips getting wider. "Sex. I'll stop looking."

"You don't have to stop." He moved back to the bed. "Just let's do other things as well. Feel free to tell me how awesome it is too, I won't stop you."

"It's—"

That was as far as I got as *ding, ding, ding* sounded and we entered round two.

Words turned into a moan as his mouth sealed mine. And with my hands no longer restricted, I used my newfound freedom to explore.

"Oh my God." At least that is what I intended to say, though I couldn't be sure it wasn't just garbled nonsense. "You are so freaking hot."

I didn't even care how it sounded—he *was* hot. His body deserved its own cathedral, a place where we could congregate and worship, which is what I planned to do with every part of my body.

He lowered his mouth, skimming my ear. "I love that you think so, but right now I don't give a shit." His voice raw. "You're beautiful and I want to be inside of you."

I doubted the fires of Hell were any hotter than what was burning through me.

"Yes."

Give me a pen and let me sign away my soul because whatever happened after this would be worth it. I'd completely lost the ability to think past the next minute.

He pulled open a drawer, yanking it free from the nightstand with force as he grabbed a box with one hand and then tossed the drawer aside. My eyes stayed glued to him as it dropped to the floor with a rattle—its fate not my concern—as Ryan tore open the box and grabbed a condom.

I wasn't sure whether to lean back and enjoy the show or offer to help as he slid on the condom, his impressive cock getting a stroke as he moved closer.

But my mental debate didn't last long, his mouth back on mine as his hands lost interest on himself and moved to me.

Holy shit he was hot.

Every single touch was like fire on my skin as our bodies moved in a silent game of *Twister* on the bed. Hands, feet, mouths—everywhere, as I gave up thinking and handed control over to my libido.

"Lila." My name half growl, half groan as he grabbed my knees, my legs falling apart like they'd been given a command.

"You're so beautiful. Your body is so fucking perfect." His hand shifted to my pussy, my wetness coating his fingers.

"No more foreplay." I shook my head, not willing to wait another second. "I need you. Please, I can't wait."

My body was so primed anything more than penetration was going to be overkill, and unnecessarily cruel.

He didn't hesitate, pushing inside me in a rush as I moaned into his mouth.

So good.

This was so fucking good.

I arched my back, feeling the fullness of him as he started to grind, keeping himself inside me as he circled his hips.

I had resisted casual sex, believing my mind needed the emotional connection in order for my body to feel good. I didn't think I even had the ability to detach. But as Ryan *touched* me, *kissed* me, *fucked* me, I could think of nothing other than that moment. And *all of it* felt amazing.

His mouth dropped from my lips, moving to my neck as he sucked against my skin. My fingernails bit into his back as I wrapped my legs around his waist, the friction not enough.

"Fuck." His hands anchored themselves at my waist as he

rocked with desperate swings of his hips, our eyes catching.

That hunger, the *need*, I could see he was feeling it too. And in that moment nothing existed but the two of us and that bed.

I was going to explode.

My body ached in sweet delicious pain as he pounded into me, hard and fast and frenzied. My skin went slick with sweat as I bucked underneath him, frantic with urgency with each slide of his cock.

"Lila."

My name.

He said everything he needed to say with just that one word. It made me feel sexy and beautiful and powerful, the vibration in his throat unlatching whatever little self-control I had left.

"Ryan, I need—"

I couldn't finish, not sure what I actually *needed*. But I knew I wanted more of him, more of everything he had to give me.

"I know what you need." He drove in deeper, filling me so completely that I exploded around him.

My body shook, my orgasm washing over me in a heated rush and engulfing me whole as I turned to liquid beneath him. He didn't stop, thrusting and stroking my body as I came further unraveled.

"Yes, yes," I panted, unable to move as echoes of pleasure rippled through my limbs.

I was positive he'd broken me, that my ability to get up and walk was no longer, and I didn't care. The damage positively worth it as I watched his jaw tense and his grip around me tighten.

"I need to come." The words strangled in his throat as he bucked against me. "I don't want this to end but I need to come."

An echo of regret flashed through his eyes as his powerful body lost its internal war with biology and he shouted my name. Every part of me tightened, feeling the rush of his release, sending me spiraling along with him. His body covered me in a hard, weighty blanket as rapid breaths pushed out from both of our lips.

He was no man.

He was some sort of divine being descended from deities, sent to earth for the pleasure of women. Stories would be written and songs sung of his legend, with his sexual mastery spoken in whispered reverence for all eternity.

"I want to stay buried in you," he moaned into my neck. "I imagined this a million times and not once did it ever feel this good."

My cheeks hurt as a smile I couldn't stop broke across my face. I wasn't sure if it was the multiple orgasms or that I had been better than he'd imagined. Maybe it was so great he'd want to do it again; I know I sure as hell did. "It was pretty good for me too, I don't think I've ever come three times before."

I couldn't remember the last time I'd even come twice, my orgasms usually hard earned. But nothing even remotely close to what I'd just had.

"Princess, are you telling me I'm your first?" He lifted his head, the pride almost exploding across his features. "Because I know I can do better."

"Yes, it was a first for me. It's been a while, I probably had a few banked." I pushed roughly against his strong, action-figure chest.

"Well, now I'm just going to have to prove myself, aren't I?" His head dipped, nipping my shoulder. "You're going to have so many orgasms, Lila, you're going to need to beg me to stop."

"I bet I don't." I wasn't at all confident in that statement but the very idea thrilled me more than it should. And one thing I didn't do was back down from a challenge.

"Well, that is a bet I'm going to take." A mischievous grin spread across his lips. "Let's see if we can't recalibrate your personal best."

CHAPTER #8

SEX WITH DEITIES came at a price, with my body aching in ways a couple of Motrin wasn't going to fix. In the end neither of us had tapped out, our bet coming to an impasse as exhaustion took over and we both fell asleep. I wasn't confident to guess who closed their eyes first, but I assumed it had probably been me.

And while spending the night in his arms and his bed sounded like a really good idea, I didn't want to risk it being weird in the morning. We'd had sex—amazing sex—and it wasn't something I was going to regret, but he was also a friend and intricately woven into the life of my best friend.

It was not something I could afford to screw up.

So when he turned and finally unwrapped his arms from around my body, I quietly and discreetly picked up my clothes, redressed and slipped out of his cottage. And I managed to get back inside the main house undetected despite almost tripping the alarm either Eric or Tia had set in my absence. Thank God, I'd remembered the code from the last time I visited, it would have really sucked to get so far only to be thwarted by a bunch of sensors.

Sleep came easier than expected. I didn't think, didn't contemplate and didn't analyze as I curled my body and gave away to fatigue, falling into a state closely resembling a coma. And if I dreamed of anything, I didn't remember it when I woke up the next morning.

I expected to feel awkward, for sanity to have prevailed and remind myself why I didn't sleep with men I wasn't actively dating. But oddly, it didn't come. I wasn't worried about seeing Ryan, confident he'd had enough one-night stands to play it cool.

Maybe I had my prostituting grandma to thank for some obscure recessive gene, and I'd had the ability to have sex and *not* get emotionally attached all along. Or maybe adults *could* have casual sex and it not descend into a nightmare.

Oh, and if my brain thought I'd not noticed I'd gone from *one-night stand* to *casual sex* in two beats, then it was an idiot. Which could only mean I was thinking about it being more than just a once off. My body had already made up its mind. And speaking about either of them—and effectively myself—in the third person probably wasn't a good sign. Did I mention dear old Grandma died in her early fifties with a serious case of dementia? My genealogical profile was a freaking nightmare.

"Good morning." Tia handed me a cup of coffee as I entered the kitchen. "Sleep okay?"

Ordinarily I'd assume her question was loaded, that she'd somehow had the ability to smell the sex off me. But Tia, while usually perceptive, was a terrible liar. So, either she was too tied up in her own bliss to notice mine, or I was incredible at playing it cool. Meh, it could have gone either way.

"So good." My academy award winning performance slipping as I hid my smile behind the cup.

The coffee tasted better this morning, *brighter* almost, hmm interesting. "I didn't want to bug you guys last night, so I just went to bed. I know when Eric's shooting you don't get a lot of alone time."

"Yeah, thanks for that. I did mean to check on you, but I got distracted." Her smile not even attempting to hide that distraction had been wild monkey sex with her hot boyfriend. "How did things go last night with Ryan?"

"What?" I laughed, my acting career all but over as I tried to cover my shock. "What are you talking about?"

"Didn't you two go stake out Dean Watt's house? I know we had a few drinks last night but I'm not totally losing my mind."

"Oohhhhh, that!" Oh praise Jesus, thank you holy mercies. "Yes, yeah, we did do that." Relief flowed through me with the conversation's change in direction. "Although it wasn't so much of a stake out as a setup, Ryan knows him and the whole thing was a charade. But I did get to meet him and he's agreed to help me with my story. But it's going to be top secret. No one will know it's him."

If there was anyone I trusted with my life and my reputation, it was Tia. So I knew it went without saying that anything work related wasn't discussed outside the two of us. And like she'd demonstrated by keeping Ryan's true occupation undisclosed, you could count on her to keep it in the vault.

She leaned in closer, her smile inching at the corners. "An undercover operation. That sounds like so much fun; let me know if you need help with the research. My column has already been turned in for this week, there's only so much you can write about whether anal bleaching is the onset of society's downfall."

Anyone else and that conversation would have received a stern look and a very hasty goodbye. But while my grindstone had been *The Times*, Tia was a columnist for *The New York Post*. Which meant she could write about whatever the hell she wanted. And while I sometimes envied her, there was no way I could consistently be that creative. I didn't have that kind of comedic timing. No, I was better suited to reporting, facts and their interpretation.

"Thanks, sweet cheeks." I gave her a one-armed hug. "But I

think I'm good for now."

"Fine, don't utilize my stellar CSI skills." She sighed, her acting skills also terrible as she attempted pretending to be annoyed. "I would have rocked it. Are you going to ask Eric?"

It was my turn to sigh. "I don't know, T. I don't want him feeling obligated."

"Feeling obligated for what?" Eric's voice entered the room before he did. His casual stroll and smile making their appearance a few seconds later. "Is this a secret meeting or can anyone join?"

"I didn't want you to feel obligated to talk to me for my story," I volunteered. "You're already letting me stay in your house, it's a lot to ask."

He walked straight over to Tia, wrapping his arms around her. "Firstly, you know you're always welcome here. And I'm a big boy, I can say no when I want to."

"He can, and he does," Tia added.

"So, it's something you would consider?"

He was probably the most logical source, but I in no way assumed he was a sure thing. In Hollywood circles, Eric was huge. It would give the story better credibility and make others more likely to want to be involved, but his friendship and respect were worth more to me. "All names and identifying information will be suppressed but given our connection, people will probably guess you're involved."

He threw his head back in a throaty laugh. "Well, luckily I don't care what people think, so whatever you want to ask, you can ask."

"Yay." I put down my coffee cup and did a little victory jig. This story was going to be awesome. "I'll compile some questions. Let me know when you have a break in your schedule in the next few days and I'll make time."

"I've got late shoots for the next few days, but if it can wait until the weekend, we can do it then?"

"Sure, sounds like a plan."

"Great." Eric planted a quick kiss on Tia followed by a smile as his attention returned to me. "Why don't you ask Ryan to introduce you to a few other people around town. He'll know who's most likely to be interested."

And unlike Tia, his smile wasn't one of ignorance. Neither was the pointed look or the lingering grin that had yet to disappear. I wasn't sure how much he knew, but he knew something.

"Ryan tell you?" I went the honest route considering there wasn't much point denying it.

"I told you not to mention it." Tia elbowed him, playfully.

"You know too?" I stared at Tia. Wow, I had totally misjudged that one, maybe the sex had shaken something loose last night because I was totally off my game. "I can't believe you knew and didn't say anything."

Eric shook his head, biting back his grin. "For the record, Ryan denied it. You forgot to reengage the alarm after you came in last night and I got a call from the security company. I assumed."

Foiled by technology.

It seemed my self-praise over remembering to disengage the alarm was premature because forgetting to turn it back on was just as bad. I guess it was only a matter of time. If not the alarm, it would have been the security cameras. I'm sure they captured my early morning reentry from every angle.

"Well. So. Yeah." For someone who made her living with words, I sure had a shortage of them.

"I didn't bring it up to be an asshole, you are both adults and it's none of my business." And honestly, he didn't look annoyed and or bothered by it. "Just reset the alarm next time so I don't get a two a.m. wake-up call."

"Thanks." I grinned, biting my lip.

Would there even be a next time? I hadn't shot the idea down, so there was that. Although he probably had some say in it and I wasn't sure that now we'd finally done *it* that the thrill of the chase was gone and he'd move on. Or not, maybe we could play together a little while longer.

"Don't mention it. I've got to get to the studio." He shrugged giving Tia another kiss. "Want to walk me out?" The raised eyebrow hinted he was looking for more than the peck on the lips he'd just given her.

"Don't hold back on my account." I held my hands up backing away. "I'm going back upstairs to start working. You guys do whatever crazy morning ritual you need. I was never here," I whispered, disappearing around the corner and headed to my bedroom.

I was a lot of things, but embarrassed wasn't one of them. Sure, I felt like a dumbass, and clearly should not plan any heists while riding high on endorphins, but in a way I was glad they knew. Strangely relieved.

I had been so concerned about everyone's reaction for nothing. Eric didn't have a problem with me getting up close and personal with his friend and security detail, and Tia wasn't all weird about it either. And Eric giving his blessing and support to my story could only mean good things. I pinched my arm quickly just to be sure I hadn't in fact fallen into a coma and all of this was some strange and intricate psychological illusion.

Ouch. Nope, it was real.

"Good morning, hot shot." Ryan rapped at the doorjamb of my bedroom, the door left open in my distraction. "You need me to do some intros this morning? Any special requests?"

God, he was gorgeous. His hair still wet from a shower, pushed back with just a few strands falling in front of his face. His beautiful relaxed smile framed by light stubble, which did wonderful things for his jaw.

"Hey, um yeah. That would be great. Look, about last night."

Did we talk about it? I mean, we should, right? Discuss what happened and what was going to happen in the future. Or was that bad form? I wished there was some kind of rulebook.

"You want to talk about last night? Or do you want to talk about this morning when you left?" He strode into my room closing the door behind him. His smile no less dazzling than before. "Because last night needs no discussion. You and your body were perfection." His eyes rolled over my body before they came back to mine. "So, if you're going to ask me to forget it happened, sorry but no can do. But if you want to tell me why you didn't want to spend the night, I'm all ears."

He moved to the bed, sitting on the edge as he looked on with interest. He didn't seem mad or hurt, just curious.

"Okay," I joined him on the bed, hoping this time around I'd keep my clothes on. "So, I don't usually do *that*."

"Sex?" He raised a brow, a hint of humor in his voice.

"Sex and then leave."

"So, that was another first, interesting." He rubbed his chin thoughtfully, the edges of his lips curling. "I don't feel so good about that one as I did about the multiple orgasms, but go on."

We'd been flirting with each other since the day we'd met over four months ago. I had been drinking at Tia's apartment and he offered to drive me home. In a haze of slightly clouded judgment I'd tried to kiss him but he refused, saying he needed to be sure I was sober. All the assurances in the world wouldn't sway him otherwise. Of course when the haze had lifted, I felt a little stupid considering I was one-night stand deficient and he wasn't interested in a relationship. Not that we'd talked about it back then. No, he'd walked me to my door and had seen me safely inside and then left without so much as a hug. Of course, all the information had come later and I was thankful for his self-control. But I'd made excuses to hug him after that first time which he thankfully reciprocated.

No kissing though, I already knew I was on a slippery slope.

"Come on, Ryan, it's obvious I'm attracted to you. I think I've fantasized about having sex with you at least a dozen times."

"Just a dozen?" He pretended to look hurt, his grin the tip-off he wasn't.

My shoulder knocked him playfully. "You want to hear this or what?"

"Yes, yes. Go on, tell me about all those fantasies."

"Anyway." I ignored his suggestion and continued with my original train of thought. "I'm not used to doing the casual thing, I usually have a boyfriend. This is unchartered territory, complicated because we're friends."

"Princess, I'm going to let you in on a secret." His arm moved around my waist bringing me in closer. "Nothing we're doing is complicated. We had sex. I think we both can agree it was good sex and I'd very much like to do it again. Many times, at least until you have to board the plane. We should probably stop before we get to the airport though, FAA regulations being what they are and all. But if that's not your jam, that's cool too. Whatever you want to do is fine, but we're always going to be friends."

"How can you know that?"

Out of the seven people I'd had sex with, I was friends with exactly ZERO. Not a one. It's not like I hated them and actively spewed curses at them, hoping they developed some kind of weird funky genital infection. Well, there might have been a couple of those but the vast majority I just sort of defriended.

He leaned in and whispered, his lips skirting the shell of my ear. "You know too much, you either stay my friend or I have to kill you. Getting rid of bodies is hard work, I'd really rather not."

I laughed, my voice echoing off the walls as I laid my head on his shoulder. I liked being with him like this, so uncomplicated, so easy. I knew the sex part was probably temporary, but if it was mutually beneficial then why should it matter? He wasn't using me if it's what I wanted, and it was *definitely* what I wanted.

"I'll keep that in mind." I bit my lip, looking up at him with an innocent smile. So maybe I still enjoyed flirting with him, sue me. "Eric mentioned you might be able to introduce me to some people, some other potential candidates for my story."

"Eric is such an asshole." He cursed under his breath as he rolled his eyes. "Always trying to take credit for my good work. That's what I was coming up here to suggest, and had you spent the night, I would have seen you first. Now *he* looks like the fucking hero."

I laughed again, unable to ignore how adorable he was. "If it makes you feel better, I don't think he's a hero."

His smirk returned. "Keep talking."

"And I'm grateful for your help," I added.

"*Eternally* grateful or just *regular* grateful?" His face completely serious except for the smile. "On a sliding scale, how are you rating it?"

I clutched my hands to my chest. "Eternally and desperately grateful."

"Good, I like that level." He nodded in satisfaction. "And if I'm honest, it's probably my sweet spot. I work best when people are eternally and desperately grateful."

I shook my head, shoving his shoulder as I attempted to look hurt. "Oh so I'm just one of the masses, how many people are you helping?"

"Relax, I'm very selective." His voice so smooth that at that moment he probably could have convinced me of anything. "It's a small list."

"Yeah, I'm sure."

Deep down I knew it was the same unspoken game we usually played. We both flirted shamelessly, feelings exaggerated for theatrics. And as much as I told myself I was a grown woman who didn't need to play games, I relished it. I didn't have to be articulate or funny or smart or beautiful or any of the other adjectives society dictated I should be. It was just me and him. Talking. Being silly. And sometimes being sexy. I don't think I'd ever had that with a man. Probably why us dating wouldn't work out long term. Though I would definitely miss the sex.

"You zoning?" Ryan waved his hand in front of my face, making me blink. "Now would be a good time to tell me you were fantasizing about me, we need to get my numbers up." A beautiful smile spread across his lips.

"What if I wasn't?" I laughed, even though technically I had been thinking about him. Just probably not in the way he was hoping.

"Lila, have I taught you nothing?" He shook his head and sighed. "Lie to me."

I took a deep breath, blowing out slowly. Hoping if I sounded bored, it might hide the truth. That I did think about him. All the time. And not just sexually. "Fine, I was thinking about you. Every time I daydream, it's always about you."

"A for effort, but your execution was terrible." He scoffed. "I'm not sure I believe it."

I wanted to argue, tell him my delivery had been fantastic but I didn't get a chance. His mouth was on mine, teasing my lips apart with his tongue as he kissed me.

A moan escaped my mouth, giving him access as his hand wrapped around my neck.

It was sooooo good.

Soooooooo *good*.

With a mix of teasing nibbles and deep desperate pulls, he knew exactly what to do and when to do it. My lips and body were at his command, and I *wanted* him to take me.

I whimpered, feeling my nipples pebble underneath my bra as I gripped his biceps tight, my fingernails digging into his skin. In my gut, a knot tightened; the throbbing between my legs almost unbearable as his mouth hungered over mine.

I wanted to touch him, to drop my hands down to his jeans and see if he was hard. To wrap my hand around his shaft and squeeze, feeling the pulse of his cock hammer in between my fingers while I stroked him. To watch his eyes get wide with desperation as I pumped—both hard and soft, fast and then slow—driving him crazy like his kisses were doing to me.

Inside, I was burning. *Burning* for him and for the release his mouth was promising. I was so close already and all he'd done was kiss me.

And just as abruptly as the kiss had started, it ended. Ryan pulled his mouth away from my swollen lips, my breath pushing out in short uncontrolled bursts. I probably looked deranged, my fingernails still embedded in his skin—*that* was definitely going to leave a mark—as I tried to work out what was happening.

"Now, you *will* be thinking of me." He lowered his mouth, two petal soft kisses finding their mark on mine. "And you won't have to lie."

"That wasn't fair." I panted, confused if he had only been trying to prove a point or if that kiss and its intentions had been what I'd been feeling.

"I'm sorry, Lila. I never said this was going to be fair." He kissed me again softly. "And I've been thinking about your mouth all morning."

There was so much in that statement I didn't understand, and worst of all, I wasn't sure if I knew what I *wanted* it to mean. And for the first time ever, I just let it go. Wanting the moment more than I wanted the truth.

"I like that you were thinking of me," I told him honestly, my eyes floating down to his lips, wanting them back on me. "Maybe we can revisit those thoughts later. When we're alone."

"I was hoping you'd see it my way." He leaned in and sucked the skin between my shoulder and neck. "Once with you isn't enough."

He was right about that.

I wasn't sure thirty times would be enough.

"So let me get some work done, and then we'll play." My fingers threaded through his hair playfully.

His brows skirted with his hairline, his trademark smugness disappearing as my words surprised him as much as they did me.

Did I mean it? Could I actually do this? To be honest I wasn't sure but part of me was dying to find out.

"I like this plan." His smile reappeared, his fingers knotting with mine as he brought my knuckles to his lips. "Do you want to head out, see if we can't find you some more willing victims?"

God, he was adorable. Most men were either cute or sexy, but he managed to see-saw between the two in a combo that was both heartwarming and erotic. It shouldn't have been possible, and more importantly, shouldn't have been allowed.

I rolled my eyes. "If you call them that, they are probably going to say no."

"Please, Lila. Haven't you noticed?" He barked out a laugh. "No one says no to me."

He didn't have to convince me. I'd seen firsthand what a flash of his smile or his cool charm could accomplish. He could pied-piper me and the rest of the population right off a cliff if we weren't careful. It should have terrified me, but it didn't. And I liked that.

"Let me send this proposal off to my editor first and then we can go scout for some more participants. The more we can get nailed down, the easier it will be to write it."

"Cool." He lifted off the bed, coming to his feet. "Let me go check in with Eric and make sure he doesn't need anything before we go."

Oh, yeah. That.

It was easy to overlook that Ryan worked for Eric. Things be-tween them were always so relaxed, not typical of an employer and employee. But it didn't mean that he didn't have more important things to do than go AWOL with me for an entire day.

"Or we could do an hour, maybe do some more tomorrow if you have time," I offered, feeling a little stupid I'd been so pre-sumptuous.

"I'm positive it's not going to be a problem." He shook his head, shooting down my suggestion. "Eric's filming all day and as long as Tia isn't going to get herself into any trouble, we're good. I'm all yours."

I'm all yours.

I pretended I didn't love those words.

"Great, I'll be right here." *Excited and waiting*, I didn't add.

"Be back in a minute." He winked, opening the door and disappearing into the hall.

It was all going to be great, I told myself.

Better than great.

Pity I didn't know if I was talking about the story or me.

CHAPTER #9

SURPRISINGLY, DICK LOVED my pitch.

I had barely sent my proposal email when my phone rang, his irritating and bristling voice on the other end of the line. I could almost smell the coffee breath from here.

"You think you can gather enough material for a series?" I heard the squeak of his office chair.

"Assuming I get the number of celebrities I want, yes. I have two that are locked in but I'll have a better idea this evening."

I wasn't sure if it was my artistic integrity—for the story to be more than a few paragraphs and byline—or it was the idea of hanging around a little longer in L.A. that made me pitch it to Dick as a three-part series.

Each installment would focus on a couple different celebrities, but also highlight an issue. Invasion of privacy was the most obvious but I wanted to explore some other topics. Things like bad investments—both money and people—and knowing who you could really trust with your wealth and your reputation. As well as lighter ones, like relationships and sex. Did movie stars use Tinder? 70's-style key parties? Get their agent to find them a date through a look-book?

Dick hmmed into the phone. "I like it. I want real grit though. Don't give me a fluff piece on some poor little rich boy. And for God's sake, don't make it too depressing. It's the art's section, not the obituaries."

"It won't be depressing." God forbid we give our readers something intelligent with their side of amusement. "It will be thought-provoking and entertaining."

"Fine, make sure you turn in your draft on time. I want it to run in Sunday's edition."

"I'll turn it in by Friday. It will give us time to fix it if we need." But we wouldn't. I was going to write the best article Dick had ever seen. And besides, Saturday was the gala and I didn't want the deadline hanging over my head.

"Good. Don't disappoint me."

His warmth and reassurance so touching, I was pretty sure he was raised by a pack of wolves. "Thanks for the pep talk, Dick. Always a pleasure."

"Goddamn it, Lila." I imagined his face turning red and that vein at the side of his neck bulging. "It's Richard."

"Yep. That's what I said. Tootles."

I hung up the phone, pleased I had the rubber stamp of approval and that I had successfully gotten under Dick's skin from the other side of the country. It really was a talent. If only I got paid for it, then I'd be able to afford my own house in the hills.

"You all good?" Ryan appeared in my doorway, sliding his phone into his back pocket. "Eric is about to leave for the studio and Tia says she's going to get a jump on her next column. Means it's just me and you, baby."

"Yay!" I jumped excitedly from my bed, tossing my cell phone aside but stopping short of hugging him. "All systems go on my end, and I convinced Dick to let me do it as a series, so that means I'll be sticking around a few more weeks."

"You just couldn't bear to leave me, huh?" He pulled me in, not having the same concerns I'd had about hugging. "Understandable."

"Oh, yeah." I tapped my chin like I was deep in thought and it hadn't even occurred to me that it would give us more time. "I guess that means we will probably see more of each other. Huh. Well that's cool." I shrugged nonchalantly.

His brows rose as his gaze dropped to study me, his scrutiny almost making me blush.

"Do I need to kiss you again?" His lips hovered above mine, threatening me with a tentative touch. "It will mean we probably won't make it out the door, but you'll only have yourself to blame. You and your lies." His lips curled, still in striking distance.

I batted my eyelashes, my hands running up the length of his amazing chest. "I thought you wanted me to lie to you."

"You have so very much to learn," he whispered, pulling back his lips, denying me the kiss I had actually wanted. "We should go."

I agreed, my head nodding though I hadn't moved. "Yes, we should."

Nothing good would come of us being alone and that close to a bed. It sure as hell wouldn't help me make my deadline. So leaving would have been the responsible and reasonable thing to do. Those two things always seemed to be in short supply lately.

"Stop looking at me like that, Lila." He backed away slowly, smirking as he waved his finger in the air. "I'm a person, not a piece of meat."

"My apologies." I wasn't the least bit sorry. "I'll keep my meaty stares to myself."

He laughed, waiting on the other side of the doorway. "You can try, but we both know you won't be able to help yourself."

I ignored the truth in his statement, grabbing my phone, purse and note pad. I had scribbled a few preliminary questions and hoped to build on them by the end of the day. And with everything

I needed gathered, we headed out of the house to where his Hummer was parked out front.

"You know, this must be a bitch to drive." I slid into the passenger seat, glad I wasn't responsible for having to park something that was basically the size of my first apartment. "This thing is huge."

"Now with the compliments." He closed the door, starting the engine with a grin. "I should tell you to stop but I like hearing those words come out of your mouth. Maybe you can say it again, this time use my name."

"Be serious." I pushed his shoulder gently. "If I didn't know otherwise, I might think you were compensating for something."

Let me be clear, even if he drove an eighteen-wheeler it wouldn't be *compensating*.

"Oh, you're hilarious." He laughed, pulling out onto the road. "But no, I just like Hummers. Insert your dirty joke, princess. I've heard it all before, even made a few myself."

"It's no fun if you're expecting the innuendo, Ryan." I sighed, folding my arms across my chest.

"Fine, let's talk about something else." His eyes stayed on the road as he weaved through traffic. "Oooh, I know, tell me about your family."

It was a segue that not only had I not seen coming, but wasn't prepared for.

"My family?" I squeaked. Repeating it in case I'd heard it incorrectly.

"I mean your parents, siblings, crazy uncle doing time—shit like that." He side-eyed me as he kept driving. "Unless of course you are leading a double life and have a husband and a gaggle of kids somewhere. In which case, I don't want to know." He grimaced, pulling a funny face.

I chuckled, shaking my head. "I am not leading a double life. No secret husbands and or children."

"Phew, close one." He wiped his brow, breathing a sigh of relief. "Neither am I, looks like we're both winners today."

He was crazy.

Beautiful, adorable and incredibly sexy, but certifiable all the same.

"Okay, so what do you want to know?" I threw up my hands in defeat. "I'm an only child, my parents live in Vegas, which is where I'm originally from. I don't have any crazy uncles in jail, but my father was the sheriff until he retired last year."

It was the condensed version. The one I gave at parties or whenever the subject came up. And usually it was just enough information to satisfy curiosity so I could conveniently turn the conversation to something else.

Ryan's mouth dropped open. "Dude, your dad was a sheriff in Vegas? That's freaking cool. Was your mom in the force too? No, wait." He held his hand up, stopping me from answering. "Oh, let me guess, her name was Lola and she was a showgirl."

Oh how much easier it would have been if she was just a character in a Barry Manilow song.

"Errr. No, not exactly. She runs the family business."

Ryan nodded and asked. "Which is?"

I blew out a slow, steady breath knowing there was no way of sugar coating it.

"Prostitution."

His head wiped around so fast I was surprised we didn't hit the car in front of us. His eyes wide from shock. Or maybe horror. It was a coin toss.

"Are you fucking shitting me?"

I pointed to the traffic in front of us, not wanting my mamma's propensity to sell *ass* to be the reason I met my end. "Keep your eyes on the road. I don't want to die today."

"Please, I can drive this city with my eyes closed." He waved me off, his eyes sliding from me back to the road. "Now, on to more important things, like what the *fuck* did you just say?"

"She runs a *gentlemen's* club."

There was a reason I could count on one hand the number of people I had told of my mother's profession. Because you couldn't drop something like that and not follow up with some serious backstory. *Hey, yeah, my mom peddles sex at a brothel in Vegas; please pass the mashed potatoes*, didn't really cut it. I'll admit I tried it once and it didn't end well.

But I trusted Ryan, and I knew he wouldn't judge me. And part of me was glad I didn't have to censor that part of my life with him. So as we continued the drive, I told him the story of my hooker grandma and my entrepreneur mother while he listened with silent awe.

He looked at me and smiled, his eyes filled with almost a child-like wonder. "That is probably the most fantastic story I have ever heard. Now tell me when we're going to visit, don't even try to deny me."

I laughed, relieved my assumptions of him or what he would think of me had been correct. And he did it all without asking me whether or not *I* had ever "worked" for my mom. Which was usually the follow-up question.

"I don't usually take boys home." More like never. "My folks are a little eccentric. I love them to bits but they're an acquired taste."

I hated the way it sounded, like I was embarrassed by them. But I wasn't, really. Well not anymore. They were both loving and hard working, and had given me the best—albeit interesting—childhood a kid could have asked for. Not to mention an education that I never would have been able to afford on my own. But I hated that people saw them as a punch line, my need to protect them overwhelming, just as they'd protected me.

"Princess, I'm hurt." Ryan's hand cupped his chest right where his heart was. "Firstly, I'm not a boy, I'm a *man*." He took his eyes off the road to look back at me. "And *eccentric* are my people. If it were a town, I'd be voted mayor."

"Yeah, well you haven't met my parents."

"Which is exactly why we need to make this happen." He nodded, tapping the steering wheel as he pulled to a stop in front of a big iron gate.

"Here's an idea." He turned to face me, excitement prickling his voice. "We'll go meet my parents and I'll let my mother suitably embarrass me. She will pull out ten thousand baby photos of me—although, I will tell you I was pretty fucking adorable—and then tell you about the time I peed my pants at Little League sliding into home. Then my dad will weigh in and tell you about the time Eric and I stole his beer and got caught underage drinking and making out with the minister's daughters. A lot of Hail Marys were needed that day, probably didn't help we were in the church at the time. Ah, such fond memories." He pretended to wipe a tear from his eye.

"You're crazy, you know that?" I laughed, a little nervous and a lot excited about the prospect of him meeting my parents. "Fine, we'll go, but make sure you clear it with Eric, I already feel like I'm monopolizing your time."

"I'll check his schedule tonight, and then we make plans." He fist pumped. "This is going to be awesome."

"Yeah, yeah. Let's get through today first." I looked out the windshield to the gate that had yet to open. "I still have a story to write."

MARILYN STEAL WAS gorgeous. Classic Hollywood beauty with a face and body the camera loved. She was also a good friend of both Ryan and Eric, having starred in the same movie as Larsson not so long ago. Which was why Ryan suggested we pay her a visit and see if her goodwill would extend to me. Of course Tia—my BFF and girlfriend of her ex-costar—had used Marilyn's name inappropriately in order to get into the aforementioned movie's premiere. That in turn had her meeting her now boyfriend, so I hoped that if Marilyn knew what went down that night, it was all water under the bridge now. If not, it would be one of those times where pretending to be ignorant would be allowed.

"Ryan." She smiled warmly, pulling him into a big hug as she opened the front door. "It's been forever." Good, no hostility and or anger, Tia's Viking gods had come through for her this time.

Ryan grinned, hugging her back. "Too long." He dropped his arms, pulling me inside along with him. "I want you to meet my friend, Lila. She's the reporter I told you about."

It was hard not to be starstuck. She was stunning, but it was more than that. I had gained access to a world where I didn't belong, an invite-only party where civilians barely entered. I completely understood how Tia sometimes felt off center. It was exciting and terrifying, and I prayed I could act professional and not blow what could be my big break.

Besides, it was hard not to be on edge. Considering the last person he introduced me to we'd been actively stalking, I was worried what kind of adventure this one was going to involve.

"Hi, I'm Lila." I reintroduced myself lamely as I held out my hand. "It's lovely to meet you, thanks so much for agreeing to talk to me."

"I'm Marilyn, and it's nice to meet you too." She shook my hand; her warm hazel eyes making me feel welcome. "And I'd do almost anything for Ryan."

Yeah, he gets that a lot.

"Great." My smile widened, wondering if there were any women in L.A. who didn't fall to their knees every time Ryan walked in the room.

I couldn't even be jealous, instead slightly awed by the phenomenon. It was like he omitted some kind of pheromone, a silent but seductive mating call that women found irresistible. Of course, they had given me no reason to believe they were anything but platonic. Other than the hug they'd shared, there were no signs of intimacy. No lingering glances, no discreet touches. But clearly logic wasn't the flavor of the day as I interpreted her "anything for Ryan" as more than friendly. Because, lord knows what I'd do if he'd ask, and surely she couldn't be immune.

"Well, I don't want to take up too much of your time." I prayed my smile hadn't migrated into freak show territory. "I just wanted to ask a few questions, if that's okay."

"Of course, how rude of me." Marilyn waved her hands in the air, motioning to the room off to the side. "Come into the living room where we can sit down."

"Great." *Shit, I needed to stop saying that.*

"You guys good if I sit this out?" Ryan oddly seemed more interested in my reaction than Marilyn's.

Maybe he'd noticed me acting like a fruitcake and wondered if leaving me alone with her was a smart move.

"I'm fine, if Marilyn is fine." I mean, I didn't want her to be worried I would cut locks of her hair to stuff under my pillow or something if he left us. She was already doing me a favor by granting the interview; I didn't want to make her uncomfortable in her own home as well.

"You want to see Tom's new toy?" Marilyn folded her arms across her chest, narrowing her eyes and not looking at all surprised.

Was this where it got weird? Who was *Tom* and what *toy* were they talking about? I'll admit, my mind was conjuring up all kinds of images of a sex slave—obviously Tom—wearing a ball-gag, holding a dildo. Not that there was anything wrong with that, I named my vibrator Ryan so I wasn't in any position to talk.

"What?" Ryan did a terrible job at looking shocked. "No, I know *nothing* about the new McLaren he's acquired." His smirk told us otherwise.

"My boyfriend got a new car . . . men and their toys." She rolled her eyes contradicting my earlier assessment of both the sex slave and the dildo. Wow, got that one wrong. "It's bright orange."

"Of course it's orange." Ryan reared back in shock, genuine this time. "You don't get a car like that to blend in. It's a McLaren, not a fucking Toyota."

God, he was adorable.

I shrugged, finding myself agreeing. "If you're going to get a sports car that obscene, it has to be an obnoxious color as well."

Marilyn shook her head, possibly annoyed at the lack of female solidarity. "It's in the garage, and there's beer in the fridge but do not even breathe on that thing. He'll know."

"I'll be gentle." His words so warm and lush, I wanted to curl around them and cuddle. "And please save all the potential blackmail material for my return. I don't want to miss any of the good stuff."

He gave us a quick wave and disappeared back out the front door.

"How long have you been together?" Marilyn asked, my eyes swinging back to meet hers.

"Oh, we're not *together*." I laughed, secretly thrilled she'd made the assumption. "We're just friends. *Good* friends, and I think the world of him, but we're not dating."

Her face flushed, her cheeks pinking. "Sorry, when he called and spoke about you . . . I just assumed, sorry."

While I'd been selling Dick my pitch, Ryan had made some calls of his own. I hadn't heard the content of the conversations so guessed he'd just told them I was a friend who was doing a story. Keep it simple. Of course I assumed he might have called in a few favors, something I didn't expect but was grateful for. Other than that, I couldn't even guess what he'd told them.

"No, no, it's totally fine," I reassured her, not at all offended. If anything I was flattered she'd assumed we were a couple. "I'm sure he'd probably think it was funny too." Because he'd been pretty clear we were *friends having sex* this morning, not that I wanted or planned on mentioning that part. I preferred her to believe I was capable of being *together* with him rather than being one of the girls he was with.

Which was why curiosity got the better of me and I couldn't resist.

"So . . . what did he say?"

Marilyn's face softened, her smile returning. "It's not so much what he said, it's that he brought you here in the first place. We don't usually get to meet Ryan's *dates*. I guess it's because he doesn't hang onto them for long, and probably because he is really good at keeping it insulated, so nothing ever puts Eric or any of us at risk. You can never be too careful these days, and Ryan has always been super cautious about who he vouches for. So when he said how amazing and talented you were *and* he was bringing you here . . ." She looked at me awkwardly. "I'm sorry, I shouldn't have assumed."

Wow.

Talk about conflict.

I had no reason to feel anything about his past relationships—or whatever it was he called his non-girlfriends. But it sort of made me glad that it was different with me. Even if it was just because we were friends so I wasn't a part of that. Not that I was a part of anything else, so I shouldn't get too excited either.

Besides, he said I was amazing. I should focus on that.

"That was nice of him to say I was talented." Warmth spread through my chest. "He's such a nice guy."

I'd used the word *nice* twice in the space of a minute and

both times I hadn't meant it. He was anything but nice. Amazing, spectacular, wonderful—pick a word, any word. But my mouth wouldn't say what my mind was thinking, just a tiny bit concerned he may have said all of that just to get the interviews. Make me sound more amazing so his friends agreed. *There's this weirdo I know who needs some of your personal info* doesn't have the same powers of persuasion.

"Yeah, he's great." Another smile, one that told me she knew those nice-es were bullshit too. "Let's go chat."

We moved into her beautiful living room. It was modern and roomy, but not overly ornate. Other than a ridiculously large television, twin extra-large leather couches and a coffee table, there wasn't a lot else in the room.

She sat across from me, offering me a drink while I prepared my questions.

Initially reserved, it wasn't until after my confession about calling my boss Dick and two fruit punches later—sadly devoid of vodka—that she started to relax.

I listened intently, scribbling as much information as I could get on the pages as she spoke. All of it—fascinating. And if I asked something she didn't want to answer, we moved on to something else, the conversation flowing with ease. Meanwhile, Ryan was still MIA and I had enough from that one interview to write my entire first article.

"This has been really insightful." I packed away my note pad. "I know people in the entertainment industry aren't always treated fairly by the press, but I promise you I'll handle the information with respect." Not to mention she had trusted me without signing an NDA, based on the word of a friend. There were reporters who would give their right hand for that kind of access, and I wasn't going to blow it.

"I know." She smiled, lifting her delicate body off the couch.

"Besides, it felt good to just say what I thought for a change."

"No names or anything that can connect you to the story will be printed," I assured her again, rising to my feet. "Thank you so much for doing this."

"You ladies finished?" Ryan reappeared, his car lusting apparently over.

He'd been gone awhile, so I hoped he wasn't harboring one of those weird fetishes where he screwed a tailpipe or something. *Hey, my mother owned a brothel, remember?* I'd heard it all.

"Hey." The possibility of a funky sex fetish no longer on my mind as I resisted the urge to hug him. "I thought you were going to come back for the good parts?"

"Nah, I've heard most of them before." He nodded an acknowledgement to Marilyn before turning back to me. "Besides, I had a few phone calls I needed to deal with."

I wondered about those phone calls and what Marilyn had said when he had spoken to her about me. I pushed the thoughts aside, ignoring the excitement of my name on his lips as I watched him stroll into the room.

"Well, we're all done," I offered cheerily as he came to stand right beside me, our bodies inches apart.

I hated being this close to him and not being able to touch him. The impulse to reach out and wrap my arms around him so great, I had to remind myself to stop. We didn't do that, not out in public.

Keeping my hands locked to my side, we said goodbye to Marilyn and walked back to the car.

I didn't say anything as I slid into the passenger seat, putting on the seat belt as he started the ignition. The rumble under the hood broke the silence.

"Everything okay?" He looked over at me curiously. "You seem really quiet."

"Yes, everything is great." There was that word again. I pushed out a long breath, my hands settling in my lap. "I was just thinking."

"About me?" His head turned, a hopeful smile on his face.

"Yeah, it was about you."

I didn't lie.

I didn't want to.

"Was I doing dirty things?" he asked with a grin, keeping his eyes on the road as he took a corner.

"Always," I answered honestly, my hand moving to his thigh. "I wanted to touch you."

"You can touch me anytime you want." One of his hands dropped from the steering wheel and cupped mine. "You don't need to ask."

He had no idea what he was giving me permission to do. He couldn't know. That inside my head thoughts of him swirled uncontrollably. Not just about his body—which was amazing—but his mind and his heart. That when I thought about it, it felt so normal, even though it wasn't because what we were doing wasn't normal. Not for me anyway.

This was new, unchartered territory, and the feelings were almost confusing. Not the kind I assumed I'd be feeling for what was *supposed* to be a fling.

"Is it strange that I want to do it all the time?" I asked, needing a second opinion. "Like a few days ago, the closest we'd gotten was a hug. Now I want to crawl in your lap and suck on your neck while you drive. Not necessarily to fuck, but just touch."

He didn't need to answer that. Hearing it out loud was all the verification I needed.

It *was* strange.

"Wow, princess." He swallowed, the Adam's apple in his throat bobbing slowly as his hand gripped mine tight. "I'm not sure I could have you in my lap, sucking my neck and *not* fuck you. It would be," he coughed, clearing his throat, "difficult."

I liked that he felt that way. That something I said or did could make him lose control. Just like I seemed to whenever he was around.

"Well then, for the safety of the car and its occupants, I won't climb in your lap." My back relaxed into the seat while my hand stayed on his thigh.

I might have put a stop to the dry humping, but I wasn't going to stop touching him. Not yet, at least.

He moved my hand from his thigh to the fly of his jeans, pressing my palm against the firm ridge growing between his legs. "I could pull over."

"Tonight." My hand rubbed him through his pants, feeling him thicken. "I promise."

He moaned, widening his legs so I could get more contact. "Are you sure? Car sex can be pretty awesome."

I didn't doubt that.

I couldn't imagine any scenario where Ryan was naked where it *wasn't* awesome. His body was its own moving violation, and I wanted to be reckless with him. I loved the feel of him under my hand, stroking him through his clothes while cars beside us had no idea what I was doing.

"We shouldn't."

It was a statement but inside my head it was asked as a question. *Could we? Should we?* What would be the fallout if we did? Nothing bad, surely. I pressed harder, the heel of my palm working him as he drove.

"Responsibility wins again." He pushed out a frustrated sigh, not giving me a chance to continue my internal debate as he stilled my hand. "Fine, no car sex. It's probably just as well, you wouldn't be able to conduct another interview after I was finished."

"Oh, you think so?" I laughed, keeping my hand unmoving on his erection, amused by his smugness.

If last night was any indication, then it was completely justified, but I wasn't going to give into him that easily.

"Lila, I *know* so." He glanced to the side, a hint of a smile. "And you know it too."

He was right, I did know it and secretly I loved that he could do that to me. Unravel me, make me distracted, make me wild—all the things that would make conducting another interview impossible.

"Yes," I answered without hesitation.

His brows scrunched in confusion. "Yes?"

"I wouldn't be able to do another interview."

There was something about him that made me feel like I could tell him anything. That nothing was off limits. Whether it was telling him about my parents or admitting what sex with him would do to my body and mind. But I also knew those feelings needed to be locked up tight for now.

He was charming and charismatic and made women swoon left and right. And yes, he was a nice guy, but I wasn't convinced *I* was all that special. Not that I was lacking in self-confidence, more that this was part of his MO. He wasn't manipulative, but I also knew he had an aversion to commitment and I didn't want to misread any of it for more than what it was.

He was a good guy.

He just wasn't *my* good guy.

Begrudgingly, I moved my hand from his lap into mine with a moan of disapproval from Ryan. "Being right has never sucked so much."

CHAPTER #10

KELLY SMOKE HAD been our next stop. She was an actress with an unfortunate last name and a huge chip on her shoulder. And it took me three seconds to decide I didn't like her.

She answered the door, lighting up like a glow stick at a Berlin rave the minute she saw Ryan. Her brown wavy hair bounced as she hugged him, giving him a kiss on the cheek before she gave me a limp-wristed wave and generic "hi" with her face screwed up. The dislike, it seemed, was mutual.

I persevered, pretending to be interested as I opened up my note pad and went through the motions, but in minutes it became obvious she'd only agreed because Ryan had asked her.

Maybe they'd had a *thing* once and she was hoping for a repeat or maybe she was just optimistic, but she didn't take her eyes off him once. Not even when I was asking her questions. Instead, she spent the entire fifteen minutes acting cagey and giving me one or two-word answers while she stared—creepily—at Ryan.

I gave up when she started giving me recycled gossip and bragging about her shiny new convertible. She was exactly the stereotype I was trying to disprove with her fake Instagram life and manufactured Twitter feed.

So it came as no surprise when I thanked her for her time, telling her I had all I needed and wrapped it up early.

She pushed out her tits and gave Ryan a suggestive smile, but to his credit he just thanked her like I had and we left.

Part of me wanted to ask him about her, curious if they'd shared history, but I didn't ask. Better to not know. Instead, we returned to our easy conversation.

With Eric shooting into the night, Tia had decided to go visit him on set for dinner. She asked if I wanted to join her but I knew deep down she probably didn't want the company. So I stayed home while Ryan drove her to the studio.

Meanwhile, I ate Chinese food alone at my laptop while I worked. It wasn't all bad, I got most of the framework for my article in place and even got a first draft. It was going to need more attention tomorrow but it beat sitting around and waiting for Ryan to come home.

That didn't mean I couldn't multitask. I sat by the window casually looking at the stars—at least that's what I pretended to look at—and I worked. So of course the minute I saw headlights reflect off the glass, my heart started thumping like an idiot.

Saving my work, I shut my laptop and ran down the stairs with a stupid grin on my face.

"Heeeeey." I tried to hide my disappointment when the door opened and Tia was by herself.

"Hey, yourself." Tia laughed, closing the door behind her and engaging both the lock and the alarm. Not something you did when you were expecting company.

"Eric going to be late?" I asked, more interested in why Ryan hadn't come in with her. My eyes still on the door.

"Yeah, he'll be shooting till about three." She pressed her back to the door, smiling. "Why don't you just ask me?"

"Ask you what?" I turned my attention to her, wondering if

there was more to the conversation I had missed. I'd been concen-
trating more on the door than what she was saying; the probability
was better than average she had said something else.

She folded her arms across her chest with a big smile inching
at her lips. "Where Ryan is and why he didn't come in with me?"

I cringed, wondering when I'd become so transparent. "It's
that obvious?"

"Come on, I know you." She laughed, waving her finger in
the air. "And you're not usually waiting at the door to welcome
me home."

"I swear," I shook my head, not even having the decency to
be embarrassed, "I've got it bad. It's like I'm obsessed. Can you
believe I sat by the fucking window, waiting for him to come home?
Who does that?"

"Umm, hello?" She waved her hand, throwing her head back
in a laugh. "Do I need to remind you of all the crazy stuff I did
when I first met Eric? You sat by a window? You're not even close
to major leagues yet."

"T, I'm not even going to try and compete with your kind of
crazy." I threw my arms around her, hugging my best friend. "So
tell me, what do you know?"

She patted me on the back, giggling. "He went to go get
dessert."

"Huh?"

I pulled back, unwrapping my arms as my eyes narrowed. I
wasn't sure if that was code for something or if perhaps I should
know what that meant? But he went to get dessert? Nope, I still
had no idea.

"When we were at the studio he mentioned that he hated you
were eating dinner alone," she threw over her shoulder. She moved
away to the door and motioned for me to follow her into the living
room. "And even though I told him you were fine and it gave you

an opportunity to work—Lord knows I've been there, trying to fit in writing between dealing with infatuation—but he wanted to make it up to you." Her body fell messily onto the couch, her arms and legs stretching as she continued. "So, he asked me what your favorite dessert was. I'll admit when he said dessert, I though he meant sex. I mean, you would think sex too, right?" She waved her hand at me, waiting for me to nod before she went on. "So I was a little surprised when he dropped me off and told me to tell you he'd be back and went to go get you Devil's Food cake."

"Wait, he went to go buy me a cake?" I stayed standing, too confused to sit down.

I wasn't sure if the suggestion was out of this world adorable, or crazy, considering it was close to ten at night. The tightness in my chest spreading that he was thinking about me while we weren't together.

"Yeah, I told him to pick up vanilla ice cream too because it's better like that. Honestly, I should have told him to just get the ice cream, the cake is going to take longer and I know that isn't what you really want."

And clearly I was a terrible person because she was right and I didn't want the fucking cake, annoyed with myself that my favorite dessert wasn't a milkshake from a drive thru.

"No, it's not what I really want but it's so freaking sweet, I can't even be mad."

"I know, right?" She nodded. "And if it makes you feel better, when he talked about you, he didn't mention your boobs once."

"Do I want to hear this?" I warned, not sure if it would make things better or worse. "I already have this sick obsession. I'm not sure adding to it would be a smart thing."

"Stop trying to be *smart*." She rolled her eyes; little did she know there was no chance of that. "Sure, he's probably dated—or his version of the word—a lot, but he isn't a bad guy. If he was an asshole, I'd be the first person to warn you off."

"I know, I know." I purposely didn't dwell on his past sexual history, the idea not one I wanted to spend too much time with. "He is not an asshole."

"Okay." She yawned, exaggerating her fatigue as she stretched out her arms. "Well, I'm just going to pretend that I am really tired so you can go run off and enjoy your *cake*." She used her fingers like little talking marks for the word. "He's with Eric all day tomorrow so we can eat cookies and gossip all day. And I'm going to want all the details, you owe me." She gave me a pointed look as she rose off the couch. "Good details, Lila. You're a reporter, I know you know how."

She waved, disappearing out of the room while I sat there with what was left of my scattered thoughts.

Keeping with the theme of the night—I didn't care if it made me sound pathetic—I sat in front of the window and waited until the headlights reappeared. Luckily for the good of all mankind, his mission to procure cake and ice cream hadn't taken long, the rumble of his Hummer stopping as he pulled into the garage.

A surge of excitement shot up my spine as I ran Tom-Cruise-Mission-Impossible style to the back of the house where the double glass doors led to the backyard.

Remembering to disengage the alarm—and cursing its existence—I unlocked the glass doors, flinging them open to see his shadowy figure on the opposite side of the pool moving toward his cottage.

"Ryan," I yelled, my attempt to casually call out his name abandoned as soon as the security lighting illuminated his face.

He stopped, turning to face me while in his hands he held a plastic bag and a box.

A smile that could melt the entire surface area of Antarctica spread across his face. "Princess, I was just about to call you."

I didn't think, running the rest of the distance across the grass until I was standing with him in front of his door.

"Open the door," I whispered, taking the cake and the ice cream out of his hands so he could take care of the lock. My heart beating so fast I was worried I might be having a heart attack.

He didn't waste time, unlocking the door and yanking it open, turning on the light as he tossed his keys onto the side table. The cake and ice cream were pulled from my hands as they joined his keys, their purpose forgotten as our bodies moved closer.

"Kiss me." My voice so needy and thin I barely recognized it.

"Fuck." Ryan pulled me in, slamming the door shut and pressing my body against the wall beside it. "I want you so badly, Lila."

"Then take me."

His head lowered, brushing his lips against mine, my mouth parting for him as I moaned.

"Fuck," he cursed, dominating my mouth as his hands moved to my breasts. "You are so beautiful, Lila."

I wanted to respond, to tell him how hot he made me, but the words got stuck in my throat. I had nothing, incapacitated by his mouth and his body as he swallowed my moan.

My fingers wrapped around the thin fabric of his T-shirt, yanking at it until it was lifted off his body. I wanted his skin on mine so badly I thought I would explode.

My breaths came out in short bursts, pulling my lips away from his just for a second to ground out, "I need you."

"I know, I know." He kneed apart my legs, his body settled between my thighs. "I need you too." The hard ridge of his cock pressing against my clit.

Hands ripped at clothing as his jeans and my dress got tossed to the floor in a heated rush. Next was my bra, his fingers flicking it free while I worked on his boxer briefs. Our bodies were quickly stripped, clothes discarded without care or concern as I heard the sound of fabric tear. I was pretty sure that had been my panties and they weren't going to be wearable later, but I didn't care.

Instead, I focused on his mouth and where it moved on me.

My neck. My chest. The swell of my breasts.

His tongue flicked across my nipple as I sucked in a breath, the feeling making my skin tingle. My fingers dug into his shoulders as little whimpers came out of my mouth, his lips and tongue taking turns as he teased me.

"I bet I could make you come just like this. Up against the wall." He breathed on my skin, my pussy so wet and ready that one sweep of his thumb would have undone me completely.

"Yes. Yes," I whimpered, not sure if I was agreeing with him or if that's what I wanted, my body writhing while he pressed against me. "Please make me come."

One of his hands dropped from my breast, plunging two fingers inside of me while his mouth moved back up to my neck. "I love the noises you make. I love those little sounds you give me when you're close," he mumbled against my skin. "I want them all, and to know it's because of what I'm doing to you."

In blind lust I reached down for his cock, my fingers closing around as much of his girth as I could. I squeezed, my one-handed grip tight as I pumped him. "I love that I make you so hard."

"Yes, that's it." He groaned, his fingers moving faster as he sucked the skin between my neck and shoulder. I felt the slight sting of teeth as his mouth shifted higher. "Harder, I like it when you squeeze me tight."

My hand slid up and down his shaft trying to find a rhythm while his thumb circled my clit. The sensations completely over-whelming me as his mouth and hands owned my body. I couldn't hold on any longer, my legs starting to shake as I fisted his cock, the glide up and down no longer possible.

"I'm going to—" The air was sucked out of my lungs as my

body became hypersensitive, every cell awake as I struggled to breathe.

"I want to feel it, Lila. Come for me."

He didn't need to ask, my release unstoppable as my legs buckled underneath me, completely overcome.

"I—I—"

My mouth opened and closed with a soundless yell, my head hitting the drywall as I shattered apart. My body convulsed as his arm reached around my waist and grabbed me, stopping me from falling to the floor as my body continued to pulse.

"I love that." He lapped at my collarbone. "I could listen and watch you come all day long. But I'm so greedy, Lila. I want it again and this time I want to feel it on my cock."

My fingers were still gripped around his painfully hard length, my feet struggling to find purchase as I kissed him. Our lips fused as we shared the same desperate breath. His fingers slid out of me, his hands finding a better purpose as they hauled me off the floor and pulled me tight against his body.

"I want you inside of me." My voice tore from my throat as my arms wrapped around his neck. "Now. Don't make me beg."

He cursed out my name, his legs taking steady strides across the floor while he cradled my body in his arms. "You won't have to beg, princess. I'm going to give you exactly what you need."

His footsteps were heavy as we entered his bedroom, the light from the living room just enough to see as he tossed me roughly onto his bed.

My back arched, my knees falling apart as I watched him open the drawer of his nightstand and pull out a condom.

"Let me." I held out my hand, my fingers desperate to touch him again. "I want to slide it on you."

"You're fucking killing me, Lila," he gritted out from his tight jaw, tearing open the packet before handing over the latex.

The muscles in his abs tensed as I moved closer to his dick, my lips hovering over the head before I pulled him into my mouth.

His fingers knotted in my hair as he exhaled with a sharp, "Fuck."

I felt his grip tighten as I sucked, a tiny bite of pain against my scalp while he pulled and it drove me freaking crazy.

My mouth lollipopped him, licking and sucking while fisting him with one hand, the other, clutching the condom I had yet to put on him.

"Lila, put it on me." His voice so raw it was barely recognizable. "Put on the damn condom before I come in your mouth."

With a wet pop, he yanked his hips back, pulling himself from my lips, his hungry eyes stalking me from above. "Do it, or I will."

We'd both suffered enough, heat radiated from my body as my fingers stretched the condom over the head of his cock and covered his length. I could almost feel him vibrating as I pumped him twice, smoothing down the latex.

The minute he was covered, he was on me. The mattress compressed under his weight, his muscles contracted as he pulled apart my knees and pumped into me.

"Lila." He pushed out my name on a breath, pulling out and then thrusting back into me, slowly and deliberately. Each drag of his cock deeper and harder as I twisted against him, an uncontrollable moan escaping from my lips.

The friction between us got me so close I could feel myself teeter on the edge of pleasure and pain I didn't want to end. And yet I was desperate for the release, my body and mind disconnected completely as I tried to hold on a little longer.

"Ryan, I'm almost there."

"I know, I can feel how tight you are around me."

Words whispered into each other's skin as my arms locked around his torso, holding on as he pumped into me.

The tendons in his arms flexed as he repositioned my body, tilting my pelvis so he could drive in deeper, harder, faster. Each time giving me just a little bit more until I couldn't hold out any longer, the sensation in my body snapping like a rubber band.

"Ryan."

It was more of a shout than his name, my fingernails digging into his skin as I came apart. Over and over again, like a wave that wouldn't break.

Tumbling.

Falling.

Flying.

I splintered into a million pieces, shards of my body and mind tossed into a spin as I struggled to maintain my grip.

Every part of him tensed as he blew out a guttural, "fuck." His weight heavy against me as he exploded, pumping into me as his hot breath tickled my neck.

"Lila."

He said it again and again, my name getting lost in the sound of the freight train of his breath and his release. And it was the most beautiful thing I'd ever heard.

I didn't move.

I couldn't.

Just wanting to feel it all a little bit longer as our breathing started to slow.

"So." He was the first to speak, peppering soft kisses on my jaw as he made his way to my mouth. "The ice cream is probably melted."

I laughed, my hands still wrapped around him as my body gently shook. "I'd rather have you than the ice cream." My teeth toyed with his bottom lip.

"Good." His mouth sealed mine, his kisses less urgent—slower, like he was trying to savor me. "Because I really enjoyed watching you melt instead."

Wow.

Did my heart just squeeze?

I was sure something was going on inside my chest that wasn't normal.

"You are all kinds of smooth, aren't you?" I beamed, my smile so wide my cheeks were probably going to split apart.

"What can I say?" He shifted, sliding out of me. "You inspire me. Don't move." He kissed my shoulder. "I'll be right back."

He went first to the bathroom, the water running a few moments before he remerged still naked minus the condom. A wicked grin played on his lips as he turned on the lamp beside the bed while I watched with interest.

"Get into the bed." His hand griped the comforter waiting for me to roll to the side so he could pull it down. "I'll get in with you in a second."

He disappeared out of the bedroom back into the main part of the cottage. I heard the rustle of the plastic bag and the opening and shutting of drawers before he returned carrying the cake box and a fork.

"The ice cream is almost soup." He strode in slowly, sliding into bed beside me, and opening the cake box. "But the cake is still edible."

"We're going to eat cake in bed?"

"No, I'm going to feed you cake in bed." He forked off a piece of cake and lifted it to my lips. "Open."

My mouth did exactly as he commanded, parting as the decadent chocolate cake played on my tongue. It was sinful and delicious—and the cake wasn't bad either.

"Soooo good," I moaned, closing my eyes to enjoy the mouthful. "You know, you keep giving me orgasms followed by cake and I'll probably never leave."

Shit.

I hadn't meant to say that out loud. It was too much too soon and the last thing I needed was for him to assume I was going to turn into a clingy pest who overstayed their welcome. That was a misstep I wouldn't be making again.

"Really?" He looked at me curiously, probably trying to work out whether to run now or let me finish dessert.

After all, he went to so much trouble to get it and I was in his bed, it was probably easier to kick me out in an hour or two. More democratic. Although I wasn't sure what the etiquette was on flings, maybe I was the one who was supposed to leave.

And this is why I basically sucked at casual sex. It took just as much mental and emotional energy as a regular relationship with the added risk of an STD.

"Well, it's really good cake." I laughed, hoping he didn't see my panic. "I can already feel my ass getting bigger."

That was not a lie. The cake was divine, and probably like five million calories. I was going to have to go for a run tomorrow just to work it off. Not that I cared how long or how many miles it would take, today totally would have been worth it. For the cake I mean, I was talking about the cake.

He stopped, looking puzzled at the empty fork before loading it up again, his hand moving back to my mouth. "Why do women do that? Worry so much about their ass?"

"What?" I mumbled, a mouth full of glorious cake, the chocolate covering my tongue.

"Why are women so preoccupied about their bodies, their ass, gaining a couple of extra pounds? It's always been so curious to me."

"Well," I swallowed, the deliciousness lingering even though it was gone. "I guess as much as women want to believe they're okay, we're bombarded with the notion of perfection. It's tough to see magazines and movies, or the people dubbed "the most beautiful" and for it not to affect you on some level."

It wasn't something I obsessed over. And even though I was an educated woman with a decent self-esteem, and knew most of it was bullshit—Photoshop had a lot to answer for—part of me still bought into the lie.

"I guess," I shook my head, my vulnerability peeking through, "there's a fucked up side to all of us that just wants us to feel beautiful."

What the hell was I saying?

This was too personal, too deep and not at all sexy. Couldn't I have just let him believe I was clingy? No, instead I had acted like a vain psycho case with confidence issues.

Bravo, Lila, brav-fucking-o.

Oh, and I needed to stop eating. Not because I was actually worried about my ass, that was the least of my problems. That Devil's food cake was aptly named—a menace and the work of evil—with the chocolate-induced endorphins making me talk like I'd been injected with truth serum.

"I get that to some point." He shrugged, again filling the fork with cake as he continued his interrogation. *Lord help me not to say anything else.* "But do you know what a guy thinks about when he sees a naked woman in front of him?"

"Hmm?" I mumbled, clamping my mouth shut as I tried to save myself and the possibility of further betraying the sisterhood. Who knew what he would ask me and what information I would offer up? The combination of men and cake couldn't be trusted.

"When a woman is in front of a guy, naked, they're not thinking about whether her ass is big or whether she looks like a photo they saw in a magazine." He offered another forkful, which my mouth shamelessly accepted. It was going to be my downfall for sure. "They're thinking *holy shit, there's a naked woman in front of me; I hope I get to touch her.* Trust me, we're simple creatures. Too fat, too thin, too this, too that—our brains only see one thing. Beautiful. So don't worry about your ass or any other part of your body, because you're fucking perfect."

I stopped eating.

My mouth froze as I searched his face for sarcasm or humor, anything to prove what he was telling me was a lie. A joke at my expense, a prank, using my vulnerability against me for some kind of sport.

Because generally, men weren't this honest. Not any men I'd ever dated. Even my dad—who was one of the most honest people I knew—told my mom she looked great in that corduroy skirt, and she'd looked hideous. It was a crime against clothing. So the idea that Ryan was letting me in on some man secret was just as crazy.

"Why are you telling me this?" I asked, wanting to know if this was where I was hooded and carried to some dark dungeon for an ancient male ritualistic sacrifice. I knew those societies existed, I just never pegged Ryan as a member.

"Because I wanted you to know. I hate that you would even think that about yourself. There are men who would give their left testicle to be with you, Lila."

I was so confused.

Between him, the sex, the cake, and the situation—years of education did absolutely nothing for me as I sat there dumbfounded. Too baffled to speak, and not confident enough to laugh it off.

Was it because we were friends? The mutual sharing of information part of the friends-with-benefits agreement I had somehow wound up in? Was it so we were more adequately prepared for a relationship with someone else when it ended? Was he already trying to soften the blow, the mention of other guys—a hint that was where my future was heading?

It was more than I could process, my heart desperate to just accept the words at face value even though I knew it would be a mistake.

"Well." I found my voice, staring into his gorgeous brown eyes and at his perfect face. "You'll be happy to know no testicular forfeitures are required. I'll let everyone keep their balls for now."

"Good." He laughed, his beautiful lips magically appearing against mine.

I don't know how he did that. Did I blink? Or was I hypnotized, entranced by everything that was *him*. In any case, I didn't mind, loving the feel of his mouth on mine, even if I was still confused.

"We need to eat more cake." He found the abandoned fork and proceeded with the sweet inquisition. Any hope I had for maintaining control over the situation was diminishing by the second.

My hand grabbed his, a last-ditch effort to exercise some restraint. "You haven't had any yet."

"I intend to," he grinned, pressing the cake to my lips and then using his tongue to lick off the thick gooey icing. "Mmm, you're right. This cake is delicious."

I was in some serious shit.

CHAPTER #11

I HAD BEEN in some questionable situations in my time. I mean, my mother owned a brothel for Christ's sake. Prostitutes came to our house and shared holidays with us—one even tutored me in math—so dealing with the bizarre didn't faze me. My best friend Tia also played fast and loose with ridiculous—probably one of the reasons we got along so well—so I should have been well and truly ready to deal with whatever life threw at me.

The truth was, I was not.

An entire week had been spent in L.A. interviewing celebrities—we'd gone back to visit Dean as well as some other friends of Eric's—and writing, as well as being with Ryan in a bliss that shouldn't have been legal.

Living in a mansion by day like Bruce Wayne, working on my story, and then at night I turned into Batman—if Batman was a woman with an insatiable sexual appetite. Or maybe Ryan was Batman? I didn't know which, but neither of us needed fancy gadgets, even if most of the time I felt like I was leading a fantasy double life.

And while I loved spending time with Tia and laughing over a box of Milano's, it was usually done on the *other* side of the country.

My new normal had a way of intersecting with my old one, which just unnerved me rather than comforted me.

And no matter how many times I told myself it was all totally fine, it was not. Even Dick—my asshole boss with a permanent case of I-hate-everyone's—was acting strange, loving my first draft and telling me to keep up the good work.

Not even Tia or Eric could be counted on for the reality check. The talk of *you-two-hooking-up-better-not-screw-things-up-between-our-little-dynamic*, completely MIA. And they had to have been thinking it, surely. I mean, it had the potential to be epic-level messy, why wasn't anyone concerned?

Something deep and dark was at work here, lulling me into a false sense of contentment and calm, and it couldn't be trusted. That, or the conspiracy theorists were right, and we had been moved to an alternate universe. I needed to check in on CERN and their Large Hadron Collider. Where was a damn physicist when you needed one?

"I know I've already seen the dress, but it gets no less awesome the second time around." Ryan's eyes rolled up and down my body, his expression heated. "Not sure how I'm supposed to keep from mauling you like an animal. We may need to come up with some kind of strategy."

My feet tentatively took the last couple of stairs, conscious my range of motion was hindered by my tight but gorgeous Herve Leger gown. The new shoes weren't helping either, the heels higher than I was used to.

I strode over to him, adjusting his tie, which really didn't need adjusting. "You look pretty damn edible yourself. I love this on you." My hands smoothed down the lapels of his tuxedo.

A man in a well-made suit was my kryptonite. While Ryan in casual clothes was nothing short of smoldering sexy—I enjoyed a pair of jeans and a T-shirt just like the next girl—there was something about those tailored layers that did things to me sexually. Like inviting me to unwrap it like a present, and I very much wanted to tear it apart to get to my gift inside.

He wasn't the only one who would need a strategy; I was going to need to cuff my hands together to stop myself from touching him. That he didn't seem to mind only made the situation worse.

"We can ditch them once we get there you know." His lips found their way to my neck as his hand playfully grabbed my ass. "There's more security at this thing than a G7 Summit, as long as I'm back for the pick-up, I don't need to be there."

"Eric wants you to be there," I reminded him, not wanting to be the reason he shirked his responsibilities, even if it did give me a secret thrill. "And what's my excuse for going missing? I'm not in the habit of bailing on a friend."

Honestly, I'm sure Tia wouldn't have cared. She would have given me a knowing smile and nod and probably done the very same thing. Chances were, the reason why she and Eric hadn't come downstairs yet was because they were doing some mauling of their own. Eric anywhere in the vicinity was Tia's weakness, but put the man in a suit and we were probably going to be late.

But I needed to protect myself, keep my feelings in check even if I loved being part of the craziness.

Ryan and I were *not* a couple. We were friends who slept together, and when I went back to New York, chances were we'd go back to just being friends.

The kind that didn't see each other naked or have sex.

Which was totally fine.

Or at least that's what I needed to convince myself of, because giving him up entirely was not a scenario I was ready to deal with.

"Fine, fine, break my heart, Lila." His eye roll negated by his smile. "We'll be responsible."

"Your effort has been noted and you will be rewarded." This

time it was my turn to squeeze his ass. It was the tux's fault. And I very much liked touching his body.

He chuckled, kissing my forehead. "The rewards make everything worth it. Let me go bring the car around, and while I'm doing that you should also make sure you have some condoms packed. I said we'd be responsible, that didn't mean I'd behave."

My hand shot to my mouth, pretending to be scandalized. "Ryan, in public, really?"

"No one will see anything, I promise." His voice rumbled as he took a step back. "I have two in my wallet, but with you and that dress we're going to need reinforcements."

I pushed lightly against his chest, not mentioning the two condoms I had already stashed in my clutch. "Go, we'll discuss my feelings on public fornication later."

He pouted but left, leaving me standing in the foyer while I waited for Eric and Tia to come down. They were definitely having sex; no one took *that* long to get ready.

As for Ryan, I needed to concentrate on how the experience would be a great learning tool for me. It was a gift. To be able to have my fling with irresponsibility with someone who wouldn't hurt me or treat me like a whore. And not read what I was feeling as anything other than friendship. It was easy to forget what he said at the start and believe that it had turned into more. But that was because as sexy and mouthwatering gorgeous as Ryan was, he had a good heart too.

Such a good, *good* heart.

And he was honest. He didn't pretend to be someone he wasn't or speak around the truth. He said what he meant and meant what he said. So when he did eventually settle down—if that day ever came—the woman he chose would be lucky beyond measure. And the rest of us, just glad we got to have him for a while. Because I would rather have had a few weeks with him than a year with an asshole who'd pretend and tell me what he thought I wanted to hear.

"Sorry," Tia called from the top of the stairs, adjusting her earring as Eric came up behind her. "I couldn't find something."

From the smile on her lips I'd say she was lying, although it didn't seem like her usual I-just-had-sex grin. No, her smile was something entirely more dangerous. She'd been talking—and possibly scheming—instead. And worse than that was I assumed that the man with his hand around her waist was in on it. No prizes for guessing what that *something* was. Ryan and me, at the top of her list.

I laughed, watching them descend the stairs. "You two fool no one."

"What?" Tia asked with a show of faux shock, her acting ability still leaving a lot to be desired. "I have no idea what you could possibly mean."

"Oh, your delay wasn't intentional? Tell me, what were the two of you looking for?" My hands were anchored at my hips as my raised eyebrow challenged her.

"A movie script I misplaced," Eric offered, and considering he was an actor he too was doing a terrible job of convincing me. If I had to hedge a bet, I'd say he wasn't even trying.

"Yes, a script." Tia clapped her hands together, her face brimming with excitement. "This guy—totally hot—meets this girl and even though they are from different worlds, they are meant to be together. And there is a misunderstanding about what each of them wants even though it's an epic love story. So when she is forced to leave, he pursues her but she didn't know it. And then meets some other guy who she thinks she's in love with, but is totally wrong for her but didn't know the first guy was still interested. And she didn't get any of the letters he sent her so didn't know it was more than just a summer romance until they reunite and he kisses her in the rain." She petered out, looking proudly to Eric who was shaking his head trying to bite back his grin.

Tia really, *really* sucked at lying.

"Hmmm." I pretended I was fooled by her verbal spill of the synopsis. "Sounds remarkably like *The Notebook*, I didn't know they were considering a remake."

I wasn't even going to touch the epic love story portion of her spiel. Last time I watched it, Noah and Allie were in an actual relationship, not just having hot sex until one of them had to leave.

"Err, no, it's not *The Notebook*." Tia laughed, tugging nervously at her earring. "It just sounds sort of similar. You know Hollywood, no original ideas."

"Yeah, I'll bet." I glared at her, not as annoyed as I pretended to be. "You can tell me all about it in the car. Ryan should be around the front by now."

"Oh, I think that is pretty much all I remember," Tia added, looking to Eric to bail her out.

"Yeah, it was a rough draft. Needs a lot of work." Eric nipped at Tia's bare shoulder. "Hey, do you mind if I sit up front? There's some stuff Ryan and I need to go over."

Not sure why he was asking for permission. It was his car, his friend—I was just a guest. I wasn't about to say no, even if I preferred to sit beside Ryan.

"Sure, of course. It will give Tia and I a chance to *chat*." Just hopefully not about any other movie scripts and or her idea on what she thought was happening.

Tia nodded, her face lighting up with excitement. "Yes, we will talk about all the things." I wasn't convinced she wasn't going to try another angle.

Ryan pulled open the door, the idling car parked right outside. "The car awaits, my Lord." His outstretched arm gesturing toward the Hummer.

"You have serious issues, my friend." Eric punched Ryan playfully in the arm. "I'm not sure whether to kick your ass or give you a raise half the time."

Ryan smiled, his fist making contact with Eric's bicep. "Dude, always more money. I'm fucking indispensable, and for what you're paying me now, you should be embarrassed."

The whole exchange made me giggle, loving how much they obviously seemed to care for each other. It probably would have been easier if he wasn't so charming. I imagined his ex-lovers met on Tuesdays in a coffee shop somewhere and lamented how amazing he was, but none of their perfect vaginas had managed to bewitch him enough to stay. I was probably going to need the number and location for future reference.

"Don't listen to him, Lila." Eric shook his head, laughing. "I know heart surgeons who make less than he does."

Ryan leaned into me, mock whispering, "He would be lost without me."

"And on that note." Eric nodded toward the door. "Let's go before I decide to drive myself."

Eric and Tia made their way to the car while Ryan waited at the door. "After you, princess. I'm going to pretend to be polite so I can stare at your ass when you walk out."

"You are so bad." I playfully smacked him in the chest with my clutch as I walked to the car, Ryan locking the front door before joining us.

He didn't question the seating arrangements, easing into the front like it was business as usual. I guess I was the only one who was disappointed, hmmm, good to know.

"So, what did Dick say about your article?" Tia asked as we pulled out from Eric's driveway to the big iron gates.

I smiled, feeling the rock of the car as we continued onto the road. "He loved it, he didn't ask for any content changes, so it went straight to the copy editor. I think he was either high or didn't know who he was talking to. He never accepts my submissions on the first round. It comes out in tomorrow's edition."

The process had been too easy so I was still waiting for the other shoe to drop.

"Wow, the Sunday *Times*." Tia squeezed my hand. "That's huge."

"Let's not get too excited." I sighed. "He could just as easily change his mind next week and dump me to Wednesday's edition, buried behind film screening times."

The danger was real. Dick once pulled one of our political correspondents from The White House for reasons unknown and reassigned him to the metro section. The guy had a masters in Political Science and ended up writing about golf courses in the Bronx. Lucky for me, there wasn't much lower I could drop. Although, I heard the food section had an opening.

We continued talking about me and my article, while Eric discussed his film schedule with Ryan. It took a lot of talent to keep my end of the conversation going while I eavesdropped on theirs, thankfully I was the master of nodding and adding in words when I wasn't really paying attention. I guess I did have something to thank Dick for.

Eric needed to do a couple of location shots next week in Santa Cruz and didn't want to be driving back and forth all week so was staying up there for a few days. The studio wanted to use their own security so Ryan wasn't needed. He mentioned they hadn't decided if Tia was going with him or staying in L.A. but they would work out the finer details tomorrow.

"So, what do you think?"

Oh shit, maybe I wasn't as talented as I thought because Tia was looking at me like she knew I didn't know the answer to whatever it was she was asking.

She was right; I didn't even have a clue. "I'm sorry, T, I missed that. What did you say?"

"I said, I was thinking of going to Santa Cruz with Eric for a few days, but I wanted to see what your plans were for next week. I can hang in L.A. if you'd prefer."

So at some point the conversations had intersected, Eric and Ryan's and ours, being about the same thing. Which should have made it easier to keep track of, pity it didn't.

"T, it's fine," I reassured her, feeling a little guilty our time recently had been limited. "I do interviews or researching during the day so we don't get a lot of time anyway. I'm sorry, you must think I'm a shitty friend."

She reached across the seat, grabbing my hand and giving it a squeeze. "Hey, I knew you were coming here for work. I'm just happy for whatever time we get. Which is why if you want me to stick around, I will."

God, I don't know what I ever did to deserve a friend like her. She was the sister I never had and no matter where she moved to, I knew we'd be friends forever.

"No, you should go." I squeezed back, touched she would sacrifice her own happiness for me. "It will be fun. No point sitting around here when I'm working all day and Eric's gone."

"She has a point," Eric called over his shoulder, making it clear the indecision had been solely on her part.

Tia smiled, beaming at Eric. "So, I guess I'm going then."

I tried not to get too excited at the prospect of spending time alone with Ryan. That was assuming he didn't decide to use the time off to take up a hobby or go back to his original one—women. Big assumption on my part he'd want to hang around, even more so that he would want to spend every single hour with me. I'd hate to imagine the amount of booty calls he'd passed up, the thought alone making my stomach turn.

"When do you leave?" I asked, genuinely interested and trying to focus my thoughts on something positive.

"Monday morning. I need to be there for Tuesday," Eric answered. "We'll be back by Friday night, Saturday morning at the latest. I have a meeting with Roman Sunday night to go over some contracts."

"Great." Tia sounded a little too excited at the news of seeing him. "I had one of the guys in legal at *The Post* draw up a bogus lawsuit against me. I'm going to see if he is as good a lawyer as he claims to be." She rubbed her hands together. "Dave and Nick are in on it too."

"You enjoy tormenting Roman more than you should." Eric laughed, shaking his head.

"Oh Eric, I enjoy tormenting *all* your brothers in equal parts. They never had a sister, consider it my duty." Her smile filled with pride as she straightened in her seat.

Ryan cleared his throat, his eyes meeting mine in the rearview mirror. "Sounds like a perfect time for us to go to Vegas, if you ask me."

Tia laughed, her voice raising an octave. "Oh my God, you're going to Vegas? Please tell me you're going to see your parents!"

"That's kind of the reason why he has this burning need to go." I rolled my eyes, both excited and nervous. I had no idea how this was going to play out. Literally, no idea.

The prospect of bringing any friend—let alone a man—home was unnerving. My parents were an acquired taste, but I guess it was easier knowing there was no potential for anything long term and we were just friends like I was with Tia. Maybe it would be a good thing, do wonders for my personal growth.

"Bullshit," Ryan called from the front. "She had to almost beg me to go. I'm a good boy. I'm not used to being around such debauchery—sex, money, alcohol. I have genuine fear for my soul." His hand flailed dramatically.

"She told you, huh?" Eric turned to Ryan, shaking his head

with a laugh.

"Dude, I'm so freaking excited about it, I am going to overlook the fact you already knew," he shot back, not even trying to hide how pleased he was.

His excitement niggled at me a little, probably because I assumed he was thrilled because we were visiting my mother's brothel. That was the reason he'd wanted to go, right? To see the prostitutes, maybe—God, I hoped not—sample the product. Did I offer? Give him the option to sleep with one of them if he wanted? It's not like he was mine to keep. And unlike someone else, a prostitute would only give him her body, there wouldn't be any emotion involved. Not that it helped, the thought of him with anyone still ate at me even if it was irrational.

"You know, I get a family discount too," I added like an idiot. "Who knows where things might end up?"

I officially hated myself, more so when the huge grin spread across his face.

He glanced over at Eric, wiping away fake tears. "I think Lila might be my soul mate."

He didn't mean that.

It was a joke—said off the cuff—something he did all the time. And I knew those words weren't real. And if I was honest, they weren't funny either. That the idea I would allow him to sleep with someone else had won me the title. Not that I had any right to be angry about it; I'd volunteered myself for the position, suggested it even. He was just doing what he always did and playing right along with me. Besides, who even knew if *soul mates* existed? Maybe the joke was on me, waiting for that one true love who probably wouldn't be coming.

I laughed, a little annoyed at myself that a couple of words that seemed so insignificant could rattle me. "I'll try not to be too much of a bad influence. It will be difficult though, you're so easily led astray." I refused to let a stupid joke ruin my night and my mood, now wasn't the time to get sensitive.

"It's not being led if he goes willingly." Eric looked back at me. "You're going to need to apologize to your parents in advance and tell them I'll cover any damage this idiot causes—physical or emotional."

"Lies, they are going to love me." Ryan smacked the steering wheel in fake annoyance. "And if you behave yourself you might get invited to our wedding. Unless Lila can't wait and we elope while we're there. I'll leave it up to my future bride to decide."

More words he didn't mean.

These ones stinging just a little bit more.

"Wow, soul mate to future bride in less than a minute, chances are I'll be your ex-wife before we even make it to the gala." I forced myself to laugh, still hating the idea it was a joke as I continued to play the game like he was.

"More lies." Ryan waved his hand, slowing in front of a row of cars. "You would never be able to leave me, I'm too loveable."

No, I shook my head silently.

He was wrong.

It would be him leaving, not me.

THE DOLBY BALLROOM was a sea of white, gold and red. Pristine, crisp linen-covered tables topped with intricate and bold centerpieces, the lighting low and intimate as celebrities mulled around.

My eyes widened as we were directed to our table, people I'd seen in films or magazines literally a shoulder-width apart. It made it easier to forget the conversation in the car, being overwhelmed by all that star power in one room.

"If anyone ever wanted to cripple Hollywood, this room would be the place to do it," I whispered to Tia, my head whipping around seeing more famous people than I even knew existed. "Is that Jake Durant?" My eyes almost bulged as the tall, blond sex symbol laughed a few feet away.

"Stop being so impressed, Lila." Ryan pressed his hand against my back, leading me to my chair. "Jake is an arrogant piece of shit, not worth your attention or your adulation. Besides, you should be saving that of all for me. I can be a very jealous man."

"Shhh." I waved him off, my attention still on Jake. "He's taller than he looks in the movies, is there a rule you have to be over six feet or something?"

Eric—who topped the charts at six-four—laughed, his arm around Tia's waist. "No, but it helps."

"I'll say," Tia responded dreamily, her obsession with height restricted to one particular movie star.

"Can you introduce me?" I turned to Ryan, his hand still on me. "I know the chances of him agreeing to an interview are slim but if he said yes, it would be amazing."

"You don't need him." Ryan seemed irritated, his tone sharp while his trademark smile was missing in action. "And more importantly, you don't want him. I'm serious, Lila. He's an asshole."

My eyes moved from Jake, no longer interested in him as I focused on Ryan. A man who usually hopped from one joke to the next suddenly seemed serious. "Wow, okay."

"Just keep away from him." Ryan shoved his hands in his pockets, his body tense. "I'm taking a walk, be back in a few." His head nodded to Eric, a silent conversation happening between them.

"Yep, we'll be here." He pulled out Tia's chair and waited for her to sit before joining her.

I grabbed Ryan's arm, latching onto it before he had a chance to leave. "Do you want me to come with you?"

"If you want." He shrugged with little commitment.

My arm looped around his as I gave him a smile. "Yes, I want."

"Okay, then." His body seemed to relax as we walked away from the table.

"So," I waited until we had moved out of the main room and into a smaller foyer area, "you want to tell me what happened back there?"

He stopped, studying me. "Depends on who I'm talking to, is this Lila the reporter or just Lila?"

Ouch, well okay then.

I shouldn't have been annoyed at the suggestion, after all it was part of my job to take what I'd learnt and turn it into news. But I knew the line, and I hoped Ryan saw that too. While I wasn't as tight-lipped as he was—he'd made keeping his mouth shut an art form—I never spoke about Tia or Eric other than in casual vague terms. And even then only to people I trusted.

But there was something about the look in his eyes that made me forgive the barb, knowing it was more important to find out the underlying *why* rather than rake him over the coals for being a dick. I'd do that later if needed, and as long as he didn't pull the reporter crap again, I'd give him this one free pass.

I wrapped my arms around his neck, ignoring the few people who were also sharing the space. "It's Lila, your future wife." The taunt not stinging so much this time around. Maybe I had been too sensitive about it; I would definitely enjoy pretending.

He laughed, all the tension easing out of his face as his hands locked on my hips. "I'm glad you're finally seeing things my way."

"Will you tell me?" I tugged him a little closer. "I promise it's completely off the record."

He sighed, looking down on me with his beautiful brown eyes. "Jake Durant likes to use women. The fame, the money—all of it just one big lubricant to get someone in his bed. Which is fine if he was on the level with them, but he pretends like they are going to be this long-term thing and then sends them packing. Man has told so many lies, it's a wonder if he even knows the truth, and he has zero integrity. Seriously, not one ounce of fucking decency in his whole body."

His words confused me a little. He was angry because Jake slept with women? Didn't he do a similar thing? Okay, so maybe not the same in that he didn't lead them on like Jake did. And Ryan didn't use the whole fame and fortune thing as foreplay from what I knew; he didn't need to. So was it the distinction he was worried about? That he was a manwhore with a conscience and Jake wasn't?

I lowered my voice, keeping the space tight between us. "So, you're mad because he is a liar or because he can't keep it in his pants? I'm not trying to be an asshole, Ryan, I'm just trying to understand."

Sure, maybe I was over simplifying it by putting them in the same glass house. But I had nothing to work with and he'd had a pretty strong reaction for what sounded like consensual, casual sex.

Ryan shook his head and let out another sigh. "It's not about the broken hearts, Lila. You know, I haven't exactly been a model citizen and maybe there have been girls in the past that I forgot to call." I saw the flash of regret when he looked at me.

Jealousy spiked inside me, hating to hear about the other women even though I had been the one who'd asked. But I needed to know, hoping he wouldn't stop.

"But I'm not like him. They don't know what they are signing up for with Jake. A girl comes home with me, she knows *exactly* the score; *he* fucks them and then *fucks* them if they don't leave quietly." His eyes had darkened, his hands gripping me a little tighter.

My eyes widened as they spat out the words. "What do you mean *fucks* them, as in, personally?"

His eyes darted left and right, making sure we couldn't be heard. "Yeah, *personally*. Girls have lost roles, kicked off movie sets, or even passed over purely because they got into bed with him and didn't smile politely when he left them hanging. Never mind what he'd promised them in the start. And maybe they should have known better. I mean, if everyone is using everyone it's only fair, right? But he has pulled some shady shit, Lila, and ruined lives because of it."

"And you know this . . . ." It seemed like a lot of personal information, and pretty specific at that.

"Eric and I used to hang out with him, in the earlier days. Party with him. We were having a good time and I was sort of seeing this girl, so I brought her along with us."

The thought of Ryan dating anyone made my skin prickle even though it had been before I even knew him. Of course he'd dated; he wasn't a freaking monk. I also reminded myself I had dated too, and jealousy was both irrational and stupid considering we weren't even dating now.

"And then what happened?"

He took a breath, his thumb rubbing circles on my hips. "Are you sure you want to hear this?"

I don't know, do I? "Yes." My mouth made the choice for me.

"So, we were drinking, and Liv says she's going to the bathroom." The confirmation not needed that Liv was the girl he was *sort of seeing.* "And she was gone awhile so I went to check on her and found her and Jake fucking in his room."

"Oh, Ryan, I'm sorry."

Even though it had happened years ago, I hated the idea of someone hurting him. How could anyone cheat on him? He was perfect—gorgeous, smart, funny, amazing in bed—the complete package. Liv must have been crazy to throw that all away for a fling with Jake, who while was good looking himself, wasn't even close to Ryan's level of hotness.

"Nah, it's fine." He seemed not all that bothered by the

infidelity. "It wasn't anything serious. She was more of a friend, you know. The sex was kind of incidental."

Kind of like us, I guess. I felt my cheeks heat at the realization, ignoring the similarities. It wasn't about me, I reminded myself. None of this was about me.

"Still, wasn't cool," I heard myself saying, unable to comprehend sleeping with anyone else while I was sleeping with Ryan.

Even without a commitment, I just knew I couldn't be with anyone else until we were done. Hell, if I was honest I couldn't even imagine *after*.

He smiled, shaking his head as he continued. "Anyway, it was fine. They fucked and when she came out, I drove her home. She knew I knew, and was upset and apologetic. Told me he'd promised to get her in on a movie he'd just been signed to, which of course was his MO and she was in between jobs so I guess it was sort of tempting. I told her it was all cool, who am I to question anyone's choices? But obviously, I wasn't interested in the sex part anymore, so we kicked it back to just friends."

I wondered when my time came if I could find it so easy. I'm not sure that I would.

"O-kay."

His hand gripped me a little tighter, some of the anger coming back. "So of course he reneges on his deal and feeds her some bullshit about it not being the right time or some shit. So, she decides to cut her losses and tries to forget it but it turns out her little interlude with Jake wasn't so unforgettable when a couple of months later she finds out she's knocked up. She confronts him, and he tells her it's probably my kid and I should deal with it. See, I had no idea that the whole time I assumed we were *pals*, he had some fucking fixation in sleeping with women I'd been with. Some girl he had apparently wanted ended up hanging out with me instead and while he was pretending to be zen about it, he was working out a way to fuck me too. Of course, his usual methods didn't work—he couldn't get me fired or screw up Eric's career, so instead he turned his attention to anyone close to me. He was already being a douchebag, and if it happened to impact me, all the better."

So many thoughts were going through my head, and most of them weren't even about Jake. Did I even dare to ask who the father of Liv's baby was? Was it even my business? And why was it that usually I had no problem thinking of something to say and right now I was drawing a blank. I literally had nothing.

"It wasn't mine," he said when I didn't ask, his eyes spelling out he knew what I'd been thinking. "Considering we'd never had unprotected sex there was little chance, but the paternity test proved it beyond a shadow of a doubt. It was Jake's."

"Did she keep the baby?" I hated how relieved I was it hadn't been his, that I should care about something that didn't involve me.

"He gave her ten grand and told her to have an abortion and have a nice life. She did neither, and ended up suing him when the kid was born. He pays child support but Jake wanted nothing to do with his son."

"Wow. I had no idea."

You'd have thought some of it would have been leaked or something. It was widely reported he enjoyed female company, but news of an illegitimate child wasn't something I'd forget.

"He has good lawyers, lots of paperwork," Ryan explained. "And whatever trouble he runs into, he just throws cash at it. It's worked so far, but Liv wasn't an isolated case. Not the baby thing, I think after that little slip he stopped being so careless." He waved his hand clarifying that Jake didn't have a horde of unwanted children. "I mean, the special *interest* he showed in women that were close to me. He even tried to sleep with Ellen, not knowing she was my cousin. All of them screwed over—in more ways than one—just because I happened to be the common denominator. If there was any justice, his dick would contract some flesh-eating disease and fall off, sparing the rest of the civilization." He barked out a laugh.

Sounded to me that it was a miracle he *hadn't* contracted some kind of disease, flesh-eating or otherwise. Jesus, had the man not heard of STDs or karma?

"What happened to your friend Liv?" I was curious if she was still in the picture.

Ryan cursed out a breath. "Oh, that was the kicker. Because she had the nerve to challenge the asshole, he made sure her career was done. She was a makeup artist, but after he got through with her, she couldn't even get a job at a makeup counter at Macy's. She ended up tossing it in, moving back to Montana where she was originally from."

Internally I was so confused.

Annoyed that I was glad this poor girl who had exerted poor judgment and even worse impulse control was gone. She was no threat to me, yet I was relieved she was no longer in the picture. Because obviously, I was an evil person.

And then there were my feelings toward Jake, wanting to give his future prey a helping hand and take away his ability to screw anyone whether or not they were connected to Ryan or not.

As for Ryan—Lord, where did I even start?

"He sounds like a complete cocksucker." I gave Ryan a hug, just wanting to touch him.

"Yep, he is." His arms wrapping around me as he kissed the top of my head. "In a million years, he wouldn't be worthy of you."

"Stop being so charming, Ryan." I lifted my eyes to meet his. "You're going to make it difficult for other men."

He laughed, his firm, perfectly toned chest shaking against my body as he held me close. "Good, then my evil plan is working because you shouldn't be thinking about anyone but me."

CHAPTER 12

THE GALA EFFECTIVELY could have been broken up into two parts. The first—and the most formal—part, where everyone sat down acting very civilized as dinner was served.

The food was delicious, looking as beautiful as it tasted, reminding me of a few times Tia and I ate at fancy restaurants back in New York. French champagne and expensive wine was paired to each course while an orchestra played classical music. No expense had been spared.

In between the eight-course meal, money was raised through various ridiculously extravagant auction items. Mini vacations in the French Alps, the use of a helicopter—with pilot—for an entire year, cars, jewelry and possibly my favorite—a gold lamé dress previously worn by Marilyn Monroe.

It was so glamorous and beautiful, I could picture myself in it, swirling a martini. Although I almost died when bidding opened at two hundred thousand. Yeah, I didn't like it that much. My martini swirling would have to take place in the gold dress I already owned. I was fine with that, in fact I may have started practicing, three martinis in by the time we'd hit the second part of the festivities.

I wasn't sure if it was the three—maybe four, I'd lost count since I wasn't paying for them—cocktails I'd consumed or shit really did get crazy.

The light changed, as did the music, creating a more nightclub feel as the famous people relaxed and got up and danced. Men with beaked masks appeared—maybe it was time to slow down on the drinking—wandering around the room wearing black cloaks, while bikini-clad women juggled knives. It was a cross between a Stanley Kubrick movie and the circus as the music and booze raged on.

I was almost disappointed there was no overt drug use or public sexual displays. Maybe that stuff happened in a backroom somewhere. Or maybe those masked men were the gatekeepers, deciding who got to go the super-secret orgy happening elsewhere. *Yeah, I should definitely stop drinking.*

"Having fun?" Ryan breathed in my ear, his hot intoxicating scent amplified by his close proximity.

He'd had his hands on me all night and we had yet to use any of our collective condoms. But that was probably going to change very soon, judging by the way he was looking at me.

"You." I yanked his lapels, bringing his face in closer. "You need to dance with me."

"Anything you want, princess." He smirked, pushing his chair out and helping me up, his hand resting on my back just above my ass.

Tia and Eric had disappeared about an hour ago. They were dancing and drinking while I had wanted to stay at the table and people watch. Ryan—who hadn't even had a glass of wine with dinner—stayed with me, amused as I continued to suck down drinks.

As we pressed through the crowd of people, I no longer cared who was famous and who wasn't. Too distracted to give a shit, wrapping my arms around Ryan as we stepped onto the dance floor.

Our bodies swayed to the music, not enough room to actually dance as we looked into each other's eyes.

"You smell good." I nuzzled against his shirt, probably ruining it for future use with lipstick stains. I liked the idea of marking him, a signal to other women that he was mine for the night.

"Thanks." His hands lowered onto my ass. "You smell pretty good yourself."

I tilted my head, getting lost in his beautiful brown eyes as I giggled. "I want to fuck you, Ryan York."

"Right here?" He raised an eyebrow, the corners of his mouth twitching into a grin. "On the dance floor?"

"No, I don't want people seeing you naked. That's just for me." I swatted his chest playfully.

He grabbed my hands, stopping their assault. "Well then, we better find somewhere else more private."

I giggled as he spun me, anchoring his hands on my hips as my back pressed against his front. I could feel he was hard, my ass rubbing against his length before he stopped me. A long steady breath hissed from his lips.

He whispered in my ear, guiding me off the dance floor. "Just keep walking, princess."

"Go left," was his next command, as we passed a bikini-wearing woman breathing fire. "Through that door." His lips grazed the shell of my ear as my body started to vibrate with need.

It could have been the atmosphere or the alcohol or my inability to control myself when Ryan touched me, but I wanted him, and I wanted him now.

Slowly—way too slow—we moved away from the main part of the room, Ryan guiding me to a narrow hall.

"You've done this before." I wasn't sure if it was a question or a statement, too turned on to care what his answer was going to be.

"I always make sure I know the layout of a venue." His hands stayed locked around me as he whispered his answer. "Part of the job description."

Even though I shouldn't have cared, it made me feel better knowing it wasn't from doing this with someone else. Or at least, he wasn't admitting that.

We'd made it to a door when we heard moaning on the other side. There was either a wounded animal in the room or *someone* had our idea. Unless that was where the *real* party happened, and Ryan was leading me to a sex dungeon. He never specified why he needed to know the layout of the venue. My eyes widened as his hand tugged on the door handle.

Light from the hallway flooded what looked to be a janitor's storage room. And next to the neatly stacked shelves of toilet paper and hand sanitizers were no wounded animals.

Instead, there was a naked woman—makeup and hair a mess—splayed out on the table while a man in a suit fucked her hard. He didn't even stop when the light hit them, just driving into her with his back to us.

Oh shit.

I recognized that suit.

And judging by the under-his-breath "fuck" Ryan cursed out, he knew it too.

Jake looked over his shoulder, his smile immediate. "Ryan, fancy meeting you here."

"Yeah, it's a fucking pleasure." The edge in Ryan's voice suggested otherwise.

He moved further into the room, stepping in front of me as he looked at the disheveled woman on the table. "You okay, Mara?"

Wow. I wasn't sure if I was more surprised he knew her name or kept his eyes on her face even though she had a very spectacular set of tits.

"I-I'm f-fine." Her face flushed with embarrassment. "I was just—" She gave up, her explanation not needed considering it had been obvious.

"You want her after me?" Jake smirked. "I'll swap her for yours, she looks new." The asshole had the nerve to wink at me while he was still balls-deep in someone else.

"You're a real piece of work, Durant." Ryan barked out a cold laugh, completely devoid of humor as his head shook. "You have a better chance of breathing underwater than you do getting anywhere near her." His body tensed as his hand reached for mine.

"Come on, York." Jake thrust into Mara. "It will be just like old times, you loosen them up for me. You know I don't mind getting your sloppy seconds."

Ryan turned, his face completely unreadable. "Lila, can you wait for me out in the hall?"

"No." It came out of my mouth so fast I almost surprised myself. "It's been a while since I've seen a big dick with a small penis, paradoxes intrigue me."

As much as I appreciated Ryan feeling the need to protect me, I wasn't going anywhere. Firstly, because Jake Durant was a pig and I hated men who treated women like meat. Even the prostitutes who worked with my mom weren't handed around like freaking party favors like this asshole was offering. And secondly, because I had some protective feelings of my own. I might be blonde and slim, but I grew up in Vegas and lived in Brooklyn. If Jake even breathed in Ryan's direction, I'd poke his eyes out with the nail file stashed inside my purse.

"Small penis?" Jake hissed, losing interest in Mara as he pulled out of her and turned to us, the penis in question on display. "Does that look small to you?"

He grabbed it in his hand and stroked.

Okay, so it wasn't a micro penis like I'd imagined, but it certainly wasn't something to brag about. I'd say at most, it was average sized, possibly five and a half inches? And his girth left a lot to be desired. So, where he got the idea his manhood was impressive was beyond me. Although in saying that, I now felt I had my own scientific proof that there was no correlation between height and size. Always a silver lining.

"Is that fully erect?" I laughed, my eyes squinted like they couldn't quite see. "Oh, I'm so sorry, Mara." I turned to the naked woman, her hands reaching for her clothes to cover her exposed skin. "You might have been better off just using your hands."

In the short time I'd known Ryan, I'd never seen him speechless. His mouth opened and then closed again, looking confused as he focused on me.

"We'd love to stay and chat but I'm already bored." I fake yawned, tugging on Ryan's sleeve. "But, Jake, if you want a good cosmetic surgeon's details I can help you out. My best friend's brother-in-law could totally hook you up with a penile implant. He works in Manhattan, but so worth the trip. Okay, tootles." I finger waved at my gob-smacked audience as I pushed Ryan back into the hall and closed the door.

"What are you doing?" Ryan seemed dazed as I pulled him away from the storage room.

I wasn't sure if we were traveling closer to the direction of the party or somewhere else—the absence of signage wasn't helping—but at least there was no danger of seeing Jake's lack of snake any longer.

"I don't actually know if Will does penile implants." I kept him moving, my eyes focused straight ahead. "I mean he does amazing boob jobs, so if nothing else he can give Jake a decent pair of tits."

"I'm not talking about Tia's brother-in-law." He grabbed me, pushing me up against the wall. His hold was firm but his voice was soft, the anger from his eyes gone, and in their place concern. "I mean, why didn't you let me handle that?"

"Because you probably would have hit him. And he totally deserved it; I'll even admit I contemplated violence as well." I felt liquid in his arms, my body soft against his. "But you know he would have filed an assault charge, and him being an asshole isn't a valid defense. Besides, I thought hurting his pride would do more damage."

Ryan shook his head, skating his nose up against mine before gently brushing my lips with a kiss. "You are incredible."

"No, I'm selfish." My fingers tiptoed up the length of his chest as I looked at him from under my lashes. "I can't have sex with you if you're in jail. I was only thinking of myself."

I wanted to distract him, for him to forget about Jake and leave the anger back in that room.

He kissed me again, a little deeper this time, his teeth playing with my bottom lip. "Lies. You are a lot of things, but selfish isn't one of them. Is it wrong that I'm incredibly turned on right now?"

His body pressed against me, the hard length in his pants serving as evidence in case there was any doubt.

I arched into him, loving that he was as turned on as I was, that he was right there with me in that moment. "Considering if I was wearing panties right now they would probably be drenched, I'd say it's not wrong at all."

He stilled, his smile dropping as he sucked in a harsh breath. "What do you mean *if* you were wearing panties?"

"The dress is fitted." I shrugged, biting my lip suggestively. "I didn't want you to see a panty line and I've never been a huge fan of G-strings."

His eyes narrowed, looking down at my dress before meeting my eyes. "Are you telling me that underneath that dress you're not wearing *anything*?"

"Yep, I had to forgo the bra as well. I didn't want the whole look to be undone by a rogue strap."

"Christ, Lila." He took a step back, his hand raking roughly through his hair. "How the hell am I supposed to get through the rest of the night knowing that?"

His chest heaved with heavy breaths as his eyes rolled down the length of my body. I loved their attention, how they darkened as they moved back up to my face.

"It was supposed to be a surprise. Lucky for you the night is almost over," I whispered, poking him playfully in the chest.

"Oh, you think so, huh?" He pulled me away from the wall, my body hitting his wall of muscle, the bulge in his pants noticeably larger. "The night isn't even close to being over for either of us."

IT HAD BEEN almost impossible not to have sex in the hall.

We were alone—well, as alone as two people could be when there were a few hundred people a few feet away—with the space deserted.

But instead of getting down and dirty up against a wall like I had been ready to do, Ryan kissed me one more time and led me back to the main room.

I was disappointed and sexually frustrated, but I didn't complain, knowing in a few hours I'd be in his arms and in his bed. It was a really good compromise and one I didn't have to wait too long for with Eric and Tia both ready to leave by the time we got back.

Eric and Tia sat in the backseat of the Hummer while I rode upfront with Ryan. I had my hands on him the entire time, squeezing his thigh and inching my hand closer to his crotch whenever I got the opportunity.

When we got back to the house, I didn't even bother heading to my room, waving Tia and Eric goodbye as I followed Ryan into his cottage.

"Jesus, Lila." Ryan thrust into me, my hands steading myself as he rocked.

We had barely got inside when he pushed me up against his

sofa, lifting my dress and going down on me. His tongue had worshiped me, making me come before he unzipped, put on a condom and pushed into me hard. Neither of us had bothered to undress, the time required more than we were willing to wait.

"Ryan, I'm going to come." My eyes shut tight as yet another orgasm ripped through me, my body shattering as he drove into me from behind.

"Fuck, I love feeling you come." One hand gripped my waist, while the other lay flat against my back. "I love the way you squeeze me hard right before, erupting into pulses as you go over. I love the way it feels along my cock, and knowing it's all for me."

His strokes were slow and steady, dragging himself in and out of me with unbelievable control as my legs shook, barely able to support my own weight.

"That's it, baby." A rush of air pushed through his lips. "Give me everything." He stilled as if absorbing me.

I was dizzy, absolutely intoxicated by him as I tried to slow my heart rate, the fitted dress tight against my chest making it harder to suck in air.

It was so quiet, just the sound of our breathing punching through the darkness, his still-hard length buried inside of me.

"I want you in my bed, Lila," he growled, lowering his lips to my ear. "I want to take my time with the next one I give you."

It was too much.

I had already had two, to ask for anything more would be greedy.

But I wanted it.

More of him.

And not just physically, which was the only way I could have him right now.

I felt him pull out, teasing the seam of my ass with the head of his cock while his hand pressed against my bare skin, everything amplified in the dark.

Then came my zipper, first the metal trill as it slid down my back, then the soft rush of air as it parted, exposing my spine. He didn't ask, taking the hem that was bunched up against my waist in his hands and lifting it over my head.

His fingers came back to settle on my hips, his lips kissing the base of my neck before spinning me around to face him.

"God, you're beautiful." His mouth skated around my collarbone, little nibbles making their way up my throat.

"You can barely see anything it's so dark." My hands reached out to touch him, the definition of his chest, ripples under my fingertips.

"I can see everything." He pulled me closer, his lips hitting mine. "Now come to my bed."

CHAPTER #13

TIA AND ERIC had left late Sunday, trying to avoid Monday morning traffic on their way to Santa Cruz, so we decided to do the same.

Loading up the Hummer with snacks, sodas and an epic playlist curated by yours truly, we made the trek along I-15 to my hometown.

My parents were thrilled at the impromptu visit and even more excited I was bringing someone home with me. I think my mother texted me twenty times on the drive over, asking me a million questions about *Tia's boyfriend's friend*, careful not to call him something I hadn't.

"So, your folks never had any more kids?" Ryan asked, opening his mouth like a baby bird so I could feed him more fries. Apparently, the snacks I'd packed weren't substantial enough, a burger stop needed about an hour and half out of L.A.

I laughed as he licked the salt off my fingers, wondering how someone who ate like he did could stay in such good shape. "Nope, my mom had to have a hysterectomy after I was born. They didn't get much of a choice."

"Wow, that blows. Still, had to be cool not to have to share your toys." He opened his mouth, ready for me to shove more food in.

"I didn't think about it much to be honest. It's all I really knew."
I let my fingers linger in his mouth a little, loving his lips closing
around them and sucking. I'm not sure why I'd suddenly turned
into a deviant, I could only blame the California sunshine and the
large amount of sex I was having.

"It wasn't until I got to school that I really understood what a
brother or sister was," I continued, taking a sip of soda. "Some of
the girls who worked for my mom had kids, so I still had plenty of
little people around me growing up. What about you? We spoke
about your parents—which we still need to visit as part of this
deal—but you never told me about your siblings."

"Two sisters and a brother," he announced proudly. "My parents were clearly masochists or didn't watch a lot of television."

"Wow, four of you! Your poor mother." I angled the straw
of my Coke so he could have a drink. "So, where do you fit in?"

He took a sip, swallowing before smirking. "The youngest,
you think they would have had all those kids if they'd had me first?
Nope, obviously they stopped when they got to perfection."

I shook my head with complete lack of surprise. "You have
the biggest ego I have ever seen."

"Aw, princess." He grabbed my hand, kissing my knuckles.
"You *know* it's not just my ego."

Well, there he had a point and was certainly not getting any
arguments from me. No complaints either.

"So, I was wondering." It was my turn to ask a question or
two. "Why do you call me princess?"

He laughed, his eyes flicking to me and then back to the road.
"You really want to know?"

"It better not be because you think I'm a diva," I warned,
knowing I hadn't displayed anything close to diva-like behavior.

"Nope." He shook his head giving me nothing. "If you're a
pain in the ass, I've never seen it."

"Then what?"

I didn't look or act like royalty. Unless monarchs these days were getting around in casual clothes and drank a lot, then there was possibly a similarity. I wasn't knowledgeable enough about global aristocracies to know for sure.

His lips twisted, fighting the grin. "I call you princess after Princess Peach."

Errrrr, what?

"I'm sorry?"

"Princess Peach? Mario Karts? Oh my God, Lila, please tell me you played Nintendo as a kid." He looked horrified, shaking his head in disbelief.

This was about computer games? I scoured the recesses of my mind trying to find a common thread and came up with nothing.

"I had a PlayStation I barely turned on and when I did, I was more a Tekken kind of girl." I shrugged, computer games never really my thing. "I liked beating people up. I felt it gave you life skills."

He nodded in approval. "This makes sense actually."

I'm glad it made sense to someone, because I still had no idea.

"So, what do *I* have to do with an inferior gaming console?"

He hissed out a breath, narrowing his eyes as he waved his finger accusingly at me. "Easy there, Lila, I don't want our marriage to be over before it's even begun. I will not have you speaking ill of my fondest childhood memories."

"You have serious issues." I rolled my eyes, ignoring the marriage comment and his look of disapproval. "Please go on."

"I was like obsessed with Princess Peach when I was a kid. Like seriously *obsessed*. Pretty sure she was the first girl I jerked off to. And the first time I saw you, all those feelings came flooding back."

"Ewwww." I punched him in the arm. "I don't know what's worse, that you found a cartoon game sexual or that I remind you of jerking off in your younger days. I think I would have preferred you thought I was high maintenance."

"Don't tell me you don't think it's fucking adorable, Lila," he warned. "Because that is as charming as it gets."

"Clearly we have very different ideas then," I lied, because deep down I did think it was adorable, and a little thrilled he'd sort of admitted he was maybe obsessed with me. I didn't even care it was most likely only sexual, it was *awesome* and I secretly loved it.

He held his hand up. "I'll ignore that right now because I'm driving and we'll continue this discussion later." A grin playing on his lips. "Okay, so now that we've got the basics down, let's start on the fun stuff."

I folded my arms across my chest, knowing exactly where it was heading. "Let me guess? First sexual experience?"

"Jesus, Lila." He laughed. "I was going to start with kiss but if you insist, sex it is."

I sighed, knowing I was probably never going to hear the end of it. My first time hadn't been wonderful and it wasn't something I was going to forget in a hurry. And sadly, not because it was awesome.

"I figured I'd just get it out the way. I'm sure it's going to amuse you."

He glanced over at me, absolutely beaming. "Princess, I can only imagine. Proceed." The wave of his hand indicating he was ready.

I leaned back and looked out the windshield, the landscape passing us in a blur while I prepared for my mortification. "So, I was sixteen, and I was seeing this guy from school. My parents didn't know I had started dating, so I had to go behind their back. Not that what we were doing was anywhere close to actual dating. We'd been to the movies a few times and made out, he'd stuck his hand up my shirt and I'd felt his dick, that kind of thing."

He coughed, shifting in his seat. "I'm seriously getting hard right now."

"Oh, shut up." I covered my face with my hands, partly regretting even starting the conversation.

I could have easily lied, made some story up about fumbling in the dark in the backseat of someone's car. But noooooo, I had to tell him the truth, a story that had only been told one other time.

"So anyway, I decide we were going to have sex."

"A woman who knows what she wants, I like it." He nodded, approvingly.

Ignoring him, I continued. "I snuck into The North Star—which is my mom's place—and stole some handcuffs in an effort to make things more interesting. Both of us were virgins and I may have oversold my confidence a tiny bit."

"Sixteen-year-old Lila was a naughty girl." He laughed, his finger waving in my direction. "See, I was right about you. You are totally going to lead me astray."

"Anyway." I blew out a breath, purposely not making eye contact. "I invited him back to my house after school one day. Dad was still at the Sheriff's station and Mom was doing inventory at The North Star, so I knew I had a good couple of hours." I neglected to add that realistically it was about one hour and fifty minutes longer than I needed, but I digress.

"And neither of us really knew what to do, so we start kissing and touching and he gets hard. We get the condom on—because if it's one thing my mother taught me, it was safe sex—then I tell him to handcuff me." I swallowed, just the memory of the day making me want to vomit.

"Please tell me you had a key." Although from the tone of his voice I was guessing he was hoping for the opposite.

"Oh yeah, the key wasn't the issue. Instead of just positioning my arms above my head, he thought it would be a good idea to add another element of excitement and lock them through the bedpost. Problem with that was I couldn't lie on my back and my shoulders were on a weird awkward angle. It was far from sexy and not even close to comfortable, but I didn't want him to think I was chickening out, so I pretended everything was fine. Which it was, until he pushed into me and I wasn't ready.

"There'd been zero foreplay and we weren't smart enough to think of lube, so when he went in fast—he explained later he figured it would be easier for both of us—my whole body contorted in pain. Inadvertently, I wrenched my restrained arms, which dislocated my shoulder. He panicked, pulling out of me and coming in the condom while trying to free my arms. And if that wasn't bad enough, it had been a day my dad had decided to come home . . . early."

Ryan started laughing uncontrollably. "Holy shit."

"We had managed to get one of my arms free and pull up the sheet before my dad walked in. Of course, by then it was too late, he'd heard screaming coming from my room so he bolted in, gun drawn, threatening to shoot poor Damon."

Ryan was barely able to keep the car on the road, his body shaking as he roared with laughter. "Oh my God, Lila."

"It was terrible. I was trying to explain that I wasn't being taken against my will, and the only crime we'd committed was being stupid. Meanwhile, I was howling in pain and Damon started crying, thinking he was going to die. We never did see each other after that. I'm pretty sure he's still in therapy."

"Oh, princess." He wiped the tears from his eyes. "That was the best story ever."

"Yeah, yeah, whatever." I waved him off, folding my arms across my chest. "I'm surprised it didn't turn me off sex for life. I was almost eighteen before I tried again. Between that, and boys thinking I was easy if they knew what my mother did, I was celibate for most of my teens. Okay, your turn." I poked him in the arm, ready for him to do show and tell.

"I don't know, Lila. I'm feeling a little inadequate. My first time was boring as hell."

"I highly doubt that." I rolled my eyes. "Just spill already."

He smiled smugly. "Fine, I was fifteen, she was sixteen and my next-door neighbor."

"This already sounds like a bad porno."

"Not even close." He laughed. "I snuck into her bedroom one night and we ended up having sex. I think I lasted about five minutes."

I coughed, having difficulty imagining a time Ryan wasn't amazing at sex. "Well, at least that's no longer a problem for you."

"Yep, and thank God for that."

Yeah, I'll say.

The conversation shifted to unimportant stuff. Ryan told me more about growing up and then going to work for Eric, while I reciprocated with my version of childhood tales and career path. The miles passed easily as we discussed everything and nothing.

He made everything feel so uncomplicated, the road trip ending too soon as we pulled up to my parents' house in the suburbs.

I took a deep breath as we parked in the driveway, the security light left on to welcome us.

"Baby!" My mom was out the door before we'd even climbed the first step. She threw her arms around me, squeezing me so tight it made it difficult to breathe before pulling back to study at me. "You look amazing. I'm so glad you decided to visit."

While neither of my parents had ever tried to discourage me from leaving and finding my own way, they made sure to show how much they missed me whenever I came back.

"I'm glad I came too." I squeezed her hand, glad she had waited up for our arrival. "Mom, this is my friend, Ryan." I stepped aside, making room for him beside us.

My mother was in her fifties but had stopped aging sometime around her thirtieth birthday. She slathered herself in anti-aging cream, ate organic, and ran five miles every day. And she looked stunning even at ten o'clock at night, her blonde hair twisted into a neat bun while wearing a fitted navy dress and a pair of red flats.

"Well hello, Ryan. So nice to meet you." She held out her hand politely, like she was having an audience with the mayor.

"The pleasure is all mine, Mrs. Callan." He returned her handshake, treating her to one of his amazing smiles.

"Please call me, Jen." Mom laughed, leaning in a little closer. "Mrs. Callan is my mother-in-law. She wears printed cotton housedresses and smells like mothballs, and I'm almost positive she's tried to kill me three times."

"Mom." I glared, hoping we could at least make it inside the door before we hung out all our family crazy.

"Fine, fine," she conceded, giving me a small reprieve. "Let's go inside and say hello to your dad. He's just as excited as I am to see you." She gave us a not-so-secretive smile as she turned, her hips swishing as she moved to the front door. All my talk of *he's not my boyfriend* apparently having been ignored as she looked at Ryan with wonder. "Just go ahead and leave your luggage in the car, Andy will help you get it later."

Ryan smirked, lowering his voice as he followed me inside the doorway. "Your mom is seriously awesome."

"Don't start," I whispered back, elbowing him in the ribs as we walked down the hallway toward the dining room.

My mom gave me a sympathetic smile before we walked in the room. "I tried to stop him."

I literally held my breath.

Oh. Shit.

This was so *not* a good idea.

While most fathers were skilled at giving people the third degree, mine had turned it into an art form. There he was, sitting at the dining room table, polishing a hunting rifle causally while laid out in front of him was enough weaponry to take over a small nation.

"Dad." I glared, hoping my subliminal messages of please-act-normal were getting through. I wasn't hopeful when he didn't lower the rifle.

"Pumpkin." The barrel snapped shut, his eyes drifting from me to Ryan. "Your mother told me you were bringing home a guest."

Ryan was going to turn around and run any minute now. Tell me how wonderful the road trip was, how great I was but he had a *thing* in L.A. that he just had to get back for.

Any second.

"Pleased to meet you, Sir. I'm Ryan."

I must have blinked. Or had a stroke, something that would have rendered me unconscious for a few minutes. And in those few moments—forever lost to the black hole or whatever was at work—Ryan had disappeared from my side and had approached my father. Casually. With his hand extended. Ignoring the militia paraphernalia spread on the table like hors d'oeuvres for a rebel army.

The handshake was not accepted as my father instead jacked up his spine, meeting Ryan eye to eye. "My daughter pregnant, Ryan?"

Please, God, if you are up there, help me out here.

"Dad!" It fired out of my mouth, my hands firmly on my hips. "Of course I'm not pregnant."

His eyes tracked me, looking intently at my stomach like he could ultrasound detect a fetus. "You sure?"

"Yes, I'm positive. And please put the guns away." I grabbed the double-barrel shotgun out of his hands, double checking it wasn't loaded—this was my father we're talking about, you could never be sure—and placed it on the table with all its scary brothers and sisters.

"Okay, Okay." My dad relented, wiping his palm on the side of his pants before finally giving Ryan his hand. "My name is Andy, but you can call me Sheriff Callan."

Please, God, just a little help.

"You're not a sheriff anymore, Dad, you retired," I reminded him, before turning to Ryan and mouthing a silent *I'm sorry.*

"Andy, behave." My mom chuckled, lifting a handgun and rubbing her manicured finger on the wood. "And clear all these guns off the table, you'll ruin the varnish." Straightening, she smiled, gesturing to the dining room chairs. "Why don't you kids sit down, I'll get some refreshments. Beer okay, Ryan?"

"Yep, a beer would be great. Thank you." He nodded, holding out a chair and waiting for me to sit down.

I lowered my body slowly, watching my dad gather up his cache as Ryan stayed standing.

"That's a lot of firepower you got there, you need a hand?" He waited, looking for the okay from my dad before touching anything.

Dad stopped, eyeing Ryan hard. "You know guns?"

Ryan didn't flinch, and if he was uncomfortable he wasn't showing it. "I've had weapons training but I don't carry. I have a Beretta I'm fond of in a safe back home."

My dad relaxed, his stance softening as he nodded to Ryan, allowing him to help. "Beretta makes a fine nine millimeter. I've got a couple myself."

And with that, the risk of someone being shot was exponentially lowered as they cleared the table.

I still had yet to breathe a sigh of relief; too worried that Ryan was alone with my father and the Second Amendment to relax as my mother returned, beers in hand.

"I like him." She lowered the beers, taking a seat next to the chair my father had vacated. "He's very handsome."

"Yes, he is," I agreed. "But we're just friends."

While my dad liked to use old school interrogation techniques, my mother was more psychological. I guess that was why she was so good at what she did, and could read people better than anyone.

"If you say so." Her raised eyebrow hinted I was either doing a terrible job selling it, or she wasn't buying. "Should I go ahead and make up the guest room then?" And damn if she didn't smile.

"Okay, okay, we're sleeping together, but that's it." My eyes scanned the hall, listening for the sound of footsteps. "Don't make a big deal about it."

She shrugged, picking up her beer and taking a sip. "No big deal."

Yeah, right.

I didn't have time for further rebuttal, interrupted by Ryan and my father's return. Thankfully no one was sporting a flesh wound, so that was a plus.

"Let's sit and have a beer." He clapped his hand on Ryan's shoulder, the animosity completely gone. "And then I'll help you get those bags out of the car. You guys must be tired."

"Thanks, Andy." Ryan slid into the seat beside me and clinked bottles with my dad. The unmistakable waft of smugness lingering in the air.

"Everything okay?" Translation: *what the hell is going on?*

Ryan lifted the bottle to his lips. "Just peachy."

His words didn't ease me; if anything they made me more on edge.

"Great," I muttered under my breath, wishing I was drinking something a hell of a lot stronger than beer.

Mom asked if we had any plans while we were in Vegas and thankfully Ryan didn't mention checking out her fine establishment. I then steered the conversation safely away from anything dangerous by telling them about my new story and how excited I was about finally getting to write something decent. Of course, my mom had some suggestions on follow-up stories, a couple hadn't been all that bad.

I was curious how far I could push the boundaries of the "art" section but writing a think piece on how the condom industry had adapted to latex allergies and anaphylaxis probably wouldn't be Dick's idea of words well spent. Maybe I could toss that idea to Tia, it was too good to ignore.

After we finished our beers, we went back out to the Hummer and grabbed our bags. Mom and Dad decided to head to bed, promising to catch up with us for breakfast while Ryan and I made our way up the stairs to my childhood room.

While most parents liked to preserve the space their children left—a virtual time capsule—my parents had decided to redecorate. Instead of the pale pink walls I remembered as a child, they had been recovered in a pale blue. The drapes were now charcoal. But there was *one* thing that had remained the same.

Ryan took one look at my four-poster bed and started grinning. "So, let me ask you something." He lowered himself onto the mattress, testing it with a few good bounces before continuing. "Other than your ill-fated first time, any other guys been up here with you?"

I coughed out a laugh, leaning against the wall as I watched him at the scene of the crime. "Are you kidding? After that first time I didn't bring any guy within a ten-mile radius of this house. No, no one else has been up here."

I knew when to quit while I was ahead, and also wanted to save myself from a lifetime of therapy.

"You feel like being nostalgic?" He pulled a pair of handcuffs from his pocket, twirling one of the cuffs around his fingers.

My smiled widened, joining him on the bed. "You just randomly happen to have a pair of handcuffs with you?"

"Nope, I stole them from your dad. He had a couple of pairs with all the guns, and unless he does a stocktake every night, I doubt he'll notice they're gone."

No mention was made on why my father would have hand-cuffs, which were no longer necessary considering he was no longer the Law. Or maybe Ryan had already been told, my dad proud he was ready for when the civil uprising happened and heathens started looting and acting like thugs. It was one of his favorite bedtime stories. In any case, he wouldn't be missing a pair tonight, but they would definitely have to go back first thing tomorrow.

My fingers played with the metal, memories of a pair just like them and the room flooding back. "I'm not sure recreating one of the most traumatic experiences of my young adult life is something I want to do."

"No?" He pouted, looking disappointed. "Is there another experience you'd like me to recreate instead?"

It was strange, but even in the hypothetical I didn't want to think about the past with Ryan. I didn't want to think about other men I'd been with, or other women for him. I wanted it to be just us.

Here.

Now.

"No." I pulled the handcuffs from his fingers, placing them on my nightstand. "How about we do something new instead?"

He looked at me with a curious expression, his hands wrapping around my waist. "Like?"

I shifted into his lap, straddling him while my fingers played with his hair. His beautiful brown eyes tracked me as my mouth lowered down onto his with all the confidence that my sixteen year-old virgin self hadn't had.

"How about we get naked and take it from there."

"That is the best plan ever."

CHAPTER #14

"GOOD MORNING, PRINCESS." I felt his lips at the back of my neck. "You want to get up and go sightseeing?

"Ugh," I groaned, not getting enough sleep after our *try something new* exercise last night. One of us probably needed to go to the gym a little more. And here was a hint, it wasn't the one who was all perky about being awake in the morning.

My eyes stayed shut, feeling his hands glide slowly down my back. "You mean like the Hoover Dam and the Grand Canyon? Because there is no way I'm going to the strip." My enthusiasm for field trips at an all-time low.

"God, you're adorable." He laughed, his hands going lower, skirting the top of my ass. "This isn't middle school, Lila. No, I was thinking more along the lines of showing me where you hung out, went to school, that kind of stuff. I want the full Lila Callan tour. I expect commentary too, embarrassing stories are a plus."

An irrational wave of panic washed over me, stilling me. Why did he want to know all that stuff? Not even Tia, who had come with me to visit my parents, had that kind of information. Not because I didn't trust her, but I just felt that stuff was best left in the past. Growing up, I had been slightly awkward, uncoordinated, and didn't have a lot of friends. I was happy of course, but I liked this version of myself better.

"Can't we just go to the brothel instead?" I flopped onto my back, the sheet slipping to reveal my breasts. I wasn't above using them as a distraction.

Plus, wasn't The North Star the reason why we had come in the first place?

My mother's fine establishment, who, since its inception, had serviced both men and women and their sexual indulgences.

He didn't miss a beat, lowering his head and kissing my breasts. "We'll get there eventually, but I want to see the other stuff too."

I had seriously underestimated him.

Not only had my breasts failed me—seriously girls, I was counting on you—but he was able to multitask. Distracting *me* with his delicious and dexterous tongue while carrying on a conversation. It was a skill I wasn't sure I possessed and it was unfair he did.

And why the hell was there a sudden change in our list of objectives?

He had been positively giddy when I'd told him what my mother did. Insisting we go to Vegas so he could experience the magic, or whatever it was he thought was going to happen. In any case, the tales of the life and times of Lila weren't on our agenda. He couldn't flip the script on me now, not when we were here.

"The other stuff is boring." I stifled the moan, eyes boring into the ceiling in an attempt to concentrate on something other than his mouth and tongue. "I know this might come as a surprise to you because I'm obviously so fascinating now." Oh, sarcasm, that was surely a win, right? "But my childhood wasn't all that interesting."

His hands moved to where his mouth had been, his body double-teaming me while my resolve floundered. "Are you kidding me? Not even taking into account your dad pulling a gun on the kid trying to deflower you—"

"Deflower? What century are you from?" Ooooo humor, that was an extra point.

He ignored me, slashing his hand through the air. "*And* the prostitutes who tutored you in math."

"Hey, some of those girls went on to get their Master's degrees with no student loans," I protested, the idea that women only sold their bodies because they didn't have any other choice was both archaic and inaccurate. "I'm not saying it was something I could do, but it worked out well for them."

He grinned, his lips moving to my mouth where he nibbled at my lower lip. "I'm illustrating a point. That even disallowing all of that—which is so far from boring, it needs a made up word or something—I bet you'd still be a hell of a lot more interesting than ninety percent of the people I grew up with."

My throat constricted, making it hard to breathe.

How could he do that? Disarm me so quickly that I lost my ability to speak and think. It was a party trick I wasn't totally comfortable with, both loving and hating it in equal parts simultaneously.

"Fine," I agreed, knowing I was powerless to stop it. He had a way of making me do things I thought I didn't want. The status—or more accurately the non-status—of our relationship, a prime example.

He laughed, tossing his head back in victory. "Don't pretend like this isn't going to be the most awesome thing ever." His hands rubbed together in villainous glee. "Now, let's go get breakfast so we can get started. I already snuck downstairs early to put back the handcuffs, I didn't want to risk your dad noticing they were gone and using them on me."

It was my turn to laugh, the thought of my dad cuffing Ryan and asking what his intentions were was hysterical.

We dressed and went downstairs to the main part of the house. My dad was already up, at the stove cooking eggs while my mom sat in the breakfast nook going over paperwork.

"Good morning, sweetheart." She lifted her head, her blonde hair still wet from the shower. "Did you both sleep well?"

My dad cleared his throat, his disapproval of the previous night's sleeping arrangements not needing to be said as he looked over his shoulder. "Eggs?"

"Thanks, Dad, we'd love some." I went and gave him a quick peck on the cheek before returning to the table. "And yes, we slept very well."

Ryan held out a chair, waiting for me to seat myself before doing so himself. He did have such amazing manners.

"I'm so glad." She reached across the table and squeezed. "I had the mattress replaced last month. I bulk bought for The North Star and figured we'd do the house too. I put extra condoms in the drawer of your nightstand as well, I got those in bulk too."

Dear. God.

The color drained from my face wondering if it was too much to ask to get through thirty minutes with my parents with some semblance of normality. I'm not asking them to be "regular" parents—they lacked the capacity and I was mostly fine with shenanigans. But surely the condom talk could have been saved for another time. Like never.

Meanwhile, my father had a coughing fit, spatula in hand waving around like he was the Pope at Christmas service, probably having a heart attack. The restocking of my bedroom drawers obviously a solo venture performed by my mother.

"Oh, relax, Andy." My mother rolled her eyes. "She's twenty-eight years old. You think she isn't having sex? At least this way she'll be safe about it."

Mortified.

Well and truly mortified.

"Mom, can we not?" I regressed to my teenage self,

remembering the time she pulled out a banana and made me latex the thing about thirty thousand times till she was satisfied I knew how. It was so much worse with an audience. And the fact Ryan was sitting there grinning, didn't help either.

"Lila, I know I didn't raise a prude. There's no need to be embarrassed, sex is normal and healthy."

"I agree, Mrs.—" Ryan caught himself, "I mean, Jen. And I applaud your frank and open relationship with your daughter."

He was sooooo not helping.

Neither was my father who had managed to compose himself—the heart attack shelved for a little while at least—enough to shoot daggers at both of us.

I reached for the jug of juice on the table, pouring out a glass for both Ryan and I. Lord, help me. "I'm not a prude. I just don't want to talk about it."

"And you don't have to, pumpkin." My dad dished out eggs onto plates before carrying them over.

"Here." He sat a plate down in front of Ryan. "They're unfertilized, I'd like to keep all the eggs at this table that way, thanks."

This time I laughed, because the situation was so ridiculous there really wasn't any other appropriate response. They weren't doing it to intentionally embarrass me; this was just them, and their version of loving me.

I waited for the noise of the chair scrapping against the floor, Ryan standing up and announcing he had to leave unexpectedly. Followed by the sound of screeching tires as he hightailed it away from the madhouse as fast as he could.

Instead, he remained in his seat, giving my dad a two-finger salute. "Heard loud and clear, Sheriff." And then tucked into his eggs like nothing had happened.

Wait a second?

Did I forget to wake up this morning and the whole scenario

was an elaborate dream sequence? Because no one was this chilled around my parents, not even me, and I was a product of their DNA.

"Eat, Lila. Your eggs will get cold." My dad dropped a kiss on the top of my head before shuffling onto the bench beside my mother and joining us for breakfast.

It was almost normal.

Well, *normal* if you didn't count the condom, sex and unfertilized eggs talk that happened a few minutes prior.

Thankfully, the rest of breakfast was smooth sailing, the conversation almost benign.

And Ryan hadn't run, which was a plus. I chalked it up to his impeccable manners—seriously who pulled out chairs for people anymore, he was pathologically polite—and assumed he would at least stick it out for the rest of the trip. I also liked to think I was amazing in bed and that in his reasoning he'd decided the sex was worth the crazy. It wasn't like he had to put up with it long term. If I had been presented with insanity that provided screaming-out-loud-white-knuckled-toe-curling orgasms, I'd probably have shrugged it off too. Hey, you could always get rid of the crazy later, but good sex was hard to come by.

After clearing the table and the dishes, we waved my mom goodbye as she headed to the "office." We told her we'd stop by at some point. Today, if we had time, if not tomorrow. I wasn't sure how long my guided tour of the ghosts of Lila past was going to take.

We hopped back into the Hummer, Ryan sliding on a pair of aviators and a smile as he reversed out of the driveway, and we headed to our first stop.

Thankfully, we didn't discuss my parents who had done their best to be mortifying. And Ryan was evidently so well trained at dealing with crazy—he lived in Hollywood after all—to react, or he was too polite to comment. Either way, I was thankful, and glad he hadn't been scared away by two people who loved me but were clearly far from normal. Of course there was still time, so I hoped he didn't spook easily.

"Turn up there on the right." I pointed up ahead.

The stop sign that used to stand so proudly on the corner had been knocked down at some point and was reclined on an angle. It didn't look recent, the grass beneath it plush and undisturbed. But like everything in the 'burbs, not much attention was given to stuff like that, people too caught up in their own lives to worry.

Most residents didn't venture into the strip unless they absolutely had to, something I told Ryan about as we pulled up to my elementary school. The brown and red brick buildings completely unchanged since I walked into its gates.

"So, there you go." I looked out of the side window, the engine still idling. "This was where my first day of school was." My hand waved, showcasing our location in case he was blind and/or stupid. I couldn't believe how nervous it was making me. "I went to pre K further down the road at the Uniting Church on Lark Street. Trust me, drop off in the mornings was a barrel of laughs for the dads who'd previously visited The North Star." I chuckled, remembering how it only occurred to me years later that the men making hasty exits were probably customers.

Most people judged, possibly even blamed my mom for providing the service. But she wasn't their moral compass, and at least the women who worked for her were safe. Something that couldn't be said a few miles down into town.

Ryan grabbed my hand, bringing to his lips and kissing my knuckles. "Did little Lila like school?"

"She did for the most part. I liked the learning, the kids—not always." I sighed. Being tall and blonde wasn't always a virtue, especially when you hadn't grown into your body yet. "We should probably get going to the next stop, classes are in session and we don't want to look like we're casing the place or stalking kids."

"Ah, yes." He nodded, throwing the car into gear as we pulled away. "Good point."

We cruised past my middle school—very uneventful few years and no reason to stop—and then finally to my old high school.

The massive sign at the front advertised the Coyotes—their football team—who were currently on a losing streak.

I cringed. "I tried out to be a cheerleader my freshman year."

"Wow." He swallowed, his eyes darkening. "You just want to make all my fantasies come true, princess, don't you?"

My hand shoved his shoulder as I laughed. "Ugh, so predictable. You know I'll expect this in return. If I'm forced to revisit this, then you're going to have to do it too."

It wasn't something we'd spoken about seriously. Just a vague promise he would adequately embarrass himself when he introduced me to his family. So, there was nothing to stop him from reneging later if he wanted to.

"Princess." He let out a sigh, shaking his head before his eyes caught mine. "I was a god in high school. Telling you about it will only make me look better."

"I can totally see that."

And I could.

He had a confidence about him that wasn't learned, like he'd been born with an innate sense of self-assurance. Sure, possibly some arrogance, but he made it look so goddamn adorable. No one in their right mind would write him off as a cocky asshole.

"Ironically, I made the squad. I had grown into my body then and wasn't so much a mess of arms and legs. But after about a week of teasing my hair into a high ponytail and slapping on a massive shiny bow, I realized it wasn't for me. Too much cheer—in the team, not me."

Ryan laughed as he took his foot off the brake and left my old high school in the rearview mirror.

As the car rolled through the streets, we chatted about me finding my love for journalism and my dream of seeing my name in print.

I pointed out familiar streets, directing him to a local Italian joint that was open for lunch. It seemed like a good time to take a break.

"So." Ryan clapped, rubbing his hands together as he beamed. "What about the important stuff? First kiss, first date—I want the director's cut of this tour." The amazing cheese pizza in front of us remained ignored.

"Ugh. Why am I being punished?" I groaned, my head dropping down to my hands with more drama than was needed I peeked through my fingers and saw he was smiling. "If it's because of my parents, then you only have yourself to blame. I tried to warn you."

"Your parents are great," he said without a hint of sarcasm. "They obviously love you very much. Thanks for giving me the chance to meet them."

My hands slipped into my lap as I studied him in greater detail, his sincerity both heartwarming and unexpected.

"You're welcome." The words got stuck in my throat, over-whelmed by the intimacy we were sharing. This wasn't the kind of conversation I was expecting or used to. It felt almost too personal, exposing me in a way I wasn't sure if I was comfortable with. We were friends who slept together, and I was already starting to feel things I shouldn't. And if I knew he meant those words beyond just being a nice guy, I would have been ecstatic. But I didn't know anything, and speculating was dangerous. This wasn't permanent and I needed to remember that.

I shifted in my seat, my eyes falling from him to the pizza. "We should eat. The pizza is going to get cold."

"Yep, and while we're doing that, you can think of new places to go. *Good* places, Lila." He grabbed a slice and lifted it to his mouth. "I'll know if you're lying."

I didn't doubt that for a second.

He seemed to have a freakish ability to *know* people. Like he was tapped into their psyche or something. Watching him work a crowd was fascinating. He was literally unflappable, able to roll with whatever situation was thrown at him with ease. And as much as I hated to admit it, he knew me better than I would have liked.

It wasn't that I didn't trust him—he'd more than proven he was a decent person—it just wasn't supposed to be that way. Not between us. It was meant to be fun and flirty, sexy even—but feelings? Nope, they were not supposed to be involved. This was exactly the kind of behavior that would lead me to get attached. To start daydreaming about things I knew couldn't happen.

"Here," I said before I could stop myself. The detailed and logical pep talk from moments ago, all but forgotten as my mouth went off script.

We hadn't agreed yet, asshole.

Well, you brought him here so clearly you'd planned this all along.

Shut up, it was just a place to eat, it has zero significance. Coincidence.

HAHAHAHAHA, you are such a liar.

God, I hoped my debate was kept internal.

He stopped chewing, looking at me strangely because a single word did not an explanation make. Who needed my parents to convince him to say goodbye? I could do that all by my damn self.

"Here, what?"

"This was where I had my first date and my first kiss."

And now I had done it, the slice in his hand lowered to the plate, his attention no longer on eating.

"Tell me everything."

Shit.

My mouth had thrown me under the bus and if I didn't elaborate he'd assume I was chicken. He wasn't to know what it meant to me, by volunteering that information. Allowing him further into my circle and if I was honest, further into my heart.

"I was sitting over there." I pointed to a booth at the back. It was empty with its faded red leather seats a shadow of their former glory. "I was fifteen, we ordered pizza by the slice and sat up there in the back. He was sixteen, and so handsome, I could barely eat."

Ryan's eyebrow rose, a questioning glance shot my way. "Go on."

"I guess because sex was so matter-of-fact around my house I wasn't really interested in boys in that way. But he was nice to me, so when he asked me out, I didn't realize it was a date."

Realistically, even now, I wasn't sure it had been intended to be either.

"Blake's dad was the deputy. He worked with mine so we'd known each other for years. I assumed he was thanking me for helping him with his reading comprehension. But halfway through dinner he leaned over and kissed me." I laughed, the whole experience hysterical. "It was so awkward, I was mid chew and our mouths were so greasy from the pizza."

"Pfft." He folded his arms across his chest, leaning back against his chair. "Amateur."

I leveled him with a stare, it might not have been a lasting relationship but Blake had been nice. "We were kids, it was sweet. But zero chemistry. Maybe it was the pizza grease." I shrugged, remembering not being disappointed by the lack of spark. I guess even then I had been pretty pragmatic.

"It wasn't the pizza grease." He reached across, his lips brushing against mine.

Whatever fireworks I'd missed the first time certainly weren't lacking now as I leaned closer, giving him more of my mouth. My tongue swept over his lips, tasting the mix of salty and sweet and hungering for more.

I moaned, tilting my head in an effort to get more contact, my fingers locked around the edge of the table as my knuckles went white.

"Easy," he whispered against my mouth, his voice raw. "I'm almost positive Sheriff Andy doesn't want to have to bail us out of jail later."

I smiled, my tongue sliding across the seam of his lips before I pulled away. "You started it."

"Yeah, I did." He slowly kissed my retreating mouth again. "I knew you would eventually corrupt me, I just didn't expect it would happen this fast."

A laugh traveled up my throat, peppering the air as I tossed my napkin at him. "I think you will find it is the other way around."

"Lies." He had the nerve to look indignant. "But we should finish our lunch, we still need to see the movie theater where Damon got to second base."

"You have a sickness, you know." I laughed, picking up a slice and biting into it.

He grinned watching me eat. "Normal is highly overrated."

CHAPTER #15

WE EVENTUALLY GOT to the movie theater.

It was at a strip mall not far from my parents' house and where I'd spent most of my time as a teenager.

We bought tickets to a four o'clock showing of some action movie neither of us cared about and sat up in the back in the dark where we made out. He pulled my T-shirt free of my jeans and slid his hand up to my breasts. His mouth dominated mine as he pushed down the cup of my bra, rolling my nipples between his fingers as I bit back a moan.

Not to be outdone, I discreetly unzipped his pants, my fingers finding their way to his very hard cock. I stroked him through his underwear, the heel of my hand pressed against his length and I felt him get harder.

"Fuck." The word getting lost between his throat and his jaw the minute my fingers touched his naked skin, his feet kicking out in front of him to give me more access.

We were almost alone, a few people scattered through the theater who were too busy shoveling popcorn in their mouths with their eyes glued to the screen. No one cared what we were doing as we enjoyed our private bubble.

The low glow from the screen gave me just enough light to see the muscles in his neck flex, his jaw locked tight as I gave him a slow and steady stroke.

"Lila." His hand cupped mine, holding it still as his chest moved up and down with each breath.

"Shhhh," I whispered in the dark, biting my lip as I gave him another firm stroke.

His body tensed but his grip on me relaxed, the slide up and down his cock made a little easier as my hand disappeared inside his pants.

I loved feeling the tightness of his abs as my fingers curled around him, the breath pushing out of his lips as he let me have control, dictating the tempo.

The low ache increased between my legs. He wasn't even touching me anymore and I could feel myself get wetter, my mouth dying to savor him.

He was so beautiful.

The light from the movie screen flashed across his face and I watched him in profile as his eyes blinked slowly, half-raised lids giving me just enough of a view of his gorgeous brown eyes. They were wild, needy as he turned his head and looked at me.

Heat raged through my core as my mouth hovered closer, needing to touch him in some way too, kissing him with full lips.

A groan vibrated against his throat, his eyes closing as his tongue invaded my mouth. I loved it, feeling his hips buck against my hand while I squeezed tighter.

"Lila."

Never had I heard my name with so much worship, both a prayer and a beg in the same breath. My lips moved to this neck where I felt the hammering of his pulse beneath his skin.

I could make him come.

Right here, right now, in the dark while people were a few

feet away.

I could do it, and he wouldn't stop me.

Power and lust licked at my skin, wanting to replace my hand with my body and feel him inside me. I wanted those rocks of his hips to be against mine, to feel the heat of his breath as I took him deeper.

His lips grazed the shell of my ear, his hand grabbing my wrist. "You're making me fucking crazy."

The grin spread across my lips as a weird sense of pride bloomed inside me. He had started this game, tried to tease me in the dark but I had been the one who was victorious. He was the one tapping out when I would have gone all the way.

With his fingers still locked around my wrist, I pulled my hand from his jeans. He let go, shaking his head at me as he adjusted himself and zipped. A long deep exhale audible as he shuffled in his seat.

"You want to get out of here?" he breathed against my ear, his hot breath tickling my skin.

It's not like we were watching the movie. I couldn't even tell you what it was called, let alone what it was about.

"Yeah," I whispered back in the dark.

Slowly, we both rose, shuffling out of the aisle and exiting to the main part of the theater.

"Nice." I glanced down at the very obvious bulge at the front of Ryan's pants. There was a benefit to no longer being in the dark.

"So cruel." Ryan reared back, clasping his hands to his chest while pretending to look hurt and disgusted. "To mock me. But sure, go ahead and admire your handiwork." He held his hand up dramatically. "Meanwhile, I think I've lost circulation to my balls."

While my arousal was easier to hide, it didn't mean it wasn't there as well. I was just as hot and bothered as he was, but the female anatomy was just far more superior.

"You could have stopped me anytime, you know." My shoulder knocked his, basking in my own smugness.

"And turn you away from touching my cock?" His look of shock intensified as he leaned in closer, dropping his voice to a whisper. "I don't even know if I can do that."

"Well, sweet cakes." I tugged on his arm, pulling him back toward the direction of the car. "I'll keep my hands to myself for the rest of the afternoon, how's that?"

He shook his head, pulling his car keys from his pocket. "Not a solution, Lila. And not one I'm happy to endorse."

We pushed out the double doors and out into the afternoon sun, the weather warmer than I was used to for October. Our feet fell into rhythm as we walked out to the parking lot, his blacker-than-black Hummer not far away.

"So, do you want to—" The sentence left as unfinished as he trapped me between a wall of Ryan York delicious muscle and the big black car.

"Do I want to put my fingers down your jeans and see if you're wet?" He cocked his head to the side, running his hard length against me. "Yeah, I'd like to do that."

"We're in a parking lot." My lame, half-hearted rebuttal ignored as he kissed me, silencing any other protests I might have.

He needn't have worried, parking lot or not, I wasn't going to stop him.

His hands planted themselves on either side of my body while his lips took want they wanted. Lucky for me, it was exactly what I wanted too.

And he wasn't gentle.

The weight of his body pressed against me while his hot and demanding mouth continued its assault. First taking and then giving, the subtle nips and sucks against my lips making it almost impossible to breathe, let alone think.

If I'd been in control in the theatre, his hands were well and truly locked on the wheel here. Anything, I would have done anything for it not to stop. For him to kiss me like that for hours.

"Lila? Is that you?"

No, it's not, I wanted to scream, not acknowledging the female voice or the clearing of the throat. Maybe If I ignored her—whoever she was—she would go away, and I could fall further into the oblivion.

"Lila Callan?"

Because my effort to ignore her wasn't clear enough the first time, she had to say my full name to force my hand. The interrupter insistent that she get my attention.

Before I could stop it, the sweet, sweet weight pressed against me eased, lifting and leaving me feeling empty and disappointed.

It better be the Virgin Mary looking for a place at the inn or something, or I was going to be pissed.

Ryan twisted around, the shift of his body giving me the ability to see who had been interrupting.

"Mary?" I squinted my eyes, almost in disbelief.

Her face lit up, the smile hitting her eyes as she nodded her head. "I knew it was you. Oh my God, it's been forever."

It was a *Mary,* just not the virgin one; her black hair framed her face like a veil in a humorous twist of irony.

"Heeeeeey."

I tried to pretend like I hadn't just been sucking Ryan's face off in the parking lot and remember the last time I'd seen her. Graduation? No, it was after, when I came back to visit my freshman year of college.

"So . . ." I adjusted my T-shirt and affixed a smile. "This is Ryan." I game-show waved at the confused man who I'd been dry humping a few minutes before. "How have you been?"

"Errrr." She stalled out, no doubt blinded by all that sexiness that hit you like a blast heater. "Hi, Ryan, I'm Mary."

"Hi." His smile not helping the situation as he eased himself beside me.

"I've been great." She grinned, the question of her welfare answered as she continued to look at him, her eyes doing that thing where she tried to imagine him without his clothes. Okay, I didn't know for sure, but I couldn't be the only one who did that.

"That's wonderful," I lied, wondering how long I had to keep the conversation going in order to appear polite. "We were just leaving actually."

Fine, so I failed miserably at politeness, my two minutes probably ruder than I wanted to be.

Mary and I had sort of been friends growing up, not the kind you'd call if you were hiding a body but a friend nonetheless.

"Oh, don't go," she whined, pouting with what looked like genuine disappointment. "I haven't seen you in forever and you hardly ever come back home. Your mom told me what a big time reporter you are. *The New York Times*? Wow, you really made it."

She looked at me with such respect and adoration it was hard to not to feel guilt. Guilt, because I wished it was true, and guilt, because she was being nice and I was ready to blow her off for a quickie with Ryan.

"I'm not that big a deal, Mary." The idea of lying to her too overwhelming. "I write for the art's section. I don't get the major stories."

"Are you kidding?" She laughed, shaking her head in disbelief. "Honey, you got out of here. I got pregnant my first year of college and ended up working at my sister-in-law's beauty salon. *You* did awesome."

My eyes peeled back, like I was seeing her for the first time. "Wow, you had a baby?"

"Three, actually. Once the seal was broken, they kinda kept

happening. It's okay though, I love those cheeky bastards." She smiled proudly, like she hadn't just told me she'd given birth to three humans *and* was the same age as me.

"Wow. I mean, wow."

Yep, words failed me as I tried to imagine myself giving up my dream, to be a parent. I had been way too selfish, the idea of it happening even now, almost terrifying me.

"So, you see," she waved her hand matter of factly, "we need to catch up. You should come by the house and have dinner. Besides, I'm positive Blake would love to see you. His dad and yours still go out to the firing range every other weekend, so we're always hearing about you."

"Blake? As in Blake Harvey?" As in the deputy's son who took me on my first date and gave me my first kiss? *That* was the guy who knocked her up three times?

Wow, I'd seriously dodged a bullet with him. Given the obvious efficiency of his swimmers, I'm surprised I hadn't been impregnated by his kiss. Well, it had been lackluster and there had been a table in between us, thank God for small mercies.

"Yeah, we got married just before Tyler was born. He's working as a mechanic down on Crane Street."

"Ummmm." My brain stalled for an answer.

It would be weird, right? Not because of our fifteen-minute relationship—if you could even call it that—but because I hadn't seen Blake since I'd left for college. And even though our dads were still firm friends, neither of my parents were gossips so I had no idea what anyone in the town was up to.

"We'd love to," Ryan volunteered, giving our commitment to dinner before I'd had a chance to nix the idea.

"Didn't you want do that other *thing*?" My head jerked to the car, a not so discreet hint that maybe this wasn't such a good idea.

"That can wait." He waved it off, completely unconcerned.

"I'd love for us to catch up with your friends."

"Great." This was the opposite of great. "Sure, Mary, we'd love to come, but only if you're sure it's no imposition."

She laughed, her pretty hazel eyes watering. "Lila, I have three boys. Short of you firing a canon in my living room, nothing would be an imposition. Plus, I would love some grown-up time and have adult conversation. All I seem to do these days is talk about the kids."

"Okay then, well I guess we'll follow you?" I asked, not having the faintest idea where she lived.

"Yep, sure thing." She shook her car keys, "I'm just three rows over. I'll circle back."

"Awesome." Not. My mouth thinned into a tight line as I watched her saunter off, excited about our impending dinner.

"You." My hands pushed against Ryan's chest. "Are a menace. What were you thinking agreeing to dinner?"

A smile that could only mean trouble spread across his lips. "C'mon, Lila. She was so desperate to spend time with you. Have a heart. Besides, you met a bunch of my friends. Hell, I even let you interview them."

"They weren't social occasions, that was work. This is different." I wasn't sure why I was trying to rationalize it, it's not like anything could be changed now.

"We should probably get in the car." His grin widened. "We don't want to keep Mary waiting."

"Ugh, you're impossible." I huffed, stomping like a five-year-old to the passenger side and climbing in. "Impossible."

"It will be great, I promise." He slid into the driver's seat, resting his hand on my knee. "It's good to brag a little. I do it all the time." He laughed, pointing out the obvious. "Be proud of what you've done. And I get you moved away and you're not the same girl who left this place, but it's part of who you are."

I hated when he talked logic, especially since what he was saying was so fucking obvious I should have been able to see it myself.

I wasn't always the best person at seeing things the ways others did, not for myself anyway. It wasn't a confidence thing, I knew I was smart and I was good at what I did. And when it came to work, there was no bigger advocate for myself than me. But I'd been so busy pushing forward, I sometimes forgot to stop and smell the roses and appreciate how far I'd come. I needed to be better at it, to see the good things I already had.

"This better not be about meeting Blake." I narrowed my eyes, trying to look annoyed but his blindingly adorable smile making it difficult. "I know you're playing dumb right now, but you know full well it's the very same Blake who gave me my first kiss."

"A complete bonus." He leaned across the center console and gave me a kiss. "I love the 'Burbs, it's so easy to run into people."

I just shook my head, the "whatever" muttered under my breath as Mary's white sedan came into view. She gave us a friendly wave and then waited for us to pull out and follow.

Mary's house wasn't far at all, literally a few turns away from the mall on a street similar to where she used to live. Actually, it was the *same* street, and the *same* house. The siding that had been green before was now white, but other than that, it was identical to the last time I had been there.

"You're living with your parents." It had come out of my mouth before I had a chance to stop it, my effort in trying to be polite still pulling up short.

Mary smiled, ignoring my rudeness as she unlocked her front door. "Nah, we got Mom and Dad situated in a duplex in a retirement community. My mom hated sitting home every day, and she was driving my dad nuts. They're happier where they are now and they get to do salsa dancing and play bingo every day of the week. It's like they're teenagers again. Well, except for the bingo part."

"That's great." I wasn't sure what the appropriate response was supposed to be. Was it good when parents went on permanent spring break? Mary's straight-laced dad doing the *Mambo* wasn't something I could imagine. I guess the bingo was a safe. "It's good they get to socialize."

"Yeah, plus we never would have been able to afford a house on our own." She pushed open the door, holding it ajar with her hip. "Come in, but excuse the mess, I wasn't expecting company."

"I'm sure it's fine." I laughed, waving my hand dismissively.

Famous. Last. Words.

My smile dropped the minute I'd stepped across the threshold.

It looked like a crime scene, or a house that had been burglarized, with every square inch of the carpet covered with toys or clothes or—I had no idea what the other stuff was.

"Let me just pick up." Mary tossed her keys and bag onto a worn armchair and started to pile things into her arms. "Although, not sure why I bother. Blake will be home with the boys in a few minutes and the place will just look like a hurricane came through again." She shrugged, chuckling to herself as she started to expose what the floor looked like underneath.

"Here, let me help you." I got down on my knees, picking up random items and not knowing what to do with them. "Ryan?" I turned to see he'd already grabbed an empty box, tossing in toys as he gave me a wink.

"You guys." Mary beamed, her eyes misting in appreciation. "Thank you so much. But I invited you here for dinner, not to help me clean."

"It's fine, we're fine." I grabbed what looked to have been a hamster in a former life and held it up for inspection. "Do you want this anywhere special?"

"Oh, that's Connor's pet." Mary held out her hand, waiting for me to pass it over before arranging it carefully on top of the television. "He wanted a cat but I'm allergic so he carries *that* around and pretends it's his cat. I got it from the fabric store at the mall, best three dollars I ever spent."

We had barely got the room looking respectable—and less like it had been ransacked by the FBI—when the door flung open and three small humans of varying heights and weights came barreling though at full speed.

"Mama," the smallest one screamed, arms outstretched as he threw his body with little regard for his safety at Mary.

"I don't want to eat your boogers!" the bigger one hollered, the booger-feeder middle one running after him with his finger extended.

"Hey, babe, we're ho—" Blake stalled out, standing frozen in the doorway with three backpacks piled in his arms. "Shit, Lila?"

"Shit, shit, shit," screamed booger middle, shaking his ass in the older one's face. "Shit, shit, shit, shit."

"Stop that," Mary snapped, grabbing the nose-picking *shit* repeater with one hand as she shifted the little one to a hip. It was like watching Cirque De Soleil, hands and feet flying, and everything balancing precariously. "I've told you we don't say that word, it's an adult word."

"Hey." I waved, not sure if I should be wrangling kids or offering to help Blake with the bags he was carrying. "Mary saw me in the parking lot of the mall and invited us for dinner."

A smiled spread across his face as he dropped the backpacks where he stood and closed the front door. "That's great. It's so good to see you."

He moved closer, his eyes shifting to Ryan as he awkwardly extended his arm in a half hug, half shoulder tap. "It's been too long."

"It has." I nodded, accepting his hybrid hug, not wanting it to be any more awkward than it already was.

"I'm Ryan." He held out his hand, obviously immune to the craziness, completely unfazed. "I'm here with Lila."

"Hey, Ryan. Good to meet you, Blake."

Hands were shaken, pleasantries exchanged, while one of the kids—and since we were in Vegas, I was putting my money on the middle one—screamed that he needed to poop. Mary corralled the two smaller ones and shuffled them out of the room as the older one, completely uninterested in us, grabbed his iPad and sat down.

"It's sort of crazy before bedtime." Blake shrugged. "Mary is a lot better at it than me."

Blake's face still held the same warmth and kindness it had always had, but he looked older than his years. Deep-set lines crinkled when he smiled and his hair was graying at the temples. His once fit body had softened, a beer belly where his abs used to be, but you could tell he loved his wife and his brood.

Tyler was the oldest at ten, and by all accounts the quieter, more serious one. Chase—the giver of boogers—was five, and I didn't need confirmation to know he was the loudest and most challenging. Then lastly came Connor, he was three. And while he fit somewhere in the middle of the other two in temperament, he was equally as skilled as Chase in making a mess. Something we witnessed as he dumped the entire box of toys Ryan had picked up all over the floor when he and Mary returned to the living room.

"I'm going to fire up the grill," Blake announced, giving Mary a kiss on the cheek as he walked past. "Ryan, want to join me outside for a beer?"

Ryan rose to his feet, giving my hand a squeeze. "Sounds good to me." He looked around at the boys who had managed to destroy the living room in the few minutes they'd been in it. "Actually, I think *all* the men should join us. Building fire is important men's business."

Three heads snapped up, eyes widening in expectation as they halted the Hunger Games death match they'd been playing on the floor in front of us.

"Are you sure?" Mary looked at Ryan like he had offered to strip naked and run through her suburban street. "That's a lot of people getting close to a flame. It might be a bit of a handful to control."

"Nonsense." Ryan slashed his hand through the air, turning his body to the tiny humans, looming like a giant. "We're going to listen carefully and learn how to roast dinosaur flesh like the cavemen before us."

"We're having dinosaur for dinner?" Chase's eyes got wide, mouth strained open as he sucked in excited breaths.

"Let's go outside with your dad and discuss it." Ryan's head tilted toward the door as all three boys scampered to their feet and ran out to their father.

"Enjoy, ladies." His hand tipped at his head as he walked backward toward the door. "We're going to hunt and gather."

Mary looked she was about to burst into tears with gratitude. And if Ryan ever needed a president for his fan club, I was sure she would fight to the death for the honor.

"Oh my God, he's amazing." She grabbed my hand squeezing it hard. "I mean, I love Blake, but not only is Ryan the hottest man I've ever seen, but he's a-mazing.

Yes, *amazing* was used twice, extra emphasis on the second.

"He's pretty amazing."

Great, now I was saying it. Not like I could argue though, he certainly lived up to the adjective.

"How long have you been dating? When did you meet? Is he always this wonderful?" Questions were rapidly fired in my direction as my brain stalled on the first.

"We're not—" I stopped myself, clearing my throat before I continued. "Not long, it's new. We had friends in common, and yes, he's always wonderful."

I waited to be struck down or for my pants to burst into flames as I perpetuated the lie. I wasn't even sure why I did it, the alternate truth flying out of my mouth like it belonged there. Mocking me.

"Well, honey, you need to put a ring on it," she tut-tutted, her head tipping in the direction of the backyard. "Men like that don't grow on trees. Either snap him up or someone else will."

"Thanks."

I failed to mention he wasn't mine to *snap up*, and I was sure he would find someone to do it promptly and often, the minute I flew home.

"Don't mention it." She smiled, proud like she'd given the secret to eternal life. "Oh and I hope you're okay with burgers and hotdogs? I probably should have asked, but as much as I would love to get fancy, the kids won't eat much else."

Thankfully, Mary left the *me and my need to put a ring on it* conversation behind, her attention now on getting the table set and a wineglass in her hand.

"Burgers and hotdogs are fine. Please don't go to any fuss."

I helped her with both the table and the wine—I could use a drink myself—as we waited for Blake, Ryan and the three cyclones to return with their seared animal flesh to present as their offering.

It was easy to see how different our lives were. While it was true we hadn't been close, it had been no secret she had always harbored dreams of being a fashion designer, and working with some of the big fashion houses. New York had been a dream for her too; the idea of getting out of town was one of the few things we'd had in common. But obviously after the first pregnancy, none of that had happened.

What was really surprising to me was, even though she had some sadness about not following her chosen path, there didn't seem to be any regret. And possibly she was putting on a show for my benefit, but as she spoke about Blake and the boys, she seemed *genuinely* happy. Didn't even seem sad that she'd given up New York and her dreams. Not at all. Instead, she seemed to have embraced the new direction and loved her life with wicked abandon.

"Don't you miss it though? The clothes, the glamour, the idea of living in Manhattan?" I asked, finding the concept of giving up a life's dream just unfathomable. "You'd wanted it for so long, how do you just switch it off and not be resentful?"

I wasn't trying to be an asshole, I just couldn't conceptualize it. Like how—when the dust settled and you woke up to an alternate life you didn't choose—part of you wasn't—even if it were just a tiny bit—bitter.

"Are you kidding? It was a job, Lila." She looked at me like I was the one sprouting crazy talk. "One I can always do later if I want to. If it had been really important to me, I would have found a way to make it work. But in the end, the boys gave me more joy than dressing people on a runway. And have you seen how old those designers are? Maybe when the kids are in school fulltime, I might go back to college, or there's night school and online classes. I made a choice and I'm okay with it. I get to go to work, get paid and when I come home, it's my own time. I'm too happy living life to worry about what might have been."

She sounded so convinced, so positive she was happy knee-deep in testosterone, that I had to wonder if there wasn't a vent some-where pumping out mind-altering drugs into the oxygen source.

Maybe it was possible?

To change your hopes and dreams, and *still* be fulfilled.

Maybe I would adjust too if I had to?

Or maybe those mind-altering drugs were affecting me too.

CHAPTER #16

I HADN'T REALIZED when we'd agreed to dinner we were also signing up for a show.

Each kid took turns screaming, crying or tossing food; our time at the table reminiscent of running a medieval gauntlet where you prayed to make it through unscathed. We weren't so lucky, with Conner—the youngest—standing up on his chair, pulling down his pants and proudly telling us he had a penis.

At least he used the proper word, although I don't think that was any consolation to Mary who was doubly horrified when Chase joined his brother in the show and tell.

We stayed a little longer, the conversation easier when the hellions had left the table to get ready for bed. I talked about my job and life in New York, and Ryan told them about his exciting—and fictional—personal training business. They didn't blink, eating up every word he said with wide-eyed wonder.

But that was exactly what you got with Ryan. He was captivating, magnetic and undeniably awesome. His voice was as enthralling as his beautiful face, topped off with a warm and funny personality and it was easy to be charmed.

Which is why, even though they were exhausted from putting

three overexcited and protesting children to bed—I shit you not, it took almost two hours before they were out for the count—they were disappointed when we left. Our goodbyes at the door met with sadness, even from Blake who I suspected had a serious man-crush on Ryan.

"Don't take this the wrong way." I waved goodbye as we backed out of their drive. "But do you mind if we just cuddle tonight?"

Ryan laughed, tilting his head toward me as we drove away. "It's good birth control, huh? Have to admit, not super interested in sex right now either."

"Oh, thank God." I felt my shoulders easing, the breathing returning to normal. "I didn't want you to think it was you, but if I see another penis tonight I might scream. Clearly by that demonstration, the fascination with that starts early."

"That's because they're awesome. You just need them in the right context," he responded smugly.

Well, at least that was something we could agree on. Context was everything, not that it helped the current state of my libido. Meanwhile, my reproductive organs were cowering in a corner, giving thanks to my mother and those thirty thousand bananas she'd made me condom.

"Is that something you want?" I watched him curiously, a genuine interest in his answer.

"What, to show you my cock?" A cheeky grin spread across his face. "Yeah, I do."

I had totally walked into that one. I rolled my eyes, clarifying what I was asking. "No, to have kids? Do you want kids?"

It was probably too personal a question to ask and not something I probably had a right to know. That was the kind of conversation you shared with your special someone—i.e. a real *girlfriend,* not a friend with benefits—when there was a possibility of the two of you actually having children. But if he was thrown by my question, he didn't show it. Didn't even flinch, with the same relaxed smile on his face as we turned into the driveway of my parents' house.

"Yeah, eventually. Not now, I want to spend a lot of time on the practice, but when the time's right, for sure. Don't you?"

"I haven't really thought about it, to be honest." I shrugged, the possibility that I'd meet someone I'd even want to procreate with felt so far in the future; it had never been given any thought. "I don't know, maybe?"

"Maybe is a good answer." Ryan nodded, satisfied. "Gives you time to think on it later, reevaluate the circumstances." He knotted his fingers into mine, bringing my knuckles to his lips.

"I just . . ." The words sounded almost too selfish to say out loud. "I just don't want to stop being me. Mary gave away everything, her career, her life. I'm not sure I could do that. Does that make me sound like an asshole?"

"No, of course not." He laughed, his thumb rubbing over my knuckles. "Don't freak out."

"I know. I know."

Not sure why I was on the verge of hyperventilating but if I had to guess, it wasn't just the idea of being responsible for another human being. There was something else, something deeper, unnerving me.

"Now let's go inside before your dad assumes we're fucking in the car and comes out with a shotgun." He glanced out of the windshield, eyeing our surroundings. "I'm cool with not having kids right now, but I'd like the choice further down the line."

"You're probably right." I laughed, surprised my dad wasn't already out the door shining the flashlight through the window. "Let's go inside."

DAD—WHO EVEN TWELVE months later was still adjusting to

retirement—was out cold on the couch. He had a big day out fishing and playing cards with a couple of his buddies and had apparently passed out sometime after dinner. His arms were splayed, his legs hanging off the edge while he softly snored.

Mom, on the other hand, was awake, curled up in her favorite chair reading a book with a glass of wine in her hand. It was almost out of a Norman Rockwell painting—well, if he'd been more contemporary—except for the big box of oversized dildos at her feet. Apparently, she'd received a shipment earlier.

So, leaving Mom to her book and her dildos, and dad to his slumber, Ryan and I went to my room. Where we weren't going to have sex. It had been the first time since we'd started that we'd actually stopped.

Instead, we laid in the bed, under the covers, facing each other in the dark.

"We should probably head back to L.A. tomorrow, or Wednesday at the latest. I want to try to get another interview done this week if we can."

There was an echo of disappointment in my voice. I was finally working on a story I was excited about and I was almost dreading going back. Not because of the story per se, but because I knew each day I worked on it would draw our time slowly to a close.

"If that's what you want. We still have the week after, right?" He must have sensed it too, avoiding my end date as his thumb rubbed small circles against my hip. "Besides, Tia and Eric won't be back till the end of the week so we'll have the whole place to ourselves, it would be silly to squander the opportunity."

"What ever will we do?" I asked as my excitement spiked, loving the opportunity to be this close to him and just talk. Work could wait until we got back, I didn't want to ruin the feel-good vibe we had going on with reality.

"Throw a massive party and trash the joint." He laughed,

bringing me in closer and kissing the top of my head.

"You are so full of shit." My fingers pressed against his naked chest pushing against those tight muscles playfully. "You would never do that."

He sighed, pretending to be disappointed. "There's a first time for everything, princess. Maybe I'm just lulling him into a false sense of security."

"Or maybe." I pressed my lips to his chest, the words spoken into his skin. "You're a really good person who wouldn't betray a friend like that. And neither would I."

His fingers brushed through my hair, getting all the way to the ends before taking another pass. It was so relaxing, my body completely at ease as I shuffled snuggly into the crock of his arm.

There were no expectations.

No pressure.

Like we were in a bubble and nothing outside of us mattered. I loved it.

And as much as I loved the hot sex—his body doing things to mine better than any man had—it was possible I loved this more.

We were friends.

Real friends.

And I knew the feelings I was starting to have for him weren't the kind I should be having.

Not for a fling, anyway.

"You still need to take me to meet your family." I sighed, digging in deeper. Hey, it's not like it could get any worse, right? The damage was already done. "And I expect the full Ryan tour as well."

I felt his soft kisses against my temple. "That was the plan. My mom doesn't have dildos though," he chuckled, "but she has a million nick-knacks she's collected from yard sales and antiquing. She's almost positive one of these days she's going to buy a painting for thirty-three cents and it ends up being a Picasso."

I laughed, loving hearing about his mother. "Maybe she will find a Picasso, and then she'll have shown you."

"Oh my God," he gasped, his hand stopping its gentle sweep of my hair. "That's exactly what she said. Maybe getting the two of you together is a bad idea."

We stayed like that for hours.

In the dark.

Just talking.

Sometimes we kissed. Slow and leisurely, letting each part of our mouths make contact as we savored the moments. I couldn't hurry, needing each second to last longer, for each kiss to be a little deeper, and for his touch to linger on my skin for hours.

And if I thought the kissing was amazing, lying beside him was even better. It wasn't sexual, our bodies intertwined for no other reason than to just be together. The heat of his skin against mine as we laid in each other's arms, the strumming of our pulses—all of it a feeling of closeness I'd never experienced.

And just before I closed my eyes, the sound of his steady heart beat pressed against my ear, I knew those feelings I was scared of having, had already happened.

God help me.

I was falling in love with him.

CHAPTER #17

I SLEPT SO soundly.

My body completely shut down as I gave myself to the tranquility of sleep. I didn't think, didn't dream, didn't move—my arms remaining tightly wound around Ryan York's perfect body as I woke from a sleep that was worthy of a fairy tale. Except there were no birds chirping melodic tunes as they circled around my head, because that would be weird.

There was no lingering in bed either. I woke up to his slow and delicious kisses before he chuckled that I was making him hard, shuffling out from between the sheets to go take a shower from the bathroom across the hall.

It would have been easy to slip in there with him. To join him underneath the hot spray and kiss him some more. To feel his hands on my slick skin as I drank him in just a little longer.

But as much as I wanted to—the ache in my body to be close to him almost unbearable—I knew we needed the distance more.

I needed to sort through these feelings—ones that had been growing for some time and I had now just realized—and try to work out how to tell him. Or more to the point, *if* I told him.

So, after he slipped back into my room—small beads of

dampness clinging to his spectacular chest—with a towel slung low around his waist, I performed the impossible task of going to the bathroom alone.

It was there where I finally took a breath, my hand swiping across the steam-covered mirror to reveal my reflection.

We had to stay friends.

No matter what happened after—non-predictably, me going home and this, whatever *this* is ending—we had to still be friends.

I wanted him in my life more than I wanted him in my bed, and I desperately didn't want to lose what we had. What we'd *always* seemed to have, even before we slept together the first time.

"HEY, ARE YOU ready to go?"

Unlike him, I had remembered to bring a change of clothes with me, saving myself from having to parade half naked on the walk back in. There was no thrill in teasing him today, not when I'd only be teasing myself.

"Yep." He watched me brush out my hair while he sat on the edge of the bed. "Where's the tour heading to today?"

"Well, considering the main reason we came here was to see my mother's brothel, I assumed we'd go to The North Star."

I understood the curiosity and the excitement, and I wanted him to see it too. It had been something I shared with so few, but as I'd already shared more with him than I did with most, it felt right for him to see this too. Besides, my mother had worked her ass off to grow her business, while raising herself for the most part, and I was proud of that.

He pulled me closer, his hands wrapping around my waist. "We don't have to, if you don't want to."

"Why wouldn't I want to?" I laughed, his statement making no sense. "You were the one who said," my voice lowered, imitating him. "I *shouldn't deny you.*"

"Yeah, I know. But if you wanted to do something else, we could do that."

I knew avoidance when I saw it, and it was sitting right in front of me.

What I didn't know was why?

"I want to show this to you." My fingers played with his still damp hair. "I know we joked about it at the start, but I trust you with this. So, if you want to see—"

"I want to see."

"Then we'll go." I gave him a quick peck on the lips and grabbed my purse.

We had missed breakfast, with both my parents MIA by the time we'd made it downstairs. So, deciding to have breakfast on the road, Ryan grabbed his keys, and we headed out the door.

The North Star was a couple of streets over from the famous Vegas strip. Nestled among the casino, bars, hotels and strip clubs, was my mom's shining jewel.

It had been in the same location ever since I could remember it, renovated a couple of times with no expense having been spared. Even though most people only spent an hour or two within its walls, my mother wanted it be stylish and elegant—a classy establishment in an oasis of cheap and nasty.

A buzzer needed to be pressed, with armed, large, and scary looking security opening the double reinforced iron doors before you were granted entry.

"Lila." The seven-foot-tall, square-jawed, man-giant popped a smile as he let us in. "Here to see your mom?"

"Hi, Adam." I waved, pulling Ryan inside as the door closed behind us. "This is my friend, Ryan."

Adam eyed Ryan hard, skeptical as he assessed him. He wasn't used to me bringing strangers, especially ones who looked like they could give him a run for his money if he decided to cause a problem.

"It's okay, he's with me. He works in security," I reassured him, trying to diffuse the tension.

Adam's shoulders rolled, giving Ryan a chin tip and a nod of approval. "Hey dude, how's it going?"

"Hey, really good," Ryan responded, looking around fascinated. "Is that door bulletproof?"

I watched Adam's jaw tighten, like he wasn't sure if he should be answering or not. I'd only ever vouched for one other person at The North Star and that had been Tia, and only after knowing her a while. But as my mouth opened, I didn't have any hesitation. "He's one of us, Adam. It's okay."

Ryan looked at me strangely having no idea what those words meant. Especially not to me, and how few times I'd said them. Thankfully, he didn't ask, saving me from telling him more than I was ready to say right now.

Adam grinned, probably pleased someone wanted to talk to him about something other than the girls. "Yep, sure is. Will pretty much hold back anything except a rocket launcher or bazooka." Adam nodded proudly. "You can't be too careful out here. People are drunk or high and most are packing. Plus, if the world goes to shit and there is some kind of uprising, this is the place to be. It's a fortress."

"That's insane." Ryan's palms pressed against the metal, his fingers running along it.

"Windows are all resistant too," Adam continued, spilling his knowledge like a museum tour guide. "Plus, the girls all enter and exit via an undercover garage out back. No one gets in unless they're supposed to be here."

When I said it was my mom's shining jewel, I wasn't kidding. Not only had she sunk a whole heap of money into making the place look good, she went above and beyond to make sure all her girls were safe and respected. Which was probably the reason why so many "working" women begged to work at The North Star. And why despite a million other places men could go in Vegas to scratch that itch, they still rang that buzzer constantly, Mom able to make profit in a city where sex was sold to saturation.

"Well, it was good seeing you, Adam." My arm looped around Ryan's as I pulled him in the direction of the staircase. "We're just going to take a look around."

"Yeah sure, I'll let your mom know you're here." He grabbed the two-way hooked to his belt. "And I know I don't have to remind you to keep away from the closed doors."

I paused, sticking out my tongue and rolling my eyes. "And here I was thinking I could just go busting in on people and asking to join in. Thank God, you set me straight." I fingered waved. "I'll see you on the way out."

"Play nice, Lila," he called after me, laughing. "You know I'm only doing my job."

"I know," I called over my shoulder, pushing Ryan up the stairs.

There was soft music piping through hidden speakers as he climbed the grand wooden staircase. Ryan's eyes moved restlessly, like he was collating information to build a dossier with each step he took.

"This place looks like a fancy hotel." His eyes wide with wonder.

My hip leaned against the banister when I reached the top. "Well, in a way it is, except no one actually sleeps here. We can see a room if you want. There will be some empty ones and it's easy to sneak in."

His arms wrapped around me, leaning into whisper. "Sounds like you're talking from experience."

"I stole the handcuffs, remember?" I batted my lashes, looking at him innocently even though my earlier crime had already been confessed.

A throaty laugh bubbled up his throat as he threw his head back, the sound echoing through the empty hall. "How could I have forgotten? Please." He stood to the side, gesturing with an open hand. "Lead the way, princess."

The rooms were soundproofed so other than the soft orchestral piece still being piped through the air, we couldn't hear a sound as we strolled along the plush hallway.

At the very end were the rooms that weren't used often. My mother liked to keep a few reserved in case some VIPs happened to drop by unexpectedly. The small green light above the door handle indicated the one we'd stopped in front of wasn't in use.

I pushed open the door and flicked on the light switch, the room flooding in illumination until I dimmed it a little. Ryan stepped ahead of me, his hand gripping mine as he pulled me further into the room and closed the door behind us.

The walls were painted a deep red to match the curtains, while in the center of the room was a large bed with pristine white linens.

To the side was a small end table covered with a large ornate leather box, a welcome gift that would make a fruit basket blush. Filled with condoms, lube, and a few other helpful paraphernalia, it looked to be freshly stocked.

"The only other person I've ever brought here is Tia." I took a breath, facing him. "Not because I'm embarrassed or ashamed, but because it's too private. There are parts of me I don't want to share with anyone else."

I don't know why I was telling him. Maybe because I knew my feelings were more than sexual and I wanted him to know. Of course, it would be too obvious to just tell him outright, admit I had feelings for him that he might not reciprocate. So instead, I decided to take the coward's way out, dance around the issue, and hope he followed the line of breadcrumbs to my heart.

"Thank you," he said, pulling me closer as he tilted my chin toward him. "Thank you for sharing it with me."

My heart thumped, hopeful that maybe he felt the same way too as he took my face in his hands and kissed me.

It was soft, teasing, a whisper on my lips. And I loved it. Loved the way it made me feel, my skin humming with the touch of his hands while his mouth gently played against mine.

I didn't want to think anymore. Didn't want to know all the reasons why we couldn't be together. I wanted to be with him and have him love me.

Love me.

Not just for sex, but because there was no one else he wanted to be with. The same way I knew I felt about him.

My body pulled away from his, hesitant as I turned back toward the door and locked it. He looked at me curiously as I turned off the light and we were plunged into darkness.

"What are you doing?" He laughed, his hand reaching for me as he pulled me back toward him. My body hit the wall of muscle and I instantly sagged against him.

"This room is soundproof." My lips pressed against his throat. "Nothing we do or say can be heard outside these walls."

It was the only way I could do this, the only way I could risk exposing my heart.

In the dark.

With no one else to hear me but him.

"Is there something you want to do that you don't want anyone to hear?" He chuckled, his hands moving slowly up my back. "Because I know you're not shy, Lila."

"I'm not shy, Ryan." My lips found their way to his mouth, pressing softly against it. I couldn't rush it, needing to take my time.

"You know you can tell me anything, right?" he asked earnestly, his hands stopping mid sweep. "Whatever it is, you can talk to me about it."

It was like he knew.

Like he sensed I was desperate to tell him something, and he was reassuring me it would be okay.

Can I trust you not to hurt me? I wanted to ask, the words getting stuck in my throat, scared of the rejection, or worse, losing him entirely.

"Kiss me," is what I said instead, wanting to stay in the suspended reality just a little longer. "Just kiss me."

Tell him you love him.

Tell him that you want to be with him.

His kiss was different this time, more desperate, as he pushed me against the wall. Firm muscles pressed against me as he took my mouth, holding me hostage with his weight. I couldn't move, trapped by his body and I loved it.

Loved him.

Loved this.

"I want this." *Forever,* I finished inside my head. My fingers gripped his T-shirt in desperation. "I want you." *Forever,* again I stopped myself, only the first part being spoken out loud.

"Lila," he moaned, hitching my leg up against his hip, allowing his body to settle between the space he'd created. "God, I want you too."

It was a frenzy. Hands and lips tangled as we moved with no road map.

We didn't talk, each breath shared as our mouths stayed fused. The only sound was panting and low moans and the soft smack of our lips.

I reached down between us and felt him hard and ready, my fingers squeezing against him as his cock lengthened.

He pulled back, capturing my hand with his own and holding it against the wall above my head. His body pressing against me as his lips lifted away from mine, the air from his lips coming out in fast, heavy pants.

"Please don't hurt me." I'd said it so softly, I wasn't even sure he'd heard it. The thought that had been on constant repeat in my head finally getting vocalized whether I had wanted it to or not.

Something happened between us in the dark. Like a heavy iron lock engaging in its mechanism, I felt the shift.

Even though our bodies craved each other, this wasn't about sex.

We were too close like this.

Too close.

And I wanted to claw at him and get closer.

He hesitated, not moving as he whispered, "What did you say?"

Panic bubbled inside of me and I had no idea how to answer. I wasn't sure if he genuinely hadn't heard it or he wanted me to repeat it for further embarrassment. And I wasn't sure what his response would be.

"Should we stop? Do you not want this?" Words I didn't want to say came out anyway, because even though I didn't want to give him the choice, I was giving him one.

A chance to stop this, to stop me.

I heard the click of the light, the soft dim glow washing through the room and that was when I saw it.

His eyes.

I saw the conflict, the waring and possibly the regret.

"Lila."

It was an apology. My name, different than the way he'd said it before. And I knew, this had been a mistake.

It was supposed to be sex.

We should never have come here, not together, not like this.

We should have kept it casual, light, without complications, but instead I opened a door I had no idea if either us would walk through.

I gave him one last kiss, arching into him and feeling how hard he was for me.

He wanted my body, my friendship, but not my heart.

"It's okay," I whispered back, desperate not to lose him completely. "Some other time."

"We should probably get out of here, huh?" He kissed my jaw softly, his voice lingering with regret. "Show me the rest of the place?"

"Of course." I forced the smile, pushing down the hurt. "There's so much to see."

I took a breath and centered myself, adjusting the dress I was wearing and giving him a smile. "Wait until you see the fetish rooms, they're a special kind of awesome."

I was hurt but wouldn't allow him to see it.

Besides, if I had anyone to be angry with, that finger should be squarely point at myself.

"Hey." He grabbed my hand, squeezing it.

"Hey, yourself." I squeezed back, calling on all my reserves to sound cheery. I wasn't giving him a chance to tell me he was sorry, that he liked me but that was where it ended. "If you're not going to give me mind-numbing orgasms, we need to move on. You know I have a hard time keeping my hands to myself."

I was positive he was smarter than that. Not buying into my *everything was okay* routine. But he didn't say anything, looking at me cautiously as he unlocked the door.

"I'll give you orgasms later, I promise."

"Yep. I'm going to hold you to that too."

It hurt to smile, the shape of my lips feeling awkward on my face as I pulled open the door.

It would be okay.

It was better this way. I mean, what did I think was going to happen? He'd confessed his love for me, and then what? We both still lived on opposites sides of the country. Neither of us could pick up and move, not unless someone gave up their job. And that was something I'd never ask him to do. And something I wasn't sure I could.

"Thank you." I squeezed his hand as we walked back into the hall, the sound of the soft music eating up the horrible silence.

"Thanks for what?" he asked cautiously, probably wondering if I was going to burst into the tears.

For being honest with me before it was too late and everything was ruined between us.

For not making this weird when I know you don't feel the same way.

For saving us both from a mistake.

"For letting me share this with you."

It was simultaneously a lie and the truth.

I didn't know if I would ever bring someone here again, especially not a man. If I could trust anyone else in the future to not use it against me, and make me feel bad about myself, or to insinuate something derogatory about my mother and my family. Or maybe, even ask if he could get some kind of friend discount.

Ryan wouldn't do those things.

I loved him and trusted him, even if those feelings weren't returned.

And I was glad I got the chance.

"I'm really glad you showed me too." He brought my hands to his lips. "And it's me who should be thanking you."

God, help me, my heart was breaking, but I wouldn't be sad.

It would be okay.

I would get through this.

I would be okay.

CHAPTER #18

WE HAD SPENT more time at The North Star than expected.

My mom had found us wandering the halls and was so excited that she pulled us both in for a group hug and insisted on commandeering the remainder of the tour.

I was grateful in a way, glad for the reprieve, and loved she got a chance to show off something she was so proud of.

We even got to talk to some of the girls, who despite popular belief were not lounging around in lingerie. Yes, they were dressed in figure-hugging clothes that showcased their best assets but not unlike something you might find in a club in New York.

And all of them were so nice. Taking turns to introduce themselves and making small talk, with not one of them being inappropriately friendly toward Ryan.

See, contrary to popular thought, real "whores" don't try to steal other women's men. Sex is a business transaction, and even if they enjoy it, they aren't going to waste their time—and loss of income—seducing a man for sport. They are smarter than that, and hell of a lot more honest than most regular people. I guess that's why I had been more comfortable with them and their children than with outsiders growing up.

"Oh, I'm so glad you came to visit." My mom gave me a hug as we returned to her office. "And Ryan." It was his turn for a hug. "Thank you too."

"It was my pleasure, Jen." He returned her hug. "Thanks for having us, hopefully we'll come back soon."

I didn't want to ruin the mood by correcting him that he probably wouldn't, so instead I just smiled while my mother gave us a parting gift bag. I didn't need to look inside to know it was filled with condoms and lube and other interesting bits and pieces. It was my mother after all.

"Hey, Mom." I shifted on my feet, wondering if I was making the right decision. "I was thinking we might head back tonight. We were going to leave tomorrow anyway, but I really should get back to L.A. and finish my story."

Ryan looked at me, surprised at our apparent change in plans. I hadn't discussed going back tonight and given I had my laptop with me—even though I hadn't even looked at it since we arrived—I could easily work from here.

"Oh, are you sure, honey?" The disappointment in my mom's voice unmistakable. "You know we'd love you to stay longer. I haven't even had a chance to cook for you."

"Mom, you know you don't have to do that." My gratitude mixed with apology. "I promise I'll come back soon, when I'm not working so we can actually spend some quality time." And when I was alone so I wouldn't have to fake my happiness.

She took a deep breath, waving her finger with intent. "Okay, but only if you promise. And Ryan, you're welcome too. Oh, and bring Tia and her new man too, it's been a while since we've had a full house. Last time was when your Grandma June visited with her flying monkeys."

"Mom, Grandma June hasn't visited in years." I laughed, the first *real* laugh since Ryan and I left the room. "And those flying monkeys were her chihuahuas. I'm sure Dad wouldn't be too thrilled about you likening his mother to the wicked witch of the west."

My mother just shrugged, straightening her jacket. "If the shoe fits."

I couldn't argue; my mother wasn't wrong. "Well, we should get back to the house and start packing. Any idea of when Dad will be back? I'd like to say goodbye."

"He should be home already. He only had some morning errands to run." Her brow rose as she gave me a smile. "Maybe *he* can talk you into staying another night."

"We'll see." I gave her another hug before saying our goodbyes.

There were more hugs and goodbyes at the door with Adam shaking hands with Ryan before letting us out. He watched as we walked to the guest parking lot and get inside the car.

"You want to go back tonight?" We'd barely made it inside when Ryan turned to me and asked, "I thought we were going to drive back tomorrow?"

He didn't seem mad, more confused. Not that I blamed him, I hadn't shown any signs of wanting to leave before now. And if the truth were told, I was enjoying being here with him. But I needed to guard my heart, and I couldn't do that here, not when my defenses where down. Not stripped bare. I needed distance.

"I'm just anxious to get back and get the story fleshed out. I have to hand it in by Friday and I need time to go over my notes. Besides traffic—"

"One day isn't going to make a difference in the traffic," he pointed out, starting the ignition as he pulled out onto the main road. "Look," his voice softened, his hand coming to rest on my knee. "If this is about what happened in the room, we should talk about it."

"No, please, please don't think that." I didn't want to talk about it, hell I didn't even want to think about it. And what could be said anyway? "It has nothing to do with that. Nothing happened, I got carried away, that's all." My hand gripped his, my need to touch him at odds with my brain telling me to stop. "It's just *here*, it's easy to get caught up in things. I need to be focused. This is the first chance my editor has ever taken on me, I can't throw it away to have a good time."

It was a good excuse, and one that made sense. And hopefully one he'd understand.

He didn't answer for a while, staring out at the road in front of us. I had no idea what was going on in his mind. None.

"Okay."

"Okay?" The word surprised me, and I had no idea on what he was agreeing to.

"Okay, we'll go back." He shrugged, and we drove the rest of the way in silence.

We didn't talk when we got back to my parents' house either, going upstairs and packing what little needed repacking. It wasn't a lot, both of us done quicker than expected. I think in some way, we didn't want to prolong the inevitable. Things would be easier in L.A., clearer. And I needed to get back there ASAP.

Dad was in the kitchen, doing his best not to kill the spaghetti Bolognese he was attempting to cook for dinner. He'd taken over the cooking duties since his retirement and while he rocked breakfasts, his dinners left a lot to be desired.

"We're going to head back, Dad." I gave him a hug in case the bags in Ryan's hands weren't enough of a clue. "I have a lot of work I need to do but it was great seeing you."

"You're not leaving because of my cooking are you?" He gave me a warning look. "Because we can order out if you want. I'll even let you pick that godawful Chinese place that mocks me when I go in there."

God, I loved my parents. They were such good humans, so loving and honest, even if they were a little crazy.

"I'm not leaving because of your cooking." I gave him another hug, laughing as I shook my head. "And the people at the Chinese place aren't mocking you, Mom speaks Mandarin when she orders, they assume you know it too."

"Yeah, well I don't." He cursed softly, removing the smoking saucepan of burning ground meat from the stove. "For all I know they could be saying they are going to spit in my food."

"They wouldn't do that. But even still, we can't stay."

"Okay, sweetheart." He returned the hug before looking at Ryan. "Drive safe. Don't speed and no funny business."

"We'll be fine." I gave him a kiss before returning to the doorway. "I'll call when we reach L.A."

Ryan dropped the bags at his feet and walked over and shook my dad's hand. "Thanks for having us in your home. It's an honor to meet you."

"Yeah, well you know I have guns, so you make sure you keep honor on your mind and we'll have no problems." His hand gripped Ryan's firmly as a tight smile spread across his lips.

"Dad."

"Sorry, pumpkin." He shook his head, not sounding anywhere close to sorry. "But a man has to say what a man has to say."

"Well, I guess we'll go now." I looped my arm around Ryan's and pulled him toward the door. "I'll see you soon, I promise."

"You better, young lady," he warned as he followed us out to the front door. "You know that I hate New York, but if I have to come there, I will."

"You won't." I waved as Ryan tossed our bags into the back and slipped into the driver's seat. "I'll be back."

With my father looking on, I climbed into the car and shut the door. I knew the minute we left things would be different. Not just between Ryan and me, but different in general. They had to be.

"You ready?" Ryan asked, putting the Hummer in gear as his hands curled around the steering wheel.

"Yep, good to go." I clicked in my seat belt and relaxed into the seat. "Let's get back."

The drive back to L.A. was a stark difference to the drive up. Where we had been chatting and laughing, feeding food to each other, now we were sitting in relative silence, the stereo and the noise from the engine as our soundtrack.

"This is bullshit." Ryan was the first one to crack. "Is this the way it's going to be now? We ignore each other?"

My fingers knotted in my lap, my knuckles turning white. I hated this. "I'm sorry." I wasn't sure exactly what I was apologizing for, maybe for putting us in this stupid situation in the first place.

I wanted to rewind a few days, to go back to the way things were. To shore up the wall around my heart a little more, so the feelings didn't get through. And more than anything, I wanted to be honest with him.

"I freaked out, I'm just not used to bringing people home and things got confusing. I need to concentrate on the story. I can't blow my first big chance."

I didn't look at him, keeping my eyes glued to the road in front of us. It was more than just the view, it was what I had to do. Keep pushing forward and not looking back.

"You don't ever have to freak out because of me, ever, Lila." He reached across and grabbed my hand. "I'm glad you trusted me and I'm glad you let me in. But I don't want things turning to shit because of it."

So many words.

So many things I didn't understand.

"You're right." I took the coward's way out, wanting just to drop it. "Nothing should change."

Because that's what he wanted, right? For us to continue having fun, no strings attached? Be friends and nothing more?

"I'm sorry if things got weird, it won't happen again." And it wouldn't. I would move on and as soon as I got back to New York, things would go back to normal.

"C'mon, princess. You know I like weird." He laughed, his hand still on my knee. "I'm just saying don't shut me out."

"I won't, I promise."

It was hard saying those words, mostly because I didn't know if they were true. I wanted them to be true, to know the feeling would pass and I would look back at these past weeks and laugh. That in time, I'd find someone else who would make me feel this way. That I wouldn't be in love with someone who had become one of my closest friends.

But for now, I didn't know. And until the time that I did, I was going to fake it. What other choice did I have?

"Hey, you want to get some food?" If faking it was the plan, now would be a good time to start. "I'll feed you fries."

"Now you're talking." He turned to me and smiled. "You shuffling our driving schedule meant we were unprepared. No drinks, no snacks. I'll overlook it this one time, Lila, but as copilot, these things are your responsibility."

"Completely unforgiveable." I laughed, the happiness I was trying to feel completely empty. "But I will make it up to you with plenty of treats when you pull over."

He nodded, slashing his hand through the air like making a royal decree. "I will allow this. We may proceed."

After that, it got easier. We stopped and got burgers and other snacks and fell into a reasonable sense of normal. I made sure I talked enough, laughed enough and was engaged enough—all the *enoughs* that would help me continue my ruse.

AT SOME POINT I must have fallen asleep. The passing blur of lights and the rock of the car proved too much for my already well-established fatigue and I blinked for a second too long.

"Huh?" My eyes opened as I felt the cool night air hit my face, feeling movement even though my body was still. "What the fuck?"

"Shhh, I'm carrying you. Either tell me how big and strong I am or go back to sleep." Ryan chuckled, the soft vibrations of his chest pressing against my cheek. "My personal recommendation is big and strong. Maybe tell me how impressed you are too."

One of my eyelids cracked open, the security lighting for Eric's house throwing a harsh glow over the backyard. We had arrived and I hadn't even realized we stopped, Ryan carrying me almost to his front door before I'd noticed.

"You're so big and strong." I let myself absorb him, enjoying the fuzziness where I knew this wasn't a dream but I didn't want to deal with reality either. "And manly. Very manly."

"I know when I'm being mocked, princess." I felt myself shift in his arms. "Let me get this door unlocked."

My arms looped around his neck, giving him a kiss. "You can put me down, I think I'll be able to walk the rest of the way."

"Nope." His arms repositioned as I heard keys getting shoved into a lock. "I have my pride and you'll stay right where you are."

The door was unlocked and opened, using his foot to kick it closed when we'd walked through. Our journey continued until we got to his room, where he laid me down on his mattress, my body cushioned by its pillowy surface.

"I'm going to grab our bags out of the car." His lips brushed gently against mine. "Any special requests for when I get back?"

"Nope, just sleep." I curled over onto my side and watched as he walked away.

I could do this.

Be with him knowing there wouldn't be anything more.

I wanted this.

If this was all he had to give me.

And I refused to cry or tear myself apart because I was dumb enough to fall in love with someone who didn't love me.

With careless hands I stripped myself naked, kicking off my shoes and dumping everything onto the floor beside the bed. I'd managed to crawl underneath the covers by the time he'd made it back, my warm body against the coolness of his cotton sheets.

I watched as the smile spread across his lips as he walked slowly to the bed, his eyes on me as he casually removed his clothes, one painstaking item at a time.

His arms moved around me, shuffling me closer to his body. I loved the way I fit against him, our bodies molding into one.

"You want to sleep? Or you want something else?" His breath was hot against my ear, as his hands traveled lower.

"Not sleep." I twisted around to face him. "I want you."

"Good."

His head dipped as his lips kissed my collarbone, his tongue running up the length of my neck before our mouths met. It was slow and deliberate, taking his time with each pass of his lips.

I wanted to touch him, feel him inside of me, but I wouldn't rush it. I wanted to savor every second, like this was our last time. Because soon, I knew it would be.

He moved on top of me, his heavy weight against me as my back arched off the mattress, giving myself to him as my palms pressed against his chest. "More."

He kissed me, full on the lips, as his hands explored. Fingers ghosted over my skin just barely making contact until they reached the peak of my nipple.

"I love these." His hand closed around my breast, giving it a squeeze before his mouth gave it some attention. His lips closed around my peak, sucking and licking it as I felt myself get wetter.

"I mean." His head lifted, moving to the other. "I *really* love these."

That word I'd been desperate to hear was tossed away without a second thought and I tried not to let it cut me deeper than it already did. Knowing that to me it meant something entirely different as I closed my eyes and tried to lose myself in the moment. I wouldn't be sad, or regret this, even if he didn't feel what I did.

The attention he'd been lavishing on one my breasts was transferred to the other and then back again, taking his time to tease me with his hands and his mouth until I felt I might go insane.

"Ryan."

I was writhing underneath him, wanting more, needing more.

"The way you say my name." He growled against my skin. "Drives me freaking insane, Lila."

Unable to take it any longer, my hand slithered down my body between us. I felt him hard and ready, his thick erection pressing against my thigh just out of reach.

"Let me touch you." I wiggled, trying to reposition myself while his mouth was still on me. "I want to feel you."

A deep rumble traveled up this throat as he smiled against my skin, his body twisting to the side. My fingers curled around him, wrapping around as much of his girth as I could with one hand as I started to stroke slow.

"Mmmm." His lips moved, freeing my breast as they moved down my belly. "I love this too."

He didn't give me time to prepare, his mouth closing around my pussy as my back lifted off the mattress. His tongue lapped against my clit as my grip around him tightened.

Moving required too much concentration at this point, my brain scrambled as he slid in a finger and then a second, my body taking him in as his mouth continued its assault.

"Me." The word spilled across my lips, my body completely

liquid beneath him. "Me too."

I wasn't sure if he knew what I meant. Lord, I didn't even know if I knew what I meant.

He moved again, allowing me to keep his cock still in my hands as he twisted himself around and brought himself closer to me.

With strong even strokes I glided over the length of him, feeling him harden even more as I took him between my lips.

His body stiffened, a moan vibrating at my core as I drew him deeper in, sucking him hard as I pumped with my hand. Meanwhile, I had my own body rebellion happening. My body tingled as he lapped at me with his tongue, his fingers continued their wild frenzy inside of me.

I was on fire.

A crazy need burning out of control as I cried out, the orgasm taking hold of me completely unaware as my mouth stretched around his cock in a muffled scream.

He slowed, kissing the apex of my thighs as I continued to shudder. The small convulsions traveling through me like waves, squeezing his fingers as he pulled them out.

His hips jerked, pushing gently into my mouth and then out as he cursed out my name. "Fuck, Lila. I need to be in you." His voice so strained and raw, I barely recognized it.

I didn't have time to protest, his strength overpowering me as he pulled out from between my lips and steadied me with his weight. "I said I need to be inside of you."

He stared at me, his eyes wild as breaths tore out of him hard and out of control.

"Then stop talking about it." My hands released him, stretching out my limbs across the mattress as my voice lowered. "I want to feel you come."

His lips slammed against mine as one of his hands reached blindly at his night stand, the lamp we hadn't bothered to turn on went flying as he yanked out the drawer right off its tracks. He grabbed a condom, tossing the drawer to the floor as he tore open the packet with his teeth.

One of his hands wrapped around the base of his cock while the other covered himself with the latex. My assistance not required as he looked at me with hungry eyes, ready for me.

"Kiss me."

I didn't have to ask again, his skin pressed against mine as our lips met in a frenzy in the middle. His cock bobbed against my core, teasing against my wet seam as he thrust against me, my legs opening wider.

"Yes." I arched, my hips tilting as I felt him enter me, filling me completely in one hard and desperate thrust.

He stopped, letting me absorb him for a second before he started a slow rock, his body dictating the tempo.

I tilted and rocked and twisted against him, wanting more as he picked up speed.

More.

More.

Deeper.

Harder.

Faster.

It didn't seem enough as my fingers clawed at his back, my legs wrapping around his waist.

A strangled groan vibrated up his throat as my teeth bit into his shoulder, my body exploding as I came hard against him. I felt my nails dig into him as I held myself still, his finish coming a second after mine, our bodies shaking out of control.

I couldn't talk; my body and voice paralyzed as heated breaths pushed past my lips in uneven bursts. My skin damp and my hair a mess as my arms and legs stayed wrapped around him. His strong arms kept me steady as tiny shivers continued to rock me.

"I had wanted that to be slow," he murmured against my neck. "So much for that plan."

"Yeah, guess we both got carried away."

In more ways than one.

Slowly, he lowered me back onto the bed with our bodies slowly becoming untangled.

"I guess we did." He kissed my shoulder, rolling onto his side. "Guess I need to do better next time."

My eyes closed just breathing in the moment. "We both do."

And for once, I wasn't talking about the sex.

CHAPTER #19

WE WOKE UP late.

My face was pressed to his chest while our bodies were wrapped in tangled sheets.

Neither of us seemed in any hurry to move so we stayed in bed and kissed and touched, and had slow and passionate sex. And when it was finally time to get up, he pulled me into the shower with him where he washed my hair. The soapy water made our skin slick while the steam curtained around us in an illusion of seclusion.

We dressed, we ate, I worked.

It was remarkable how easily it became a routine, me sitting at his kitchen table on my laptop while he checked emails and fielded calls through the day.

And then at night we'd go to bed.

I was careful, allowing him to have my body and enjoying his, while remembering to guard my heart.

It sounded terrible when I said it like that, but it wasn't. I could have stopped it any time. Told him I wasn't interested, moving back into the main house and go back to flirting without sex—but I didn't.

Because I would rather have him in a limited capacity than

not at all. And because I knew the minute I got on the plane it would end anyway.

It was a purgatory I enjoyed, and part of me hated myself a little bit for it.

Not because I felt used—because I didn't.

And not because sleeping with him when I knew there was no future made me feel like a whore—because it didn't.

But because I wanted to not want him—and I couldn't.

And so passed the rest of the week. Both of us continuing on the merry-go-round that would eventually end, and neither one of us making a move to stop it.

"Your phone," Ryan mumbled against my forehead, his lips pressed against my temple. "I've ignored it the last three times, but someone is trying to get a hold of you pretty badly."

I lifted my head from his shoulder, hating the morning sun. I'd never been a morning person, and today was no exception.

My hand blindly stretched to the nightstand, reaching out to get the obnoxious piece of shit. While I kept my head on Ryan's shoulder, his fingers combing roughly through my hair as I mumbled obscenities under my breath.

"Hello." My voice was croaky, rough like I'd been gargling chainsaws the night before. "Hello." I tried again, after clearing my throat.

"Lila, I need you on a plane today." The voice boomed through the phone. "And I want you to call me the minute you hit JFK. I'll get a car to bring you straight to the office, don't worry if it's late, not like anyone around here sleeps anyway."

"Dick?" I pulled the phone away from my ear, checking the caller ID to make sure it was the regular asshole that was my boss and not some new asshole who was trying to enter the fold. My dance card was full asshole wise, I wasn't looking at add another.

"It's *Richard*." His displeasure felt through the line without the need to see his face. "So pack up and ship out, I need you back in town A-SAP."

"Wait, did something happen?" I sat up in bed, now more alert than when I'd picked up the phone. "I wasn't supposed to be back until next week. I submitted my draft last night. It should be in your inbox with plenty of time for editing for Sunday's edition."

My personal life might have left a lot to be desired, but in my professional life I was on fire. I may have been using it as a distraction—working my ass off because that was one area where shit made sense—but I knew I had turned in a quality draft. Everything had been cross-referenced, care used to make sure there was nothing to tie the story to any of the contributing sources, and it was interesting.

"That's what this is about. I read it. This is some of your best work, Lila."

I almost dropped the freaking phone as I once again checked the caller ID. Yep, still Dick. *This must be a dream or something*; I was tempted to pinch myself just to be sure.

"What did you say?" Great, now I sounded like an idiot, negating his earlier statement about my work.

Ryan shot me a questioning look, eyes focusing on me and the phone as I continued with my call.

"Don't let it go to your head. Worst thing a journalist can do is believe their own press, you should know better." His classic sunny disposition shined through, confirming it was my editor and not some imposter trying to play a joke on me.

"I wasn't, Dick, I'm just surprised."

"For Christ's sake, Lila. It's Richard." He cursed, sucking in a deep breath in and out before continuing. "Don't make me regret this before I've even given it to you."

"Regret what?" I still had no idea and not sure if it was wise to ask. Dick already disliked me, and I wasn't sure—without being able to see his face and gauge the situation firsthand—how far I could push it.

"Your last installment caused quite a stir, readers are loving playing pin the quote on the celebrity. It's like a real life game of Clue. So I want you in town for Sunday's edition and I want to discuss strategy. We get the same kind of feedback we did from last week and this series will be the last you see of the art's section."

"Wait, you're *firing* me?" I almost screamed into the phone.

Sure, I should have probably stopped calling him Dick, but telling me I did a great job only to hand me my walking orders was a low blow, even for him.

He cursed again, clearly annoyed or exasperated or maybe a little of both. "Seriously, can you just get on a damn plane and get back to New York? I'm not firing you—I'm offering you a promotion. Which I'm starting to reconsider since you're already giving me an aneurism and you haven't even accepted the position."

"I'm booking my flight now." I leapt out of bed and scrambled to my laptop, the thing not turning on fast enough. "I will be there as soon as I can and I promise nothing is going to stop me from getting on that plane."

"Good, that's what I want to hear. I figured by now you'd be bored with L.A. anyway. Those bastards are too happy for my liking, I don't trust them."

I didn't bother telling him I didn't hate L.A. or that I wasn't bored or that I hadn't been anxious to get back. Instead, I booked the first reasonable—I still had to pack and get to the airport— flight out of LAX to JFK and gave him the details. He grumbled something that resembled a goodbye and then told me a town car would be waiting at the airport for my arrival. Oh, and once again reminded me not to get a big head.

"You going to tell Tia, or you want me to do it?"

I hadn't heard him approach, convinced he was still in bed

where I'd left him when I made my mad scramble to my laptop. He'd pulled on pair of sweat pants, running his hand through his beautiful mussed up hair.

"Errr. I should do it. I know she'll be disappointed. I thought we'd have more time."

Tia wasn't the only one who would be disappointed. Even knowing this was the ultimate end game, I was still unprepared. My new forced timetable throwing my world into a spin.

"So good news, I take it? I'm assuming you aren't getting fired." He looked happy, no animosity on his face as he smiled. If he was annoyed by the early morning wake-up call, he wasn't showing it.

"No, not fired. Dick, um, my editor, really liked my story." I fumbled around the sentence, not feeling as excited about it as I had a few minutes ago. "He's offering me a promotion."

His hands rubbed up and down my arms, making my skin tingle as he looked at me. "And that was what you wanted, right?"

"Yes, it's what I wanted." Or at least what I thought I wanted.

Why the hell wasn't I ecstatic about it? Jumping off the furniture and thanking my lucky stars I was finally getting the recognition I had been fighting for. I should be happy. Why couldn't I make myself happy?

"So, we should be celebrating." He pulled me into his arms, kissing the top of my head. "How much time have we got?"

For all the happiness I didn't have, Ryan had it in spades. He looked downright euphoric, smiling from ear to ear as he asked about my fucking flight plans. Had he been biding his time? Ready to shove me out the door at the first opportunity? I knew he wasn't in love with me, but I thought we'd had some kind of connection. Something, anything, which didn't make him fucking delighted to wave goodbye to me.

"Um." My throat tightened, and for the first time I wanted to cry. "I have about four hours."

"Great, gives us time to get you packed and to the airport. Traffic is killer on Friday. Who am I kidding, airport traffic is *always* killer. Why don't you get into the shower and I'll get us some breakfast. Any preferences?"

Was he seriously asking me what I wanted to eat? Words. He had said a whole bunch of words and not one of them showed any regret or sadness that I was leaving. Sure, I didn't expect for him to get down on his knees and beg me to stay. But how could I be the only one who was hurting? It was like I had meant nothing. Literally, nothing. Like a light bulb that could easily be replaced.

Do. Not. Cry. Lila.

I summoned every single ounce of the internal will I had as I pushed down the urge to cry. I was better than that. I was stronger than that. I would not allow myself to fall apart. Not in front of him.

"I'm not that hungry." I forced the smile, turning away from him as I headed toward the shower. "I'll grab something at the airport. Thanks anyway."

My hand waved from behind as I power walked to his bathroom.

Even with the privacy of the water and the steam, I didn't allow myself to fall apart. Robotically washing my hair and my body as I went through the motions. Then drying and dressing when I got out.

Muscle memory was a wonderful thing, allowing me to get ready and packed all while my brain was disengaged. I didn't notice myself leaving Ryan's cottage and going back into the main house. Was on complete autopilot as I grabbed my suitcase and tossed things in. And was mostly oblivious when I carried my things down the stairs and left them in a neat stack right by the door.

It was only when I reached for my phone to call Tia that my soul seemed to reenter my body—the disconnect, no longer possible.

"Hey," Tia answered after the first ring. "Up early, aren't you? Still in Vegas or back in L.A.?"

I hated it had been days since we last spoke, how she even had to ask. But it was easier not to talk about what was going on—my messy feelings—with anyone, even her.

"Hey, I'm in L.A., we got back a few days ago." I moved to the couch, grateful Ryan had remained in the cottage and given me some much-needed privacy. "Actually, that's kind of why I'm calling, I need to go back to New York."

"What?" Tia's voice rose an octave, and I didn't need to see her face to know she was concerned. "Why are you leaving? Lila, if something happened you know you need to tell me. Your dad didn't try and shoot him, did he?"

"No," I laughed, glad we had at least dodged that bullet. "My parents were great. But Dick called this morning and I've been summoned."

It didn't feel great leaving out the details about Vegas. How wonderful it had been initially, and then how it turned to shit in the private room of my mother's brothel. And then we'd both ignored it, sweeping it under the carpet because I was too much of a coward to deal. So instead, I put a pin in all of that, leaving it for another day when I had the time and the emotional fortitude to talk about it. So instead I told her the reason I had to leave.

"I hate your boss." I could hear her disappointment, and part of me felt responsible. "Doesn't he know we haven't had proper girl time?"

"I doubt he cares, to be honest." I sighed, knowing Dick would probably relish in our pain and suffering. That was the kind of man he was. "But if it's any consolation, I'm sure it is killing him to be giving me a promotion. He's probably still swallowing Tums."

Tia squealed, the phone needing to be removed from my ear before I went deaf. "Oh my God! You got a promotion? What?

Where? When? This is so exciting. We need to celebrate. As soon as we're both together in the same city. Lots of drinks." Her words came out in a jumbled excited rush.

Not that Tia would ever have made me feel bad—that was one thing I knew I wouldn't have to worry about—but it didn't make me feel great about leaving so soon.

"Lots of drinks, I promise." My heart squeezed, at that moment missing her more than ever. "I'm sorry, Tia. The next time we'll have more time."

"Stop, you came for work. I knew that. It's not like you came to hang out by the pool and blew me off for someone else. It's fine. Besides, I left with Eric. So at the very least our shortage of time spent is at least half my responsibility."

"You are such a good person, Tia Monroe." The lump in my throat made it harder for me to swallow. "I swear I don't know what I would do without you in my life."

"Lila, this isn't an *I'm dying* speech, is it?" Her voice full of caution. "Like for real, I can handle you going back to New York for work. But if you have some hideous life-threatening disease and have like three days to live, you better tell me."

"I'm not dying." I shook my head, the giggle bubbling in my throat. She was probably the only person in the world who could make me laugh at a time like this. "Relax. Just sentimental."

"Well, stop that, I'm the emotional one," she fired back, an edge in her voice but zero malice. "You are the responsible one, we need to stick to our roles or the world will go to shit."

She was right, we did need to stick to our roles and I had not stuck to mine.

"Okay, I should go." I looked at my bags, still back beside the door and no sign of Ryan. "Ryan's going to give me a ride to the airport. I'll message you when I land at JFK. Dick is sending a car and everything. I might record the whole thing so I can enjoy it later, I'm positive I'll probably be overwhelmed by the shock."

"Yes, call me. And then you can tell me all about what's going on with you and Ryan," she added, not letting me off the hook as easy as I thought. "Don't think I'm going to let that slide, I know you've had a little romance happening, which is totally fine, but I want details. And if he was an asshole, I will hurt him. My loyalty is with you."

I laughed, not doubting for a second that all five-foot-four of her would take Ryan on if she'd thought he'd hurt me. She was good like that, loyal and fearless. Pity it was me who needed the ass kicking, not him.

"No need for the posse, Tia. Ryan's been fine. And we'll talk about it later, I promise. Give my love to Eric and see you soon."

We said our goodbyes, with my promise to call her tomorrow with more news. I opened the front door to see Ryan had brought his Hummer around. The big black SUV parked in front very efficiently.

Wow, he *really* couldn't wait to get rid of me. No point prolonging this any longer than I had to.

"You ready to go?" He startled me, his voice coming from behind.

I spun around and saw he was standing next to my bags, leaning up against the wall.

"Yeah, yes. I think I have everything." I adjusted my hair, securing a non-existent strand behind my ear as I watched him grab my bags. "We should go."

He moved closer, stopping when he got to the doorway I was standing in like he wanted to say something. Maybe it was to tell me goodbye or have a safe trip. Maybe it was to tell me to lose his number when I got home.

In the end he said nothing, his eyes meeting mine for what was probably a second but felt like an eternity before his gaze flicked to his waiting car and then he walked out.

Ironically, I was almost grateful. Glad there wasn't going to be some huge confrontation or longwinded farewell. I wasn't sure I could take it to be honest, so he was probably doing us both a huge favor.

So, with my smile fixed and comforted in the fact that in a few hours I'd have some much-needed distance, I climbed into the car and waited till he joined me and started the ignition.

I'd never had a problem making conversation. I could talk to anyone about virtually anything, and as a journalist, it was a skill that had served me well. It also proved to be an asset as I relaxed into the seat and started my mouth moving. The conversation was about absolutely nothing. The colder weather they'd been experiencing in New York, the state of the traffic and then when general topics started to run dry I pulled out some trivia, pointing out that we had an Ethiopian goat herder to thank for discovering coffee.

It was actually quite ridiculous, and to anyone it was obvious that I was being unreasonably chatty. But I didn't care, the ride easier with the sound of my voice in the air rather than silence.

I almost cheered in relief when we arrived at the airport, my throat starting to hurt even though I still hadn't run out of things to say.

"Thanks for the ride, Ryan." I turned, my hand giving his arm a squeeze. "And thank you so much for all the help with the story. I know some of those people only agreed because of you. So, thanks."

Shit, how many times did I thank him? I tried to stop my mouth from thanking him again.

"Um. Yeah. I'll call."

Not much better, I internally cringed, willing myself to hurry up and get out of the car.

"Lila." He grabbed my arm, stopping me from opening the

door. "I liked working with you, and I really liked spending time with you."

Was this some gentle brush off, my exit interview? *Thanks, you've been great, better luck with the next guy.* Or, *we had fun. I like you, just not enough.*

"Okay." I prayed I didn't look as confused as I felt, his words uncharacteristically odd. "Well, I'm glad." Awkward pause. "Thanks."

Shit, I said it again.

I was going to sew my mouth shut if I thanked him one more time.

Which was what I was thinking about.

When he kissed me.

It had taken me by complete surprise, my mind needing a minute to work out what the hell was going on. My body hadn't had the same problem. My stupid mouth opened for him giving him the all clear to do whatever the hell he wanted as his lips pressed against mine. His tongue stroked mine, each kiss a series of desperate pulls and deep full-mouthed caresses as his hand wrapped around my neck holding me in place.

He needn't have bothered; I wasn't going anywhere.

A traitorous moan escaped, my hands curling around his T-shirt as I gave in, hating myself for wanting it and angry at myself for not stopping it.

One more time wouldn't hurt, right? It was just a kiss, and a goodbye one at that. It's not like I hadn't been sleeping with him just hours ago, I'd make the clean break the minute I left the car.

A horn blared, the sound making me jump and reminding me I was making out in the middle of the drop off zone at LAX. Not my finest moment. And yet, I couldn't make myself regret it. Because I was an idiot who thrived on personal torture.

"I should go. I don't want to miss my flight. TSA is a nightmare." The words came out in a rush as I opened the door and pushed my body outside. You know, before I offered him a parting blowjob or something.

I'd barely got my feet on the pavement when he was out too, pulling my bags from the back and setting them down on the curb beside me.

Well . . . then. So much for a clean and easy exit.

"Let me know when you land." He waited, his eyes not giving me any kind of reprieve.

"Yep. Sure." Tight smile. "Thanks."

Goddamn it!

"Okay, goodbye." I turned, not waiting for a response as I concentrated on wheeling my suitcase as fast as I could.

I could feel his eyes on me, watching as I disappeared into the terminal, my body only relaxing when I'd passed through those glass doors.

His kiss was still on my lips, the smell of his cologne still lingering as I walked to the counter and checked in my luggage.

The bored airline staff member greeted me and embarked on a conversation I had no context with even though I was a participant. She could have asked if I was smuggling thirty Ks of Columbian cocaine for a South American drug cartel and I would have smiled and I told her that I was. Thankfully, I think she was just asking for my destination and my ID so I was saved from ending up in a back-room getting a cavity search with a latex glove wearing TSA agent.

All good things.

My good fortune continued as I was able to make it through security unscathed, arriving at my gate with enough time to stare out the window.

Sometimes the worst thing in the world was to be early. To give yourself time to sit, think and analyze.

It had been just over two weeks and so much had changed.

Ironic how I'd been so bored, craving some kind of adventure and right now, I just wanted to get back to New York and find some familiarity.

Be careful what you wish for and all that.

Life had a warped sense of humor.

CHAPTER 20

IT WAS LATE by the time I'd arrived at the office.

The flight, the time change—that transcontinental flight just never got any easier.

And there was Dick. Sipping his probably forty-fifth coffee, with a scowl that would give Jeffrey Dahmer the heebie jeebies.

"This is good work, Callan." He leaned back in his chair reading over my copy as I sat and watched on. "Not the best I've seen, but the best from you."

"All these compliments." I fanned myself, pretending to be embarrassed. "Please, Dick. I'm trying to remain humble here."

"*Richard*." His eyes narrowed, the twin rows of coffee stained teeth locking at the jaw. "And I'm gonna let that slide because you didn't shit the bed on the story, not to mention you get some sick sense of enjoyment out of my reaction, and I'm not in the mood to give you the pleasure."

I was tempted to push it further like I usually did, but my heart wasn't in it. I was tired and off my game, and not in the mood to antagonize Dick purely for sport.

Maybe this was what growing up felt like.

God, I wasn't sure I was ready for that.

"So, I still have one more week, right?"

The original pitch had been for a three part series. I hadn't interviewed Eric yet but assumed I could do that by phone. And I had enough in my notes to flesh out another week even without any more additional material.

"Yep, after this one runs, I want you to wrap it for next week." The leather from his office chair creaked as he tented his fingers in front of him. "Then I'm moving Tiffany into your position and you're shipping out."

I had been dancing around the promotion offer since I'd walked in. Not because I wasn't excited—it was probably the only thing that *did* excite me at this point—but because Dick could just as easily change his mind. And until I had a contract and a remuneration offer, I wasn't getting my hopes up. Dealt with too much disappointment as it was in the last few hours, didn't need to be borrowing more.

"So, what did you have in mind?" I asked, caution in my voice as I lowered one foot down at a time in what felt like a sea of landmines.

"Well, that was what I wanted to talk to you about." A smile that lacked warmth spread across his lips. "If you were me, where would you put yourself?"

It was like a riddle, similarly like something a serial killer would send for you to decipher before his victim died in the state forest tied to a tree.

And it wasn't because Dick hadn't made up his mind, and my new posting was open to debate. No, he wanted to see if I oversold or undersold myself. And mostly, because he enjoyed making people wriggle around like a worm on a hook.

"Well." I cleared my throat, sitting up a little straighter in my chair. At least this gave me something other than Ryan to concentrate on, so for that I was grateful. "I know we have an opening for a political correspondent."

"The White House?" His brows shot up into his receding hairline. "You want to go work in Washington?"

It was a long shot, and I knew there wasn't a chance I'd get it. And hell, I wasn't even sure I wanted it. D.C. was a nightmare, with Satan worshippers being more trustworthy than politicians. But it wasn't a question of ability. And that's what Dick wanted to know, if I had the guts to swim with the sharks while there was blood in the water.

But I wasn't running away, it had *nothing* to do with the fact working in D.C. would minimize my chances of seeing Ryan again. It was purely for my occupational growth, to further my career . . . and all that jazz.

"I have a good edge and people talk to me," I pointed out, the story that had sparked the promotion in the first place, an illustration of that. "Plus, analytically you know I'm strong."

"You weren't a political science major," he deadpanned, clearly not even entertaining the idea.

"So, neither are at least half the delegates currently serving on the Hill," I argued. "I have enough to get me through, and I'm a fast learner. Besides, I can read, what I don't know I will research."

"I'm not sending you to The White House." The wave of his hand dismissed it. "But I *am* sending you to Washington." His fingers stroked his chin.

"Oh?" I asked, trying to cover up my shock. After all, I had suggested going to fucking D.C. only a few minutes ago, acting all surprised wasn't a good look.

"I'm pulling you from your desk. You're going to be my special assignment reporter. I want in-depth interviews, expansions on headlines with a human element. But don't give me emotion without facts, I want balance."

"A special assignment reporter?" I repeated like an idiot, the words not really making sense.

"Yep, you said it yourself. People talk to you. I want the story *behind* the story." He gave me what could be my first ever genuine smile. "Senator Jacob is retiring in two weeks. The official line is he's going to enjoy his golden years or some other bullshit, but his exit seems rather hastily convenient. Those bastards at the Washington Post haven't got the jump yet, find out why."

There was no need to read between the lines; Dick was making it pretty clear what he wanted. "You want to find out if he has a mistress, or if his wife is involved in an inappropriate property deal, or if the GOP found out he likes to wear women's lingerie."

"He wears women's lingerie?" Dick's head snapped up, smile completely gone.

"Not that I know, I was assuming. He looks like the kind who would." I shrugged.

Not sure what it said about me that I thought most sixty-five-year-old conservative white guys always had something freaky in their back pocket. At least, that was their general MO at The North Star.

"Just make sure it's not gossip. I want facts." Dick picked up the coffee cup, the contents no doubt cold by now. "And if the reason is all above board, and he really does just want to enjoy a four o'clock dinner and a round of golf, give me a feel-good piece about his service to the country and all that." He waved his cup around, the implication loud and clear.

"Great."

So, basically look for skeletons and if I found none, turn his resume into a glowing account for everyone to *oh* and *ah* over.

"Hey, are you up for this?" He shot me a pointed look. "The only reason I'm even suggesting it is because of what you were able to do with those movie stars. But if you don't have the stomach for it, you can stay in the art's section."

Was he kidding?

I'd rather grab a knife from the kitchenette and perform hara-kiri than stay in the art's section. It might not be the big leagues yet but it gave me accountability and the opportunity to actually *report*.

"Yes, I'm up for this." I met his eyes, making it clear this was not beyond me. "I want this."

"Good." He nodded his head, seeming to bask in self-satisfaction. "Clear out your desk, from now on you'll work remotely. Just make sure you get me the story, turn in on time and we'll be fine. Stacey will set you up with a travel account but until then keep all your receipts. Oh, and Lila." He eyed me hard. "Do not make me regret this."

"You won't."

It wasn't just a promise to him, it was a promise to myself.

One positive about Dick was that once he was done with you, he didn't like to linger. He wanted you out of his space so he could go on syphoning the souls of small children and kicking puppies, or whatever he did in his spare time.

So, with a grunt and a dismissive chin tip, I took my cue and left his office. On my way out I packed up what little personal items I had at my desk—working in a cubical meant it was sparse of personal items anyway—and took a cab ride home to my neglected apartment in Brooklyn.

Being home didn't offer me the same comfort it usually did. It felt empty, almost lonely, which was ridiculous since I'd always preferred to live alone. I used to love the solitude, the space to do what I wanted and not have to compromise. But as I dragged my suitcase to my bedroom, I would have given anything for a friendly face.

Ignoring my lack of motivation and general moodiness, I forced myself into the shower where I turned the water up to skin-peeling hot. I pretended it was my way of adjusting to the cooler New York climate when really I just wanted to feel something other than the emptiness. It helped a little, and I didn't end up needing a skin graft, so all in all, I took it as a win.

I flopped dramatically on my bed, my body making an unsatisfying thump on the mattress as I peeled off the towel and crawled into my bed, my still damp skin sticking to the cold sheets. I didn't care, scooching down further under the covers as I fingered the glass on my phone.

I was *not* going to call.

When I'd left L.A. I had promised to let two people know when I safely arrived. With Tia, the obligatory *I'm home and I'm fine* sent the minute I touched down at JFK. She responded, glad to have heard from me and made me commit to a call in the morning. No problem at all. I was excited to tell her about my new promotion and my parole from a desk and the art's section.

But the other person who had requested notification on my *flight status*, had *not* been contacted.

It was childish not to text.

What I should have done is send a four-letter word—here—and been done with it. Instead, I ignored him, feeling he hadn't deserved my message so I wasn't giving it. Besides, why did he even care? Unless it was to make sure I had actually left so he could resume with his harem of suitors or whatever he'd done before me. Yes, that was probably it. He just wanted to make sure I hadn't changed my mind and came waltzing back in while he was trying to close the deal with someone else.

God, I was jealous.

Irrationally and stupidly jealous over a man I was never officially dating and who had made it clear was not interested in a relationship with me.

This was a new level of stupidity.

And yet, I couldn't stop.

My gut churned in knots as I imagined him kissing them.

Having sex with them.

Holding them.

GAH!

I needed to stop.

I had never obsessed over a man, and I wasn't about to start now. He was done, finished, in the past, and the best way to move on was to forget him. Besides, who knew when we'd see each other again? With any luck it would be months away when I was completely over him and his stupid ass gorgeous face.

And his horribly sexy body.

And his grotesquely humorous personality too.

All of it banished to the abyss that was my newly formed black heart.

Man, I really sucked at this.

If I wasn't even convincing myself, there was no way I could convince anyone else.

My body flopped restlessly on the mattress, tossing my phone to the other side of the bed so I wouldn't be tempted. Instead I glared at it, sending it subliminal angry messages I wanted to text. All of them ending with a very eloquent, *fuck you, Ryan York.*

And it was exactly those words that had been on my mind as I dried my eyes of my unwanted tears and I fell asleep.

IT WAS IRONIC that the phone I had successfully ignored last night was what woke me in the morning. Or maybe it was afternoon, who cared? It wasn't like I had to be anywhere important.

"Hello." I pulled the phone into my comforter cocoon, I wasn't ready to face the day just yet, so regardless of who was on the other end of the line they weren't going to be making me.

"Lila."

It was the grotesquely beautiful, appallingly sexy and horrendously perfect asshat I'd been trying to avoid.

Nice.

"What do you want, Ryan? I'm sleeping."

It was too early to be nice and I hadn't had any coffee.

"You sound awake to me."

"No, this is just an altered state." I kept my eyes shut tight, my voice coming out muffled. "The minute I hang up I will return to REM sleep where I will ride my magic unicorn into the sunset. And I believe in unicorns, Ryan. So by that definition, I am not awake."

He caught me by surprise so my defenses were down which left sarcasm as my best option. Less chance of me saying something stupid like *why don't you love me* that way.

"You sound weird, like you're under water or something." He paused. "And why didn't let me know you landed?"

"Oops, slipped my mind. I was tired. Sorry." Spoiler alert. I was not sorry. "And I'm in bed. Sleeping."

"I like you sleepy, maybe I'll call you every morning." He chuckled, his sexy voice doing its thing even from miles away. *I hated his voice.* "We can talk about unicorns and sunsets and you can lie about forgetting to message me."

"I wasn't lying." My eyes slammed open, trying to keep my tone level so I didn't sound so defensive. "I was tired."

"Okay, you were tired. Let's go with that."

"That would be because it was the truth."

"Of course it is." He didn't sound convinced, the sarcasm dripping from every word. "So, how did your meeting go with your boss?"

While his earlier words had been skeptical, the latter sounded sincere, the soft tone of his voice easing me into a sense of calm.

"Good." I took a breath, my mouth kicking into automatic

without thinking. "I need to finish the last submission for the series and then I need to make travel plans."

"Is this about your promotion?"

"Yeah, I'm going to D.C."

Damn him, I was supposed to be mad, I wasn't supposed to be telling him information.

Be mad, damn it.

"Covering a story?" he asked when I didn't elaborate.

Do not say a word. Do *not* say a word.

"Mm-hmm." I clamped my lips shut, not offering anything.

"Mmmm, sounds riveting." Only when he made those noises they sounded sexy.

Like we should be having phone sex.

Which we weren't.

Why did he make it so hard to focus?

"Look, I'm sorry I forgot to text or call," I huffed into the phone, my emotions completely scattered. "The meeting with Dick went late and all I wanted to do was have a shower and climb into bed."

And that was the truth, the whole truth, so help me God!

"Lila."

I'd never wanted to change my name as desperately as I did at that moment. I wanted him to just stop saying it. Hating the way it sounded when he did, and hating how much I liked it.

"Anyway," I interrupted, not giving him a chance to repeat it or say something else I didn't want to hear. "Isn't it like stupidly early in L.A.? Shouldn't *you* be sleeping?"

"I had some things that needed to be taken care of." *Yeah, I'll bet.* "I'll grab a nap later."

Wow, his night had been so eventful, he even needed a nap.

How nice for him.

"Well, then both of us need to sleep." It slipped out before I had a chance to stop it.

"Yep, we do."

Why did he make it sound like a dirty suggestion?

I was too tired for this game, not ready to go back to the flirting innuendo we used to enjoy. I just needed a day or two, some time to get my mind right. I just needed . . .

"Ryan, what is it you want from me?" I sighed, mentally and emotionally exhausted.

"Be honest, Lila. Did you *really* forget to call?"

You know what? He wanted honest, then he could have fucking honest. I was going to give him so much *honest* he choked on it.

"Fine, I didn't forget." Unable to stop myself as the words tumbled out in a heated rush. "I didn't want to talk to you. I was annoyed. Annoyed at you and annoyed at myself. And I know you wanted to keep things the way they were."

"What?" He had the nerve to sound surprised.

"Please don't interrupt, just listen." I figured if I didn't say it now then I was totally going to lose my nerve. "I know things were just supposed to be casual between us, and honestly, I wasn't going to push for anything more. I know it wasn't like that for you. And I'll admit." I swallowed, finding it difficult to say the words I'd been dying to say. "Maybe I got caught up in the moment and felt something more. But I promise you, I would have dealt with that."

Maybe not right away, but I would have found a way.

"But *you* were so freaking glad to be rid of me. Couldn't drive me to the airport fast enough. And then that kiss? What the hell was that? You can't just play with my emotions, Ryan. That isn't fair." I petered out, saying more than I'd intended as we sat there in silence.

So much for not causing drama. And worst of all, I couldn't stop.

This was exactly why I'd resisted sleeping with him in the first place. I knew I'd get attached. My aversion to one-night stands had been for a reason, I lacked the capacity for them. And if anything good came of this mess, it was the confirmation of that.

"You thought . . . I was trying to get rid of you?" He had the decency to sound surprised. Almost shocked. He may have decided his acting days were behind him, but he still had the skills.

Man, I was stupid.

So. So. So. Stupid.

"Kind of hard to think anything else." I closed my eyes, feeling comforted he wasn't in front of me right now. "Anyway, it doesn't matter. What's done is done and all that shit. So, let's just move on and accept it worked out for the best."

Yeah, *that* was going to happen. More likely we'd avoid each other until some random arbitrary amount of time where we pretended it never happened. And hopefully then, fall into some kind of regular friendship.

No more flirting.

No more laughing.

And definitely, no more kissing.

"So, you're just going to accept your version of events." The surprise was gone, and in its place what sounded like . . . annoyance?

"What *other* version is there?" I know I didn't imagine him pushing me out of the door with a smile on his face. Or the pitiful look of apology when we were in that room. Because both those times felt soul crushingly real to me.

"Okay."

One word.

He didn't argue, didn't try to offer an alternative, or even counter with some anger of his own.

I half expected him to tell me *see ya later*, and thank his lucky stars I was two thousand and eight hundred or so miles away.

But *okay?*

"Okay, what? What, okay?" I all but demanded, scrambling to interrupt its meaning.

Damn, he was good at this. When the phone call had started, I assumed I had the upper hand. Laying it on the line, telling him what a dick he was—well, not *really* but I wasn't going to get hung up on the technicality—and now I was feeling confused and defensive like *I* was the one who needed to apologize.

"Nothing, I was agreeing with you. Isn't that what you wanted?"

There was nothing in his voice to even give me a hint on what he was thinking. But make no mistake, men like Ryan just didn't *agree*. This was part of some kind of diabolical plan or something.

"Umm." Words failed me as I scrambled for something to say. "Sure, yeah. It's what I wanted."

What was I even saying?

I didn't want any of this, especially not the part about being confused.

"I should go. I have lots of work to do." I added quickly, "I'll call you." I cringed, the reflex response not what I'd meant to say.

"Okay then." Seriously, he was okay-ing me again? "Talk soon, bye."

That was it.

The call ended, me not having a chance to say goodbye as I stared at the phone wondering what the hell just happened.

Was there some kind of resolution in there somewhere I missed? Because it sure as shit didn't feel like it. I was hoping to feel relieved—the weight lifted off my shoulders—but *that* didn't happen.

Puzzled, and still mainly confused, I dialed Tia, ignoring it was probably too early in the morning to make a non-emergency call.

"Hello?" Her voice husky from sleep, answered on the second ring. "Lila?"

I shuffled out of my comforter cocoon, suddenly feeling more alert. "Hey, so I know it's early but I needed to talk to someone. And sorry to say, sweet cheeks, but you drew the short straw."

There was some murmuring on the line and some shuffling of sheets, and then what sounded like a kiss. "You know I'm here anytime. Just give me a second."

More shuffling, and then the sound of a door closing.

"Now, tell me everything."

I hadn't meant to spill but the minute she'd given me permission it all came tumbling out.

Ryan.

Falling in love with him.

And everything before, in between and after.

It wasn't pretty, but I was honest. And as much as I wanted to blame him, initially it hadn't been *his* fault. I should have been honest sooner, so he had the opportunity to set me straight. Maybe, I should have just been honest with myself.

"God, I'm a mess." I smothered my face into the pillow, trying to drown out the loud and repeating thoughts echoing in my head. "I keep flipping from sad to mad and then annoyed and then disappointed and then back to sad again. I don't even know what the hell I'm *supposed* to be feeling."

"Oh, Lila. I'm sorry." There was a long audible breath. "You feel however you need to feel, even if it changes minute to minute."

Great, now I was bringing us both down.

"I'm sorry." Guilt flared in me, which was just another emotion to add to an already overflowing heap. "It's early, and I should have—"

"Stop." Tia refused to let me finish. "You did exactly what you were supposed to do, and that was call me. Of course, now we need to decide on how we're going to seek retribution."

I didn't doubt for a minute she was serious. Ready to go with whatever plans of revenge I plotted with no questions asked, even if he was her boyfriend's best friend.

"Let's lay off the retribution just for a little while." After all, I wasn't sure what I wanted. Hurting him wouldn't necessarily make me feel better. "No going rogue either, Tia." The explicit directive needed if I didn't want some side vengeance delivered courtesy of my best friend.

"Fine," Tia sighed, "I won't *do* anything. As for the evil looks I'm going to shoot him, I've got no control over that."

"Evil looks are acceptable," I chuckled, imagining Ryan having to fend off some pretty heated glares. "And then when he asks if there is anything wrong, you can just tell him everything is *okay*."

Maybe then he would see how infuriating that word could be. And maybe then he'd shed some light on what he meant when he'd said it to me.

"Is that code for something? You want me to tell him every-thing is *okay*?" Tia reaffirmed, her confusion justified considering she didn't know the context.

"When I finally confronted him about how it made me feel, he *okay*-ed me."

"Hmmm." I could almost hear her mental cogs clicking over. "Like an angry *okay* or a sad *okay*?"

"Like a passive *okay*, no real emotion." I shrugged, not being able to offer anything helpful. "Like just an okay."

"O-kay."

"Ugh, not you too." I laughed. "New rule, no one is allowed to say that word."

"Now that I'm not allowed to say it, I really want to."

"Yeah, me too." I pulled the phone away from my ear, the time displayed wince worthy. It was only seven a.m., which meant it was still ridiculous o'clock for her. "I should probably let you go get some more sleep while you can. Thanks for talking to me,

Tia. It helped a lot."

"Please." The mention of sleep making her yawn. "The amount of times you've talked me off a ledge, I think you are more than past due. And I'm glad it helped. I'll call you later." Adding a sleepy goodbye before ending the call.

Well, if nothing else, at least I wasn't so sad any more. That was something to be thankful for. And I was being honest when I said talking about everything with Tia had been helpful.

I had been keeping my feelings bottled up for so long I think that had been part of my problem. That, and I hadn't had to deal with heartbreak in a really long time.

Ugh, being an adult was hard. Maybe it could wait a few more hours.

CHAPTER #21

I FARED BETTER waking up the second time.

There were no obscure *okays* via phone call, and the added sleep improved my mood a little. I was still a long way from singing about rainbows and dancing in the streets, but then that had never really been my jam anyway.

Still, I was determined I wasn't going to think about *him,* at least not for today.

So, sending a reassuring message to Tia, telling her I was in fact doing fine, I set up my laptop and started to write.

It felt good to focus on something I could control, flicking through my notepad and composing my article. All the other stuff just didn't matter. And before I'd given my mind time to wander, it was the afternoon, and I had skipped both breakfast and lunch.

There had been coffee of course, but as my stomach started to rumble, it became obvious that my body was not happy to be surviving on caffeine alone. Bodies were funny like that; eventually you needed to feed them.

And taking my own advice, I reached for the phone to order Chinese. Yes, I was predictable, sue me. But they delivered and while I wasn't crying under my comforter anymore, my appearance wasn't fit for public consumption either. Going to bed with wet hair hadn't been my smartest move.

It was just as I was about to dial, order my usual of special fried rice with chicken from *Cheng's* when my eyes caught on the very next number listed on my contacts.

Chris.

Big, jock, polo-wearing, sports writer, Chris. Who had tried to woo me with a date at the football game he was covering. Hey, at least he'd been honest. And, if I'd chosen *him* instead of Ryan for my foray into casual sex, then I wouldn't be in my current mess.

Ugh, I had done so well not thinking about him, and now I was. No, it was just a passive thought because I needed to analyze the current situation, which was about Chris. So, while not ideal, was allowed under the circumstance.

And as I continued the train of thought—about Chris, I was not fixating on Ryan—I came to the realization that maybe I should give him a call.

Chris, I meant. Definitely not Ryan.

The chances of me being interested in him romantically were almost non-existent. Actually given my current mood, I would say they were even less than that. Which, while I wasn't a mathematician, I had a fairly good idea that meant that seeing him wasn't going to send me head first into another inappropriate attraction.

Instead, it would be safe. Translation: more than likely boring. But because I no longer worked at the office anymore, I wouldn't have to deal with the uncomfortable confrontations in the elevator when I no longer returned his calls. Plus, I'd committed to calling him when I returned from L.A., so if nothing else, manners dictated I needed to. And since I was currently standing in my apartment in Brooklyn, I'd assume this qualified as me being back.

So, putting off my special fried rice with chicken for just a few minutes longer—it was still happening, there wasn't a chance

I was missing out on Chinese food—I pushed my shoulders back and dialed.

Each second it took to connect made me anxious as I fought the urge to hang up and forget the whole thing. And I was just about to chalk it up to a bad idea when the phone stopped ringing.

"Lila?"

The noise in the background made it hard to hear.

Shit.

It was a Saturday evening, and he was probably on a date or something, I really hadn't thought this through.

"Umm. Hi." I tried not to sound like an airhead whose shoe size was higher than her IQ.

"Hi, yourself." He laughed, his voice unlike mine, at total ease. "How was L.A.? I assume you're back."

"Yeah, I got in late last night. L.A. was . . . er . . . fine." Seriously, the bumbling around like an idiot routine was getting old. "It was productive, I achieved a lot," I added, not sure whether my promotion was public knowledge and if nothing else, that had been a positive to come out of the trip.

"Well, that's great. Hang on a second." I heard muffled noises like he had covered the phone with his hand. "Hey, I'm back. Sorry."

"No, no. I got caught up with work and didn't realize the time." *Or that because it was a Saturday, you would probably be out somewhere sharing a beer and some nachos with a girl called Becky with nice hair.* I didn't even care he was possibly on a date. I just didn't want to be the reason he blew off some other girl. "I can give you a call some other time."

"It's fine, Lila, really. I'm just at a bar with some friends. Watching a game."

"I thought football was on Sundays?"

"College, Syracuse is playing." There was a roar behind him. "They just scored."

"Great." At least someone was. "So, anyway, I just thought if you want to go out and have dinner sometime, that might be fun."

I hated myself.

Not because I was asking him out on a date.

But because my request lacked the confidence and seduction skills required so I didn't sound desperate. The last thing I wanted Chris to think was that I was a sure thing, or that I was sitting around in a pair of yoga pants, looking forward to an exciting dinner of Chinese food even if it were true.

"Dinner sounds good, how about tonight?"

See, he knew. Like a sniffer dog at the airport, he'd discovered my lack of social life like a bag full of blow.

"I have plans tonight." Besides the obvious—not wanting to have him think I was waiting around for his dinner invitation—I wasn't getting out of my yoga pants for anyone. "What about tomorrow night? Around seven?"

"I've got a game tomorrow. Hey, you could come?"

Great, we were back to *that* again.

"What about Monday? We could do something then, you know not deal with the rush of the weekend."

"I have a game Monday night too."

Are you kidding me? Was there a football game every single night of the week? How did this guy ever get laid? I guess he had the looks thing going for him, it probably compensated for the lack of quality time he got to spend with dates. Unless those dates were happy sitting at the fifty-yard line watching men in tight pants slap each other's asses. Huh, maybe going to a game wasn't such a bad idea?

"What about Tuesday?" I prayed the NFL had at least one day off, surely players had families they wanted to see at least once a week.

"Yep, Tuesday is good. I'll be driving back from New England, but I'll be back by four."

"Great, I'll text you the details."

"I'm looking forward to it. Talk soon."

So that was that.

I'd successfully scheduled a date and I was going to forget all about *what's his name* and all his stupid *okays*. Funnily enough, the promise of a date didn't have me feeling as pleased as I thought I would be.

At least I had a few days to psyche myself up for it.

FOR THREE DAYS I'd been in a panic.

Not because of work, I had thrown myself into that so completely I'd already finished my next article that wasn't due for another three days. So at least the fire under my ass had been good for something.

No, the feeling of impending doom I was experiencing was over my looming dinner commitment with Chris, and the feeling of I-can't-do-this which had been bubbling in me since I woke up this morning.

All those reasons I had for going out and *getting back on the horse* or whatever lame ass excuse I'd told myself, were bullshit.

I did not want to do this.

At all.

I tried to talk myself into it. Tell myself it wasn't a date, that it was just two people going out to eat. And everyone needed to eat, right? It was a basic human function. So we—Chris and I— would just be performing that basic, life-saving function together. Side by side, like teammates. Spurring each other on, making sure neither one of us was malnourished. It was really more of a public service than a date when you really thought about it. We were almost heroes.

"Ugh," I flopped onto my mattress, my arms and legs rag-dolling either side of me. I was supposed to meet him in three hours and had yet to find enough motivation to get dressed.

Instead, I rolled onto my side and stared at my phone, deciding on whether I was going to be *that* girl who was going to call and cancel.

Ryan hadn't called.

Not that I'd expected him to because we'd said everything that needed to be said. Fine, so maybe I *did* expect him to call, or *hoped* he would. Because I was a masochist and failing in my quest to forget him.

Which meant going on this stupid date was an even worse idea than I first thought. I was essentially using Chris. Taking advantage of the square-jawed, slightly narcissistic, man-child, who still dressed like he shopped at the GAP. And not for any of those reasons either. It was because I knew going into it there wasn't a chance anything was going to happen.

Just the thought of kissing him made me want to dry heave. And by anyone's standards, he was attractive, so my response was not because of external factors.

I kept telling myself he wouldn't care, that he probably wasn't even interested in anything other than getting me naked, which just made my stomach roll again.

I hated it, and right now I hated me too. That I had somehow talked myself into this mess, I was better than that.

So, while sending Chris a text and citing a fictional family emergency or a non-existent mishap was tempting, he deserved better than a cancelation via phone.

No, what I would do is go meet him as planned, tell him I was actually in love with someone else, and thank him for his time. Like an adult.

And if he still needed me to make sure his caloric intake was sufficient, I would do that. After all, we still had to eat, and I hadn't left my apartment in days. I was pretty sure my neighbors thought I was having a not-so-secret affair with the Chinese food delivery guy as well.

Shower.

I flopped onto my stomach as I eyed the bathroom with serious intent. All I had to do was harness the will to move off the mattress and start the process.

"Damn you, Ryan York," I cursed out loud as I hauled myself off the bed.

It was now or never.

The shower had made me feel marginally better and putting on makeup helped too. I made the effort even though it wasn't a date, because making myself look grotesque and hideous so he ran away screaming was cheating. Yes, I'd considered it, but we had decided I was going to be an adult so I was doing that.

Plus, there was a chance he would hightail it out of there the minute I clarified the intentions of my non-date—who breaks up with someone they aren't even dating yet?—so I wanted to look good for my Chinese food delivery man. If the neighbors were going to talk, might as well make it interesting.

I was pretty sure the tight black dress and killer heels were overkill, but it made me feel more confident so I ignored the potential mixed messages it might send. Sometimes a dress is just a dress.

Sadly, while I was feeling good and looking better, my time management skills had been a little too efficient. It meant I was ready a whole hour early, which left me to sit on my bed and ponder until it was time to go.

Which I did.

While Chris had offered to pick me up, I thought it was better to meet him there. Always have an exit strategy, and because I didn't want to give him any additional personal information.

And because I was already dealing with a decent level of didn't-want-to-go, I decided to avoid going into Manhattan on a Tuesday night. Instead I'd chosen a quiet bar in Brooklyn, ironically called Sayonara. It was either going to be a good omen or incredibly tacky, but I was hoping for more of the first.

Rather than stay in my apartment and stare at the walls that could use a fresh coat of paint, I decided it would be wise to head to Sayonara early and perhaps have a few drinks while I waited. It was a good plan, and if nothing else, a cocktail or two would help loosen me up.

A quick cab ride later and I was in the small, but relatively classy, establishment whose décor looked nothing like its oriental name implied.

I sat at the bar making sure I had a good view of the door and ordered a martini.

Or two.

They were smooth—an appreciative nod given to the bartender—and it gave me something to do in the hour before he arrived. Which, with the help of those couple of martinis, had passed a lot quicker at the bar than the few at my apartment.

"Hey." I felt a hand press along my back. "You look great."

My strategic vantage point hadn't been so great with Chris entering from a side door, and I'd missed his grand entrance. Not that it mattered; I was on my third martini and had stopped looking half an hour ago.

"Hi." I swiveled around on my stool, giving him a bright smile. "Thank you."

My eyes traveled up his tall muscular body, wondering if post-alcohol it might have a more favorable reaction, but no, my libido had hit the snooze button.

He was dressed in freshly ironed chinos, the crease down the middle of the leg razor sharp, with a pair of light brown loafers and a pale blue—yep, you guessed it—polo shirt underneath a sports coat. I wasn't sure whether I should offer him a drink or ask him when we were taking the yacht out to Cape Cod.

"Drink?" I held up mine, inviting him to take a seat. "I have a table booked for eight but thought we could sit here for a while and have a drink at the bar."

And had I not started already—consuming a few before he'd arrived—I might have cared how impersonal it all sounded. No light touches on his arm, no telling him how good he looked, no declarations of how glad I was he made it.

Instead I watched as he lowered himself onto the stool beside me and ordered a Budweiser all while staring at my cleavage.

Big mistake on the dress.

"So, how was the drive?" It was my attempt at small talk and not acting like a total bitch. "New England, right?"

"Yeah, it was good. Game was brutal." His eyebrows lifted as he once again looked at my boobs. "You should have come with me. I had a great hotel room."

So, maybe I didn't feel so bad after all. Considering he had yet to look at my eyes, even without the hotel room statement, his intentions were fairly clear.

"Yeah, I hate football. All sports, really." I took a sip of my drink, the contents of the glass not anywhere near strong enough. "But thanks anyway."

"Don't mention it." His hand was once again on my back, his hot breath uninvited in my air. "And I think you could learn to love football if you had someone to explain it to you. A real man could do that for you."

"Whoa, hold up."

I was all for being polite, and even willing to wait until he had his beer before I launched into my it's-not-you-it's-me speech. But he was trying to tell me that the reason I didn't like something was because I hadn't had a man explain it to me? No. Just. No.

"Chris," I swirled the stem of the glass in my hand, attempting a smile. "We don't know each other very well, so I'm going to ignore your last comment. But I'm going to let you in on a little hint. When a girl says she's not interested in something, ninety-nine percent of the time, you can take her at her word. It isn't because she hasn't had a man show her the way. I mean, seriously? *A real man?*" I laughed, the statement so absurd I had to repeat it myself. "Do lines like that actually work?"

"Well, yeah. Most of the time."

He looked surprised, either by the fact I had called him on his bullshit or that I hadn't fallen headfirst into his lap. I could tell the brush-off wasn't something he was used to, so subtly wasn't the way to go.

"So, let me ask you this. When you asked me out," I nodded, hoping he was following along with me, "did you think about anything other than sleeping with me?"

He rubbed his neck uncomfortably, taking a mouthful of the beer that had thankfully arrived. "I—I." Another swallow. "Isn't this the kind of thing we're supposed to talk about later?"

"Let's skip ahead. Pretend we've shared a wonderful bottle of wine and finished our tasty dinner."

He held his hand up, seemingly confused. "What kind of wine, I really don't like reds."

"Fine, it was white."

"Did we eat steak? Because that's what I was planning on ordering and if that was what I ate, I would have to drink beer."

Help me, Lord. Please. If you're up there, just let the guy follow along with the hypothetical so we could get through this in one piece.

"Chris, the food or the drink doesn't matter. You're missing the point. We're skipping ahead, *that* part has already happened.

It is no longer important."

"Does this mean we're not ordering steak and beer?"

No one could be this stupid.

He was a journalist. Some college at some point had to have given this man a degree.

And yet, here we were.

"No, we're not. This is where you tell me, you," I pointed to him, making sure there was no confusion, "were only interested in sex. And yeah, it sounds bad but at least you're honest with me. And then I," my pointer spun around, now directed at me, "tell you I was actually just using you to get over a guy I was in love with."

It was messier than I wanted it to be, the words harsher than the gentler letdown I had planned. But I'd been provoked, and I didn't think dancing around the issue was going to help me, or my cause.

I glanced up at him, trying to read the emotions on his face as the words I'd said were absorbed, the impact of them yet to be realized.

He looked at me, meeting my eyes—probably for the first time since I walked in—and took a deep breath. I felt terrible, not because I had told him the truth but because of my delivery. He wasn't a bad guy even if he had the seduction skills of a caveman.

"Oral sex."

"What?" I narrowed my eyes, wondering if I'd blacked out during part of the conversation. You know, the part where saying *oral sex* would have made sense.

He cleared his throat, shifting in his seat a little. "I wanted oral as well, not just regular sex." His eyes dropped to my mouth. "Your lips look like they'd feel nice."

I picked up my almost-empty martini glass, going back and recalculating how many I'd consumed. It had been three, right? I hoped I hadn't accidently ordered a couple of extras that had slipped from my memory and now I was dealing with clouded judgment and questionable sobriety.

"Did you hear what I said?" I leaned forward, a little worried for both of us. "Not the *you* part, obviously you have that down. Me, why I'm here."

"Some guy broke your heart." He shrugged, like it was no big deal. "I'm happy being the revenge fuck. Hell, I'll even do it in front of him if it helps."

OH. MY. GOD.

Here I'd been worried about letting him down easy when he'd been concerned about the distinction between regular sex and oral sex. Oh, and was fine with me being in love with someone else. Hell, he probably welcomed it, happy our sexual exploits weren't going to get tied up with expectations of a relationship.

"Wow." My mouth not capable of much more as my mind processed.

"Yeah and you know what, Lila." His finger grazed along my arm, as his smile widened. "I'm really glad we had this talk. I knew you were beautiful, but I had no idea you were this cool. So, now we've gotten that all straightened out, did you actually want to skip the steak and go straight to the sex? Or did you want to have some dinner first? I'm cool with either, so lady's choice."

Err . . . what?

Was he serious? No one was that clueless surely, or maybe he'd worn a polo that had been too tight around the neck and cut off blood flow to his brain.

I threw my head back and laughed. A real laugh, where my face contorted into wrinkles, my eyes wept, and it was difficult to breathe.

"Oh, Chris." I was able to choke the words out, still struggling to talk. "We're not going to do either, but I am so glad we had this talk."

I grabbed my purse and got ready to leave. All the worry about telling him, it was like a weight had been lifted off my shoulders. I mean, I still had the unrequited love thing happening, and I knew it would be a long time before I'd ever give my heart to someone but at least that was one less thing. There had to be a positive.

"So, you're going to go?" Chris grabbed my arm, stopping me from walking out. "But I said I was cool with whatever." He was so confused it was almost adorable.

"And I thank you for being so cool." I smiled at him warmly, giving him a playful knock in the bicep. "Which means you will be cool with me leaving."

My fingers gave him a wave as I sayonara-ed my way out of there.

Some blonde a few seats over had already slid into my spot by the time I'd reached the door. I was almost positive they were going to skip the steak, and good for both of them. It seemed Chris might get his blowjob after all, just not from me.

CHAPTER #22

I WAS JUST getting out of the cab when I noticed a dark SUV parked near my apartment. The shiny Escalade with tinted windows gave no clues as to who was hiding within, while my heartbeat hammered inside my chest, contemplating the possibility.

"Princess."

My fist, clasped into a ball, swung out in front of me as I spun around, the word "shit" spewing from my lips as he caught my hand before it made contact.

"Nice right hook." He held my arm, that stupid charming smile on his face. "You need to work on the swing though. I saw it coming the minute you flinched."

I had been so focused on the car and its potential occupant, I hadn't bothered to notice that Ryan York was literally behind me.

Thank God his objective wasn't to kidnap me, I'd have been bundled in the trunk before I'd realized what had happened. I blamed the three martinis. And those stupid sexy big black cars he seemed to drive.

"What are you doing here?" I stared, letting the accusations fly while my hand was still mid swing. He hadn't let it go yet, and I hadn't asked. It was sick that, despite being mad at him, I wanted him to keep touching me. Even for reasons that weren't sexual.

He lowered our hands, but kept a firm grip on me. "I was in the neighborhood. You going to try and hit me again?" The edges of his lips twitched, teasing me as he slowly unwrapped his fingers.

I almost took another swing, fluctuating between wanting to irrationally hurt him because I had been hurting and wanting to give him a reason to restrain me. I never said either of those reasons were good reasons.

My hands landed on my hips—my effort to keep them to myself—knowing he was full of shit. "You just *happened* to be in Brooklyn when you *live* in L.A.?" Yeah, I wasn't buying it.

"Sure," Ryan rolled his eyes, his arms failing dramatically. "It's fine if the movie star does it, but when I do it, it's suspect."

He accurately recalled the time Eric had done a similar thing to Tia. And I may or may not have thought him following her out here was incredibly romantic. But Eric loved Tia, so it was different.

"I'd call it more stalking than suspect but let's not get hung up on the technicalities." I held my ground, the hurt I still felt stopping me from throwing myself in his arms and kissing him. "So, other than being creepy, was there any other reason you're out here?"

"Oh, I'm not here to be creepy, princess." He took a step closer and grinned. "I'm here to prove a point."

I laughed, it was the second time tonight the giggles had gotten the better of me and I had no hope of controlling them.

"Prove a point?" I asked, wondering what *point* particular he was hoping to prove. "You know we have these things called phones?" I held my finger and thumb up to my ear in an idiotic visual display. Seriously, I hoped my neighbors weren't peeking out their windows. "You could have called me if you had such a burning desire to *prove a point.*"

Fine, so maybe I was bitter. Honestly, I was mad as hell and not all of that had been directed at him. A healthy dose of that was on my doorstep, even though he had apparently reappeared, anxious to prove a motherfucking point.

He couldn't have shown up, crawling on his knees and telling me how miserable he'd been without me. Or even, hugging me close to that amazing body of his and confessing how much he missed me. No, he did none of those things because that Ryan only existed in fantasyland. In real life, he was more concerned with being right than wanting me.

Was it too late to try to hit him again? This time I wouldn't miss.

"Can we go upstairs, or do you want to do this on the street?" He eyed the front door of my building. "Either way, I'm saying what I came here to say."

"Such drama." I rolled my eyes as I turned and unlocked the door. "We're going upstairs only because this is a nice neighborhood and I want to spare all these people your shenanigans," I called over my shoulder as I yanked open the door.

He laughed as he followed; his heavy footsteps close behind mine. "You are so considerate."

Not wanting to have to look at him—and more to the point, not trusting myself in the smaller space—I opted to take the stairs rather than the elevator as I stomped up to the fourth floor where I lived. But as I continued climbing with the adrenaline pumping through my veins, two thoughts kept tumbling in my mind.

One, why couldn't he have kissed me on the street, goddamn it? As wrong as it was to want it, I hated he came all this way just to *talk*. And two, if I'd been so worried about being in an elevator with him, how in the hell was I going to survive being with him in my apartment?

Still, it was too late now, the last landing cleared as I stopped in front of my front door. He wasn't the only one capable of drama either, my own flare displayed as I shoved my keys into the lock, flinging open my door.

"You may enter." My hand waved with a flourish as I waited for him to step inside. As long as I stayed angry I would be less tempted to throw myself at him, which is what I still wanted to do. Because obviously I was a sick, sick human being who had no sense of self-preservation.

"It's been a while since I've been in here." He watched as I followed him through, locking the door behind us. "I still remember the first time, when you tried to kiss me." The smile of satisfaction had yet to leave his face.

"Don't flatter yourself, I was drunk," I lied, remembering how sweet he'd been that night.

He'd walked me all the way up to my door and not laid a hand on me. He was sexy and I got caught up in the moment, just wanting to see if he felt as good as he looked. And now that I knew—felt and been totally consumed by his kiss—it was even harder to resist.

"Maybe." He moved closer, his thumb and his forefinger catching my chin as he tilted my head to look in my eyes. "What about now? Are you drunk?"

Stay mad at him, stay mad, goddamn it.

"No." It was a whisper, the word rushing past my lips on a soft breath.

I couldn't breathe, knowing that if he lowered his mouth and kissed me right now I would let him. I would hate myself later but right now, I would let him do it. Worse than that, I wanted him to.

As if reading my thoughts he dropped his hand, and took a step back. Like he'd been considering it but *knew* it would lead to more than a kiss. For whatever reason, he didn't seem to want that now, and whatever moment we were in had been lost.

He sunk his hands into his pockets, the smile replaced by a serious look of intent. "In that room, at your mother's—"

"Oh, please." My own moment lost as I raised my hands in defense. "We're going back there? I told you, it was a mistake."

Wasn't the humiliation of rejection enough? Why did we have to go back there?

"You think you can just listen?" His voice boomed, echoing off the walls.

It was the first time I'd ever heard him shout, the first time he'd ever seemed *really* serious. His eyes had an intensity I hadn't seen before, and if his voice wasn't enough to command attention, that fierce stare sure did.

My voice lowered, my eyes having difficulty meeting his as I shuffled on my feet, my arms tightly folded across my chest. "Fine, knock yourself out."

"You were asking for more in that room, and I know it wasn't just about sex." He was no longer shouting, with a softness in his tone that I hoped wasn't pity.

The hurt I'd felt lingered at the edges, but the anger was slowly receding. God, he was so easy to talk to. So easy to be pulled into the safe haven he seemed to offer. And like an addict desperate for her next hit, I couldn't make myself stop.

"I had a moment of weakness where I believed that maybe we could have been something. I don't know, a couple? Something? But that wasn't what you wanted." It was more honest than I wanted to be, exposing myself and my heart unnecessarily.

"We already *were* something." He ran his hand through his hair roughly. "You think I gave a rat's ass about going to Vegas to see a whorehouse? No, it was because it was connected to you. I wanted to know you, to see you."

The air escaped past my lips in a rush as my lungs struggled to expand. In all the possibilities I had calculated, I hadn't thought of this one. I knew he liked me, sure, I wasn't an idiot. But I didn't think it extended beyond friendship and a casual attraction, to think there was more was almost too good to be true. I didn't even dare to hope. But to hear he went through all of that for me? I was both elated and furious at the wasted opportunity.

There was a tightness in my throat as I tried to talk, the words choking their way out. "So, why then did you hold back?" And more to the point, why didn't he tell me?

Why didn't he give us a chance?

"Because I wasn't going to tell you that I was in love with you for the first time in a brothel, even if it was your mother's."

"You were in *love* with me?"

The world screeched to a stop.

Everything in that moment paused.

I could barely breathe, wondering if I'd heard him correctly. And yet there had been no hesitation as his eyes locked on mine when he said those words. My mind had difficulty processing, tossing around possible explanations. Maybe he meant love in a different context, like when he said he *loved* my boobs. Oh, God, did I even hope he meant it?

A slow smile twitched at his lips while he watched me wide-eyed and speechless. "Yes, first it was physical because you're beautiful, but seeing you and getting to know you, it just became more. Hell, I'm not even sure when it happened, just that it did and I couldn't stop thinking about you. And I knew you were freaked out about how it was going to work and your life changing. And I didn't want me to be the reason you needed to make the tough choice." He took a breath, the smile fading. "I was going to wait, take you somewhere that was just ours and tell you how I felt. But I ran out of time when you got the call from your boss with the promotion. How in the hell was I going to ask you to give all that up and stay with me in L.A.? I can be an asshole, Lila, but I'm not that much of a selfish prick."

"I need to sit down," I said as my hands gripped my throat,

the oxygen I was getting not enough.

He was the one who had said it was just sex. I thought it was all he wanted. All he seemed to want, but he wanted *more*?

The world was fuzzy as I moved to my couch, my body hitting the softness of the seat before I'd registered I'd lowered to it. Words I'd been dying to hear and they hadn't given me the relief I'd hoped for.

How could he love me?

"You were just going to let me go?" It wheezed out of me as my head stayed lowered, unable to look at him. How could it be so easy for him, to feel what he said he felt and then walk away? Not when we could have had a chance. "You can't tell me you did this for me, not when you didn't give me a choice."

"And what would you have said?" I felt him take a seat beside me, but he didn't touch me. "If I'd asked you stay? You think you would have given up your job? Moved? You think I didn't have something on the line too?"

There was no way I could have answered that because I didn't know. In my heart, I hoped I would have stayed. Chased a new dream or maybe given up my life in New York for a chance we might have worked out. But I was also a realist and knew that tossing away something I'd worked hard for would be stupid, especially if the relationship crashed and burned.

"I need to think." My hands scrubbed my face as my head fell into my hands.

"Okay, so think. But I'm not leaving, so you'll have to think while I'm here."

The lines between us had always been so clear. Or at least I'd thought they were. I thought he wanted the chase, the game, the women—it's what I'd assumed he was all about. And yeah, he could still be a nice guy and be sleeping around so I thought what I knew was accurate. And maybe it was, once. But he wasn't like that with me. So maybe I had been wrong the whole time. Maybe I had been wrong about what I thought he *was* and he *wanted*.

It was ridiculous, sitting in silence beside him when I just wanted to kiss him. To stop thinking so damn much and just throw caution to the wind.

"So, are you done thinking yet?" His hand was around my waist, while his lips grazed against the shell of my ear.

"No, not yet." I didn't dare look at him. He was close, so close. All I had to do was turn my head and . . .

Too late.

His mouth was on mine and I wasn't sure if it had been him or I who had started it. My body turned, inviting him in as my fingers wrapped around the fabric of his shirt and pulled him closer.

His lips smashed against mine in a heated desperation, his hands all over my body as he pressed into me. And I couldn't stop, kissing him more and deeper until we shared the same breath.

"This doesn't solve anything," I moaned in between kisses, unwilling for it to end. The beating of my heart so out of control it was possible it might explode.

"I know, but I don't have another alternative." His fingers raked through my hair as he brought my head closer. "And I can't be this close to you and not kiss you. I'm fucking dying, Lila."

I felt it too. The overwhelming need to be with him, to touch, to kiss, to have him inside of me, so primal I wanted to tear off our clothes like animals.

"We can't," I heaved, the words getting lost. "We shouldn't."

There were a lot of things we couldn't and shouldn't do. I wasn't sure exactly which ones I was referring to but not being with him at that moment wasn't it.

I yanked at his shirt, pulling it from his jeans and tearing it open. Buttons that had no business being fastened flew through the air as I pulled the two halves apart, his beautiful toned chest flexing underneath.

My mouth slithered down his neck, moving to his chest as I kissed every inch of his skin, needing more contact as my hands followed.

He didn't ask me if I was sure, instead taking my cue and yanking up my dress.

"Lila." He sucked the skin at my throat as his hand went into my underwear, his fingers instantly coated in my heat.

How could he do that? In a minute, he'd gotten my body so turned on that with a swipe of his thumb I would probably come on his hand. I writhed under him as I pulled at his belt, uncoordinated fingers tugging at the fly of his jeans as his finger plunged into me.

"Ryan."

My back arched off the couch, thrusting my hips into his hands as he yanked my panties down with his other hand. Meanwhile, my fingers were trying their best to maintain dexterity, working his jeans and boxer briefs down past his hips and freeing his cock.

He was so hard, my fingers barely wrapping around him as I gave him a long and firm pump.

"This isn't going to be gentle." His hand left me for a second and pulled out his wallet. "So I'm going to apologize in advance."

He grabbed a condom, tossing his wallet onto the coffee table as he tore open the packet with his teeth. Wrenching my hands away from him, he covered his hard length in latex, raising my hands above my head and pushing into me without warning.

"Agh," I cried out, my body barely having time to adjust as a slight bite of pain traveled through my core.

"I'm sorry." He kissed me, driving in again harder as his hands moved to my hips. "I just need you right now."

"I'm fine. Please. More." My sentence in pieces as I clawed at his skin, wanting him too. "More."

He drove into me, the permission I'd given him enough to

snap the thin thread of self-control that had been holding him back.

Our bodies rocked together faster and harder, my mouth fused to his as I came apart. My body and mind were totally consumed with him and the moment as waves of pleasure shot through my body as he swallowed my muffled screams, his release coming soon after as he exploded into me.

He collapsed onto me, his weight pinning me against the couch as I tried to suck in air and not hyperventilate.

Me.

Him.

Together.

"Well, *that* hadn't been the plan." He planted soft kisses along the arch of my neck. "Turns out, I am a selfish prick after all."

"I think I'm at least half to blame." I wrapped my arms around him, wanting to keep him close. "And be to honest, I was the one who ripped off your shirt."

He lifted his head and brought his lips to my forehead. "Give me a second."

The weight of his delicious body diminished as the curves of his chest I hadn't had time to admire moved back and he slowly pulled out. I felt the emptiness as he shifted off the couch, giving me a quick kiss before disappearing into the bathroom.

My body felt sated with parts of me delightfully sore. For days I would have loved to feel this way, but with emotions running so high and my thoughts so frayed, I wasn't able to enjoy it.

Conscious I was naked from the waist down, I tugged the hem of my dress, not bothering with the panties. They'd been tossed on the floor along with the buttons of Ryan's shirt, like souvenirs of what we'd just done. Not that I needed a reminder, I wasn't sure my mind *or* my body were going to forget that or him in a hurry.

"Just in case there was any confusion." He strolled back in, his destroyed shirt missing in action. "That wasn't a goodbye fuck."

He wasn't smiling, his eyebrows knitted as he lowered himself onto the couch. "So, whatever asshole you were on a date with tonight is going to have to be disappointed because I'm not letting you leave a second time."

I wasn't sure if I was turned on or pissed off, the warring parts of me wanting to know if he'd been following me and not caring either way. "It wasn't a date. And I wasn't aware I was under surveillance."

"You aren't, I assumed because of the dress." His hand gestured to the fitted black dress now securely in place. "I like it by the way, you can wear it when we date. At least then it won't be a wasted effort."

"Wait a second." I held my hands up, wondering what he'd decided when he'd been in the bathroom. It felt like there should have been a conversation, one that possibly I contributed to. "I'm going to deal with us *dating* in a minute, but you thought I was with another guy and your response was to have sex with me?"

"No," he said, the Adam's apple in his throat bobbing slowly as a finger ran up my arm. "My response was to find out who it was and beat him to death with his own arms. I didn't do that. Having sex with you was because I'm in love with you and I missed you, no one else is getting credit for it."

"And what if I'd already slept with *him* tonight, you were happy to be the encore?"

He'd assumed I'd been on a date, so it was conceivable that I'd decided to lose myself in a screaming orgasm with a man. Sure, it was only eight-thirty on a Tuesday night, but that didn't mean it couldn't happen. Case in point, what had transpired like five minutes after I entered my apartment.

"You wouldn't have had sex with him." He bit his bottom lip, fighting the grin. "And I bet you didn't even kiss him. I still want to beat him to death because I am positive he was thinking about it, but I wasn't worried, no."

And like me, who'd assumed things about him, he had made some assumptions about me. Although unlike me, his had been correct.

"Wow, you are so arrogant." I shook my head bewildered. I mean, he was right, I hadn't even kissed Chris, but still.

"Yeah, a little, but arrogance has nothing to do with it. How long did it take you to sleep with me? You said it yourself, you're not into casual sex so it had little to do with me being cocky and more with you being you." His fingers knotted with mine and he brought them to his lips and kissed my knuckles. "Besides, I thought you said it wasn't a date?"

"It wasn't a date." I rolled my eyes. "It was the sports guy from work who has been asking me out forever. I accepted in a moment of weakness but then when it came to going through with it, I just couldn't. So, I met him at the bar and basically told him it wasn't going to happen."

"Ahhh, the asshole." He kissed my knuckles again, casually, as he hid his grin. "What was his name again?"

"I never said." I playfully elbowed him, wondering how in the hell I'd gone from confused, to mad, to joking with him about Chris. "And I'm certainly not going to tell you now after you threatened to beat him to death with his own arms."

"Oh, come on, Lila. What if I promise not to kill him?" He pouted, followed by the most adorable set of puppy dog eyes. "I'll just smack him around a little. You know, if I really wanted to, I could find him all by myself."

"Please don't." I was almost positive he was joking, but there was a part of me that wasn't so sure.

"Fine, the asshole lives." He threw his hands up dramatically. "But only because I love you." He kissed the tip of my nose; pleased with himself he was sparing the life of a man he didn't know purely because he loved me.

"You keep saying that."

I pushed aside the absurdity of him being so jealous of someone else considering we weren't officially even dating. And how now he'd told me twice? Maybe three times that he'd loved me? Meanwhile, I had thought it a million times and had yet to say it once.

"Because it's true." His arm wrapped around me, bringing me closer to his naked chest. He had to know what his body did to me and I could only assume he was playing dirty. "Look, I'm going to be straight-up honest with you. Initially, I was extremely attracted to you, and yeah, I wanted sex. But the more I got to know you, it became less about just fucking you and more about hanging out with you. You're smart and funny and I love being with you, and the flirting was more of a game. I didn't think you'd ever say yes."

I used to think I was perceptive with decent intuition, but I had not even an inkling his feelings for me had been so involved. Yes, the initial attraction had been on both sides. He was hot, how could I not look at him with the appreciation he deserved? But he was right when he said it morphed into more. He became something else, and the flirting was more for fun. I had valued his friendship above everything else—hello, I put myself through hell the past couple of weeks trying to keep the balance—but had no idea he'd felt the same way.

"You *didn't* want to sleep with me?" My hand rested across his chest, the beating of his heart fluttering across my fingertips. If he was lying he was doing a damn good job of it.

"Of course I did. "His perfect brown eyes latched onto mine without hesitation. "I still got hard every time you walked into the room, princess, but I wanted to be in your life more. Of course, when you did say yes, there wasn't a whole lot I could do to stop myself. You were addictive, the whole package. I didn't have much choice."

I was torn between needing a break from the weight of his eyes and being unable to look away, the words coming out softer than I'd intended. "I didn't think you wanted a girlfriend."

"I didn't." His voice didn't waver as he continued with barely a pause. "I wanted *you*. It wasn't the same thing, Lila."

It felt like a million fireworks had been fired in my chest all at the same time as my eyes started to well with tears I promised myself I wouldn't cry.

"I was so in love with you." My throat tightened, needing to get the words out for so long and now that I could, being unable to stop. "I wanted to tell you but I didn't want to ruin us. God, Ryan, I don't think I've ever loved anyone like I loved you."

I wanted to curl my body around his and cry. Happy I'd finally been able to tell him how I felt. So relieved he'd felt the same way too, and mourning all of that wasted time. And hearing those words from him—telling me that he loved me—erased all the doubts. We would have made it work, if he loved me and I loved him, I would have found a way to make my work, my life, us, work.

"You're using past tense, Lila." He took my chin in his hands and brushed his lips against mine. Teasing. Soft. Just barely a kiss. "That isn't going to be acceptable for me."

The effort I had to hold back those tears was lost as my eyes started leaking. I didn't even care, allowing myself to release all that tension of the past few days and let it all out. He was right, it wasn't acceptable.

"You are my past, my present and my future tense, Ryan York. I have been, am and always will be, in love with you."

CHAPTER #23

WE'D MADE LOVE, this time slower, and with our clothes off.

And for the first time, it had been in my bed. His arms still wrapped around me as I lay peacefully on his chest.

"You know, we never visited your parents," I mumbled into his skin as he gently played with my hair. "You promised embarrassing stories, you coming here doesn't exempt you."

"Oh, you're going to meet my family. I already told them about you so short of a meteor striking the Earth, there isn't a lot that could stop it now. My mother can only be held back for so long, she's very insistent." A laugh punctuated the sentence.

I loved it like this.

Me.

Him.

Us.

"So that's where you get it from. Interesting." I lifted my head, settling into the crook of his arm. Being held had never felt this good; I could spend the next week there and not complain.

"Probably." He grinned. "So, now that we admitted we were morons, and accepted that there is no other future than together. You want to discuss how this is going to work?"

The discussion was inevitable. After all, we hadn't really talked about what was going to happen in the future other than it was going to be together. Then we'd had sex. Actually, I think we had sex *before* we'd decided, so it was easy to understand how nothing had really been worked out.

"Well, I guess since I get to work remotely with my new promotion, it makes things easier. I would still need to travel, but I don't think it will matter if I lived in New York or somewhere else."

If Tia could work for *The New York Post* and split her time between Brooklyn and L.A., surely I could do something similar.

"I'd still need to clear it with Dick, I assume. But technically, working remotely means I could be remote, right?" He hadn't specified where my desk could be other than it wouldn't be at the office.

"You think he's going to go for that?" Ryan brushed the hair off my face. "Technically, it sounds reasonable but what if you are required to remain a New York resident as terms of your employment? I'm not saying he'd pull that shit, but it's a little different than Tia's situation."

He was right about that. It was *The New York Times*, and I was an employee, not a freelance contributor. And had the possibility been posed a month or even two weeks ago, it might not have been an easy choice but I would have stayed in New York.

Now, the choice *was* easy. And not because I no longer cared about my job, but because I knew there was no reason why I couldn't have it all.

"Then I'll keep my apartment and I'll commute. There are planes that fly back and forth at least six times a day. And I know it will be a challenge, but there isn't another alternative."

"I want you to know that I'm going to step up too." His lips pressed against my forehead. "I'll work something out with Eric if I have to. If you need to stay in New York, then I'll be here as much as I can."

"You'd leave your job?" I asked, the thought having never entered my mind.

He shook his head, not sharing the same concerns I'd had. "No, not unless Eric wants that. But like you said, planes fly back and forth all day, every day. We can use studio security to fill the gaps if need be. And of course, we already have a place in both L.A. *and* New York."

"I really like your cottage." I hugged him tighter. "I think I'd like living there." It didn't hurt that it was literally a few feet away from my best friend's place, and housed the man I loved. That last part, the most important factor.

"Then that's where we'll live." He kissed the top of my head. "The landlord can be a pain in the ass sometimes, but mostly he's okay, I guess."

"Sounds like we've decided then." I rested my head back on his chest, loving the feel of his warm skin against mine.

His body gently shook as he barked out a laugh. "It was decided back in California, we both just had to wise up."

"I'm glad you came."

I'd never been the girl who wanted to be chased, and I wasn't interested in making a man jump through hoops just because. But having him fly all those miles just for me made my heart expand so much I thought it might burst.

"Hey." I shuffled up the bed, curious about something that at the time I hadn't given much thought. "So, when we were in Vegas, all the stuff you made me show you was just to get to know me better?"

At the time I assumed he wanted to torment me, draw out every one of my awkward and humiliating experiences for entertainment purposes. Not in a mean or malicious way, but for fun because Ryan enjoyed pushing my boundaries. And to be honest, as much as I pretended to have hated it at the time, I had never shared all those memories with anyone else. Hell, I didn't think I ever wanted to rehash some of those memories, but with him, it hadn't been so bad.

His teeth played with his bottom lip as a devilish look darkened his eyes. "Mostly."

"Mostly?" That was evasion if ever I heard it. "What aren't you telling me?"

He joined me, shuffling up the bed so we sat shoulder to shoulder, our bodies touching but not in a way that was sexual.

"Your first date, first kiss, the movie theatre—all stuff that I'd missed." I watched as his fists clasped and unclasped in his lap as he looked at me. "And I know you had a past before me, and I don't expect women to be virgins or any other bullshit. But I wanted to replace all of your *firsts* with other people, with *lasts* with me."

My brow scrunched in confusion wondering why he would do that. "You were building a history for me to remember when we were no longer together? That's kinda of dark."

"No," he laughed, his fingers intertwining with mine. "I wanted to be the last person you kissed there, touched there, had sex with there. So when you did go back, you'd have new memories. Ones we'd created."

"I'm not sure if that is incredibly creepy or romantic." I laughed, my heart feeling like it was three sizes too big. And God help me, I thought it was quite possibly the sweetest thing ever.

"I was going to tell you that morning when we got back to L.A." He focused on me, his trademark cockiness and sarcasm gone. "I wanted to tell you I was in love with you, but every time I tried to turn the conversation that way, you freaked out. I was going to wait until Tia got back, hoping once you had someone other than me to talk to, it might make it easier. And then that call happened. I heard what you said to your boss, I wasn't going to be the reason to hold you back."

"God, we were so dumb," I groaned, rolling into him and allowing him to wrap his arm around me. "If only we'd just said something to each other then."

"You know what, I don't regret you leaving, Lila." I felt his lips softly pressed against my temple. "I hated it, and it was the worst few days of my life but it showed me that there was no way I could live without you."

"You know, in a weird way, I feel the same. Not that I want to do that again because that was no fun, but at least we know it's for the right reasons."

And it was. Our connection wasn't an infatuation or even a sexual attraction. Fine, there was a lot of sexual attraction but it wasn't *only* that. We'd been friends, and then lovers, and then soul mates. And best of all, we didn't have to give up any of those things, we could have all three.

"Now," he stretched down to the floor where his jeans had been discarded earlier and pulled out his phone. "If one of us doesn't call Tia, we're going to have some serious issues."

"Oh yeah?" I folded my arms across my chest wondering what kind of hell she'd subjected him to. She had promised me she wouldn't say anything, but if Tia knew anything, it was a work around.

"Yeah, she's been giving me some serious evil looks for the past few days. I rewired the alarm in the cottage around the perimeter because I was convinced she was going to try to kill me while I slept." He widened his eyes in mock horror.

I threw my head back and laughed. "Yeah, that sounds like her, she's a little protective."

"Yeah, I got that." He chuckled. "Which is why I told her I was coming here. Of course, she said if she didn't hear of our happy reunion by tomorrow morning she was enlisting the help of your father and they were going to dig me a hole in the desert." He rubbed the back of his neck. "Even Eric wasn't convinced she was joking. He made me take out extra life insurance before I came out here, just in case."

"Well then, I better save your ass." I held out my hand for the phone. "I've grown rather attached to you and would hate for there to be any unfortunate mishaps. Besides, if anyone kills you, it should be me. You think I didn't learn a thing or two growing up with my parents." I narrowed my eyes, toying with him.

"Wow, princess." He tossed the phone on the bed and circled his arms around me. "I think we're both messed up because that is incredibly hot."

"Tia said before tomorrow morning, right?" I looked over Ryan's shoulder to the clock sitting on my nightstand. "Did she mean L.A. or New York time?"

"New York, I guess?" He shrugged confused as to where I was going with it. "I didn't think to specify."

"Which means we have a few hours before you're in any real danger." I wrapped my arms around his neck, watching the smile starting to form on his lips. "You want to roll the dice?" My eyebrows lifted, teasingly.

"I've always like living on the edge." He moved his mouth to my jaw, kissing up the side of my face. "Besides, I've named you the beneficiary on my new policy. You'll have to cremate me and wear me in a pendant around your neck in order to get the inheritance. Try getting a date with *that* new jewelry." He laughed against my skin.

"You are seriously twisted." My palms playfully shoved against his perfect chest, which I now had an excuse to touch as much as I wanted.

"That's right." He smirked, pulling me closer. "And I'm all yours."

FIGURING I DIDN'T want to tempt fate, I didn't wait till morning, calling Tia a few hours later. We both cried like idiots, the emotion of it all overcoming both of us as Ryan held me in his arms. I hadn't needed the phone call to know she would be happy for me but I was glad to tell her. To finally be able to say the words out loud, that I loved Ryan York. And if her eardrum-shattering squeal was anything to go by, I would assume she was pleased I'd be spending a lot more time in L.A. too.

Which just left me one more thing to deal with.

Dick.

Not the kind in Ryan's pants either.

Which is why I sent him an email and scheduled a meeting with him the next morning.

"If this is to tell me you can't cut it on the outside and you're resigning, forget it." He didn't even bother looking up as I entered the room. His eyes fixed on the laptop in front of him as I sat in the chair opposite him. "I've already replaced you in the art's section with Tiffany, and I'm not in the mood for more disappointment today."

It's was barely nine a.m., I wasn't sure how much disappointment he could have possibly experienced, but given the three empty paper coffee cups on his desk, I was assuming a decent amount.

"I'm not resigning." I cleared my throat, as I adjusted my skirt. "I'm here for another reason."

He huffed, pushed away from his desk as he looked at me with the displeasure that only Dick could. "You can't seriously be looking for a raise so soon either, the figure I gave you was more than fair."

"I wouldn't say it was more than fair." I smiled politely, knowing it would probably piss him off. What could I say? Old habits died hard. "It was appropriate considering the additional hours I will need to put in and the traveling etc."

"Yeah, yeah, then what?" He waved his hand in the air. We'd

heard rumors he'd shown patience back in 2005 but no one was still around to talk about it. "I have a paper to run."

"I'm moving to L.A." I cleared my throat, pushing my shoulders back as I met him in the eye. "I'll still go where I need to for the story and will be spending some of the time in New York, but other times, I'll be living in California."

There, I'd said it. The words pronounced confidentially and clear as I stated my intention without stuttering or hesitation.

"What?" He looked at me like he hadn't heard, and one thing about Dick was for sure, there was nothing wrong with his hearing.

"I said, I'm moving to L.A.," I annunciated more clearly, sitting up straighter in my chair.

He inhaled deeply through his nose, the air making a whistling sound as he pushed it out through his mouth, the deep lines in his forehead crinkled into a deep V.

"Lila, what did I tell you?"

I tried to cast my mind back, wishing I had taken notes. "Ummm, that you didn't trust Californians and they were too happy for your liking?"

"Besides that." He waved his hand, expecting me to throw out another one of his stellar pearls of wisdom that I probably didn't remember.

"Ummm." I shrugged, all out of ideas.

"The story." He stood up, raising his hands triumphantly in the air. "All I give a shit about is the story, and your ability to get it. Those dumbasses in HR would have my ass for saying so, but I really don't care where you live. You could buy a farm in Des Moines, Iowa and bake meth in your off time, and I wouldn't give a shit. This is *The New York Times*, Lila, I'm not here to talk about your feelings, just give me *the story*."

"Well, Dick." I joined him on my feet, elated I would have been supported in my Midwestern drug business should I choose to pursue it. "Then it's been a pleasure. And you will get your story on time, *every* time."

"For God's sake." He shook his head, his body almost levitating. "It's *Richard*."

"Right." I smiled, so much immeasurable happiness and relief filling my heart I could possibly start vomiting rainbows. "My mistake. It won't happen again."

We both knew I was lying, but in a strange way we took comfort in that.

I think, as much as Dick hated to admit it, he probably liked me. Not that he'd ever tell me, just like I would never tell him that despite being a hardass jerkface, I respected him. And he had given me the most unbelievable promotion that not only enabled me to further my professional career but also be with my new boyfriend. I should probably be thanking him, and I would, if I knew it wouldn't disappoint us both.

I picked up my handbag, my smile contained as I walked to the door and looked back over my shoulder. Saying goodbye was tempting but that wasn't my style, tipping my chin to him as I walked out of his office without being dismissed. As the door closed behind me, I could still sense his glare but not even that could stop my grin, my cheeks feeling like they might split apart.

Ryan had been instructed to wait at the coffee shop around the corner. While *The Times* did have a strict policy about non-essential staff being allowed up in the offices, I was more concerned about Ryan making good on the threat of killing or maiming Chris. And while I was oddly aroused by the idea of Ryan being all strong, manly and jealous, I figured it was better if we started our new life together without needing to go on the lam. Writing on the run would have been too much of a challenge, even for me.

"Princess." His arms enveloped me from behind the minute my feet hit the pavement. "Tell me only good news."

"I thought you were meeting me at the coffee shop?" I twisted in his arms, my lips needing to be on his.

He moaned as his lips took over, dominating my mouth as we put on a show on the sidewalk. Not that anyone cared as he sucked my bottom lip, teasing me in a way that I was almost embarrassed.

"I'm terrible at doing what I'm told," he mumbled against my mouth. "But you probably already knew that."

"You are terrible, and lucky for you I like that sort of thing." My hands grabbed at his shirt, my fingers tight against the fabric. "Want to come back to my apartment and help me pack?"

"Is that what we're calling sex now?" He laughed, his hand seductively giving my ass a squeeze. "I can't wait to *pack* with you."

"C'mon, pervert." I yanked at his shirt, pulling him toward his parked Escalade. "Take me home."

EPILOGUE

One Month Later

"LILA?"

The handle twisted as the door shook, his fist banging against the wood soon after.

"Why the hell is the door locked?" Ryan's voice piqued with interest as he once again shook the handle.

"I told you, I have a surprise." I looked at myself in the mirror, eyeing my effort and feeling a little bit stupid. I'd never been huge into role-playing but tonight was a special occasion and I wanted everything to be perfect.

"If we're celebrating *your* article, why am *I* the one getting the surprise?" he answered, his voice adorably confused.

"Because I like to mix things up," I called back. *Ha! If he only knew how much.*

My earlier trip to D.C. had been fruitful. Dick had been right about the timing of the senator's retirement. So, while he laughed about his ambition of a ten a.m. tee-off at Mar-a-Lago in Palm Beach, I uncovered the offshore account in the Caymans he'd been using to facilitate his addiction to Russian prostitutes.

It was really quite shocking. The man had been a decorated

war veteran, with a prolific career in the senate, married for over thirty years to a beautiful wife, which had produced three daughters.

Russian prostitutes? I mean, he really should have been buying American.

The IRS took issue with it too, although I think they were more concerned with the money than the hookers. Not that it mattered; the senator wasn't going to have use for either of them soon.

My exclusive had run three days ago, and my phone hadn't stopped ringing. Offers from other papers—even those "bastards" from *The Washington Post*—as well as interviews about me. It was strange to be on the other side of celebrity.

Dick did what Dick did best, told me I'd done okay but it wasn't the best he'd seen, and then gave me a raise he grumbled was probably too generous. I called him Dick about four times, so the status quo was maintained.

And my life had reached a level of fantastic that I never believed could be achieved.

I was living in a beautiful cottage in L.A. with my amazing boyfriend, which happened to be right across the backyard from my best friend. My parents were a quick—well, the quickest it had been in years—four-hour drive away and we had already been back for a visit. My dad still brandished firearms a little too enthusiastically and asked Ryan about the state of my uterus. While my mother stocked us with "goodie bags," and funnily enough, I didn't mind either.

"Are you sure you wouldn't rather go out for dinner?" Ryan asked, still on the other side of the door. "There are places we can go where you won't be bothered by the press," he added, the irony not lost on me.

"We can't go out in public with the way I'm dressed." I looked down at my body, feeling slightly self-conscious.

God, I hoped he would think it was sexy. I would probably

punch him if he laughed his ass off.

"Dressed like how?" The knocking and the jiggling of the door handle stopped. "What are you wearing?"

I was an idiot. "An outfit not fit for public consumption."

"Princess," he purred. "Those are my favorite kind. Please open the door."

I'd put off opening the door for as long as I could. Fussed with my outfit and my hair more times than was needed and looked at myself in the mirror so many times, I'd give Snow White's evil stepmother a run for her money.

It was now or never.

"Okay, but even if I look stupid, you can't laugh," I warned, my fingers hesitating on the lock. "This is the one time you are allowed to lie to me if you have to and tell me I'm sexy."

"I'm positive I'm not going to need to lie, open the door, baby."

I groaned, releasing the lock as I took a deep breath.

This had already taken too long. I threw caution to the wind as my hand pulled open the door, revealing myself in all my glory.

Ryan stood still, staring with wide eyes, open-mouthed, in utter silence.

"Say something," I demanded, moving closer, having never seen him speechless in the whole time I'd known him. "I thought—"

"Oh. My. God." His eyes steamrolled up and down the length of my body. "I think I just came in my pants."

When I'd bought the outfit, it never occurred to me to go with something *traditional* like naughty nurse or cheeky flight attendant. That just wouldn't have been us. Instead, I got a pink ball gown, white gloves, and topped my long blonde hair with a gold crown. You guessed it, I was Princess Peach.

Ryan's eyes didn't stop moving. "Princess."

"You want me to make all your dirty dreams come true?" I wrapped my arms around his neck, batting my long lashes.

"Are you kidding me?" He pulled me into his arms and lifted me off my feet. "If I didn't think it would be in extremely poor taste to ask you to marry me right before we have incredible, hot, dirty sex, I'd propose right now."

"How about this." My white-gloved finger tapped him on the nose. "You save the proposal for another day, and I promise when you ask me, I'll say yes."

"I am so in love with you." He looked at me with an intensity that made me feel like I was on fire. "And I'm holding you to that promise."

"Good, I'll look forward to it." I brushed my pretty pink lips against his. "Now, how about that incredible, hot, dirty sex you were talking about." Even under all of the puffy pink dress, I could feel him hard.

"One more question." He hesitated, rubbing his thick erection against me.

I moaned, cursing every layer of pink fabric. "Okay."

"We don't have to give the dress back, right?" His voice husky as he rocked against my core. "Pretty sure I'm going to want to keep it."

I closed my eyes absorbing his body, feeling the instant heat of my arousal flooding between my legs. "Me *and* the dress are yours forever."

"No." He kissed me. "Forever isn't long enough."

THE END

ACKNOWLEDGEMENTS

SO MANY THANK yous! To Gep, Jenna, Liam and Woodley—love you guys so very much. I know it's not easy, nothing worth having ever is.

Thank you to my amazing friends and family. Your patience, grace and support is something that defies gratitude. I love you all xx.

My agents, Kimberly Brower and Jess Dallow from Brower Literary and Management—you guys rock. Thank you for all your work behind the scenes.

To my amazing betas, MK and Danielle. We don't always agree but your feedback makes me ask more of myself. I can't thank you enough.

To Hang Le—cover designer extraordinaire, ninja, and just an amazing person—I love how easy it is to work with you and how beautiful you make my covers and teasers.

Nichole Strauss—my editor at Insight Editing—you are epically awesome. I graciously extend my humblest thanks for all the work you do. Sorry, some of those adverbs snuck back. In all seriousness, I can't thank you enough. The tight turn arounds, the date changes, the intensity—I wasn't kidding when I called you epically awesome. You are, so thanks because I know what you do and it makes me a better writer and makes me produce better work.

To Christine Borgford from Type A Formatting, you are a dream to work with. Professional, beautiful and classy—thank you for making my words look pretty.

Special thanks to my proofreaders Virginia and Rosa—your eagle eyes are lifesavers.

Authors. OMG. I can't even. There are so many of you who have become my friends that I literally need to pinch myself. It really is such a privilege to work along side you, and to know you is an even greater honor. Thank you to those who have supported, guided and talked me off a ledge.

To all the bloggers and reviewers! YOU GUYS ROCK MY MOFO'N WORLD. I don't care if your blog is 20 people or 20,000 people—you all count. Each one of you putting in time, sharing, liking, reviewing, posting—all of it helps. Don't ever think it doesn't. YOU matter. Keep going, we see you. And reader reviews, don't think your reviews are any less important. We love them all. Thank you so, so much.

I always leave thanking the readers till last because you are the person holding this book. You took the time to get here, to the end and I am so appreciative of that. I may not know your name, but feel your support and love. I hope you in turn feel my love and gratitude. Thank you for reading xx.

ABOUT THE AUTHOR

T GEPHART IS a USA Today and International bestselling author from Melbourne, Australia.

With an approach to life that is somewhat unconventional, she prefers to fly by the seat of her pants rather than adhere to some rigid roadmap. Her lack of "plan" has resulted in a rather interesting and eclectic resume, which reads more like the fiction she writes than an actual employment history. She'd tell you all about it, but the statute of limitations hasn't expired yet. But all those crazy twists and turns have led her to a career she loves—writing romantic comedy.

When she isn't filling pages with sassy and sexy characters with attitude, she's living her own reality show in the 'burbs of Melbourne with her American husband, two teenage children, and her fur child—Woodley.

She loves adventure, to laugh, travel, and strives to live her life to the fullest.

CONNECT WITH T

www.tgephart.com
Facebook
Goodreads
Twitter

BOOKS BY THIS AUTHOR

The Lexi Series

Lexi

A Twist of Fate

Twisted Views: Fate's Companion

A Leap of Faith

A Time for Hope

The Power Station Series

High Strung

Crash Ride

Back Stage

The Black Addiction Series

Slide

Sticks

Stand

#1 Series

#1 Crush

#1 Player

#1 Rival

#1 Lie

#1 Muse

#1 Love (coming 2019)

Collision Series

Train Wreck

Car Crash (coming soon)

Standalones

The Fall